CHAPTER 1:
THE CITY CALLS

WRITER: KYLE PUTTKAMMER

PENCILS AND COLORS: MARCUS WILLIAMS

INKS: RYAN SELLERS

LETTERING: BRIANA HIGGINS

BRYAN SEATON: PUBLISHER/ CEO · SHAWN GABBORIN: EDITOR IN CHIEF
JASON MARTIN: PUBLISHER-DANGER ZONE · NICOLE D'ANDRIA: MARKETING DIRECTOR/EDITOR
JIM DIETZ: SOCIAL MEDIA MANAGER · DANIELLE DAVISON: EXECUTIVE ADMINISTRATOR
CHAD CICCONI: TALKING HAIRBALL · SHAWN PRYOR: PRESIDENT OF CREATOR RELATIONS

THE QUEST FAMILY OBSERVATORY OVERLOOKING STELLAR CITY.

THERE'S NOTHING LIKE RELAXIN@ AT HOME WITH A GOOD BOOK.

BUT AS YOU CAN SEE, THIS IS NO TYPICAL HOME.

FROM HERE, I HAVE A BEAUTIFUL VIEW OF THE CITY BELOW AND THE SKIES ABOVE

TO THE CASUAL OBSERVER, IT WOULD SEEM THAT I LIVE A QUIET LIFE.

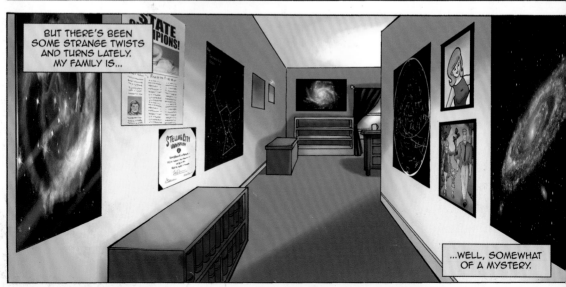

BUT THERE'S BEEN SOME STRANGE TWISTS AND TURNS LATELY. MY FAMILY IS...

...WELL, SOMEWHAT OF A MYSTERY.

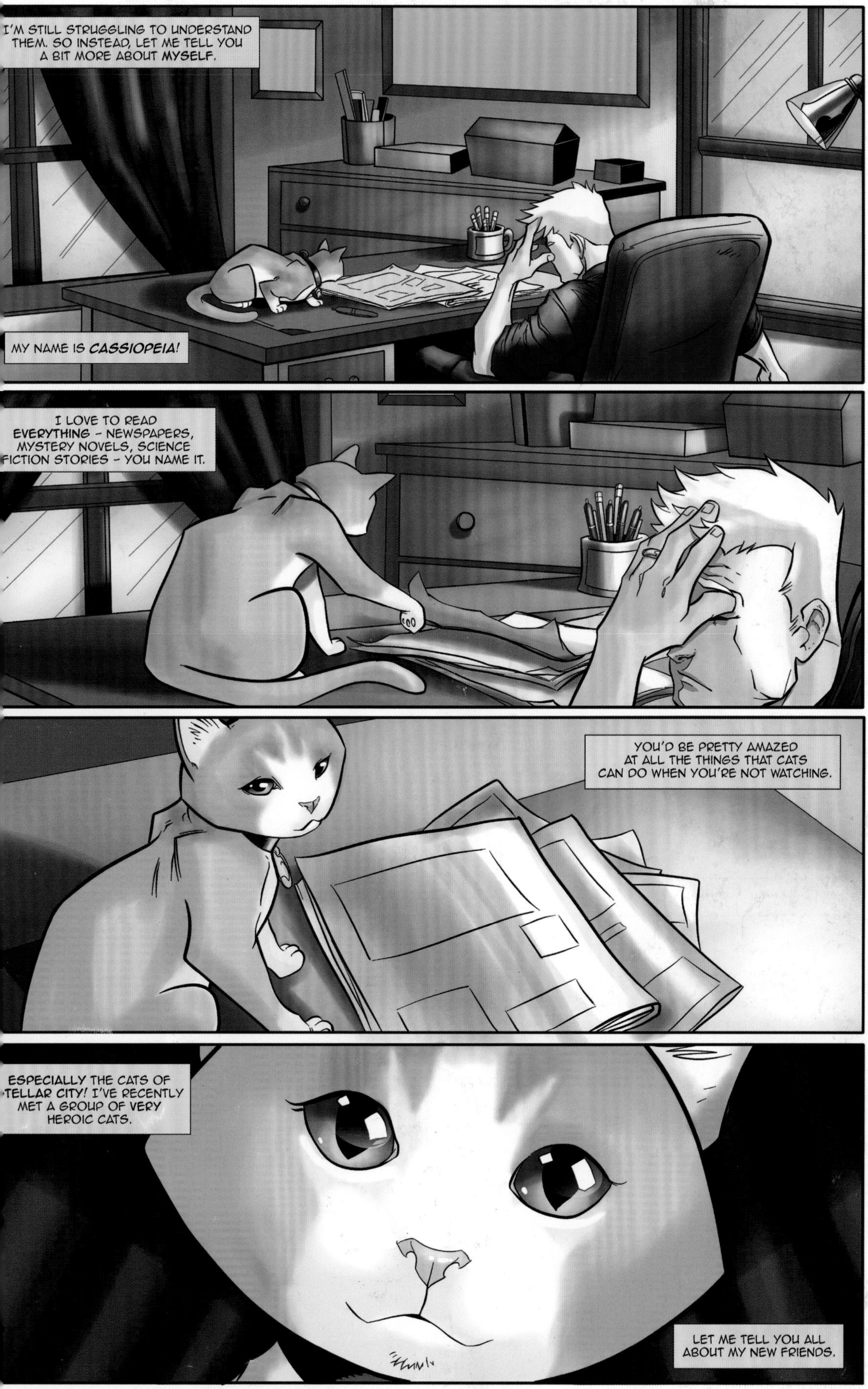

I'M STILL STRUGGLING TO UNDERSTAND THEM. SO INSTEAD, LET ME TELL YOU A BIT MORE ABOUT MYSELF.
MY NAME IS CASSIOPEIA!
I LOVE TO READ EVERYTHING - NEWSPAPERS, MYSTERY NOVELS, SCIENCE FICTION STORIES - YOU NAME IT.
YOU'D BE PRETTY AMAZED AT ALL THE THINGS THAT CATS CAN DO WHEN YOU'RE NOT WATCHING.
ESPECIALLY THE CATS OF TELLAR CITY! I'VE RECENTLY MET A GROUP OF VERY HEROIC CATS.
LET ME TELL YOU ALL ABOUT MY NEW FRIENDS.

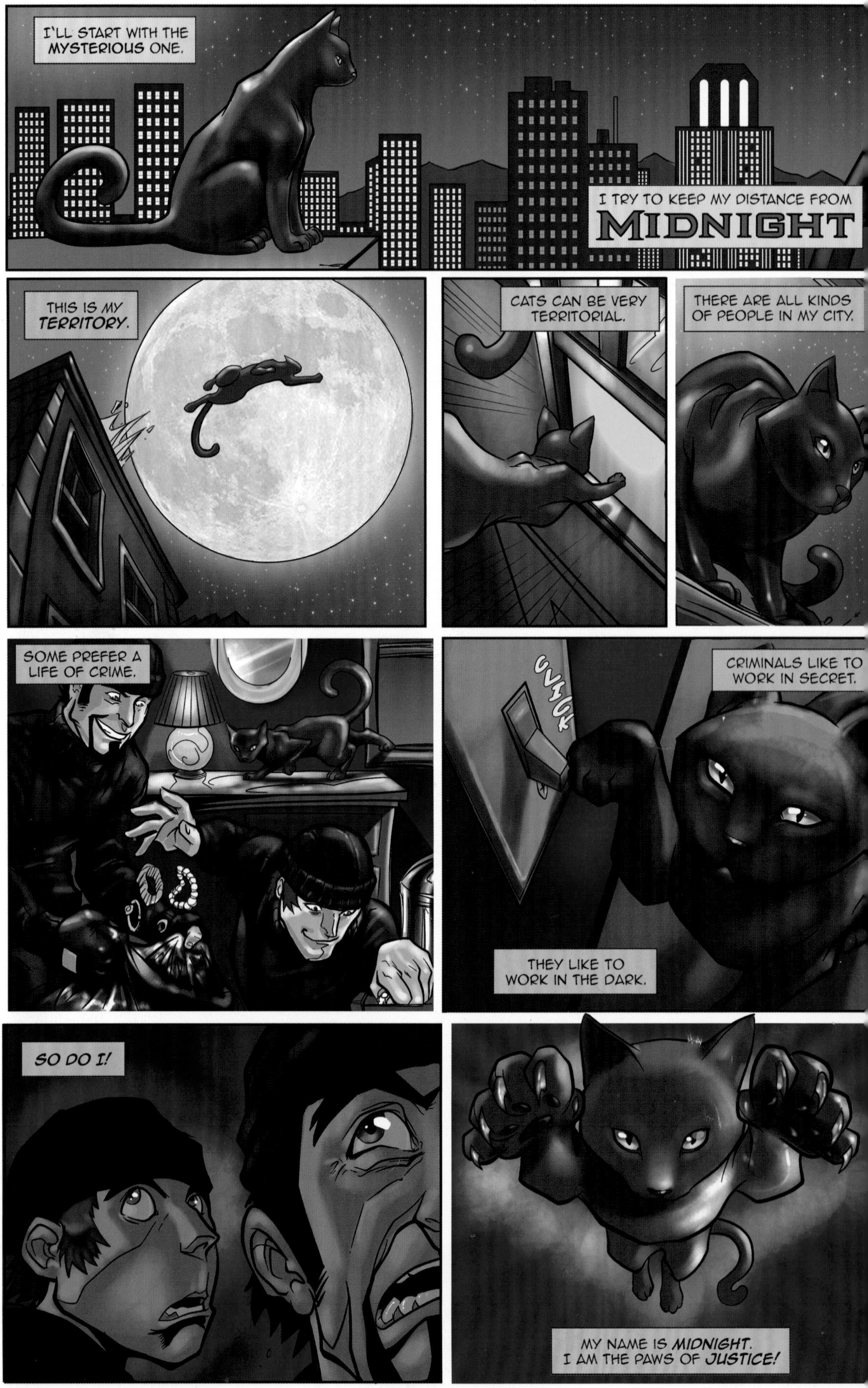

I'LL START WITH THE MYSTERIOUS ONE.
I TRY TO KEEP MY DISTANCE FROM
MIDNIGHT
THIS IS MY TERRITORY.
CATS CAN BE VERY TERRITORIAL.
THERE ARE ALL KINDS OF PEOPLE IN MY CITY.
SOME PREFER A LIFE OF CRIME.
CRIMINALS LIKE TO WORK IN SECRET.
THEY LIKE TO WORK IN THE DARK.
SO DO I!
MY NAME IS MIDNIGHT. I AM THE PAWS OF JUSTICE!

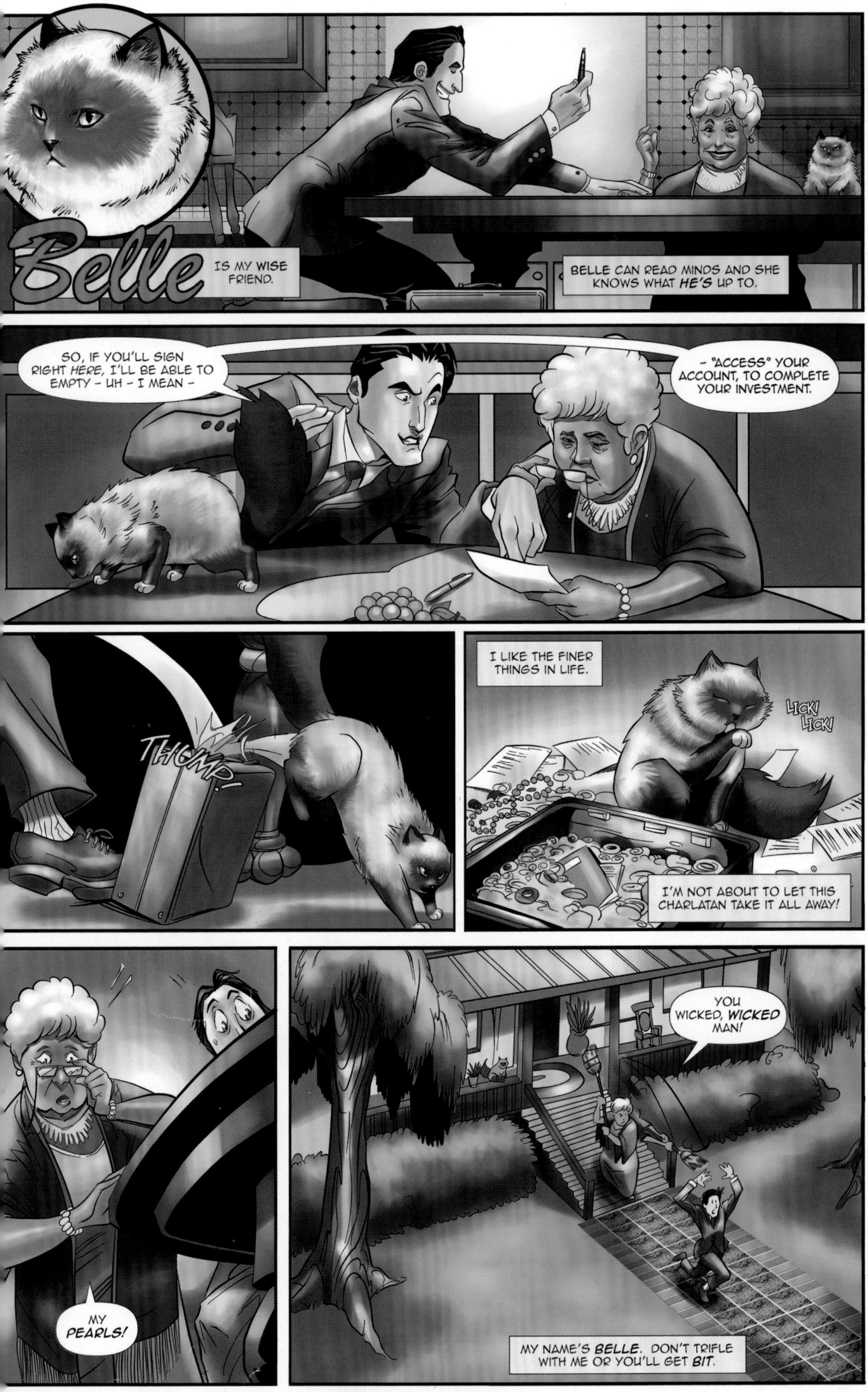

Belle
IS MY WISE FRIEND.
BELLE CAN READ MINDS AND SHE KNOWS WHAT HE'S UP TO.
SO, IF YOU'LL SIGN RIGHT HERE, I'LL BE ABLE TO EMPTY – UH – I MEAN –
– "ACCESS" YOUR ACCOUNT, TO COMPLETE YOUR INVESTMENT.
THUMP!
I LIKE THE FINER THINGS IN LIFE.
LICK! LICK!
I'M NOT ABOUT TO LET THIS CHARLATAN TAKE IT ALL AWAY!
MY PEARLS!
YOU WICKED, WICKED MAN!
MY NAME'S BELLE. DON'T TRIFLE WITH ME OR YOU'LL GET BIT.

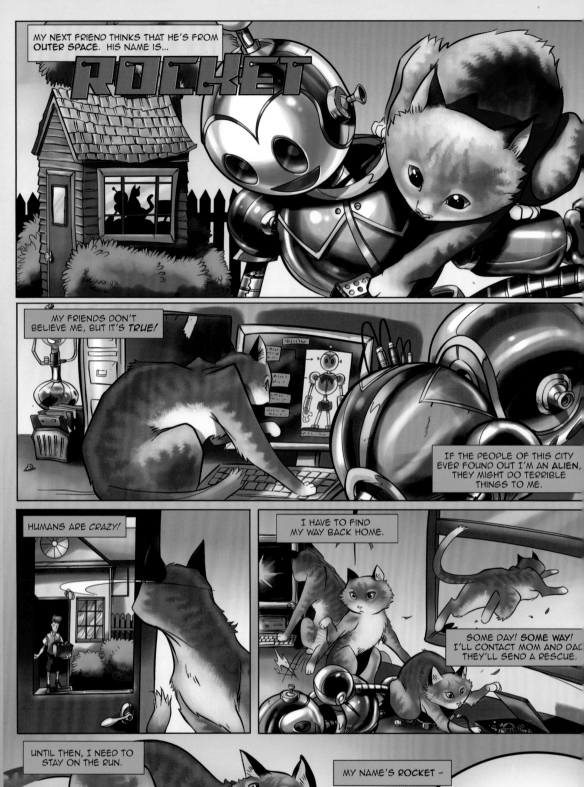

MY NEXT FRIEND THINKS THAT HE'S FROM OUTER SPACE. HIS NAME IS...

ROCKET

MY FRIENDS DON'T BELIEVE ME, BUT IT'S *TRUE!*

IF THE PEOPLE OF THIS CITY EVER FOUND OUT I'M AN ALIEN, THEY MIGHT DO TERRIBLE THINGS TO ME.

HUMANS ARE *CRAZY!*

I HAVE TO FIND MY WAY BACK HOME.

SOME DAY! SOME WAY! I'LL CONTACT MOM AND DAD THEY'LL SEND A RESCUE.

UNTIL THEN, I NEED TO STAY ON THE RUN.

MY NAME'S ROCKET –

– AND I'M *OUTTA* HERE!!

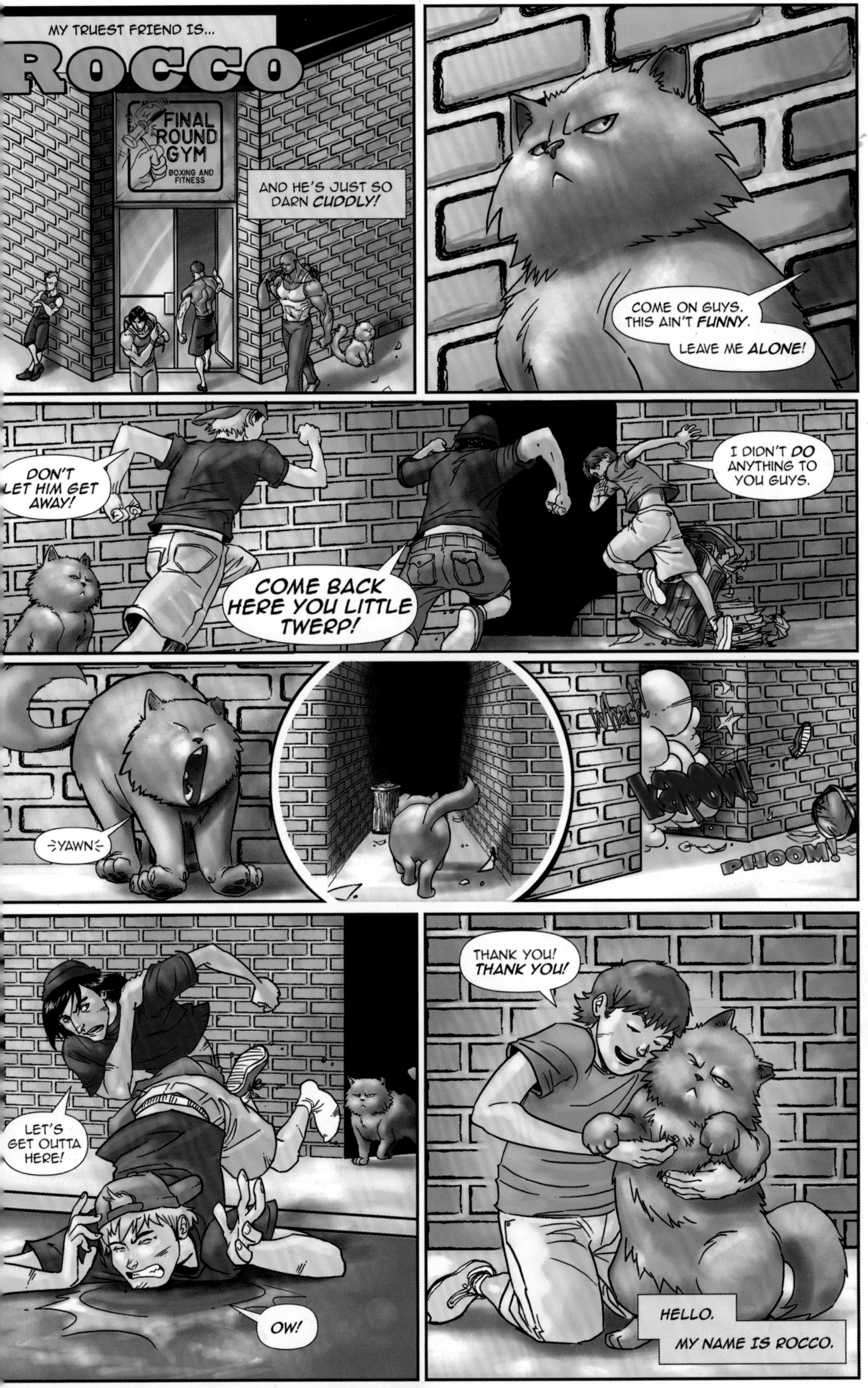
MY TRUEST FRIEND IS...
ROCCO
FINAL ROUND GYM
BOXING AND FITNESS
AND HE'S JUST SO DARN CUDDLY!
COME ON GUYS. THIS AIN'T FUNNY.
LEAVE ME ALONE!
DON'T LET HIM GET AWAY!
COME BACK HERE YOU LITTLE TWERP!
I DIDN'T DO ANYTHING TO YOU GUYS.
YAWN
whack!
KAPOW!
PHOOM!
LET'S GET OUTTA HERE!
OW!
THANK YOU! THANK YOU!
HELLO.
MY NAME IS ROCCO.

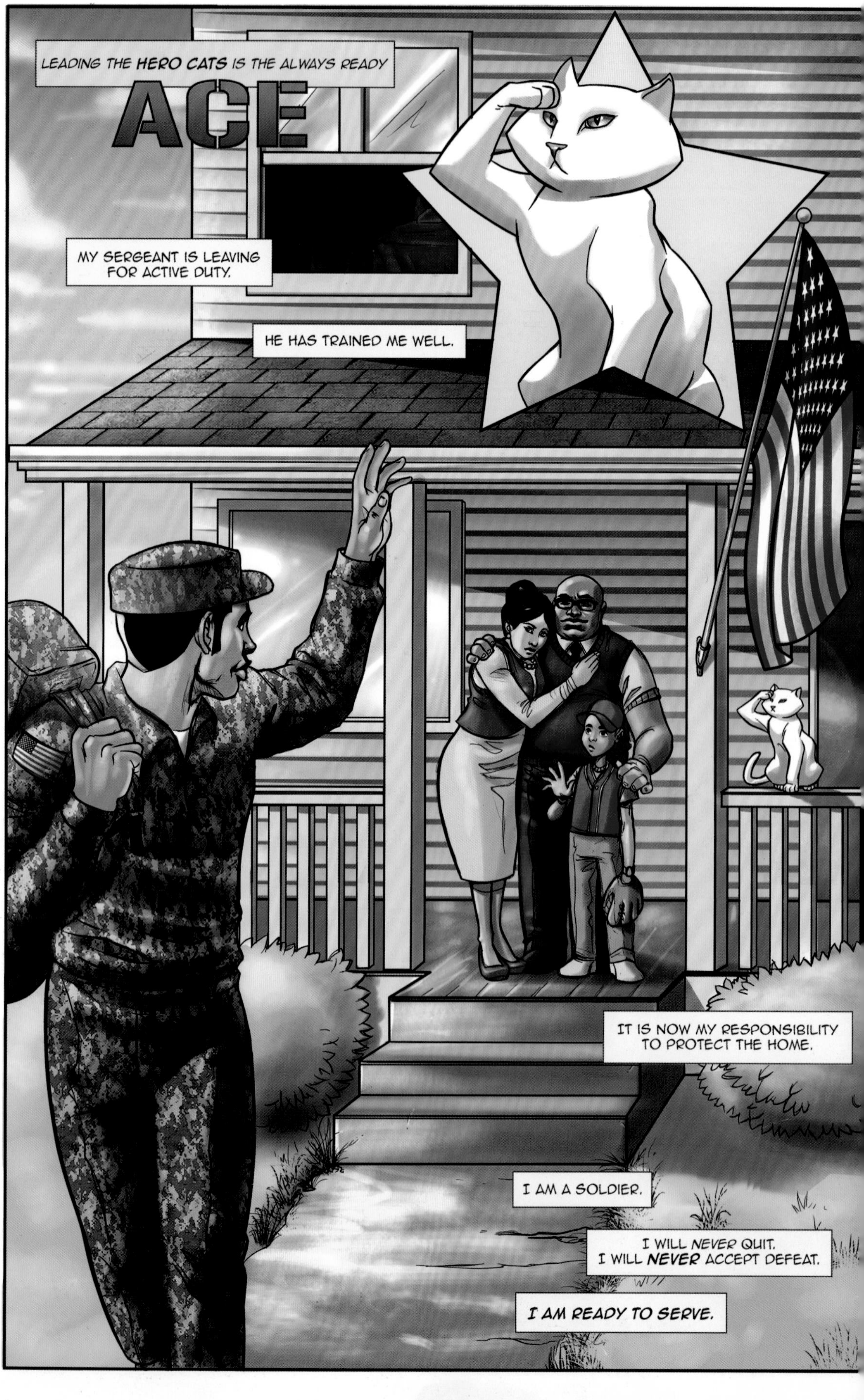
LEADING THE **HERO CATS** IS THE ALWAYS READY
ACE
MY SERGEANT IS LEAVING FOR ACTIVE DUTY.
HE HAS TRAINED ME WELL.
IT IS NOW MY RESPONSIBILITY TO PROTECT THE HOME.
I AM A SOLDIER.
I WILL *NEVER* QUIT. I WILL ***NEVER*** ACCEPT DEFEAT.
I AM READY TO SERVE.

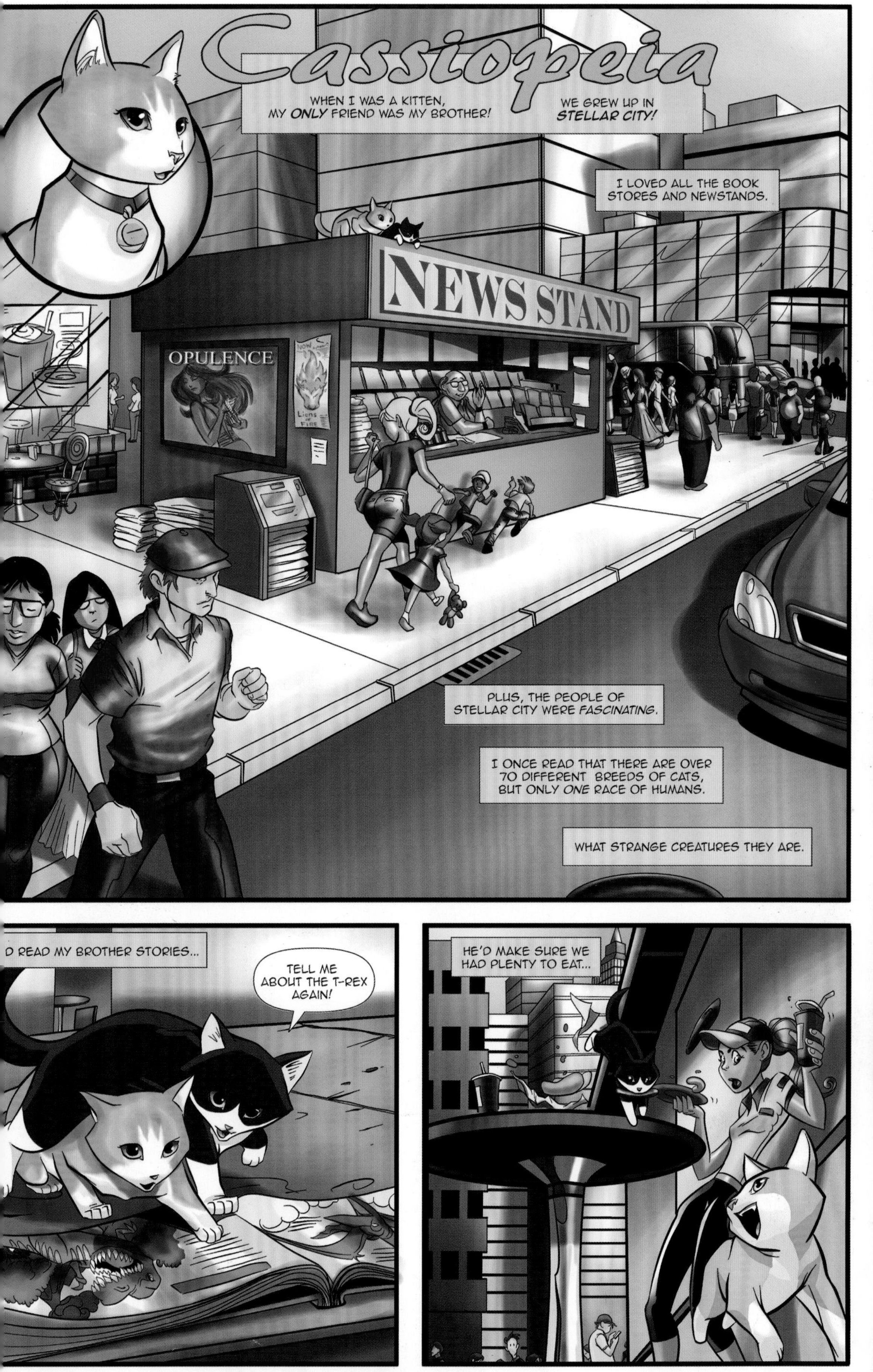
Cassiopeia
WHEN I WAS A KITTEN, MY ONLY FRIEND WAS MY BROTHER!
WE GREW UP IN STELLAR CITY!
I LOVED ALL THE BOOK STORES AND NEWSTANDS.
NEWS STAND
OPULENCE
PLUS, THE PEOPLE OF STELLAR CITY WERE FASCINATING.
I ONCE READ THAT THERE ARE OVER 70 DIFFERENT BREEDS OF CATS, BUT ONLY ONE RACE OF HUMANS.
WHAT STRANGE CREATURES THEY ARE.
D READ MY BROTHER STORIES...
TELL ME ABOUT THE T-REX AGAIN!
HE'D MAKE SURE WE HAD PLENTY TO EAT...

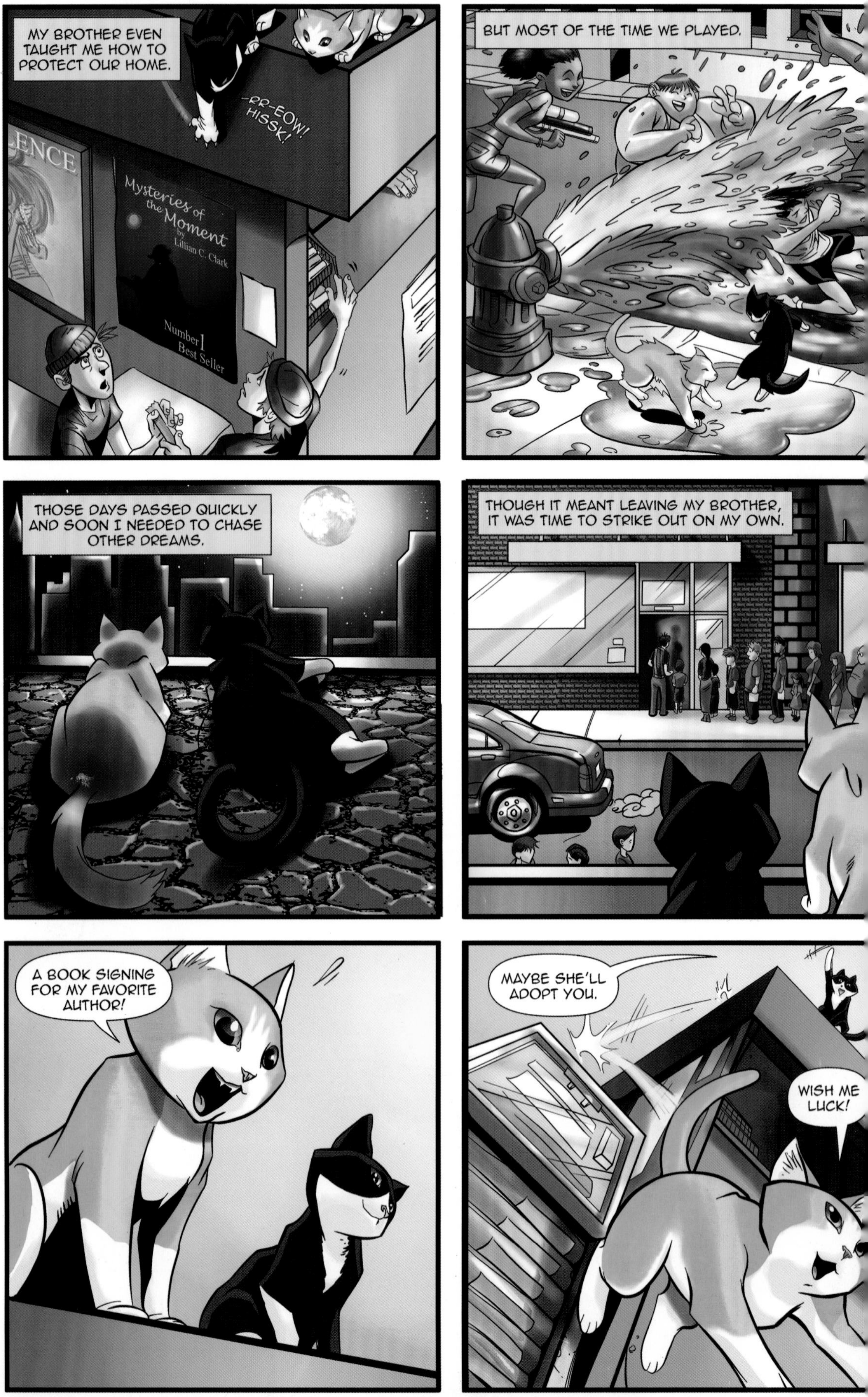

MY BROTHER EVEN TAUGHT ME HOW TO PROTECT OUR HOME.
-RR-EOW! HISSK!
Mysteries of the Moment
by Lillian C. Clark
Number 1 Best Seller
BUT MOST OF THE TIME WE PLAYED.
THOSE DAYS PASSED QUICKLY AND SOON I NEEDED TO CHASE OTHER DREAMS.
THOUGH IT MEANT LEAVING MY BROTHER, IT WAS TIME TO STRIKE OUT ON MY OWN.
A BOOK SIGNING FOR MY FAVORITE AUTHOR!
MAYBE SHE'LL ADOPT YOU.
WISH ME LUCK!

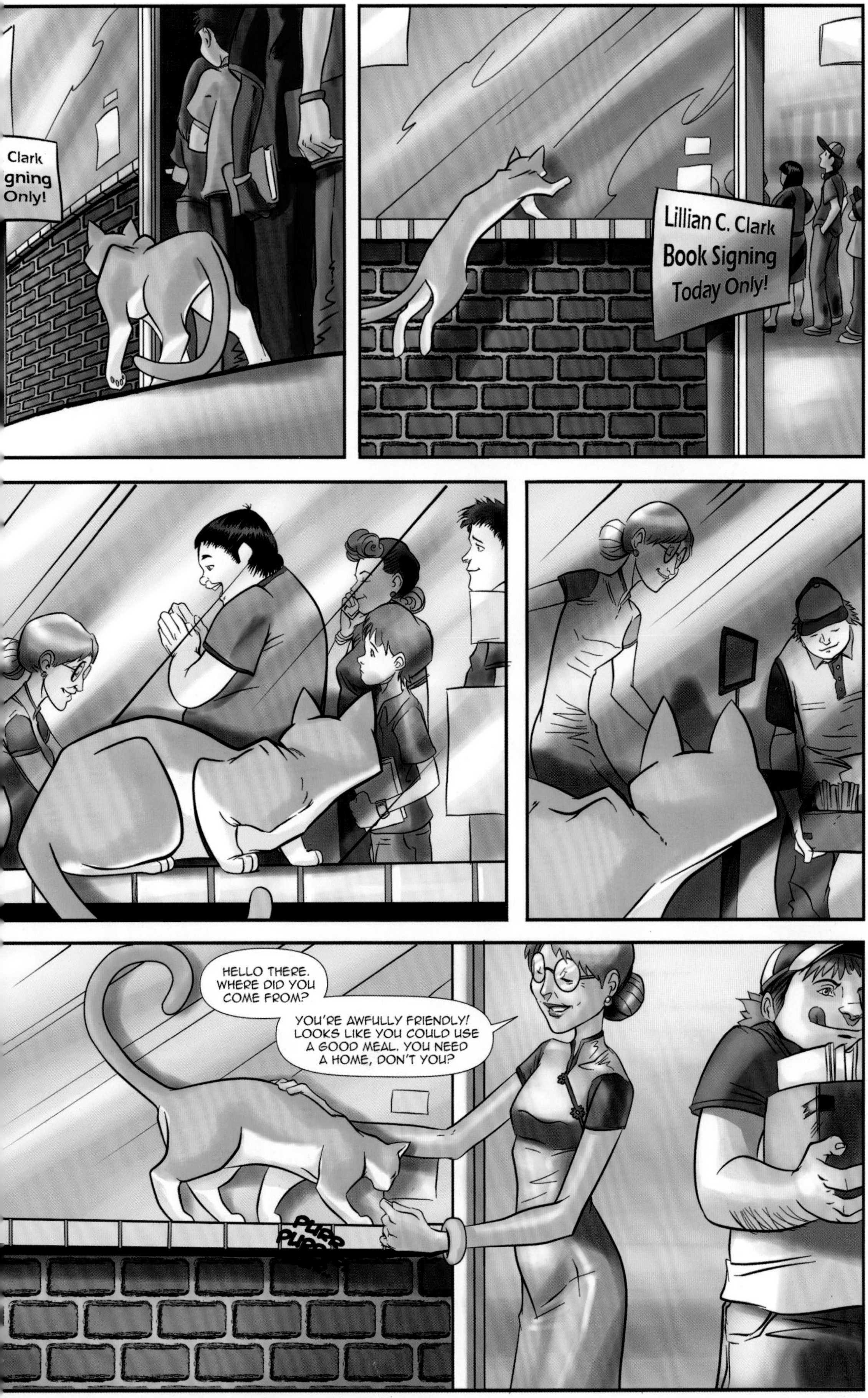
Clark
gning
Only!
Lillian C. Clark
Book Signing
Today Only!
HELLO THERE. WHERE DID YOU COME FROM?
YOU'RE AWFULLY FRIENDLY! LOOKS LIKE YOU COULD USE A GOOD MEAL. YOU NEED A HOME, DON'T YOU?
PURR

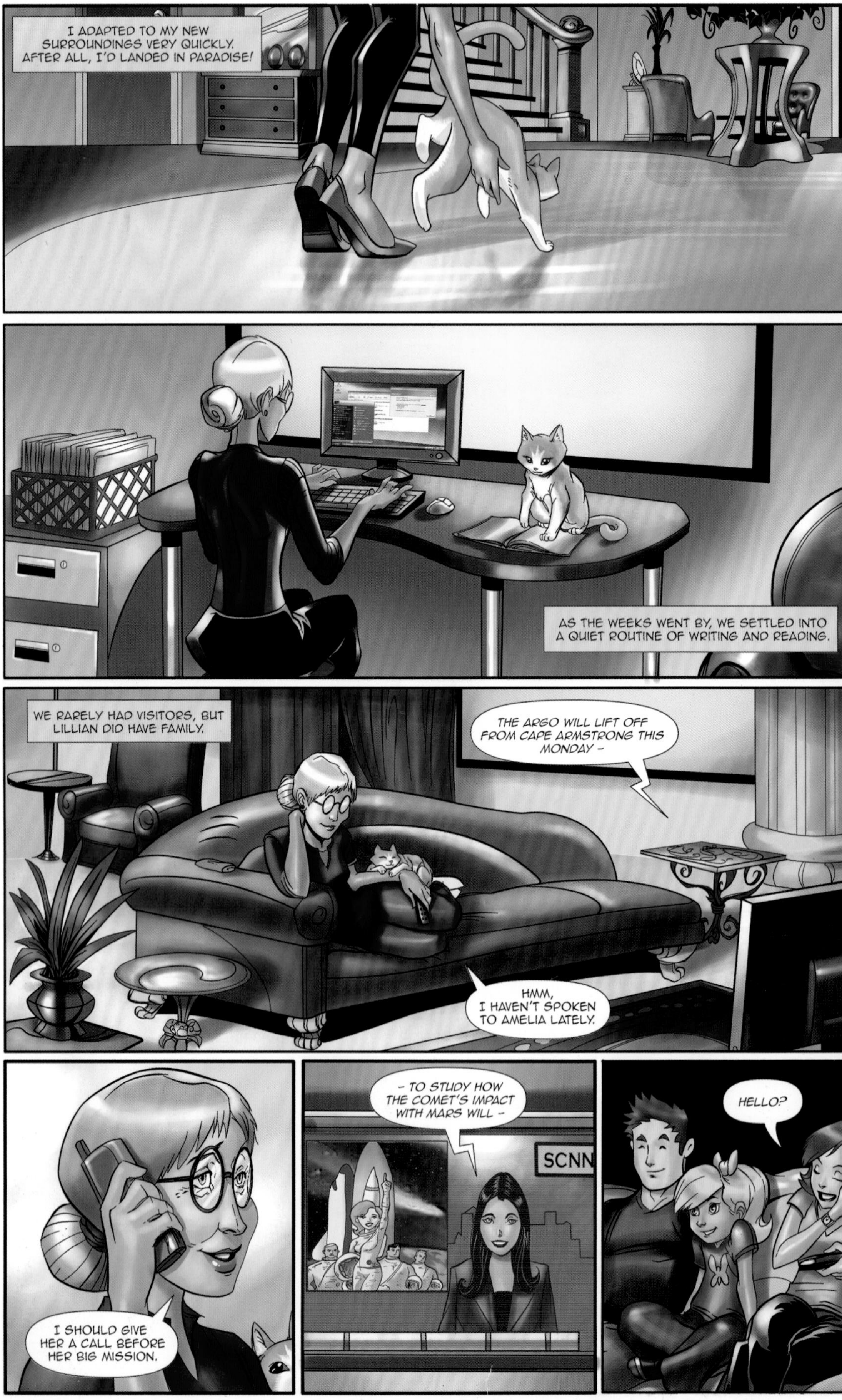
I ADAPTED TO MY NEW SURROUNDINGS VERY QUICKLY. AFTER ALL, I'D LANDED IN PARADISE!
AS THE WEEKS WENT BY, WE SETTLED INTO A QUIET ROUTINE OF WRITING AND READING.
WE RARELY HAD VISITORS, BUT LILLIAN DID HAVE FAMILY.
THE ARGO WILL LIFT OFF FROM CAPE ARMSTRONG THIS MONDAY –
HMM, I HAVEN'T SPOKEN TO AMELIA LATELY.
I SHOULD GIVE HER A CALL BEFORE HER BIG MISSION.
– TO STUDY HOW THE COMET'S IMPACT WITH MARS WILL –
SCNN
HELLO?

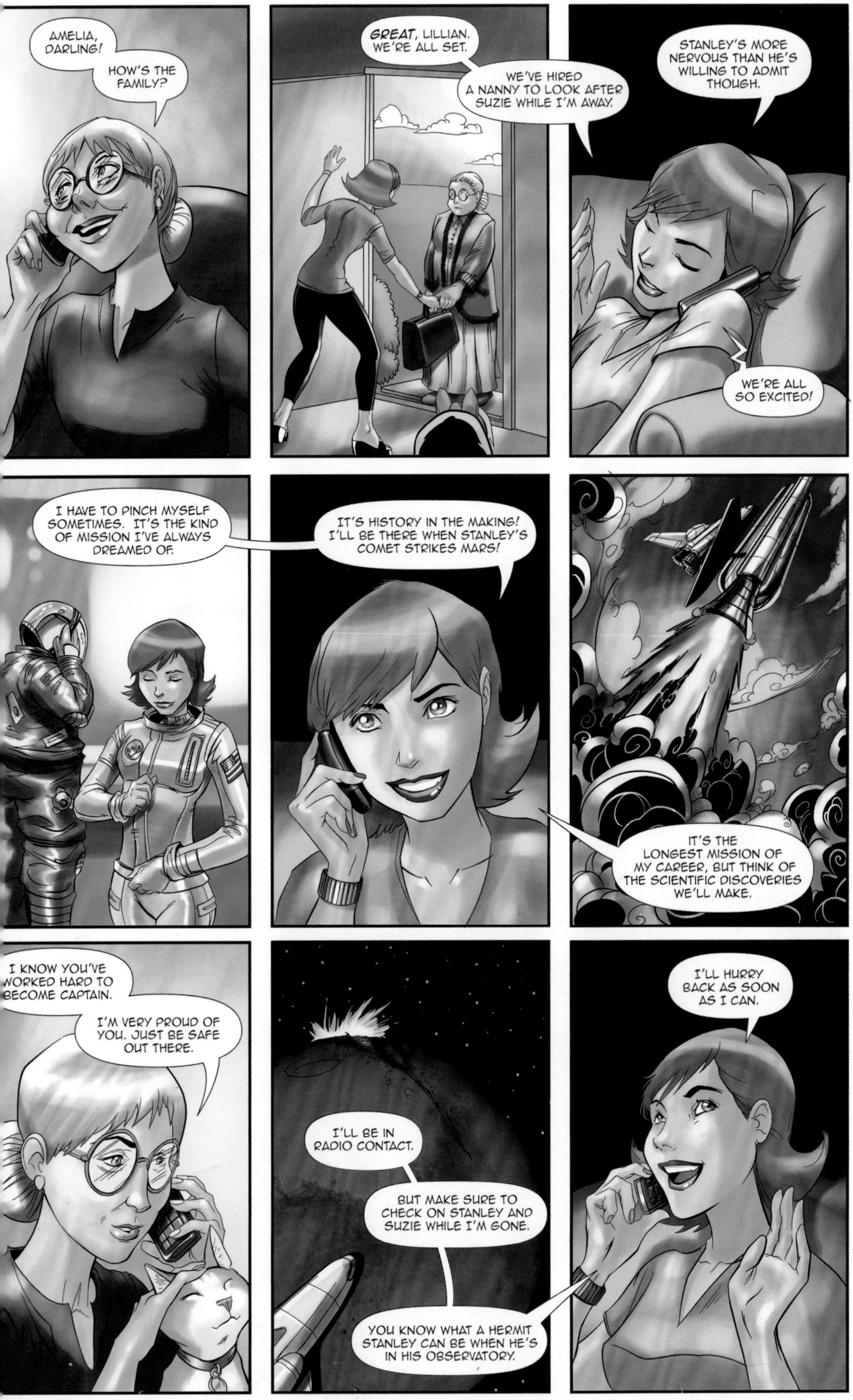
AMELIA, DARLING!
HOW'S THE FAMILY?
GREAT, LILLIAN. WE'RE ALL SET.
WE'VE HIRED A NANNY TO LOOK AFTER SUZIE WHILE I'M AWAY.
STANLEY'S MORE NERVOUS THAN HE'S WILLING TO ADMIT THOUGH.
WE'RE ALL SO EXCITED!
I HAVE TO PINCH MYSELF SOMETIMES. IT'S THE KIND OF MISSION I'VE ALWAYS DREAMED OF.
IT'S HISTORY IN THE MAKING! I'LL BE THERE WHEN STANLEY'S COMET STRIKES MARS!
IT'S THE LONGEST MISSION OF MY CAREER, BUT THINK OF THE SCIENTIFIC DISCOVERIES WE'LL MAKE.
I KNOW YOU'VE WORKED HARD TO BECOME CAPTAIN.
I'M VERY PROUD OF YOU. JUST BE SAFE OUT THERE.
I'LL BE IN RADIO CONTACT.
BUT MAKE SURE TO CHECK ON STANLEY AND SUZIE WHILE I'M GONE.
YOU KNOW WHAT A HERMIT STANLEY CAN BE WHEN HE'S IN HIS OBSERVATORY.
I'LL HURRY BACK AS SOON AS I CAN.

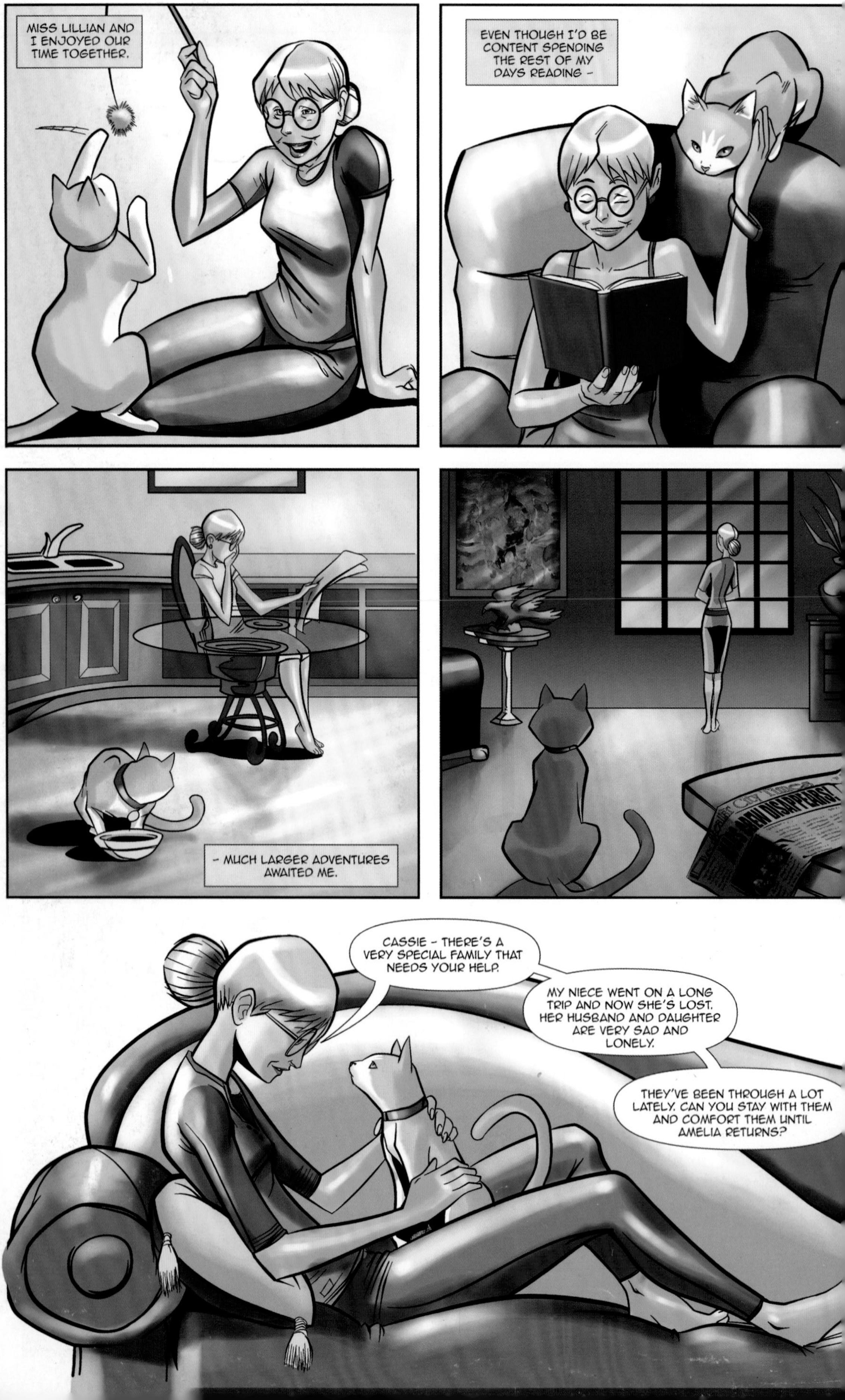
MISS LILLIAN AND I ENJOYED OUR TIME TOGETHER.
EVEN THOUGH I'D BE CONTENT SPENDING THE REST OF MY DAYS READING –
– MUCH LARGER ADVENTURES AWAITED ME.
CASSIE – THERE'S A VERY SPECIAL FAMILY THAT NEEDS YOUR HELP.
MY NIECE WENT ON A LONG TRIP AND NOW SHE'S LOST. HER HUSBAND AND DAUGHTER ARE VERY SAD AND LONELY.
THEY'VE BEEN THROUGH A LOT LATELY. CAN YOU STAY WITH THEM AND COMFORT THEM UNTIL AMELIA RETURNS?

AS MUCH AS I ENJOYED LIVING WITH MISS LILLIAN, I KNEW I WAS NEEDED ELSEWHERE.

THANK YOU FOR ADOPTING CASSIOPEIA FOR ME.

WITH ALL THE TRAVELING I DO, I JUST CAN'T WATCH AFTER HER.

WE'LL TAKE GOOD CARE OF HER.

AND I KNOW AMELIA WILL RETURN SAFELY.

WITH AS MUCH TIME AS YOU SPEND IN YOUR OBSERVATORY - YOU'LL FIND HER.

THAT'S WHEN I MET STANLEY AND SUZIE FOR THE FIRST TIME.

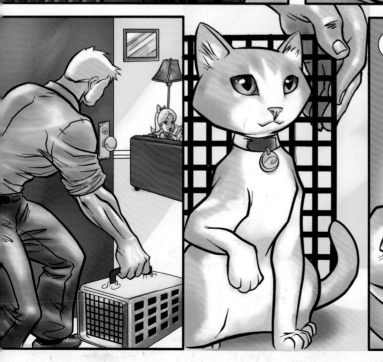

AWW, DADDY! SHE'S ADORABLE!

THAT'S WHEN I FINALLY FOUND MY HOME.

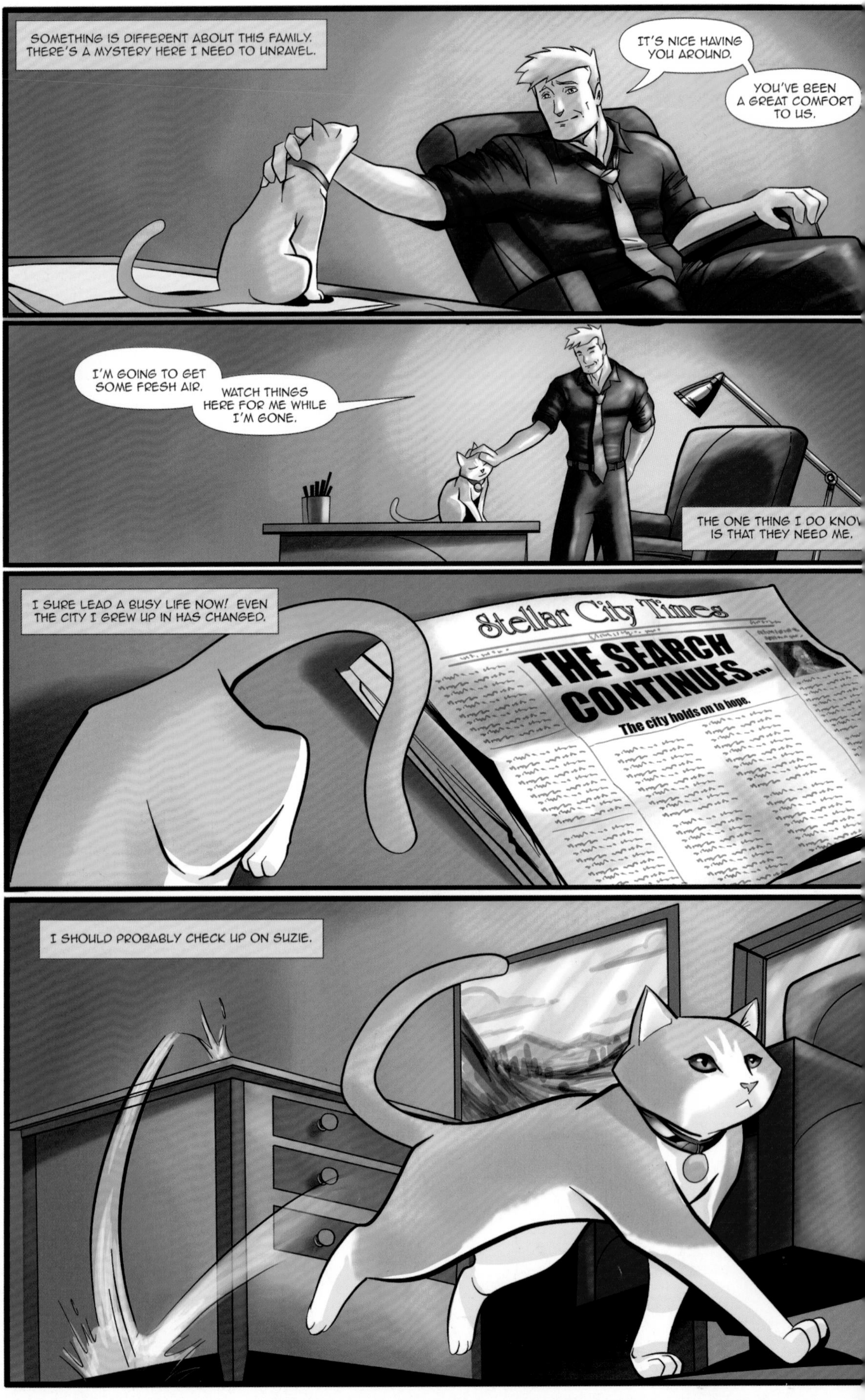
SOMETHING IS DIFFERENT ABOUT THIS FAMILY. THERE'S A MYSTERY HERE I NEED TO UNRAVEL.
IT'S NICE HAVING YOU AROUND.
YOU'VE BEEN A GREAT COMFORT TO US.
I'M GOING TO GET SOME FRESH AIR.
WATCH THINGS HERE FOR ME WHILE I'M GONE.
THE ONE THING I DO KNOW IS THAT THEY NEED ME.
I SURE LEAD A BUSY LIFE NOW! EVEN THE CITY I GREW UP IN HAS CHANGED.
Stellar City Times
THE SEARCH CONTINUES...
The city holds on to hope.
I SHOULD PROBABLY CHECK UP ON SUZIE.

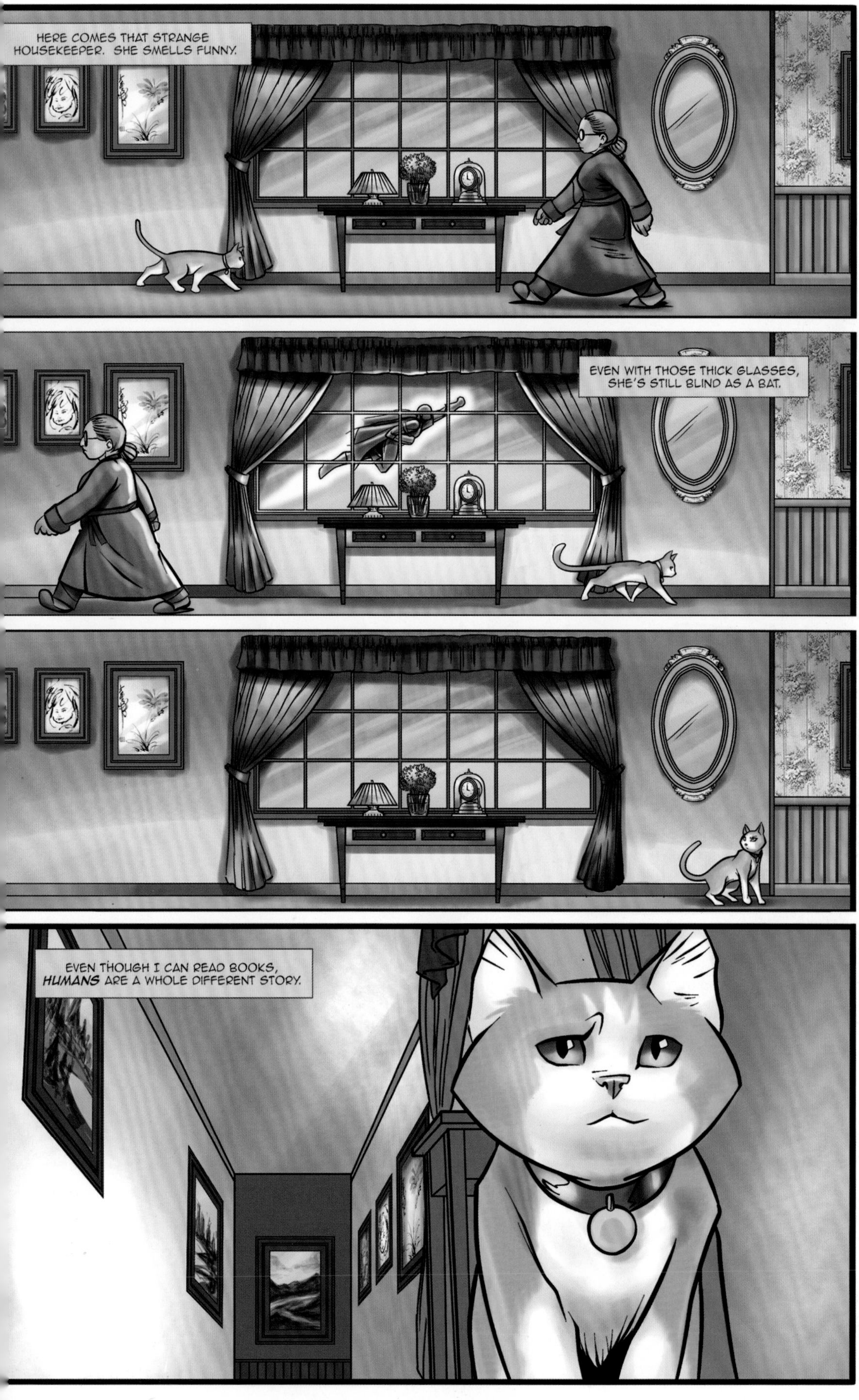
HERE COMES THAT STRANGE HOUSEKEEPER. SHE SMELLS FUNNY.
EVEN WITH THOSE THICK GLASSES, SHE'S STILL BLIND AS A BAT.
EVEN THOUGH I CAN READ BOOKS, HUMANS ARE A WHOLE DIFFERENT STORY.

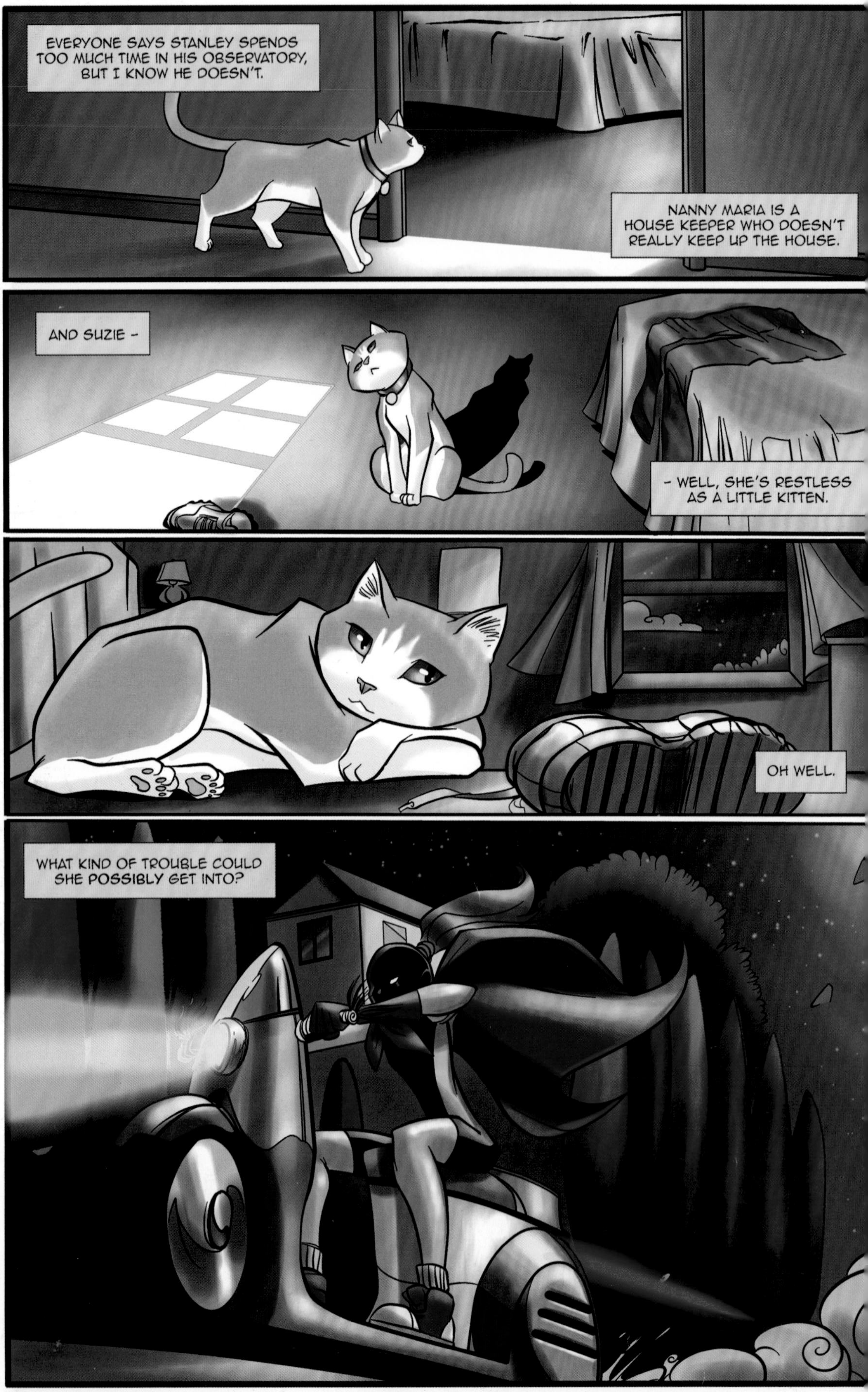
EVERYONE SAYS STANLEY SPENDS TOO MUCH TIME IN HIS OBSERVATORY, BUT I KNOW HE DOESN'T.
NANNY MARIA IS A HOUSE KEEPER WHO DOESN'T REALLY KEEP UP THE HOUSE.
AND SUZIE -
- WELL, SHE'S RESTLESS AS A LITTLE KITTEN.
OH WELL.
WHAT KIND OF TROUBLE COULD SHE POSSIBLY GET INTO?

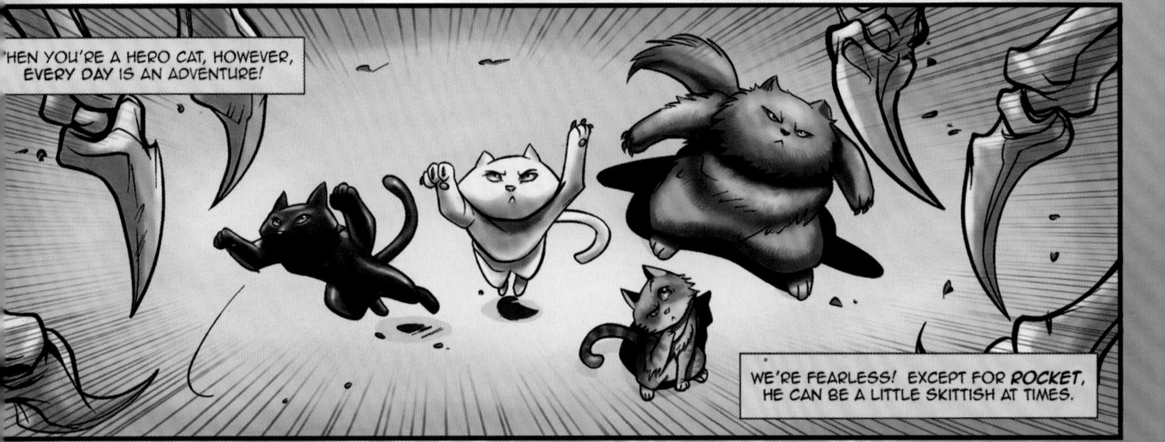

'HEN YOU'RE A HERO CAT, HOWEVER, EVERY DAY IS AN ADVENTURE!
WE'RE FEARLESS! EXCEPT FOR ROCKET, HE CAN BE A LITTLE SKITTISH AT TIMES.

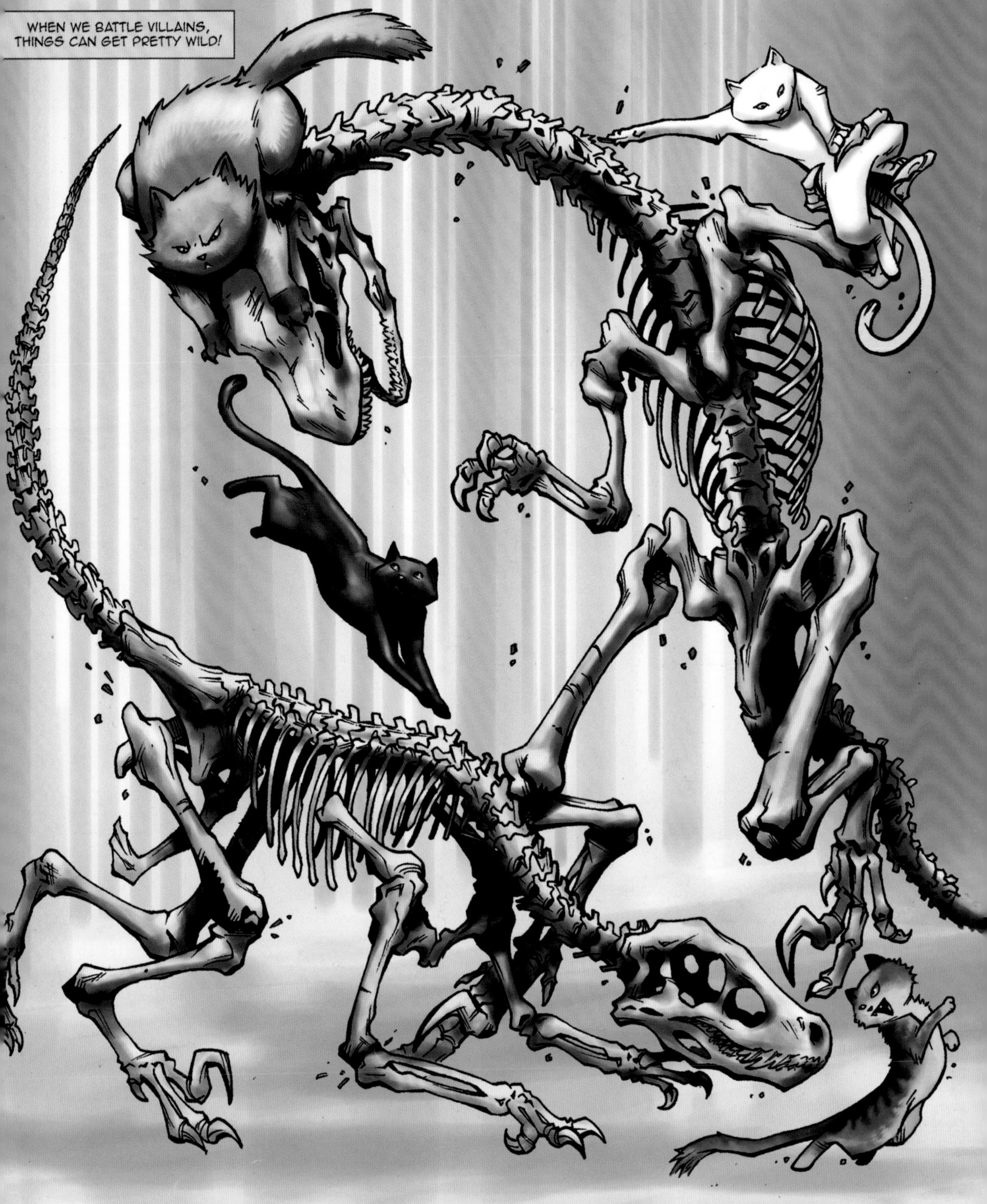

WHEN WE BATTLE VILLAINS, THINGS CAN GET PRETTY WILD!

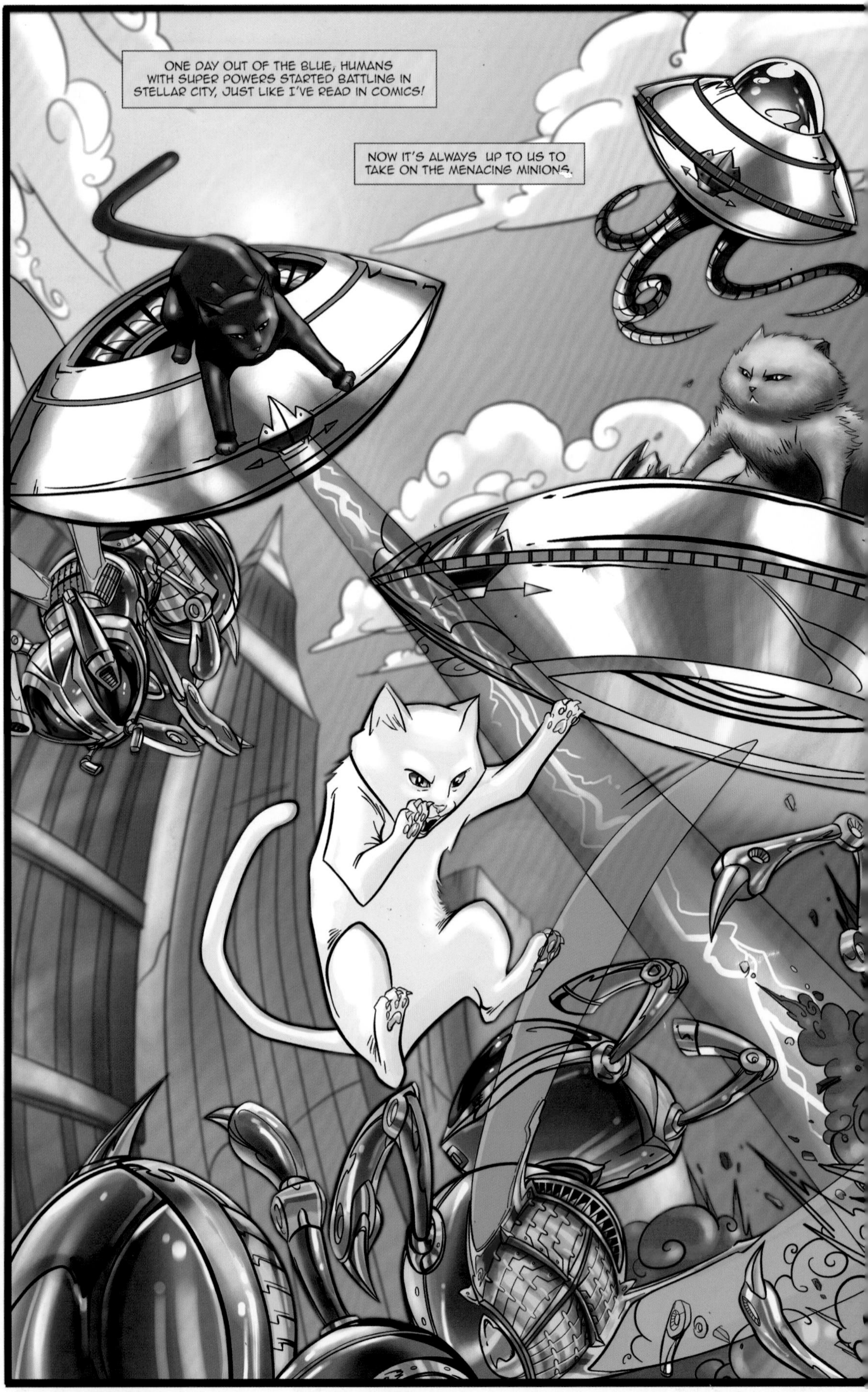
ONE DAY OUT OF THE BLUE, HUMANS WITH SUPER POWERS STARTED BATTLING IN STELLAR CITY, JUST LIKE I'VE READ IN COMICS!
NOW IT'S ALWAYS UP TO US TO TAKE ON THE MENACING MINIONS.

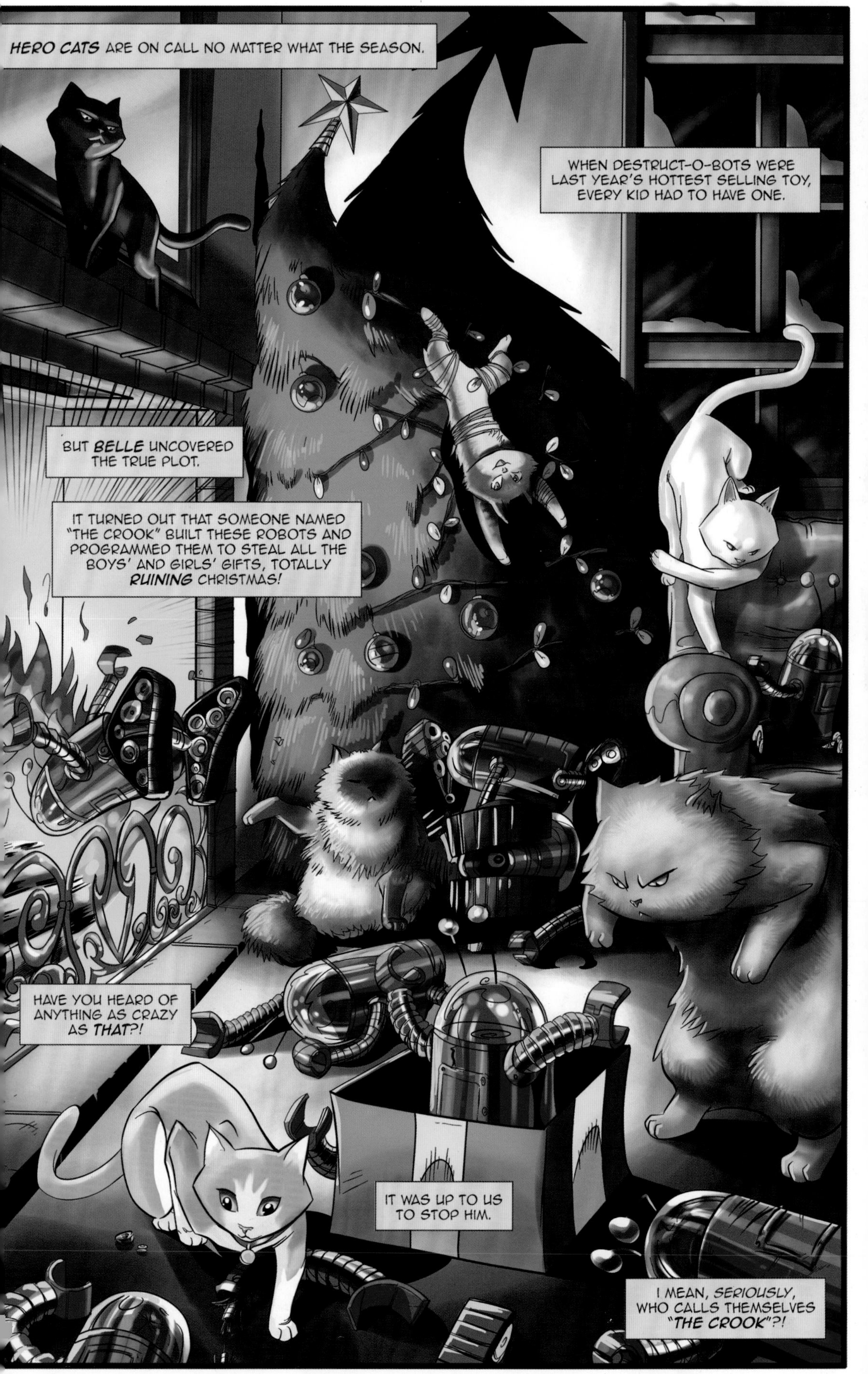
HERO CATS ARE ON CALL NO MATTER WHAT THE SEASON.
WHEN DESTRUCT-O-BOTS WERE LAST YEAR'S HOTTEST SELLING TOY, EVERY KID HAD TO HAVE ONE.
BUT BELLE UNCOVERED THE TRUE PLOT.
IT TURNED OUT THAT SOMEONE NAMED "THE CROOK" BUILT THESE ROBOTS AND PROGRAMMED THEM TO STEAL ALL THE BOYS' AND GIRLS' GIFTS, TOTALLY RUINING CHRISTMAS!
HAVE YOU HEARD OF ANYTHING AS CRAZY AS THAT?!
IT WAS UP TO US TO STOP HIM.
I MEAN, SERIOUSLY, WHO CALLS THEMSELVES "THE CROOK"?!

BUT IT'S NOT ALL WORK AND DARING EXPLOITS –

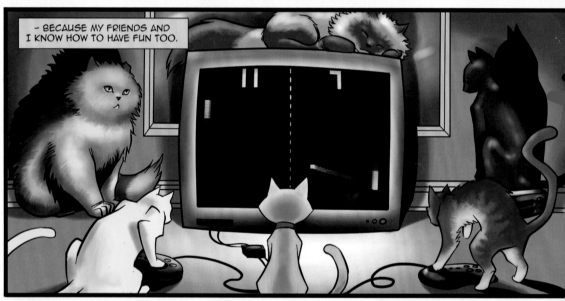

– BECAUSE MY FRIENDS AND I KNOW HOW TO HAVE FUN TOO.

SURE, WE CAN GET PRETTY COMPETITIVE –

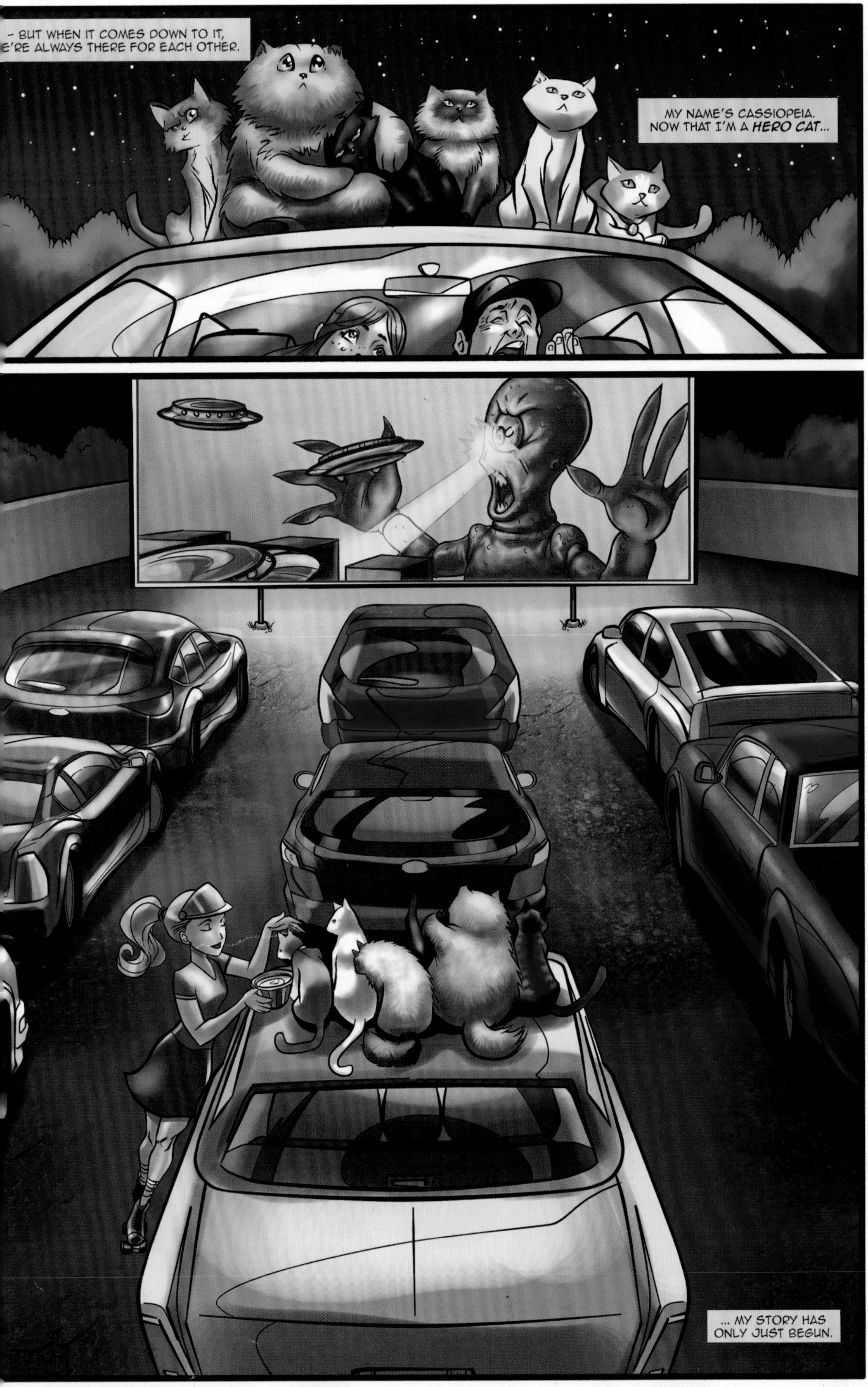
- BUT WHEN IT COMES DOWN TO IT,
E'RE ALWAYS THERE FOR EACH OTHER.
MY NAME'S CASSIOPEIA. NOW THAT I'M A **HERO CAT**...
... MY STORY HAS ONLY JUST BEGUN.

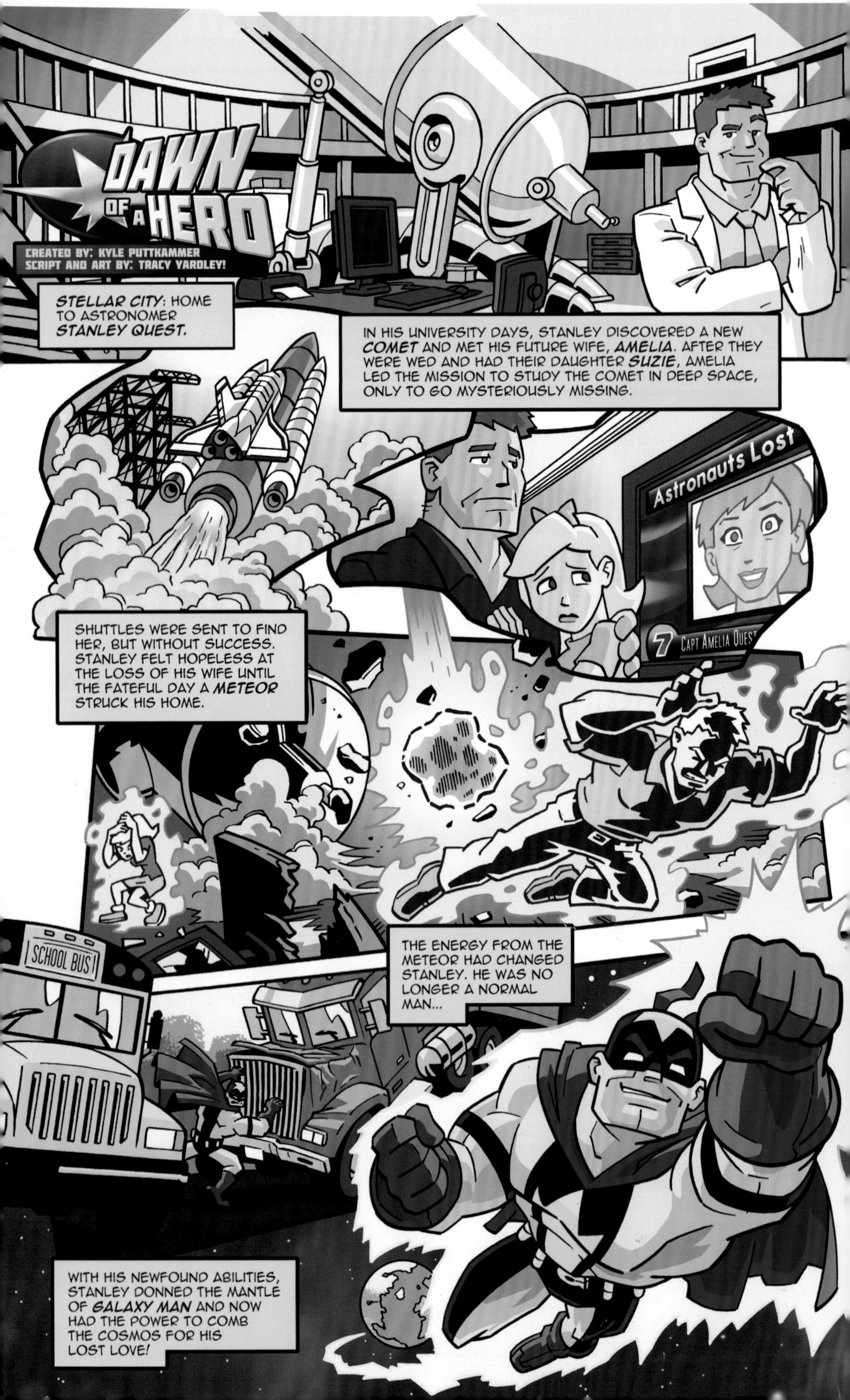
DAWN OF A HERO
CREATED BY: KYLE PUTTKAMMER
SCRIPT AND ART BY: TRACY YARDLEY!
STELLAR CITY: HOME TO ASTRONOMER STANLEY QUEST.
IN HIS UNIVERSITY DAYS, STANLEY DISCOVERED A NEW COMET AND MET HIS FUTURE WIFE, AMELIA. AFTER THEY WERE WED AND HAD THEIR DAUGHTER SUZIE, AMELIA LED THE MISSION TO STUDY THE COMET IN DEEP SPACE, ONLY TO GO MYSTERIOUSLY MISSING.
Astronauts Lost
7 CAPT AMELIA QUEST
SHUTTLES WERE SENT TO FIND HER, BUT WITHOUT SUCCESS. STANLEY FELT HOPELESS AT THE LOSS OF HIS WIFE UNTIL THE FATEFUL DAY A METEOR STRUCK HIS HOME.
SCHOOL BUS
THE ENERGY FROM THE METEOR HAD CHANGED STANLEY. HE WAS NO LONGER A NORMAL MAN...
WITH HIS NEWFOUND ABILITIES, STANLEY DONNED THE MANTLE OF GALAXY MAN AND NOW HAD THE POWER TO COMB THE COSMOS FOR HIS LOST LOVE!

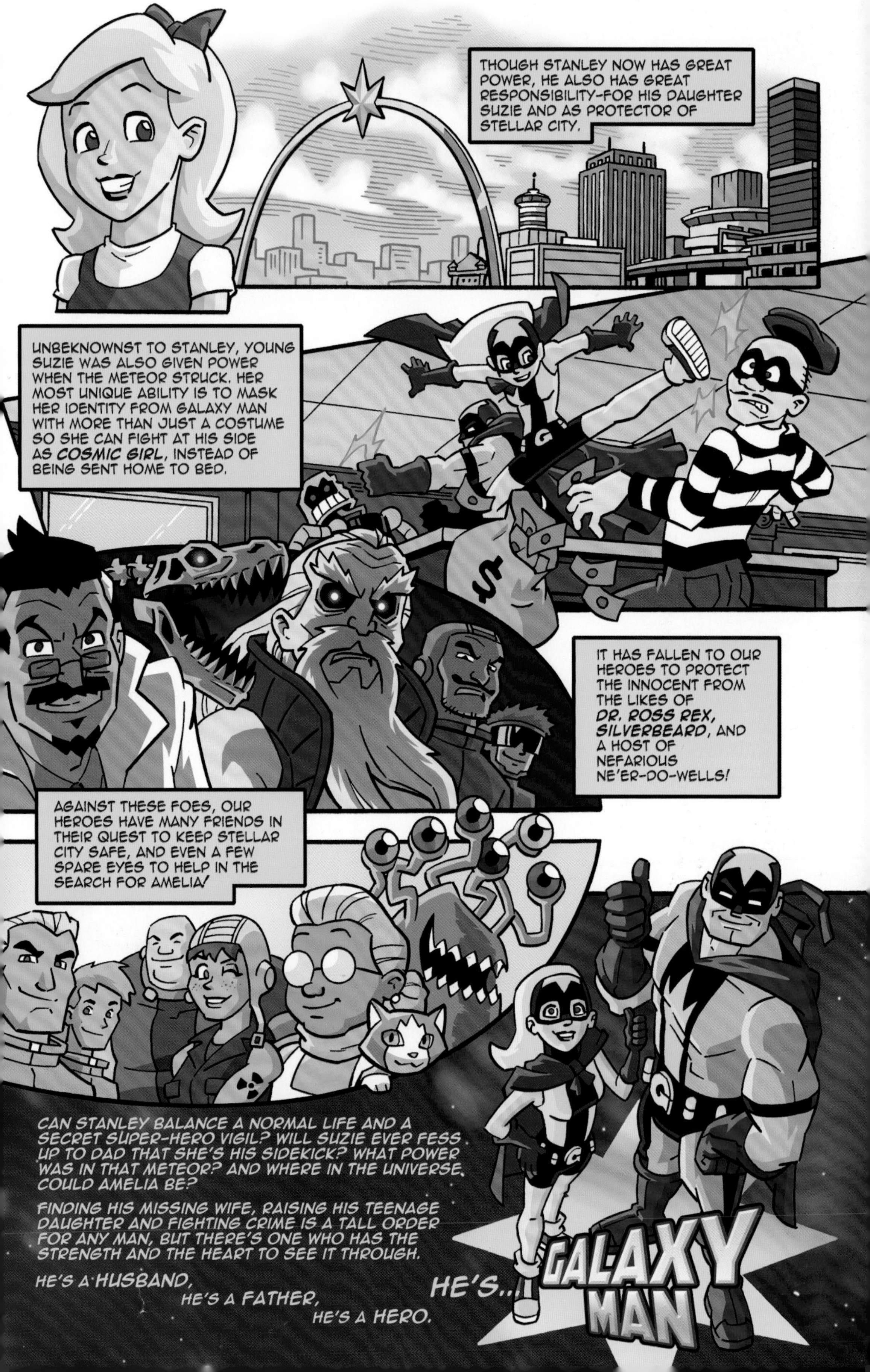
THOUGH STANLEY NOW HAS GREAT POWER, HE ALSO HAS GREAT RESPONSIBILITY–FOR HIS DAUGHTER SUZIE AND AS PROTECTOR OF STELLAR CITY.
UNBEKNOWNST TO STANLEY, YOUNG SUZIE WAS ALSO GIVEN POWER WHEN THE METEOR STRUCK. HER MOST UNIQUE ABILITY IS TO MASK HER IDENTITY FROM GALAXY MAN WITH MORE THAN JUST A COSTUME SO SHE CAN FIGHT AT HIS SIDE AS COSMIC GIRL, INSTEAD OF BEING SENT HOME TO BED.
IT HAS FALLEN TO OUR HEROES TO PROTECT THE INNOCENT FROM THE LIKES OF DR. ROSS REX, SILVERBEARD, AND A HOST OF NEFARIOUS NE'ER-DO-WELLS!
AGAINST THESE FOES, OUR HEROES HAVE MANY FRIENDS IN THEIR QUEST TO KEEP STELLAR CITY SAFE, AND EVEN A FEW SPARE EYES TO HELP IN THE SEARCH FOR AMELIA!
CAN STANLEY BALANCE A NORMAL LIFE AND A SECRET SUPER-HERO VIGIL? WILL SUZIE EVER FESS UP TO DAD THAT SHE'S HIS SIDEKICK? WHAT POWER WAS IN THAT METEOR? AND WHERE IN THE UNIVERSE COULD AMELIA BE?
FINDING HIS MISSING WIFE, RAISING HIS TEENAGE DAUGHTER AND FIGHTING CRIME IS A TALL ORDER FOR ANY MAN, BUT THERE'S ONE WHO HAS THE STRENGTH AND THE HEART TO SEE IT THROUGH.
HE'S A HUSBAND,
HE'S A FATHER,
HE'S A HERO.
HE'S...
GALAXY MAN
$

CHAPTER 2:
THE MENACE OF JOHNNY ARCADO!

WRITER: KYLE PUTTKAMMER
PENCILS: MARCUS WILLIAMS
INKS: RYAN SELLERS
COLORS: OMAKA SCHULTZ
LETTERING: BRIANA HIGGINS

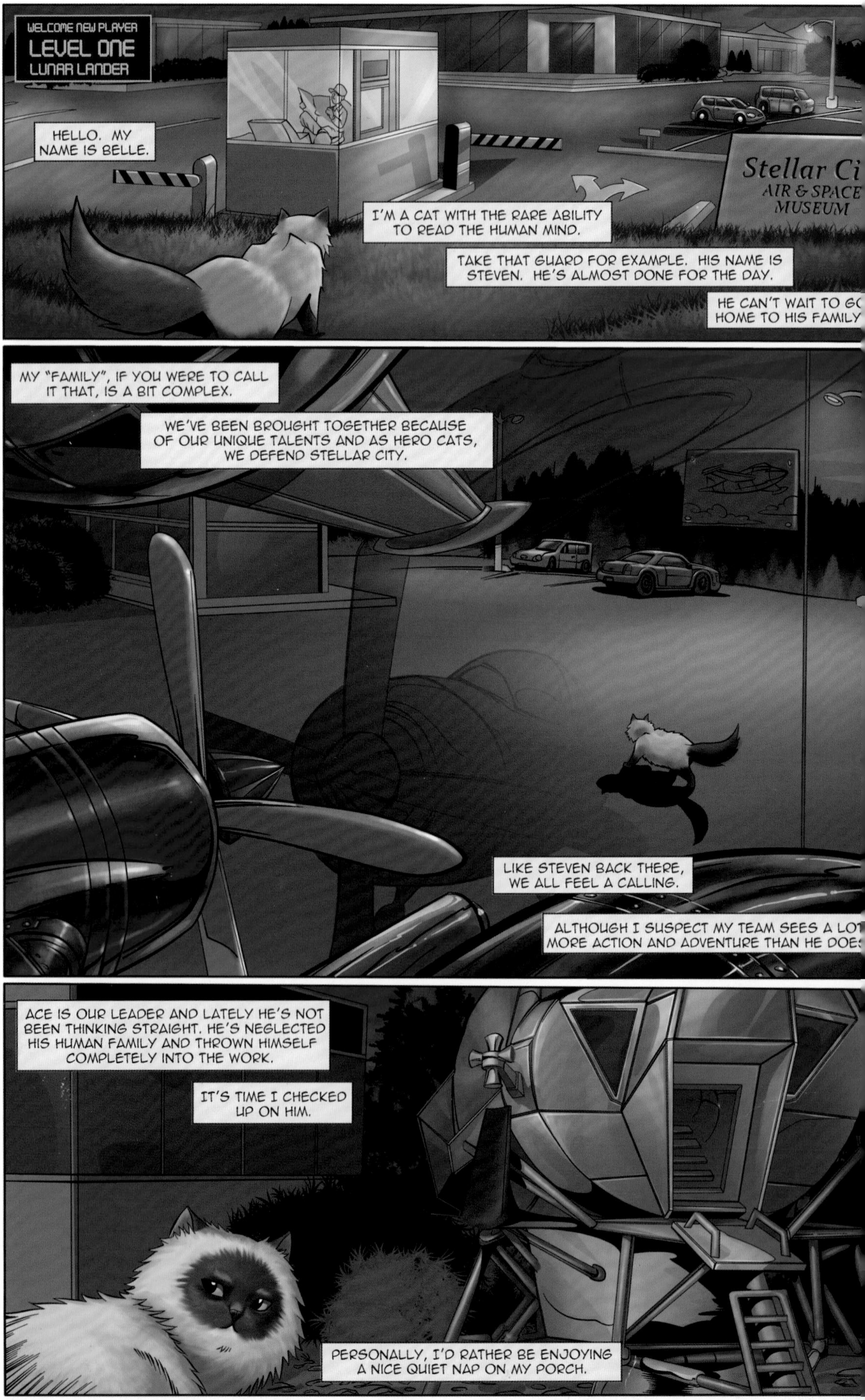

WELCOME NEW PLAYER
LEVEL ONE
LUNAR LANDER
HELLO. MY NAME IS BELLE.
Stellar Ci
AIR & SPACE
MUSEUM
I'M A CAT WITH THE RARE ABILITY TO READ THE HUMAN MIND.
TAKE THAT GUARD FOR EXAMPLE. HIS NAME IS STEVEN. HE'S ALMOST DONE FOR THE DAY.
HE CAN'T WAIT TO GO HOME TO HIS FAMILY
MY "FAMILY", IF YOU WERE TO CALL IT THAT, IS A BIT COMPLEX.
WE'VE BEEN BROUGHT TOGETHER BECAUSE OF OUR UNIQUE TALENTS AND AS HERO CATS, WE DEFEND STELLAR CITY.
LIKE STEVEN BACK THERE, WE ALL FEEL A CALLING.
ALTHOUGH I SUSPECT MY TEAM SEES A LOT MORE ACTION AND ADVENTURE THAN HE DOES
ACE IS OUR LEADER AND LATELY HE'S NOT BEEN THINKING STRAIGHT. HE'S NEGLECTED HIS HUMAN FAMILY AND THROWN HIMSELF COMPLETELY INTO THE WORK.
IT'S TIME I CHECKED UP ON HIM.
PERSONALLY, I'D RATHER BE ENJOYING A NICE QUIET NAP ON MY PORCH.

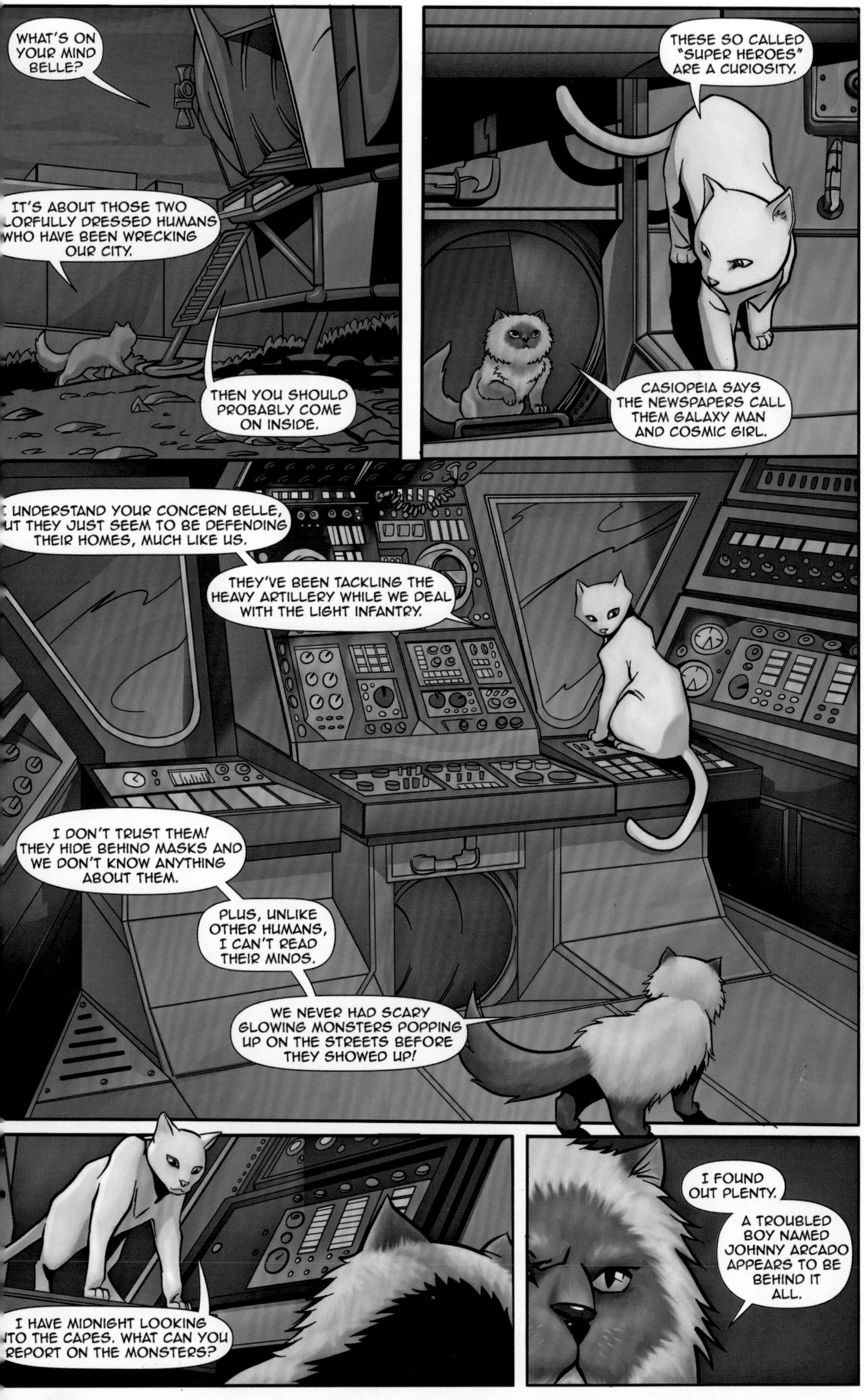
WHAT'S ON YOUR MIND BELLE?
IT'S ABOUT THOSE TWO COLORFULLY DRESSED HUMANS WHO HAVE BEEN WRECKING OUR CITY.
THEN YOU SHOULD PROBABLY COME ON INSIDE.
THESE SO CALLED "SUPER HEROES" ARE A CURIOSITY.
CASIOPEIA SAYS THE NEWSPAPERS CALL THEM GALAXY MAN AND COSMIC GIRL.
I UNDERSTAND YOUR CONCERN BELLE, BUT THEY JUST SEEM TO BE DEFENDING THEIR HOMES, MUCH LIKE US.
THEY'VE BEEN TACKLING THE HEAVY ARTILLERY WHILE WE DEAL WITH THE LIGHT INFANTRY.
I DON'T TRUST THEM! THEY HIDE BEHIND MASKS AND WE DON'T KNOW ANYTHING ABOUT THEM.
PLUS, UNLIKE OTHER HUMANS, I CAN'T READ THEIR MINDS.
WE NEVER HAD SCARY GLOWING MONSTERS POPPING UP ON THE STREETS BEFORE THEY SHOWED UP!
I HAVE MIDNIGHT LOOKING INTO THE CAPES. WHAT CAN YOU REPORT ON THE MONSTERS?
I FOUND OUT PLENTY.
A TROUBLED BOY NAMED JOHNNY ARCADO APPEARS TO BE BEHIND IT ALL.

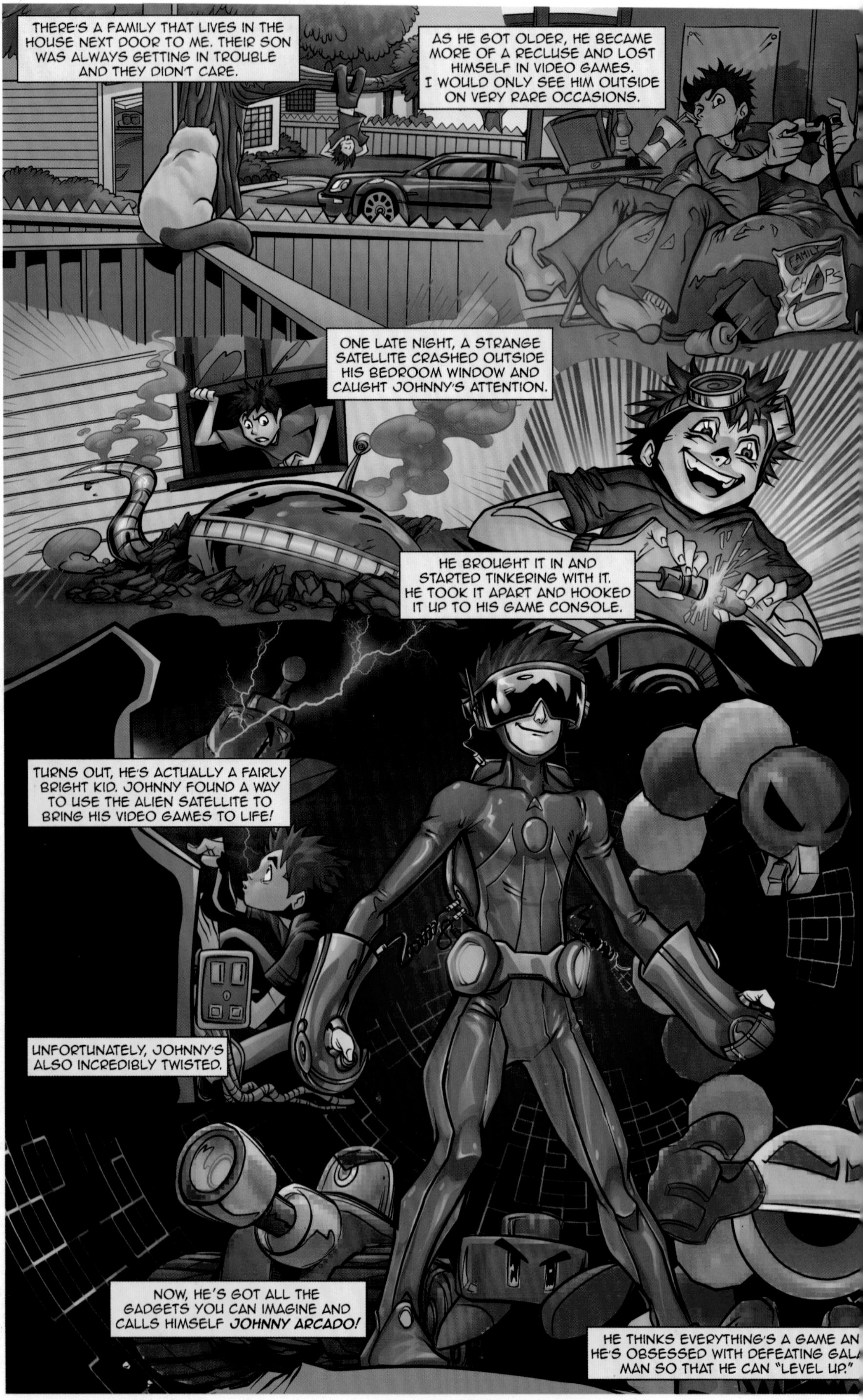
THERE'S A FAMILY THAT LIVES IN THE HOUSE NEXT DOOR TO ME. THEIR SON WAS ALWAYS GETTING IN TROUBLE AND THEY DIDN'T CARE.
AS HE GOT OLDER, HE BECAME MORE OF A RECLUSE AND LOST HIMSELF IN VIDEO GAMES. I WOULD ONLY SEE HIM OUTSIDE ON VERY RARE OCCASIONS.
FAMILY CHIPS
ONE LATE NIGHT, A STRANGE SATELLITE CRASHED OUTSIDE HIS BEDROOM WINDOW AND CAUGHT JOHNNY'S ATTENTION.
HE BROUGHT IT IN AND STARTED TINKERING WITH IT. HE TOOK IT APART AND HOOKED IT UP TO HIS GAME CONSOLE.
TURNS OUT, HE'S ACTUALLY A FAIRLY BRIGHT KID. JOHNNY FOUND A WAY TO USE THE ALIEN SATELLITE TO BRING HIS VIDEO GAMES TO LIFE!
UNFORTUNATELY, JOHNNY'S ALSO INCREDIBLY TWISTED.
NOW, HE'S GOT ALL THE GADGETS YOU CAN IMAGINE AND CALLS HIMSELF *JOHNNY ARCADO!*
HE THINKS EVERYTHING'S A GAME AN HE'S OBSESSED WITH DEFEATING GALA MAN SO THAT HE CAN "LEVEL UP."

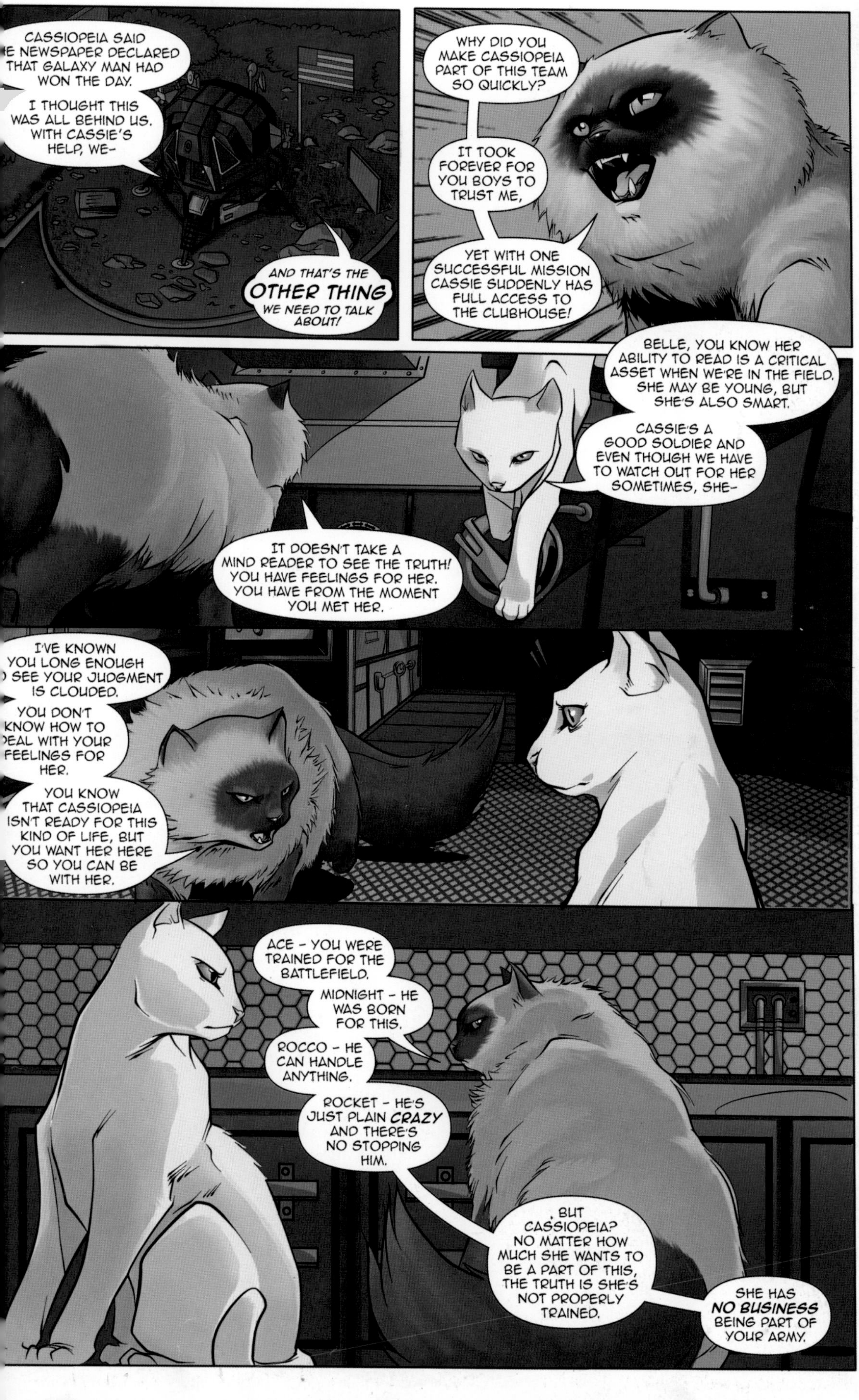
CASSIOPEIA SAID
E NEWSPAPER DECLARED THAT GALAXY MAN HAD WON THE DAY.
I THOUGHT THIS WAS ALL BEHIND US. WITH CASSIE'S HELP, WE-
AND THAT'S THE OTHER THING WE NEED TO TALK ABOUT!
WHY DID YOU MAKE CASSIOPEIA PART OF THIS TEAM SO QUICKLY?
IT TOOK FOREVER FOR YOU BOYS TO TRUST ME,
YET WITH ONE SUCCESSFUL MISSION CASSIE SUDDENLY HAS FULL ACCESS TO THE CLUBHOUSE!
BELLE, YOU KNOW HER ABILITY TO READ IS A CRITICAL ASSET WHEN WE'RE IN THE FIELD. SHE MAY BE YOUNG, BUT SHE'S ALSO SMART.
CASSIE'S A GOOD SOLDIER AND EVEN THOUGH WE HAVE TO WATCH OUT FOR HER SOMETIMES, SHE-
IT DOESN'T TAKE A MIND READER TO SEE THE TRUTH! YOU HAVE FEELINGS FOR HER. YOU HAVE FROM THE MOMENT YOU MET HER.
I'VE KNOWN YOU LONG ENOUGH
SEE YOUR JUDGMENT IS CLOUDED.
YOU DON'T KNOW HOW TO
EAL WITH YOUR
EELINGS FOR HER.
YOU KNOW THAT CASSIOPEIA ISN'T READY FOR THIS KIND OF LIFE, BUT YOU WANT HER HERE SO YOU CAN BE WITH HER.
ACE - YOU WERE TRAINED FOR THE BATTLEFIELD.
MIDNIGHT - HE WAS BORN FOR THIS.
ROCCO - HE CAN HANDLE ANYTHING.
ROCKET - HE'S JUST PLAIN CRAZY AND THERE'S NO STOPPING HIM.
. BUT CASSIOPEIA? NO MATTER HOW MUCH SHE WANTS TO BE A PART OF THIS, THE TRUTH IS SHE'S NOT PROPERLY TRAINED.
SHE HAS NO BUSINESS BEING PART OF YOUR ARMY.

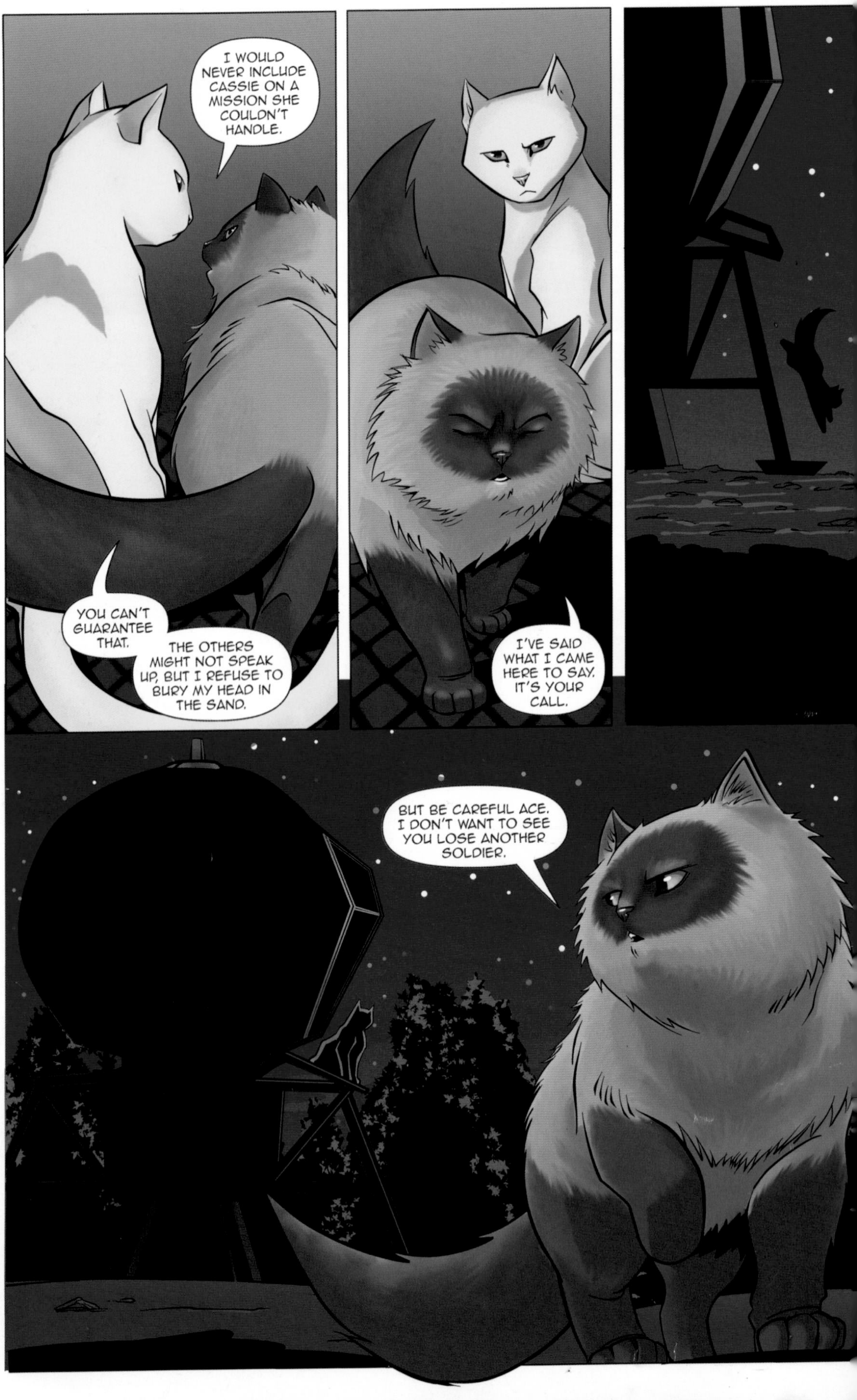
I WOULD NEVER INCLUDE CASSIE ON A MISSION SHE COULDN'T HANDLE.
YOU CAN'T GUARANTEE THAT.
THE OTHERS MIGHT NOT SPEAK UP, BUT I REFUSE TO BURY MY HEAD IN THE SAND.
I'VE SAID WHAT I CAME HERE TO SAY. IT'S YOUR CALL.
BUT BE CAREFUL ACE. I DON'T WANT TO SEE YOU LOSE ANOTHER SOLDIER.

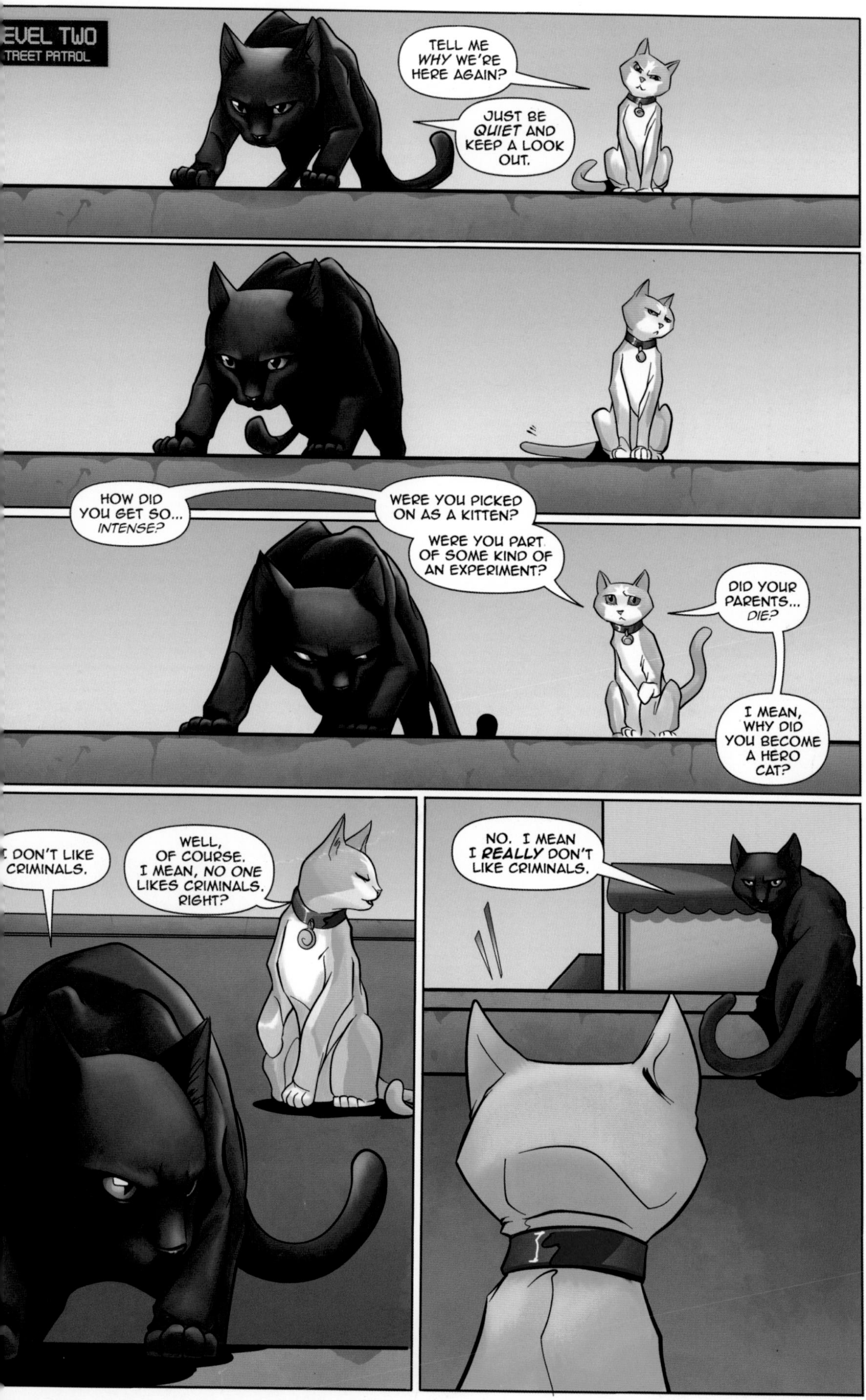

EVEL TWO
TREET PATROL
TELL ME *WHY* WE'RE HERE AGAIN?
JUST BE *QUIET* AND KEEP A LOOK OUT.
HOW DID YOU GET SO... *INTENSE?*
WERE YOU PICKED ON AS A KITTEN?
WERE YOU PART OF SOME KIND OF AN EXPERIMENT?
DID YOUR PARENTS... *DIE?*
I MEAN, WHY DID YOU BECOME A HERO CAT?
I DON'T LIKE CRIMINALS.
WELL, OF COURSE. I MEAN, NO ONE LIKES CRIMINALS. RIGHT?
NO. I MEAN I ***REALLY*** DON'T LIKE CRIMINALS.

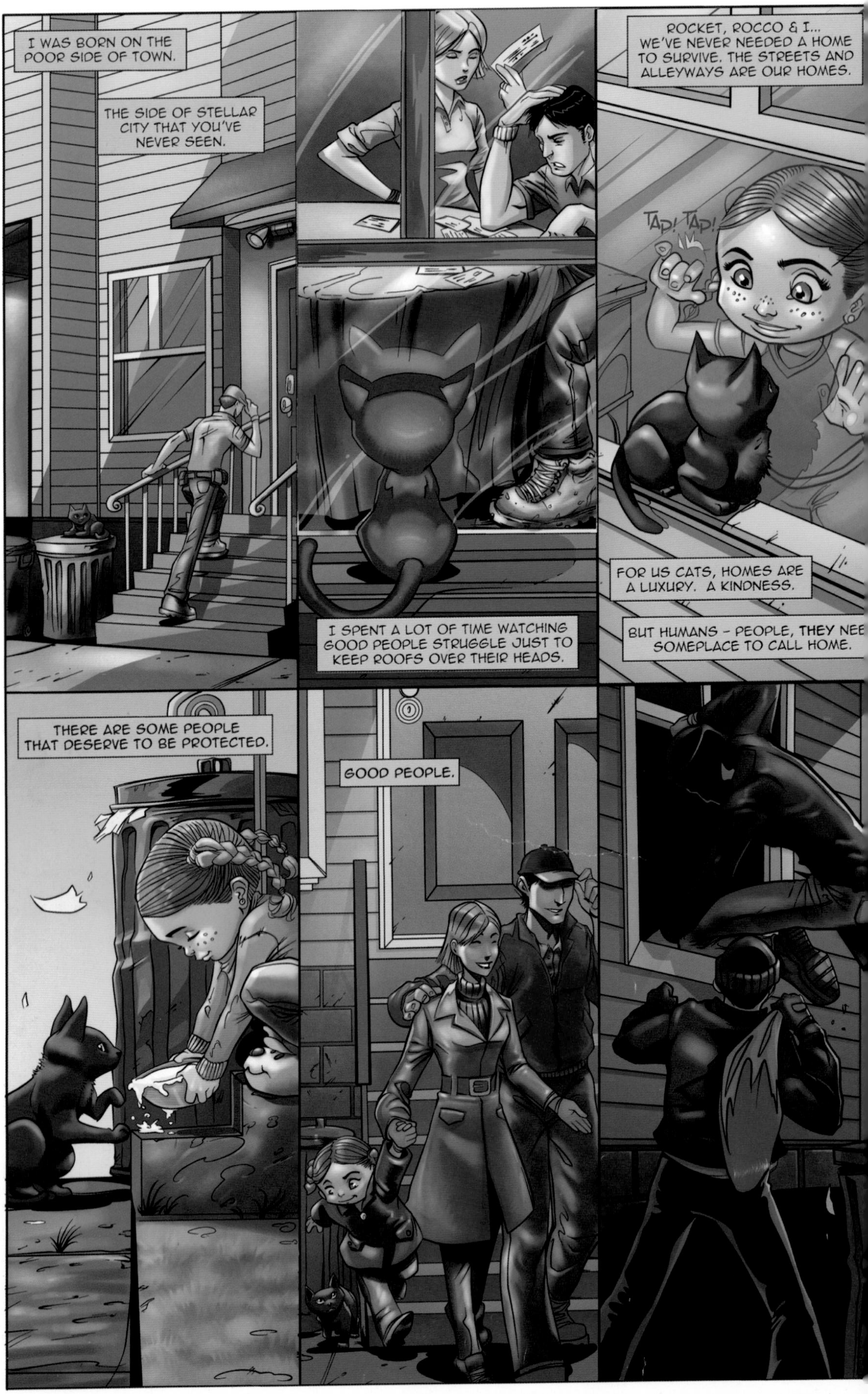
I WAS BORN ON THE POOR SIDE OF TOWN.
THE SIDE OF STELLAR CITY THAT YOU'VE NEVER SEEN.
I SPENT A LOT OF TIME WATCHING GOOD PEOPLE STRUGGLE JUST TO KEEP ROOFS OVER THEIR HEADS.
ROCKET, ROCCO & I... WE'VE NEVER NEEDED A HOME TO SURVIVE. THE STREETS AND ALLEYWAYS ARE OUR HOMES.
TAP! TAP!
FOR US CATS, HOMES ARE A LUXURY. A KINDNESS.
BUT HUMANS - PEOPLE, THEY NEE
SOMEPLACE TO CALL HOME.
THERE ARE SOME PEOPLE THAT DESERVE TO BE PROTECTED.
GOOD PEOPLE.

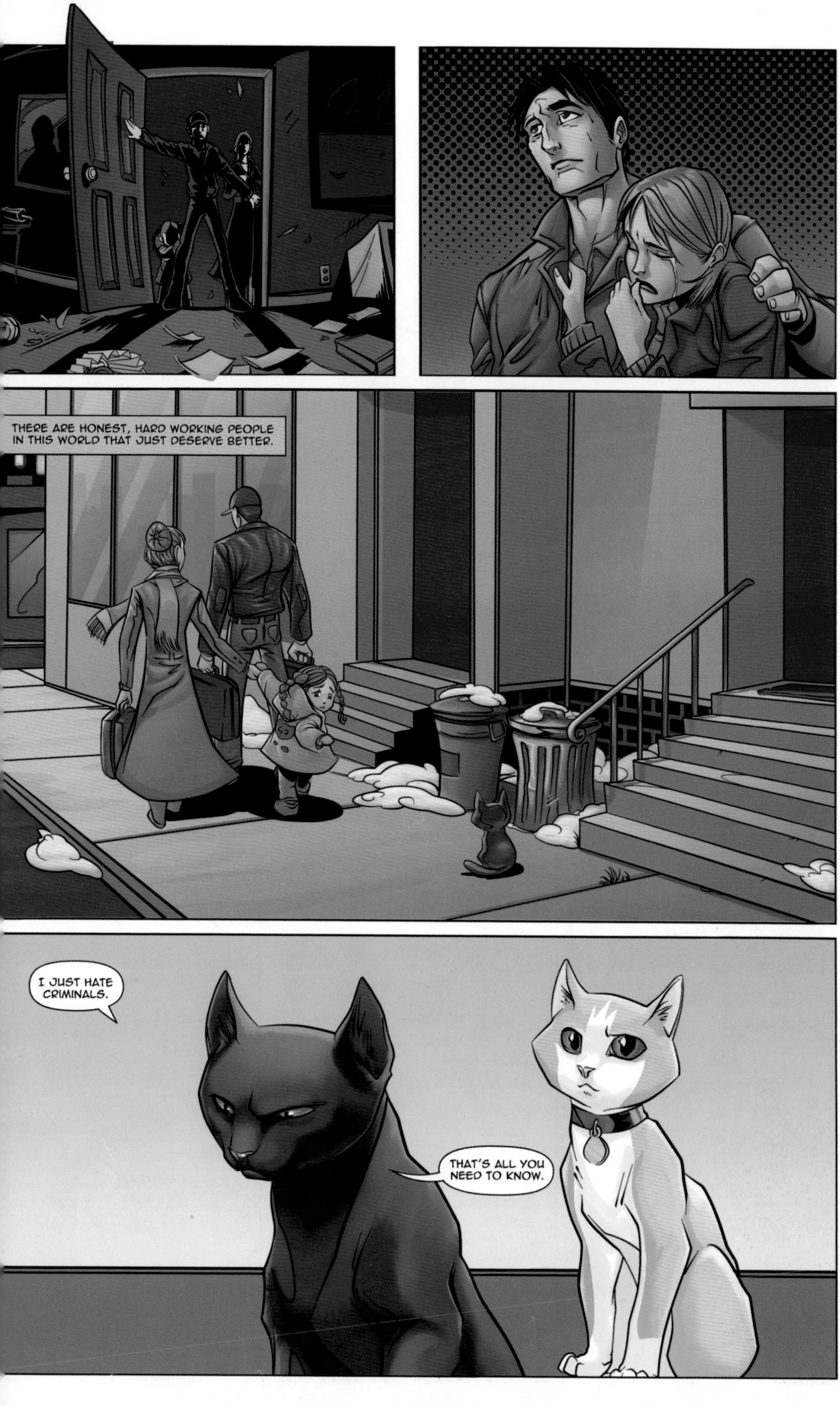
THERE ARE HONEST, HARD WORKING PEOPLE IN THIS WORLD THAT JUST DESERVE BETTER.
I JUST HATE CRIMINALS.
THAT'S ALL YOU NEED TO KNOW.

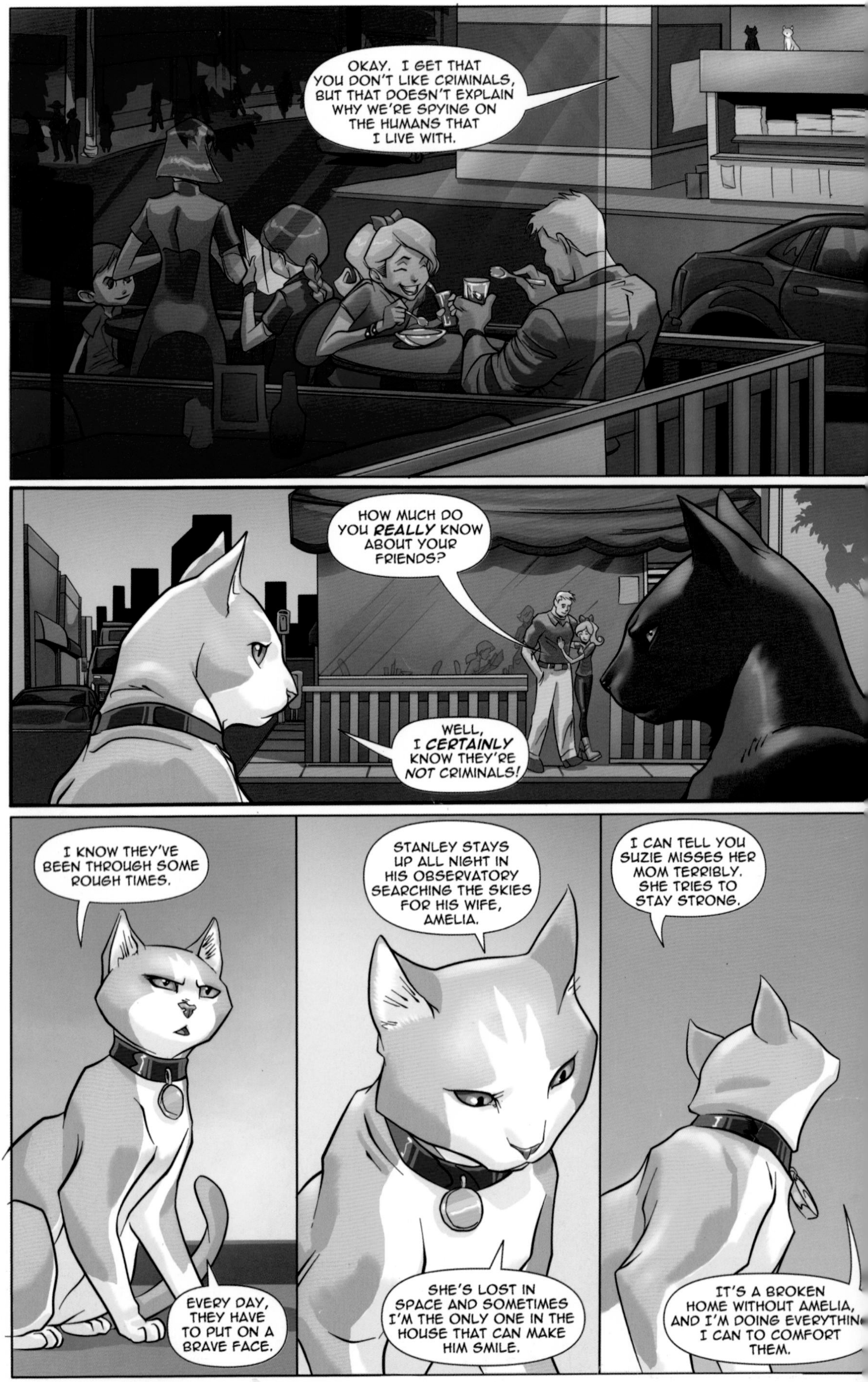
OKAY. I GET THAT YOU DON'T LIKE CRIMINALS, BUT THAT DOESN'T EXPLAIN WHY WE'RE SPYING ON THE HUMANS THAT I LIVE WITH.
HOW MUCH DO YOU *REALLY* KNOW ABOUT YOUR FRIENDS?
WELL, I *CERTAINLY* KNOW THEY'RE *NOT* CRIMINALS!
I KNOW THEY'VE BEEN THROUGH SOME ROUGH TIMES.
EVERY DAY, THEY HAVE TO PUT ON A BRAVE FACE.
STANLEY STAYS UP ALL NIGHT IN HIS OBSERVATORY SEARCHING THE SKIES FOR HIS WIFE, AMELIA.
SHE'S LOST IN SPACE AND SOMETIMES I'M THE ONLY ONE IN THE HOUSE THAT CAN MAKE HIM SMILE.
I CAN TELL YOU SUZIE MISSES HER MOM TERRIBLY. SHE TRIES TO STAY STRONG.
IT'S A BROKEN HOME WITHOUT AMELIA, AND I'M DOING EVERYTHIN I CAN TO COMFORT THEM.

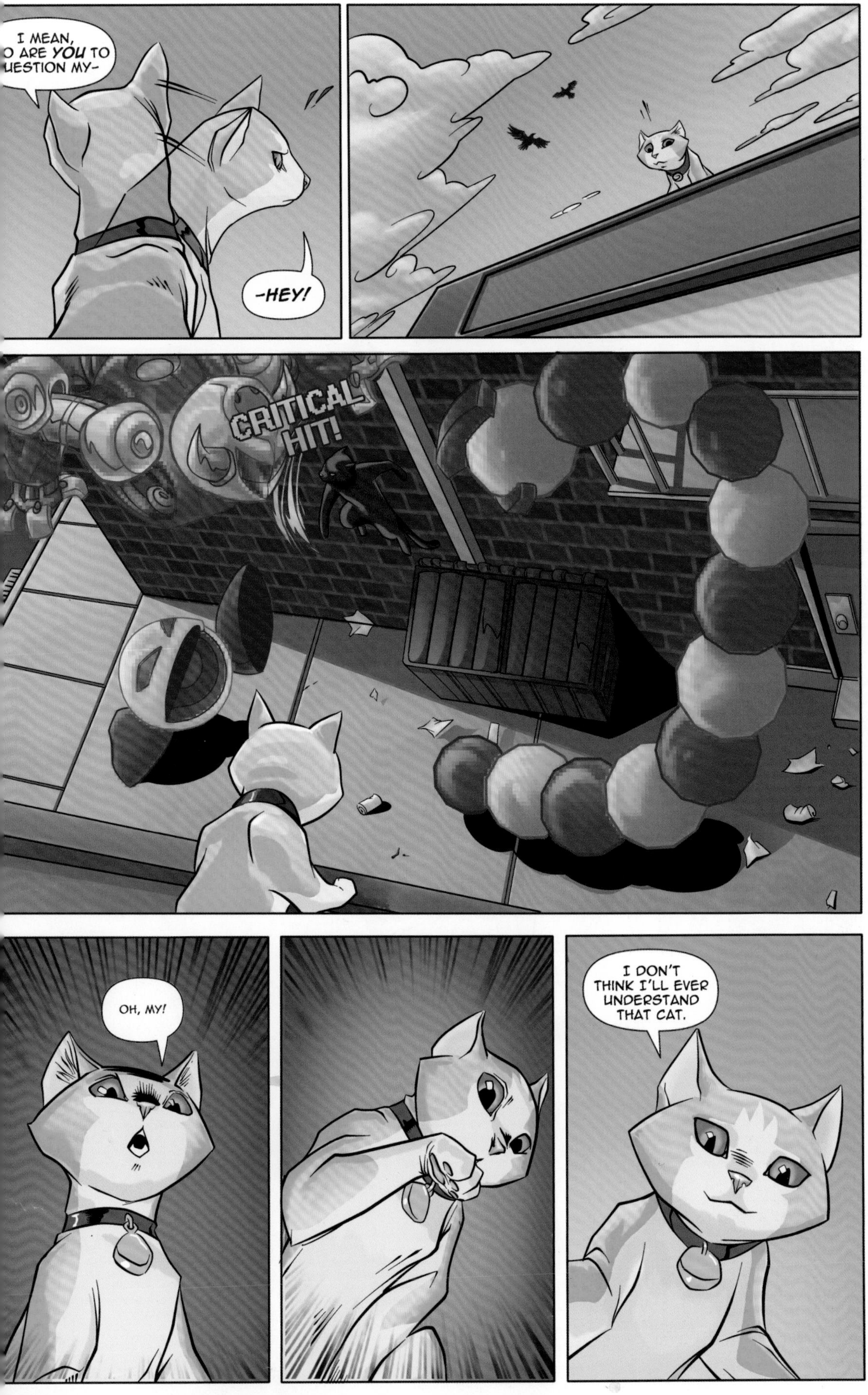
I MEAN, O ARE YOU TO UESTION MY-
-HEY!
CRITICAL HIT!
OH, MY!
I DON'T THINK I'LL EVER UNDERSTAND THAT CAT.

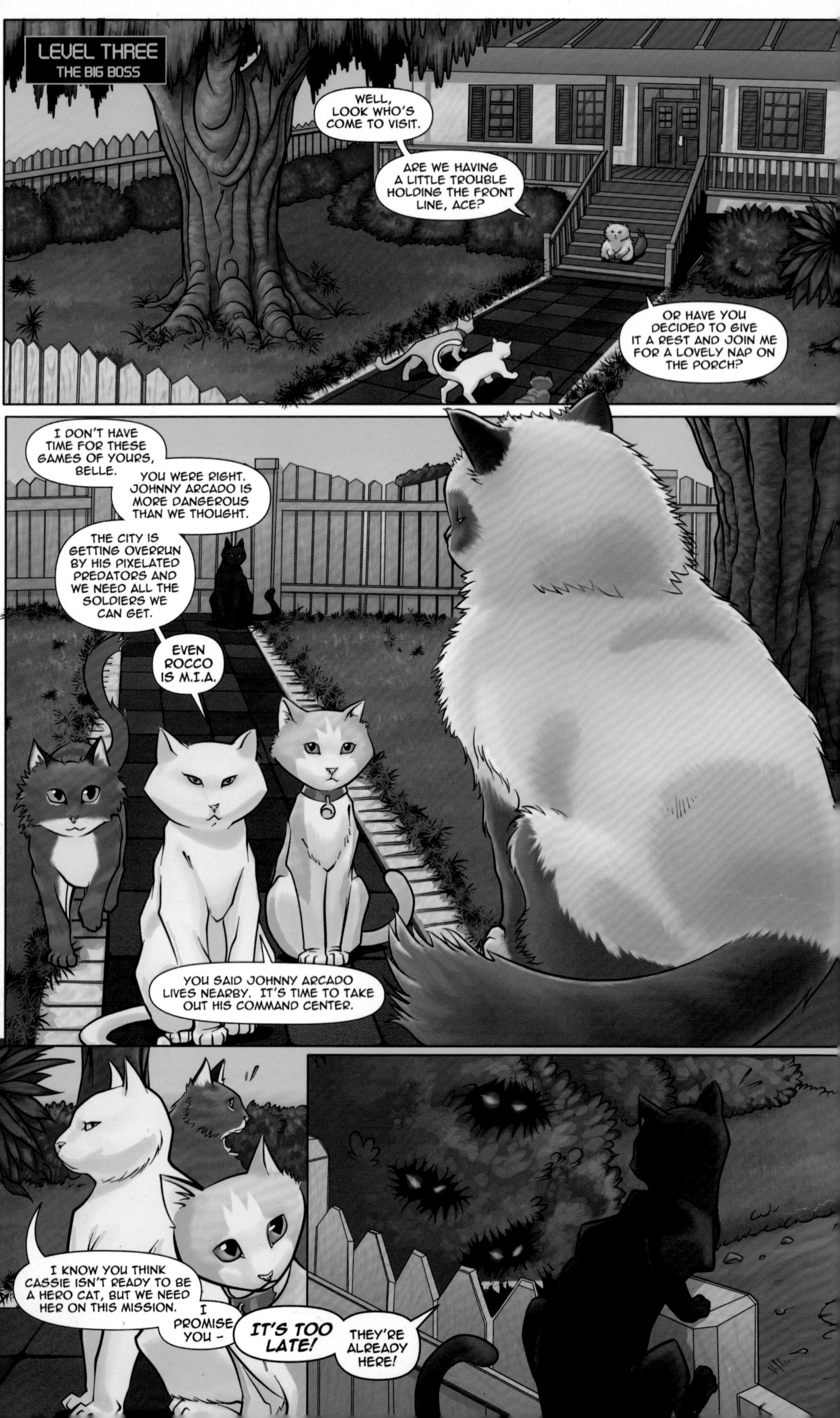
LEVEL THREE
THE BIG BOSS
WELL, LOOK WHO'S COME TO VISIT.
ARE WE HAVING A LITTLE TROUBLE HOLDING THE FRONT LINE, ACE?
OR HAVE YOU DECIDED TO GIVE IT A REST AND JOIN ME FOR A LOVELY NAP ON THE PORCH?
I DON'T HAVE TIME FOR THESE GAMES OF YOURS, BELLE.
YOU WERE RIGHT. JOHNNY ARCADO IS MORE DANGEROUS THAN WE THOUGHT.
THE CITY IS GETTING OVERRUN BY HIS PIXELATED PREDATORS AND WE NEED ALL THE SOLDIERS WE CAN GET.
EVEN ROCCO IS M.I.A.
YOU SAID JOHNNY ARCADO LIVES NEARBY. IT'S TIME TO TAKE OUT HIS COMMAND CENTER.
I KNOW YOU THINK CASSIE ISN'T READY TO BE A HERO CAT, BUT WE NEED HER ON THIS MISSION.
I PROMISE YOU -
IT'S TOO LATE!
THEY'RE ALREADY HERE!

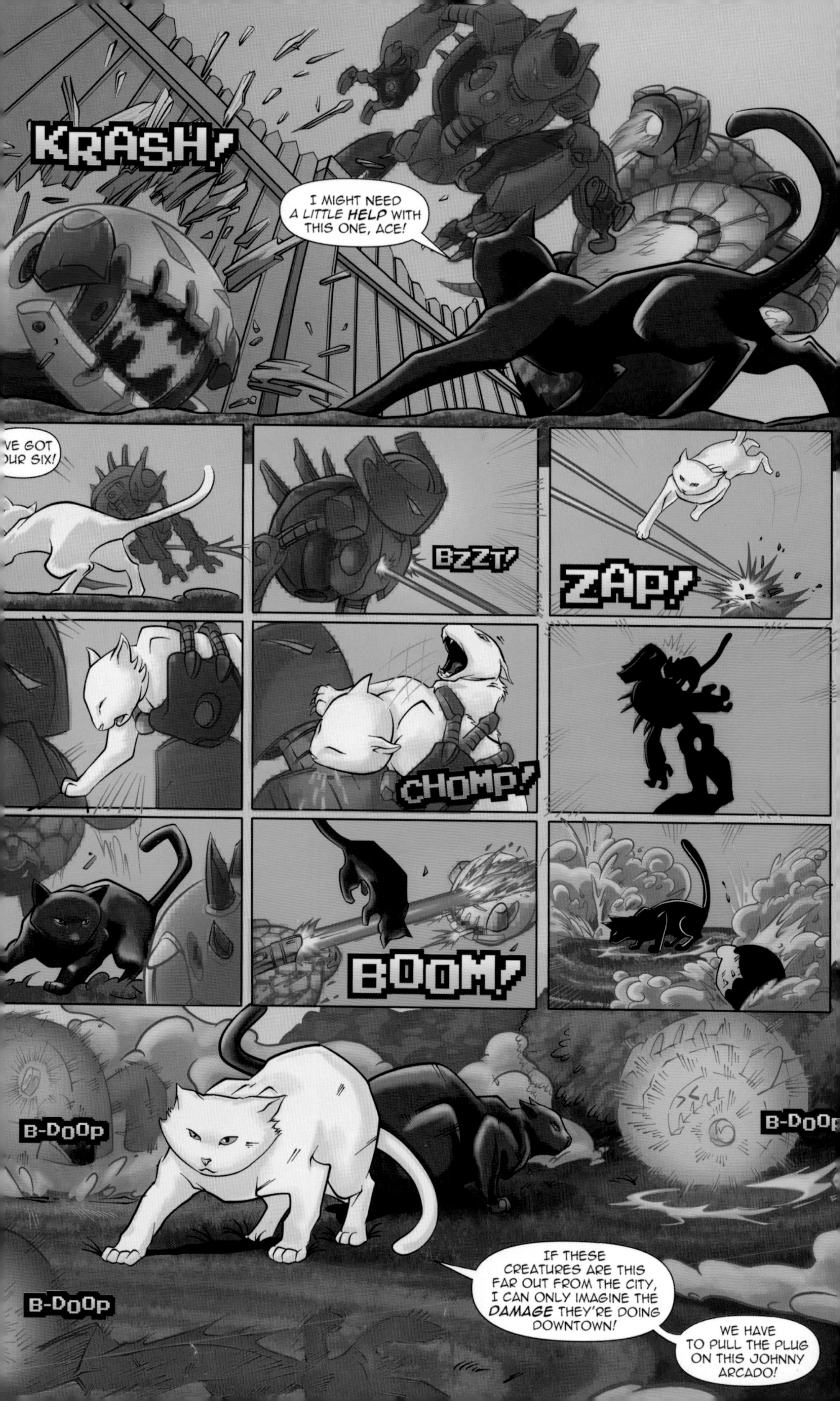
KRASH!
I MIGHT NEED A LITTLE *HELP* WITH THIS ONE, ACE!
VE GOT
UR SIX!
BZZT!
ZAP!
CHOMP!
BOOM!
B-DOOP
B-DOOP
B-DOOP
IF THESE CREATURES ARE THIS FAR OUT FROM THE CITY, I CAN ONLY IMAGINE THE *DAMAGE* THEY'RE DOING DOWNTOWN!
WE HAVE TO PULL THE PLUG ON THIS JOHNNY ARCADO!

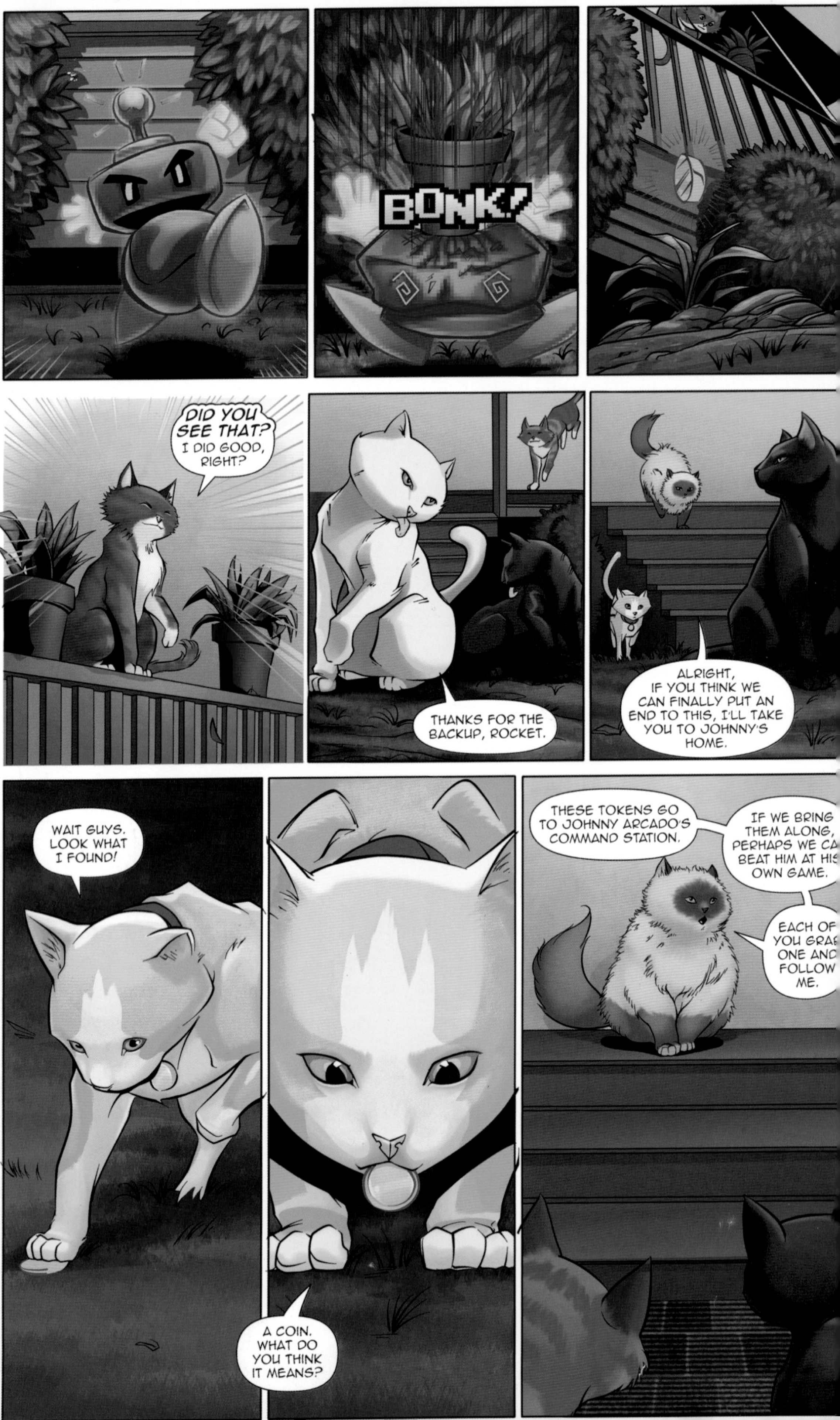
BONK!
DID YOU SEE THAT? I DID GOOD, RIGHT?
THANKS FOR THE BACKUP, ROCKET.
ALRIGHT, IF YOU THINK WE CAN FINALLY PUT AN END TO THIS, I'LL TAKE YOU TO JOHNNY'S HOME.
WAIT GUYS. LOOK WHAT I FOUND!
A COIN. WHAT DO YOU THINK IT MEANS?
THESE TOKENS GO TO JOHNNY ARCADO'S COMMAND STATION.
IF WE BRING THEM ALONG, PERHAPS WE CA BEAT HIM AT HIS OWN GAME.
EACH OF YOU GRAB ONE AND FOLLOW ME.

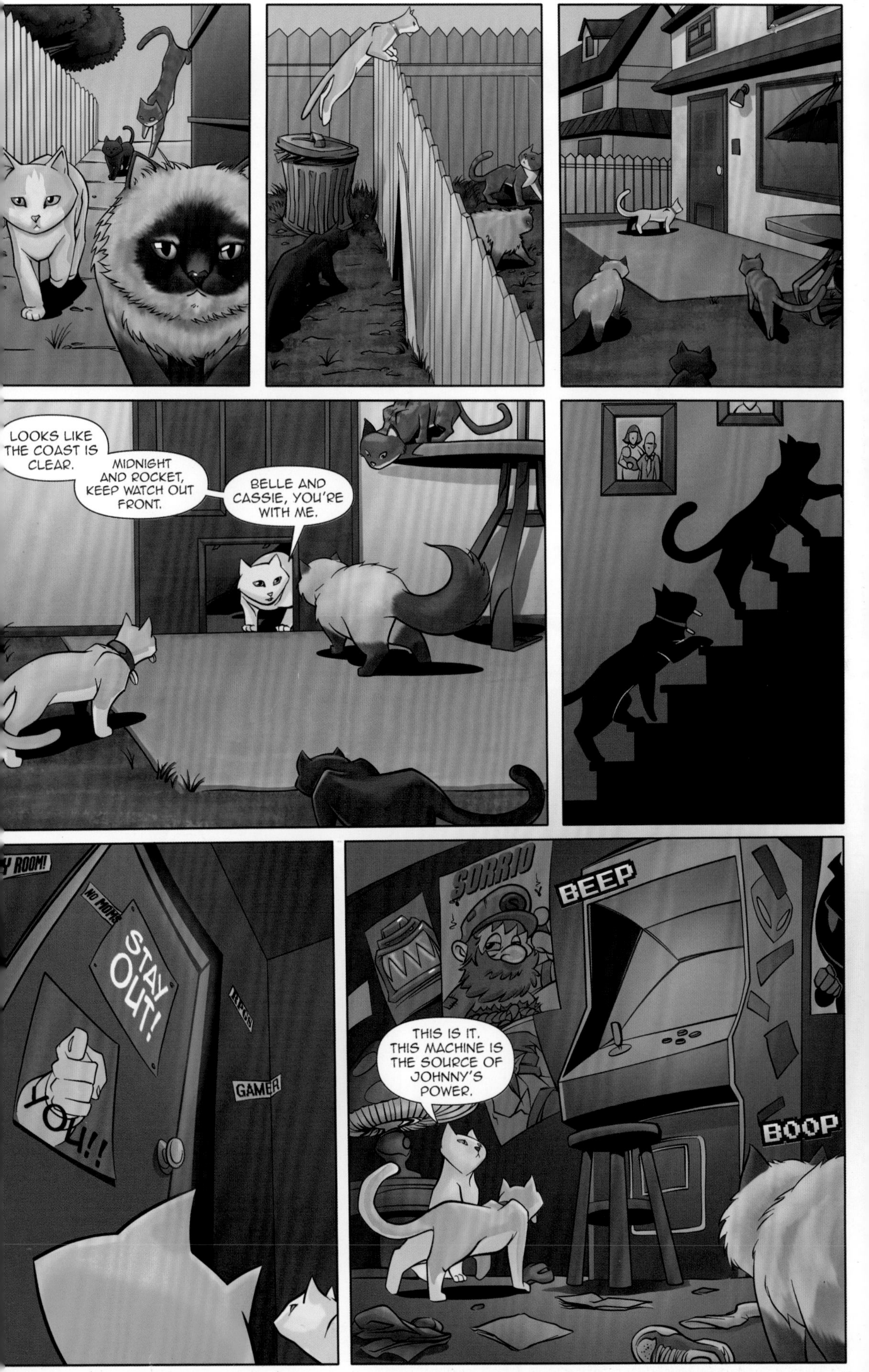

LOOKS LIKE THE COAST IS CLEAR.
MIDNIGHT AND ROCKET, KEEP WATCH OUT FRONT.
BELLE AND CASSIE, YOU'RE WITH ME.
STAY OUT!
GAMER
BEEP
THIS IS IT. THIS MACHINE IS THE SOURCE OF JOHNNY'S POWER.
BOOP

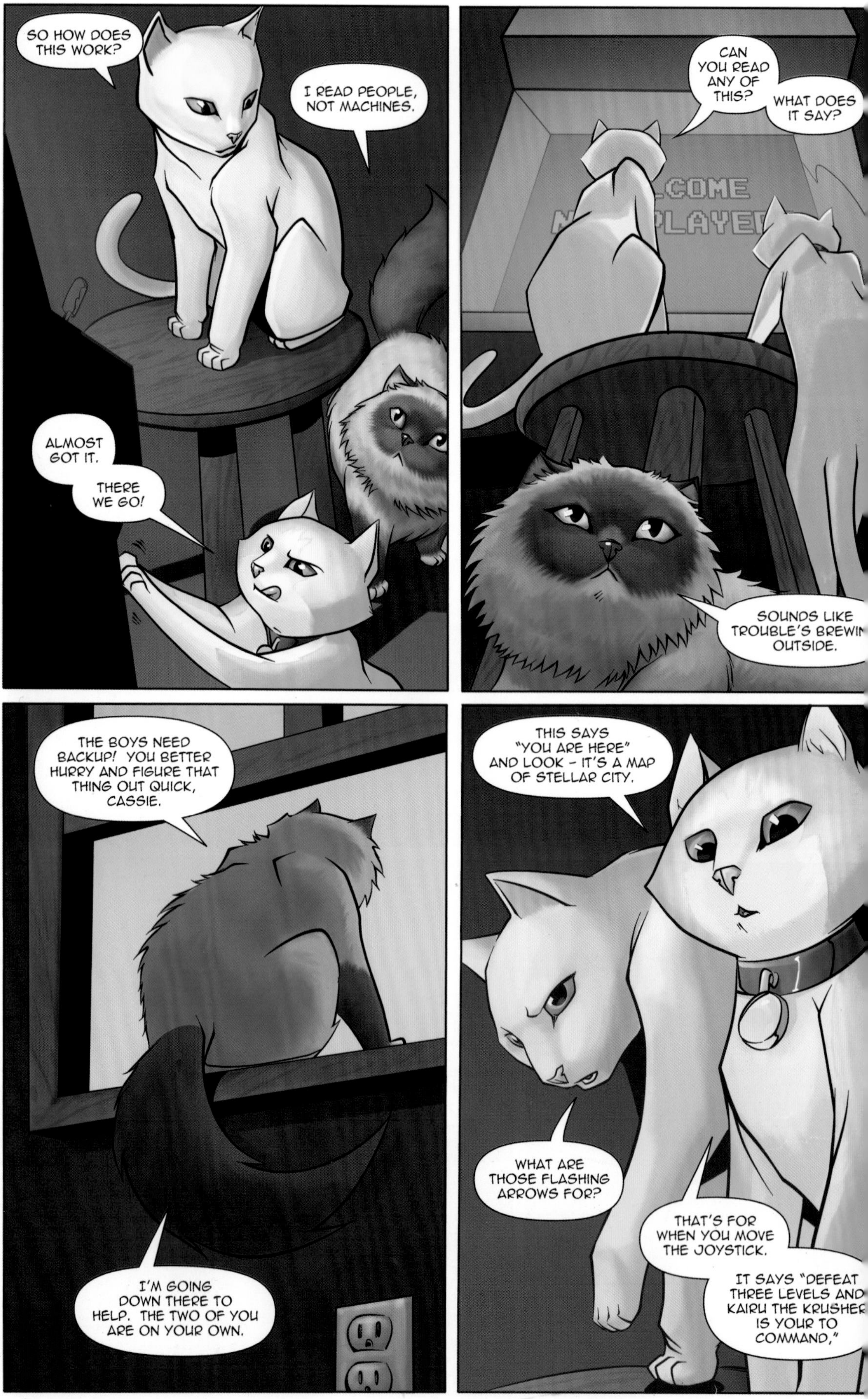
SO HOW DOES THIS WORK?
I READ PEOPLE, NOT MACHINES.
ALMOST GOT IT.
THERE WE GO!
CAN YOU READ ANY OF THIS?
WHAT DOES IT SAY?
SOUNDS LIKE TROUBLE'S BREWIN OUTSIDE.
THE BOYS NEED BACKUP! YOU BETTER HURRY AND FIGURE THAT THING OUT QUICK, CASSIE.
I'M GOING DOWN THERE TO HELP. THE TWO OF YOU ARE ON YOUR OWN.
THIS SAYS "YOU ARE HERE" AND LOOK - IT'S A MAP OF STELLAR CITY.
WHAT ARE THOSE FLASHING ARROWS FOR?
THAT'S FOR WHEN YOU MOVE THE JOYSTICK.
IT SAYS "DEFEAT THREE LEVELS AND KAIRU THE KRUSHER IS YOUR TO COMMAND,"

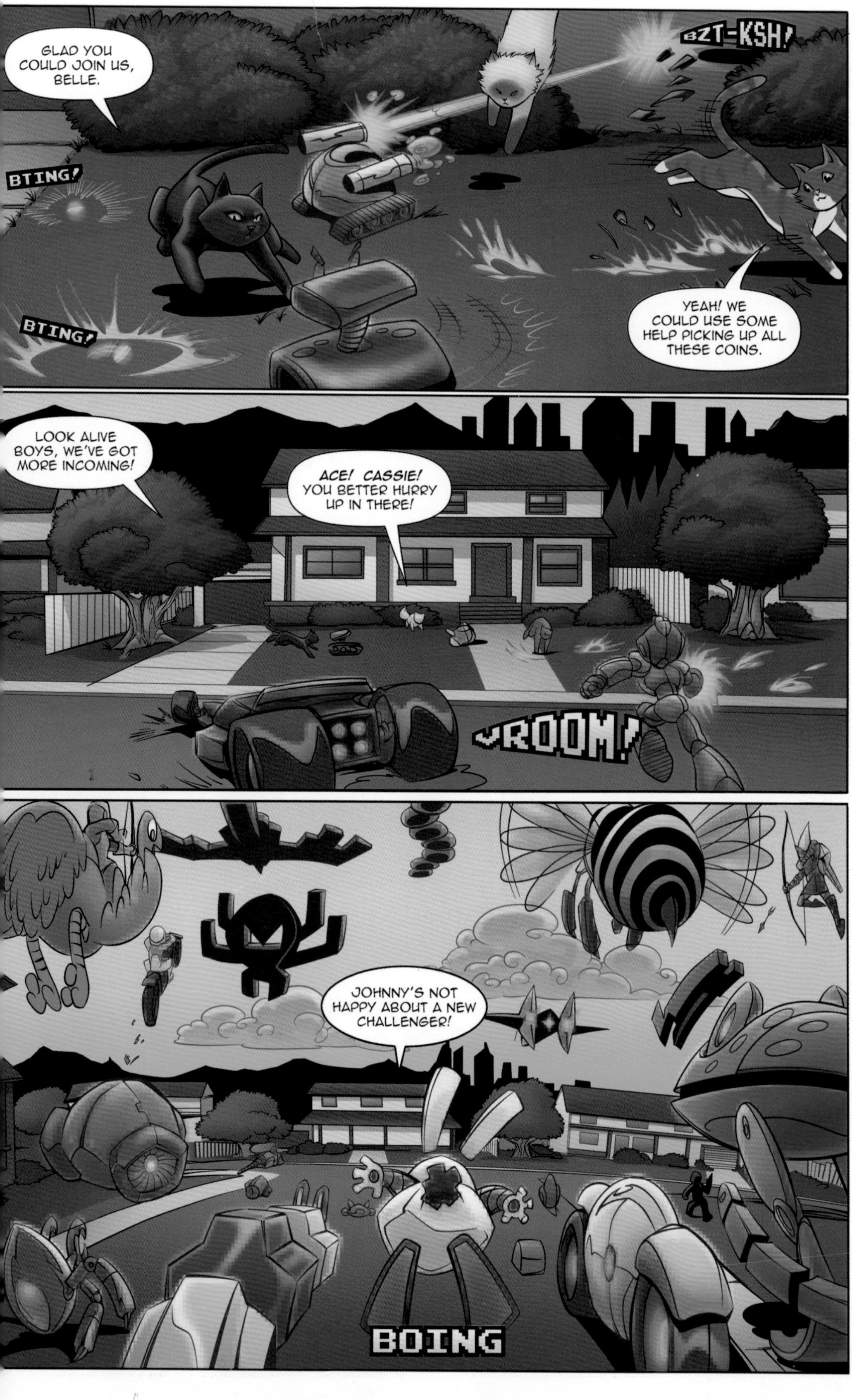
GLAD YOU COULD JOIN US, BELLE.
BZT-KSH!
BTING!
BTING!
YEAH! WE COULD USE SOME HELP PICKING UP ALL THESE COINS.
LOOK ALIVE BOYS, WE'VE GOT MORE INCOMING!
ACE! CASSIE! YOU BETTER HURRY UP IN THERE!
VROOM!
JOHNNY'S NOT HAPPY ABOUT A NEW CHALLENGER!
BOING

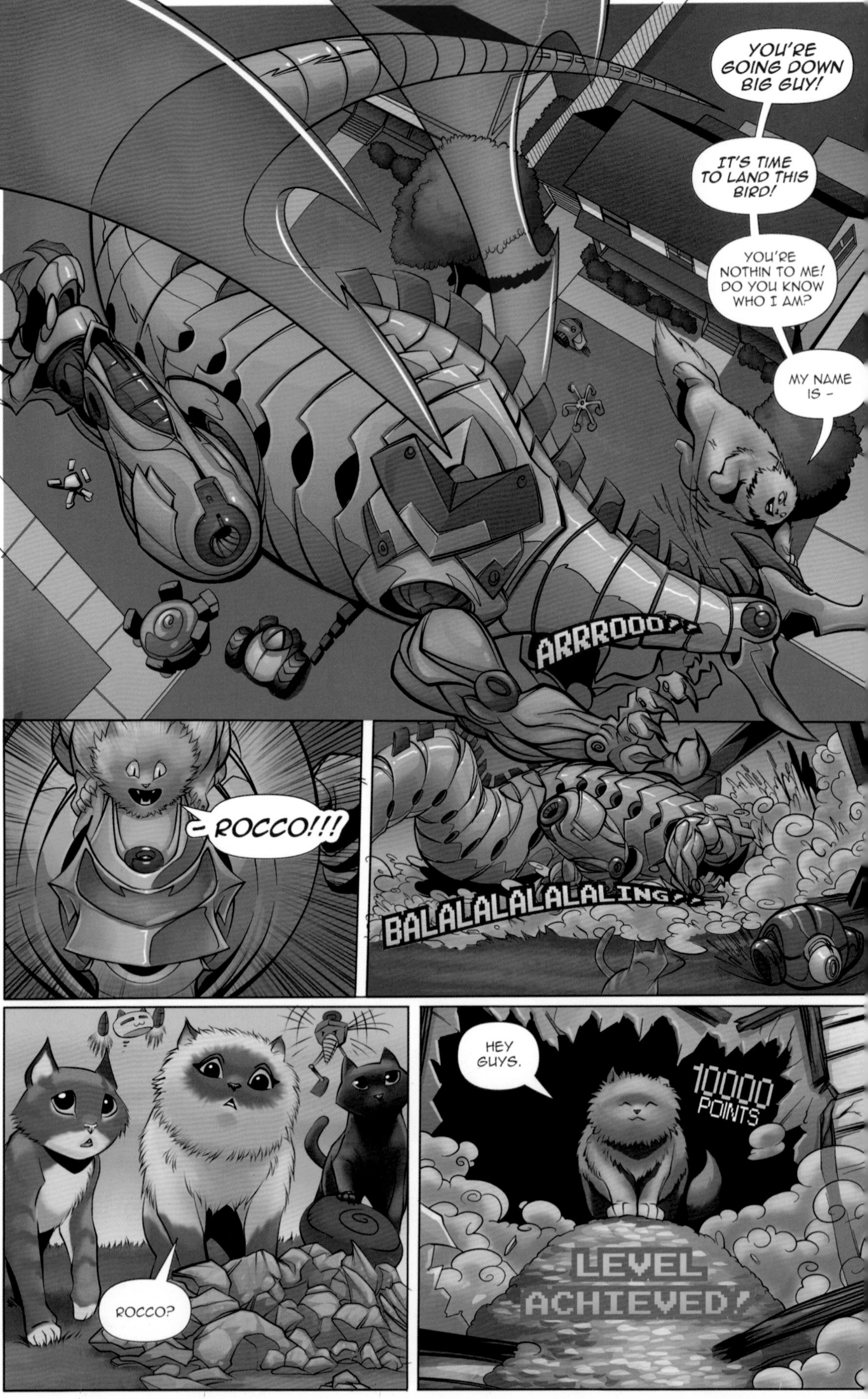
YOU'RE GOING DOWN BIG GUY!
IT'S TIME TO LAND THIS BIRD!
YOU'RE NOTHIN TO ME! DO YOU KNOW WHO I AM?
MY NAME IS –
ARRROOO!?
–ROCCO!!!
BALALALALALALING!?
HEY GUYS.
10000 POINTS
LEVEL ACHIEVED!
ROCCO?

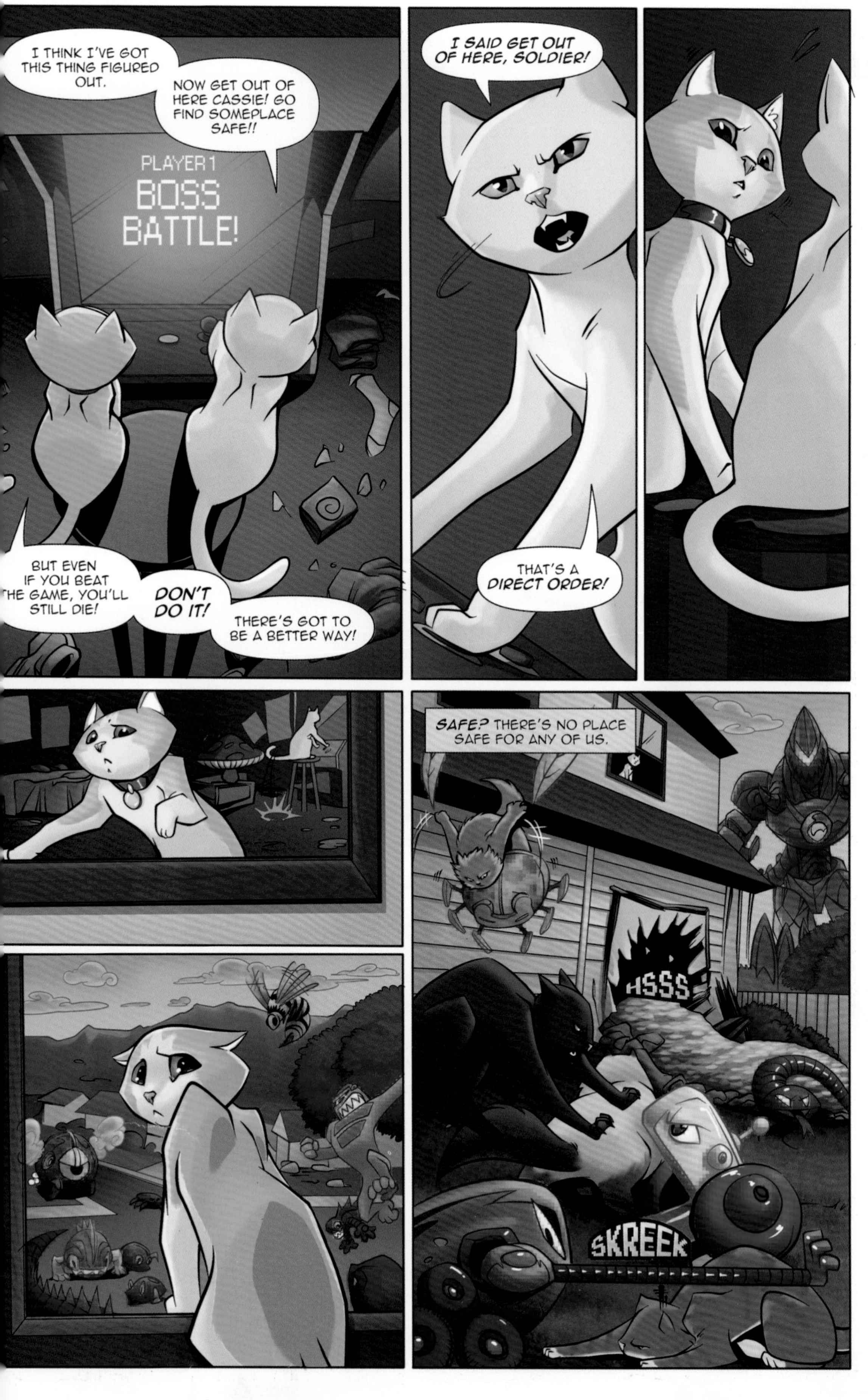
I THINK I'VE GOT THIS THING FIGURED OUT.
NOW GET OUT OF HERE CASSIE! GO FIND SOMEPLACE SAFE!!
PLAYER 1
BOSS BATTLE!
BUT EVEN IF YOU BEAT THE GAME, YOU'LL STILL DIE!
DON'T DO IT!
THERE'S GOT TO BE A BETTER WAY!
I SAID GET OUT OF HERE, SOLDIER!
THAT'S A DIRECT ORDER!
SAFE? THERE'S NO PLACE SAFE FOR ANY OF US.
HSSS
SKREEK

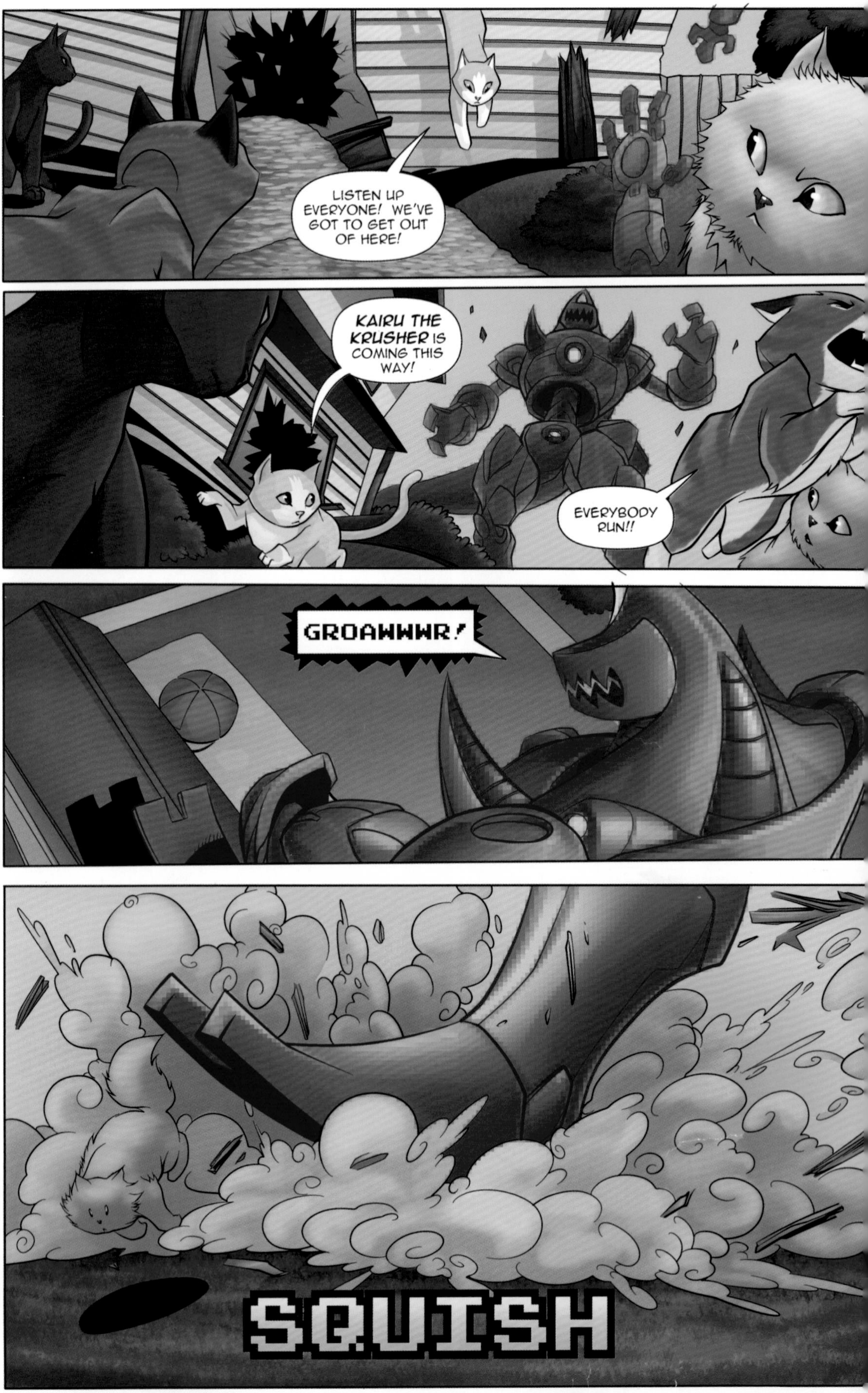
LISTEN UP EVERYONE! WE'VE GOT TO GET OUT OF HERE!
KAIRU THE KRUSHER IS COMING THIS WAY!
EVERYBODY RUN!!
GROAWWWR!
SQUISH

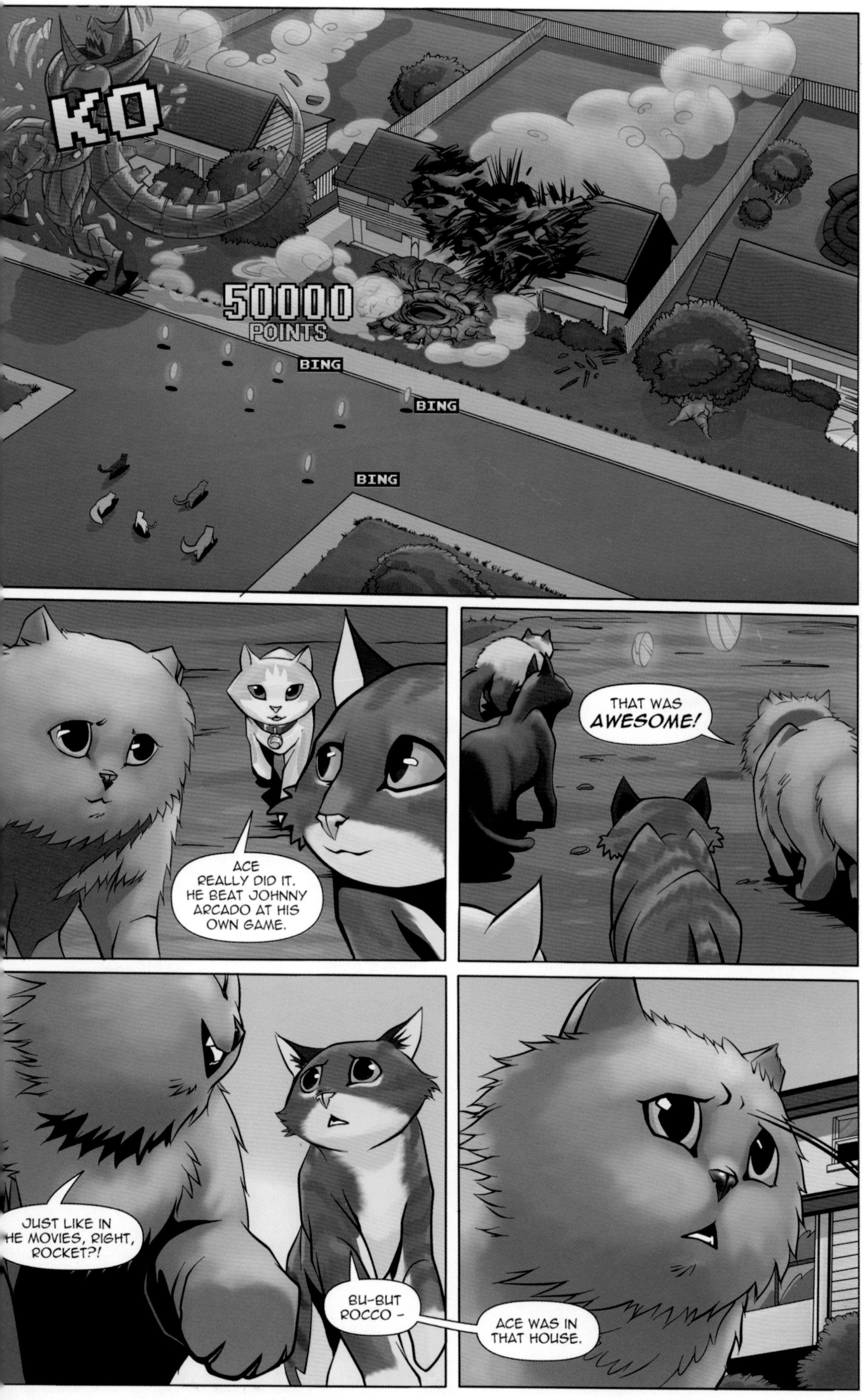
KO
50000
POINTS
BING
BING
BING
ACE REALLY DID IT. HE BEAT JOHNNY ARCADO AT HIS OWN GAME.
THAT WAS AWESOME!
JUST LIKE IN HE MOVIES, RIGHT, ROCKET?!
BU-BUT ROCCO -
ACE WAS IN THAT HOUSE.

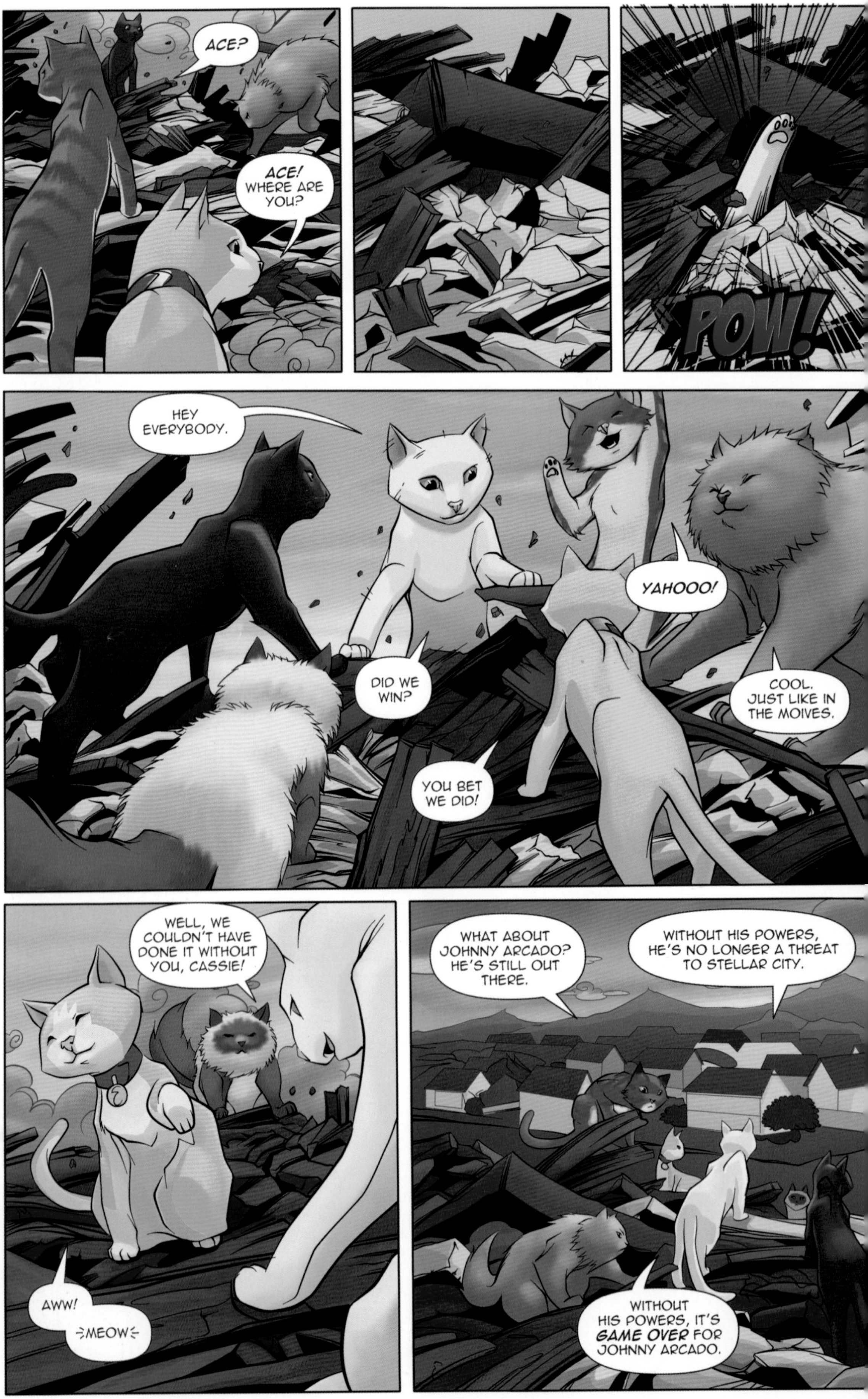
ACE?
ACE! WHERE ARE YOU?
POW!
HEY EVERYBODY.
YAHOOO!
DID WE WIN?
COOL. JUST LIKE IN THE MOIVES.
YOU BET WE DID!
WELL, WE COULDN'T HAVE DONE IT WITHOUT YOU, CASSIE!
AWW!
MEOW
WHAT ABOUT JOHNNY ARCADO? HE'S STILL OUT THERE.
WITHOUT HIS POWERS, HE'S NO LONGER A THREAT TO STELLAR CITY.
WITHOUT HIS POWERS, IT'S GAME OVER FOR JOHNNY ARCADO.

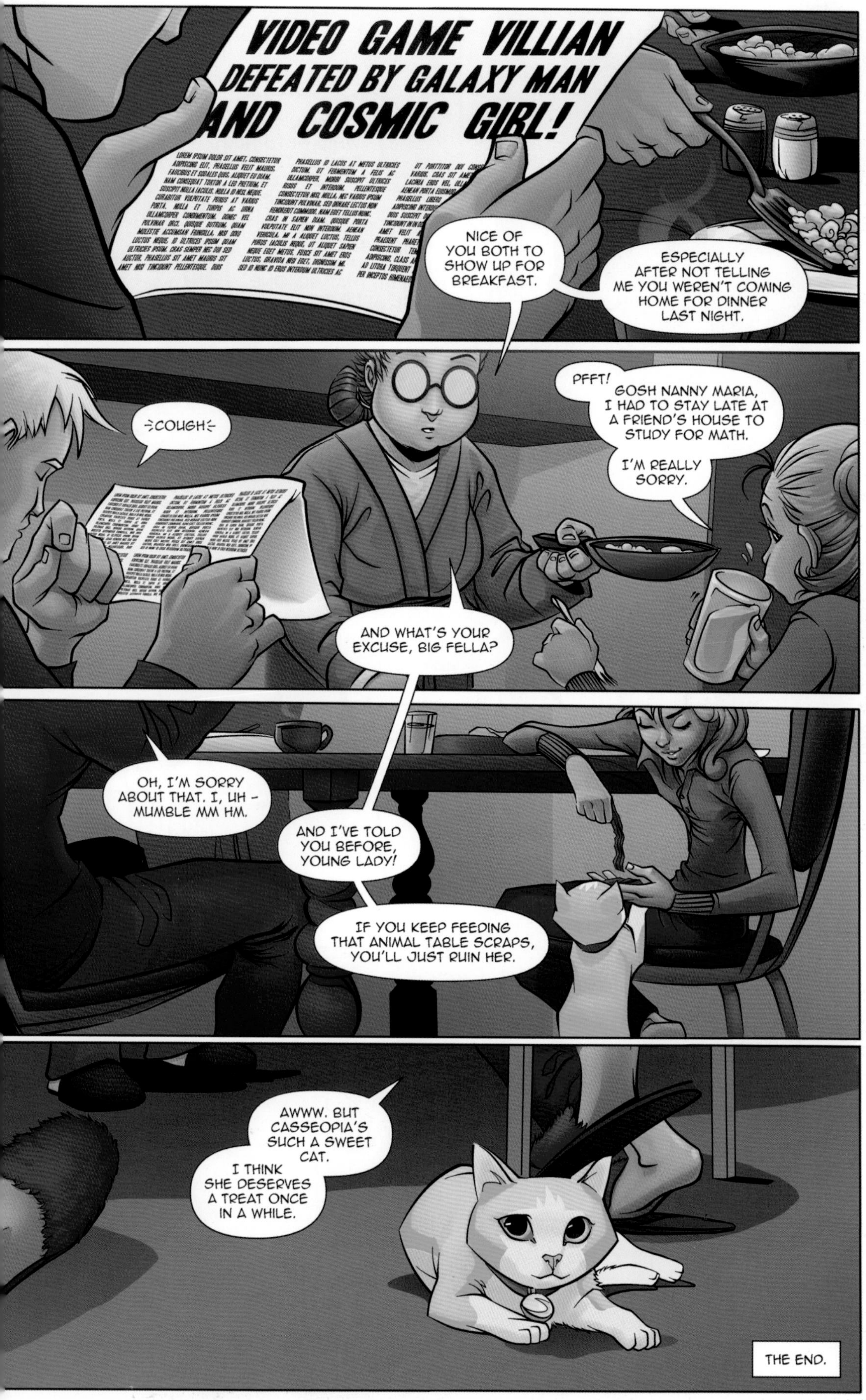
VIDEO GAME VILLIAN DEFEATED BY GALAXY MAN AND COSMIC GIRL!
NICE OF YOU BOTH TO SHOW UP FOR BREAKFAST.
ESPECIALLY AFTER NOT TELLING ME YOU WEREN'T COMING HOME FOR DINNER LAST NIGHT.
COUGH
PFFT!
GOSH NANNY MARIA, I HAD TO STAY LATE AT A FRIEND'S HOUSE TO STUDY FOR MATH.
I'M REALLY SORRY.
AND WHAT'S YOUR EXCUSE, BIG FELLA?
OH, I'M SORRY ABOUT THAT. I, UH - MUMBLE MM HM.
AND I'VE TOLD YOU BEFORE, YOUNG LADY!
IF YOU KEEP FEEDING THAT ANIMAL TABLE SCRAPS, YOU'LL JUST RUIN HER.
AWWW. BUT CASSEOPIA'S SUCH A SWEET CAT.
I THINK SHE DESERVES A TREAT ONCE IN A WHILE.
THE END.

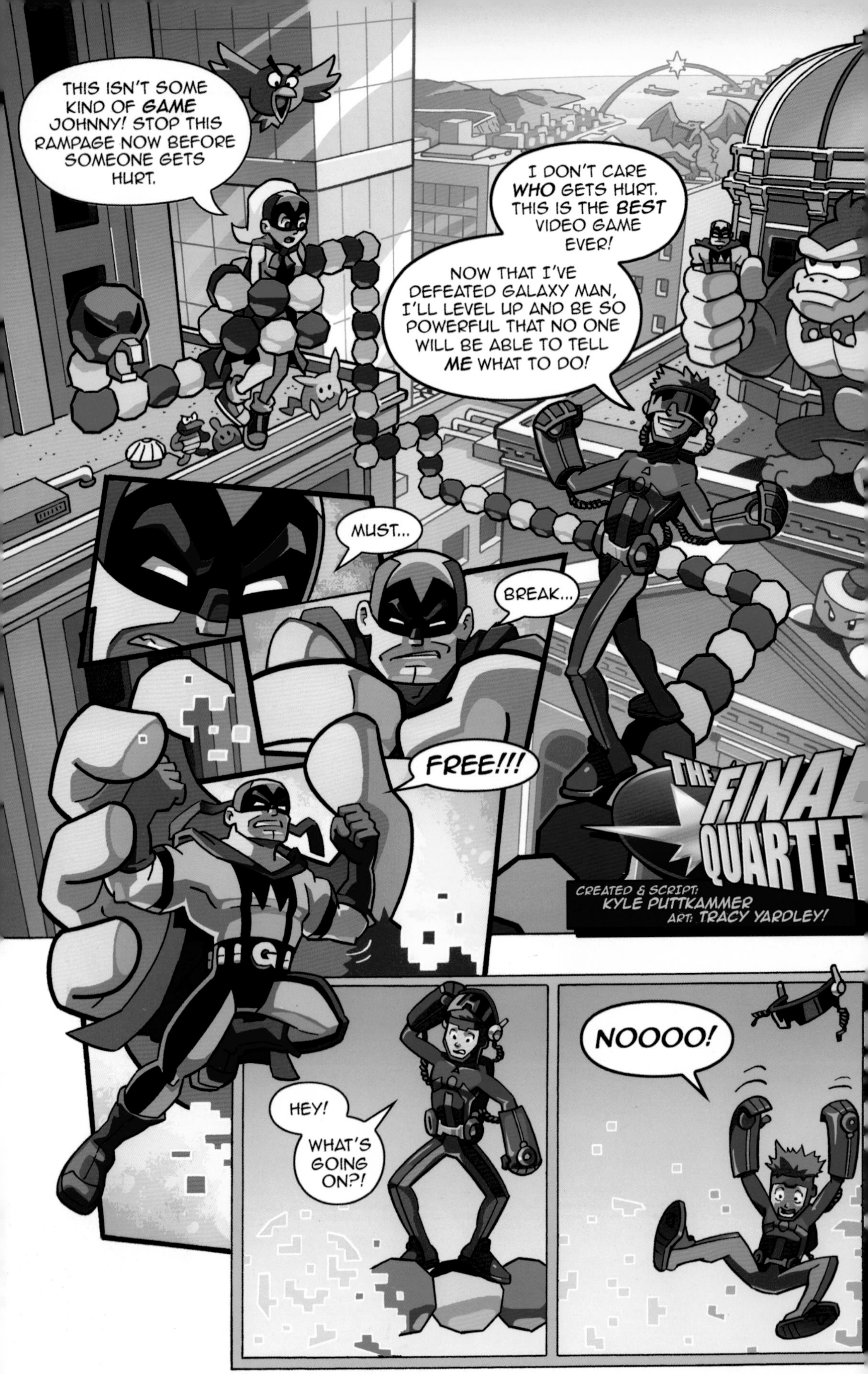
THIS ISN'T SOME KIND OF GAME JOHNNY! STOP THIS RAMPAGE NOW BEFORE SOMEONE GETS HURT.
I DON'T CARE WHO GETS HURT. THIS IS THE BEST VIDEO GAME EVER!
NOW THAT I'VE DEFEATED GALAXY MAN, I'LL LEVEL UP AND BE SO POWERFUL THAT NO ONE WILL BE ABLE TO TELL ME WHAT TO DO!
MUST...
BREAK...
FREE!!!
CREATED & SCRIPT: KYLE PUTTKAMMER
ART: TRACY YARDLEY!
HEY!
WHAT'S GOING ON?!
NOOOO!

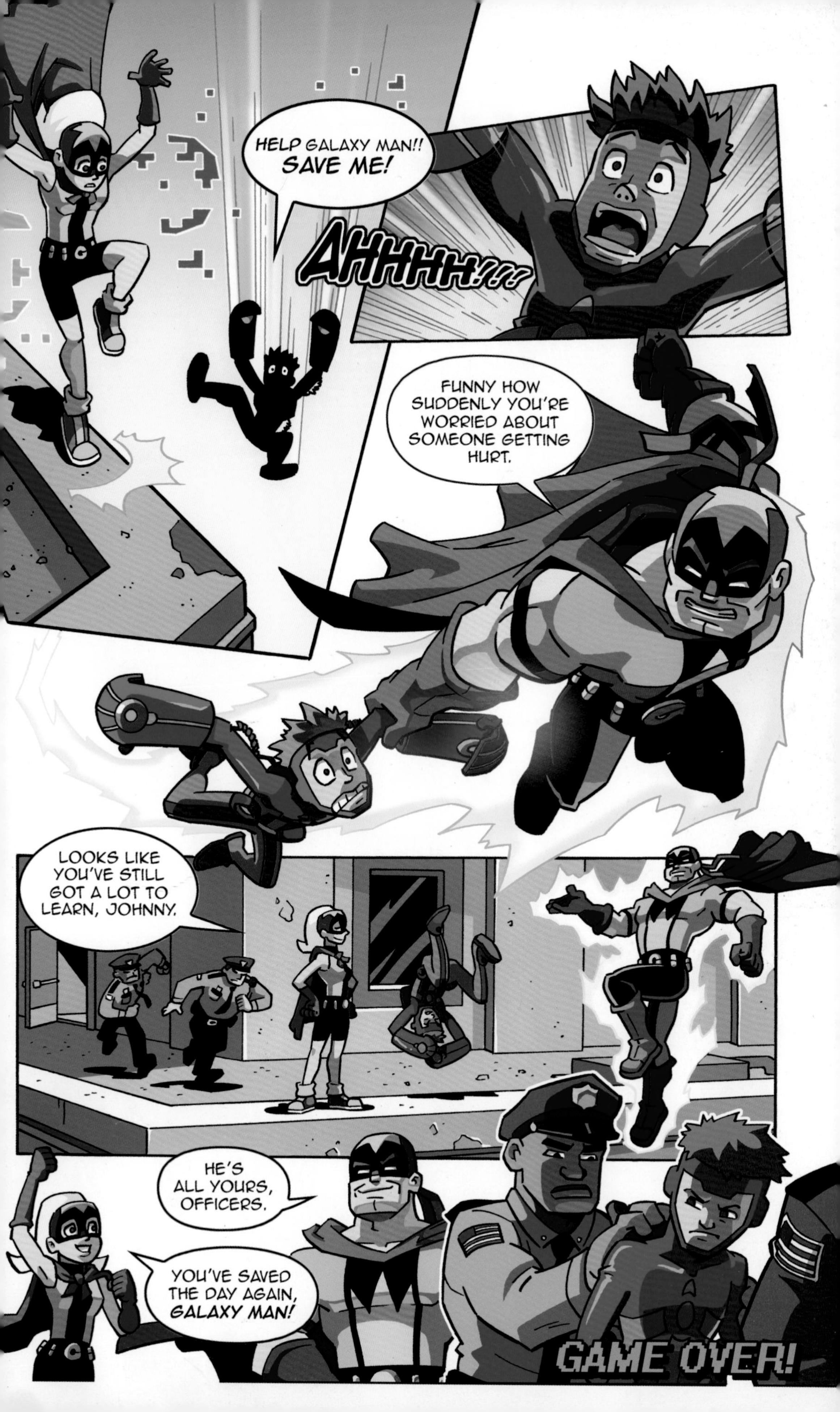
HELP GALAXY MAN!! SAVE ME!
AHHHH!?!?
FUNNY HOW SUDDENLY YOU'RE WORRIED ABOUT SOMEONE GETTING HURT.
LOOKS LIKE YOU'VE STILL GOT A LOT TO LEARN, JOHNNY.
HE'S ALL YOURS, OFFICERS.
YOU'VE SAVED THE DAY AGAIN, GALAXY MAN!
GAME OVER!

CHAPTER 3:
CASSIOPEIA'S BASIC TRAINING

WRITER: KYLE PUTTKAMMER

PENCILS: MARCUS WILLIAMS

INKS: RYAN SELLERS

COLORS: OMAKA SCHULTZ

LETTERING: BRIANA HIGGINS

EDITING: KEEK STEWART

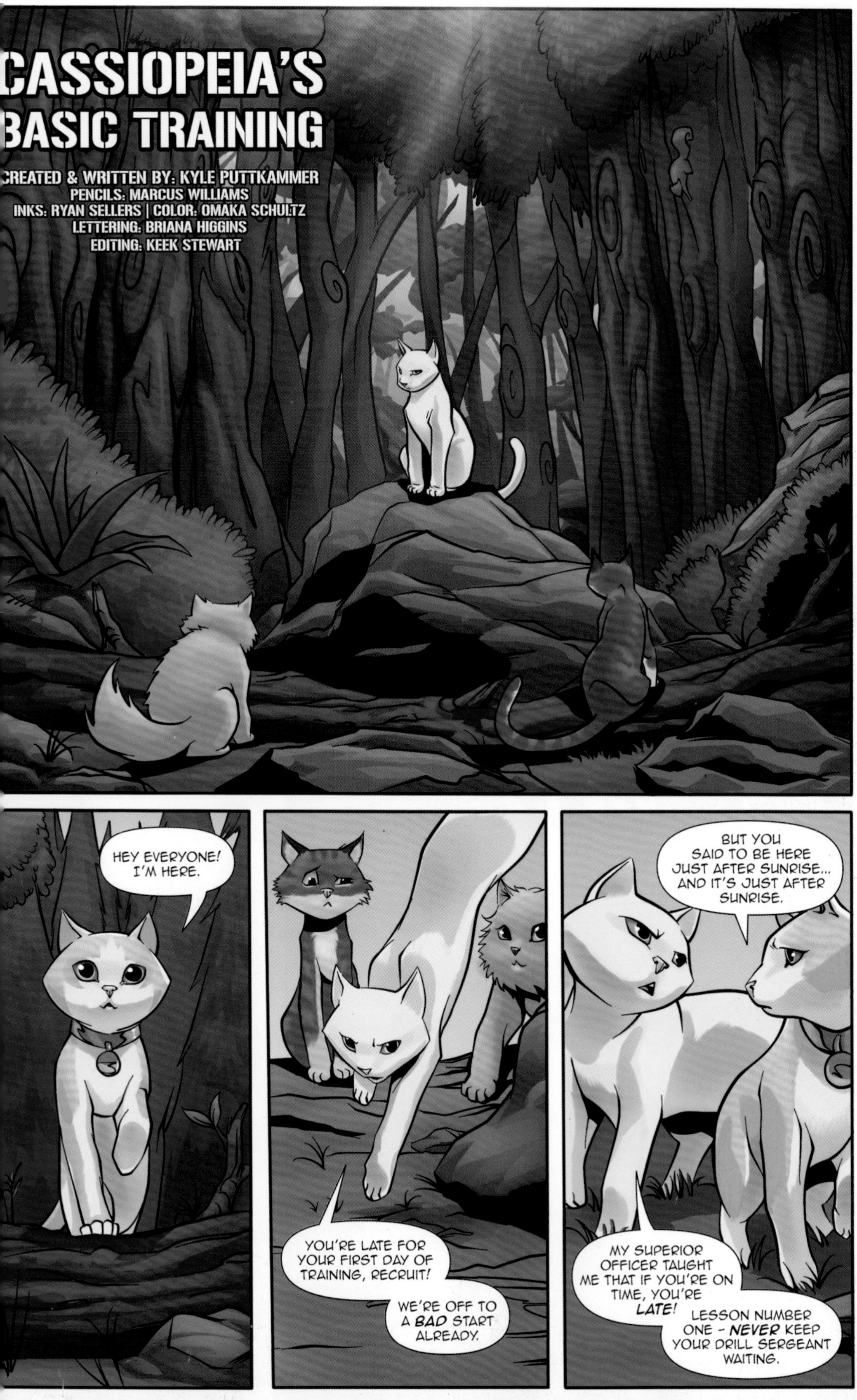
CASSIOPEIA'S
BASIC TRAINING
CREATED & WRITTEN BY: KYLE PUTTKAMMER
PENCILS: MARCUS WILLIAMS
INKS: RYAN SELLERS | COLOR: OMAKA SCHULTZ
LETTERING: BRIANA HIGGINS
EDITING: KEEK STEWART
HEY EVERYONE! I'M HERE.
YOU'RE LATE FOR YOUR FIRST DAY OF TRAINING, RECRUIT!
WE'RE OFF TO A ***BAD*** START ALREADY.
BUT YOU SAID TO BE HERE JUST AFTER SUNRISE... AND IT'S JUST AFTER SUNRISE.
MY SUPERIOR OFFICER TAUGHT ME THAT IF YOU'RE ON TIME, YOU'RE ***LATE!***
LESSON NUMBER ONE - ***NEVER*** KEEP YOUR DRILL SERGEANT WAITING.

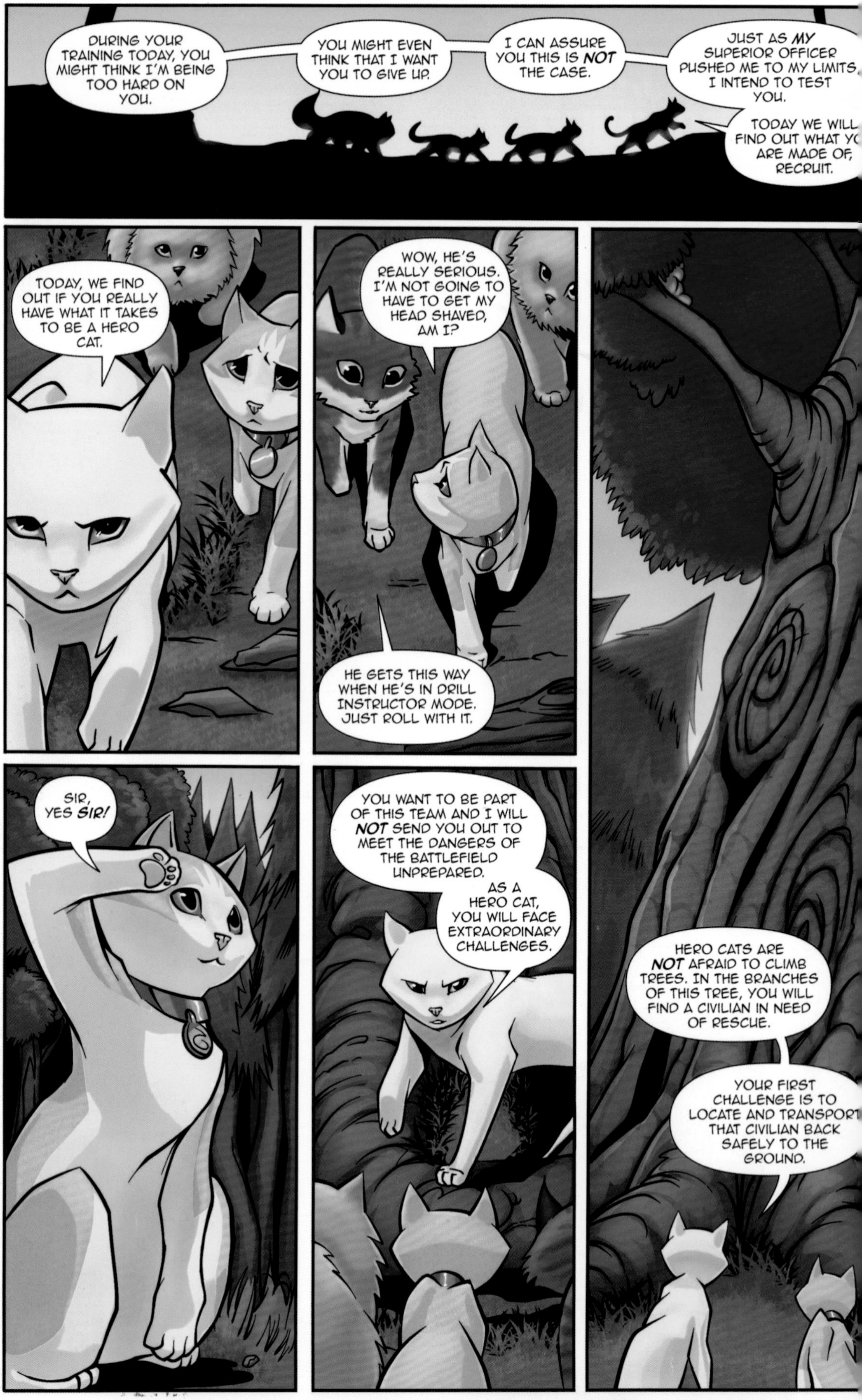
DURING YOUR TRAINING TODAY, YOU MIGHT THINK I'M BEING TOO HARD ON YOU.
YOU MIGHT EVEN THINK THAT I WANT YOU TO GIVE UP.
I CAN ASSURE YOU THIS IS NOT THE CASE.
JUST AS MY SUPERIOR OFFICER PUSHED ME TO MY LIMITS, I INTEND TO TEST YOU.
TODAY WE WILL FIND OUT WHAT YO ARE MADE OF, RECRUIT.
TODAY, WE FIND OUT IF YOU REALLY HAVE WHAT IT TAKES TO BE A HERO CAT.
WOW, HE'S REALLY SERIOUS. I'M NOT GOING TO HAVE TO GET MY HEAD SHAVED, AM I?
HE GETS THIS WAY WHEN HE'S IN DRILL INSTRUCTOR MODE. JUST ROLL WITH IT.
SIR, YES SIR!
YOU WANT TO BE PART OF THIS TEAM AND I WILL NOT SEND YOU OUT TO MEET THE DANGERS OF THE BATTLEFIELD UNPREPARED.
AS A HERO CAT, YOU WILL FACE EXTRAORDINARY CHALLENGES.
HERO CATS ARE NOT AFRAID TO CLIMB TREES. IN THE BRANCHES OF THIS TREE, YOU WILL FIND A CIVILIAN IN NEED OF RESCUE.
YOUR FIRST CHALLENGE IS TO LOCATE AND TRANSPORT THAT CIVILIAN BACK SAFELY TO THE GROUND.

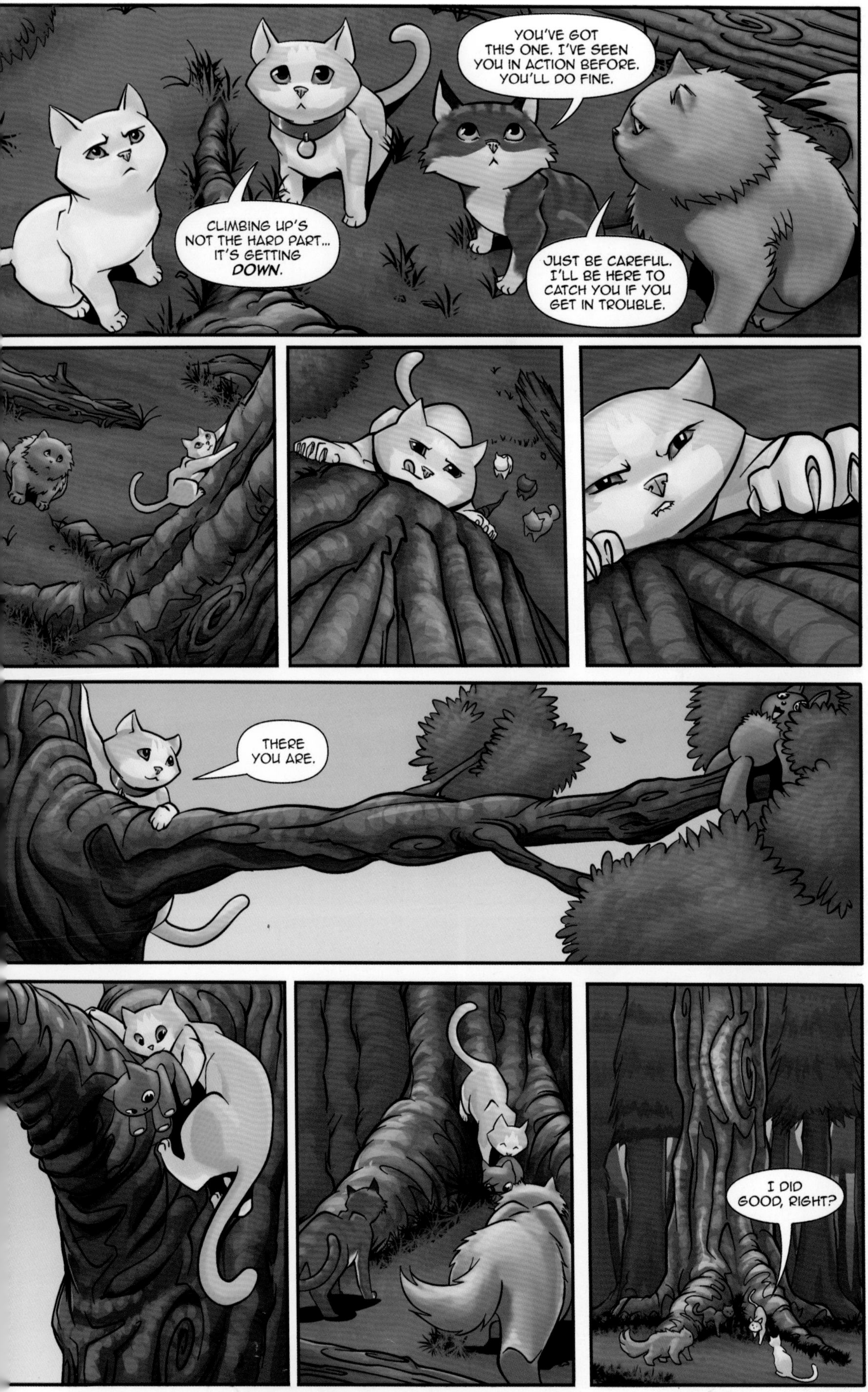

YOU'VE GOT THIS ONE. I'VE SEEN YOU IN ACTION BEFORE. YOU'LL DO FINE.
CLIMBING UP'S NOT THE HARD PART... IT'S GETTING *DOWN*.
JUST BE CAREFUL. I'LL BE HERE TO CATCH YOU IF YOU GET IN TROUBLE.
THERE YOU ARE.
I DID GOOD, RIGHT?

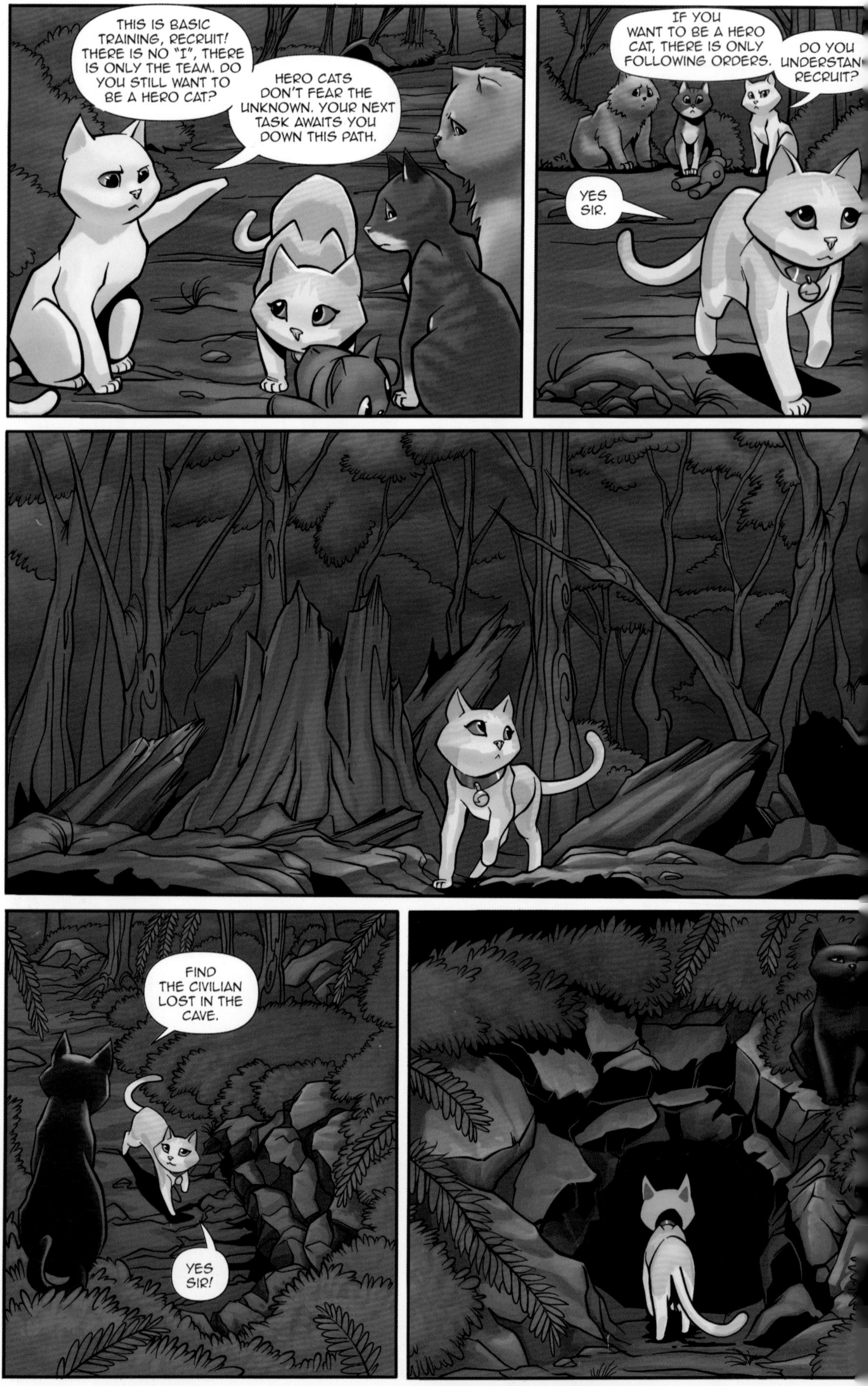
THIS IS BASIC TRAINING, RECRUIT! THERE IS NO "I", THERE IS ONLY THE TEAM. DO YOU STILL WANT TO BE A HERO CAT?
HERO CATS DON'T FEAR THE UNKNOWN. YOUR NEXT TASK AWAITS YOU DOWN THIS PATH.
IF YOU WANT TO BE A HERO CAT, THERE IS ONLY FOLLOWING ORDERS.
DO YOU UNDERSTAN RECRUIT?
YES SIR.
FIND THE CIVILIAN LOST IN THE CAVE.
YES SIR!

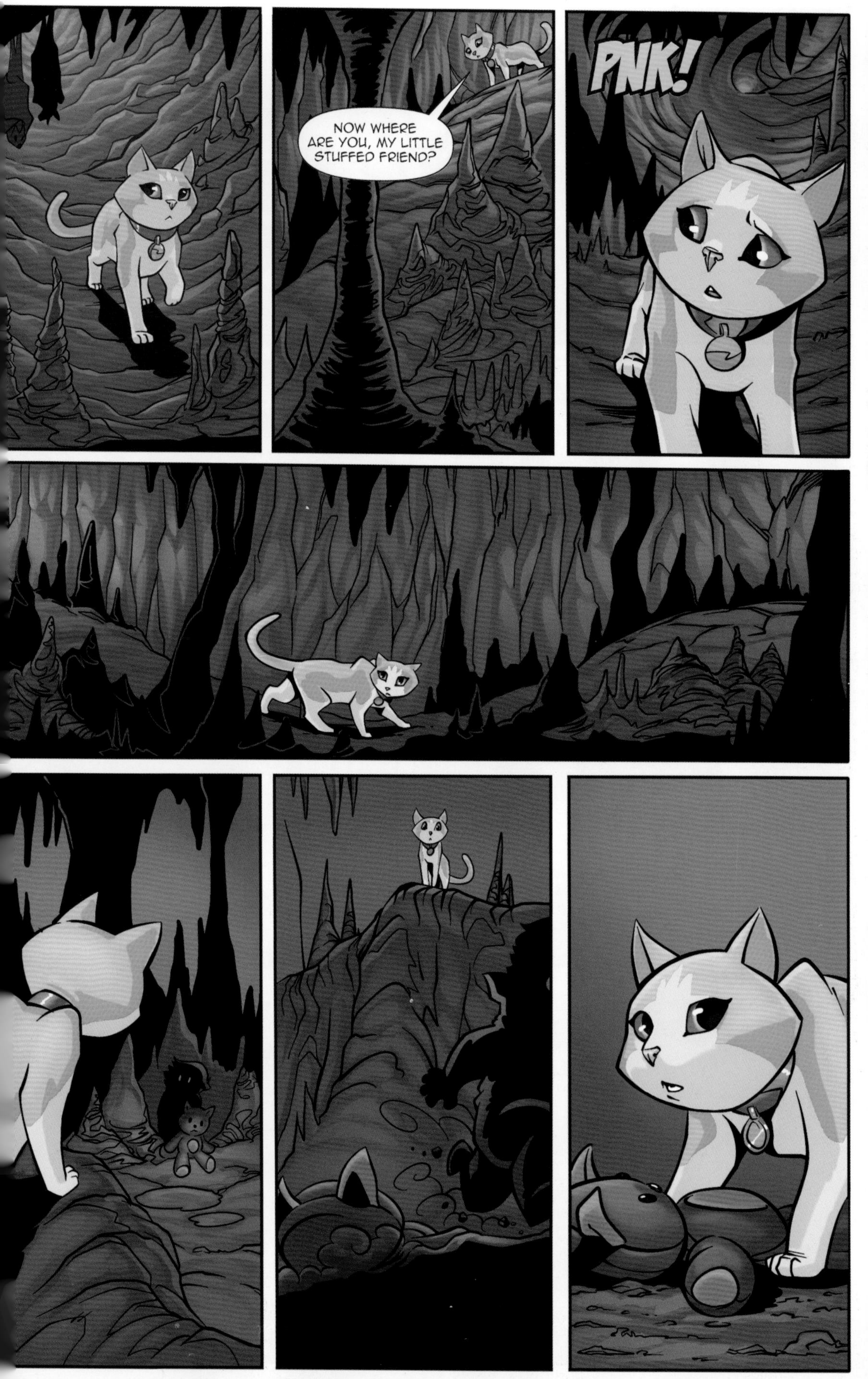

NOW WHERE ARE YOU, MY LITTLE STUFFED FRIEND?
PNK!

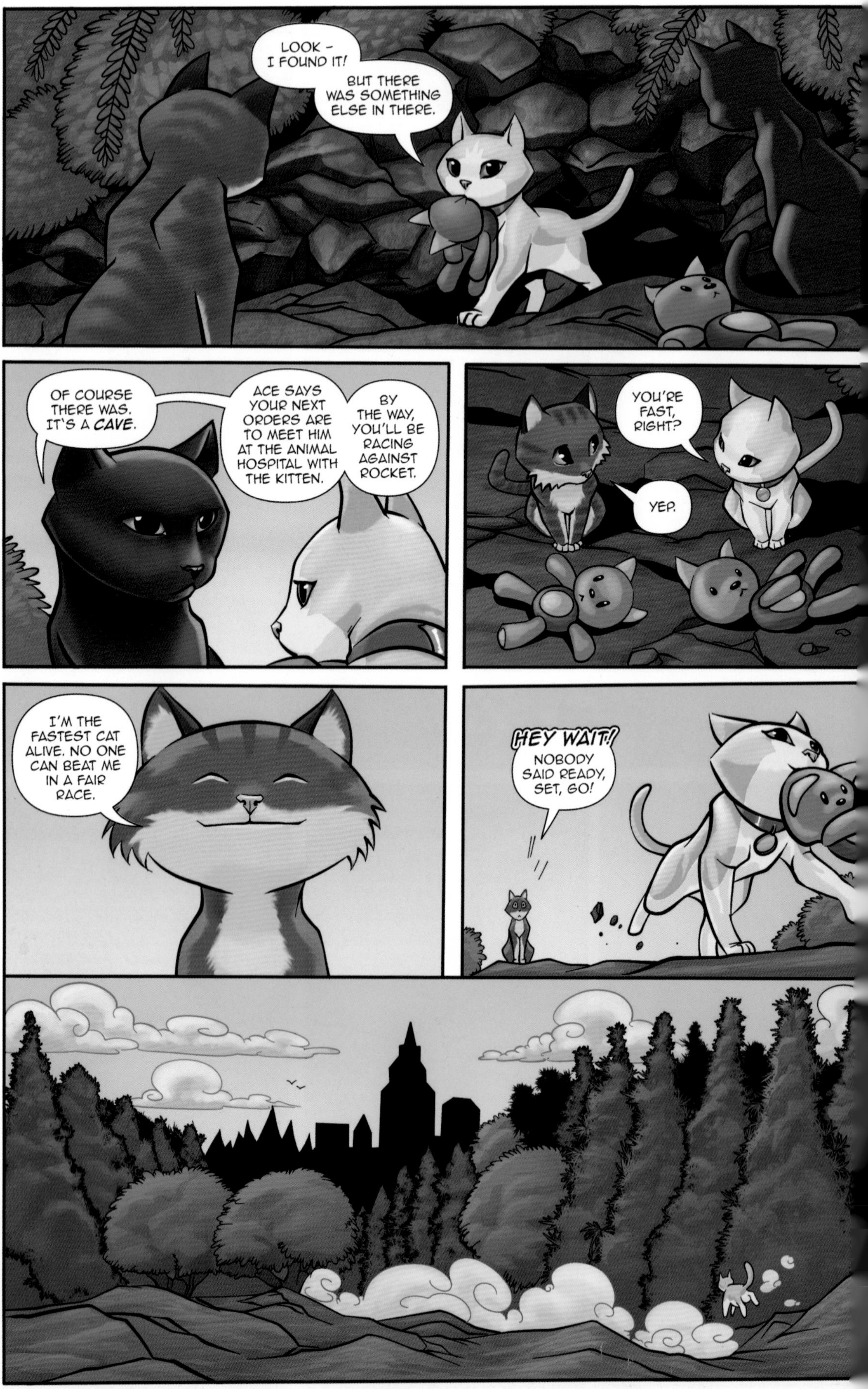
LOOK - I FOUND IT!
BUT THERE WAS SOMETHING ELSE IN THERE.
OF COURSE THERE WAS. IT'S A *CAVE*.
ACE SAYS YOUR NEXT ORDERS ARE TO MEET HIM AT THE ANIMAL HOSPITAL WITH THE KITTEN.
BY THE WAY, YOU'LL BE RACING AGAINST ROCKET.
YOU'RE FAST, RIGHT?
YEP.
I'M THE FASTEST CAT ALIVE. NO ONE CAN BEAT ME IN A FAIR RACE.
HEY WAIT!
NOBODY SAID READY, SET, GO!

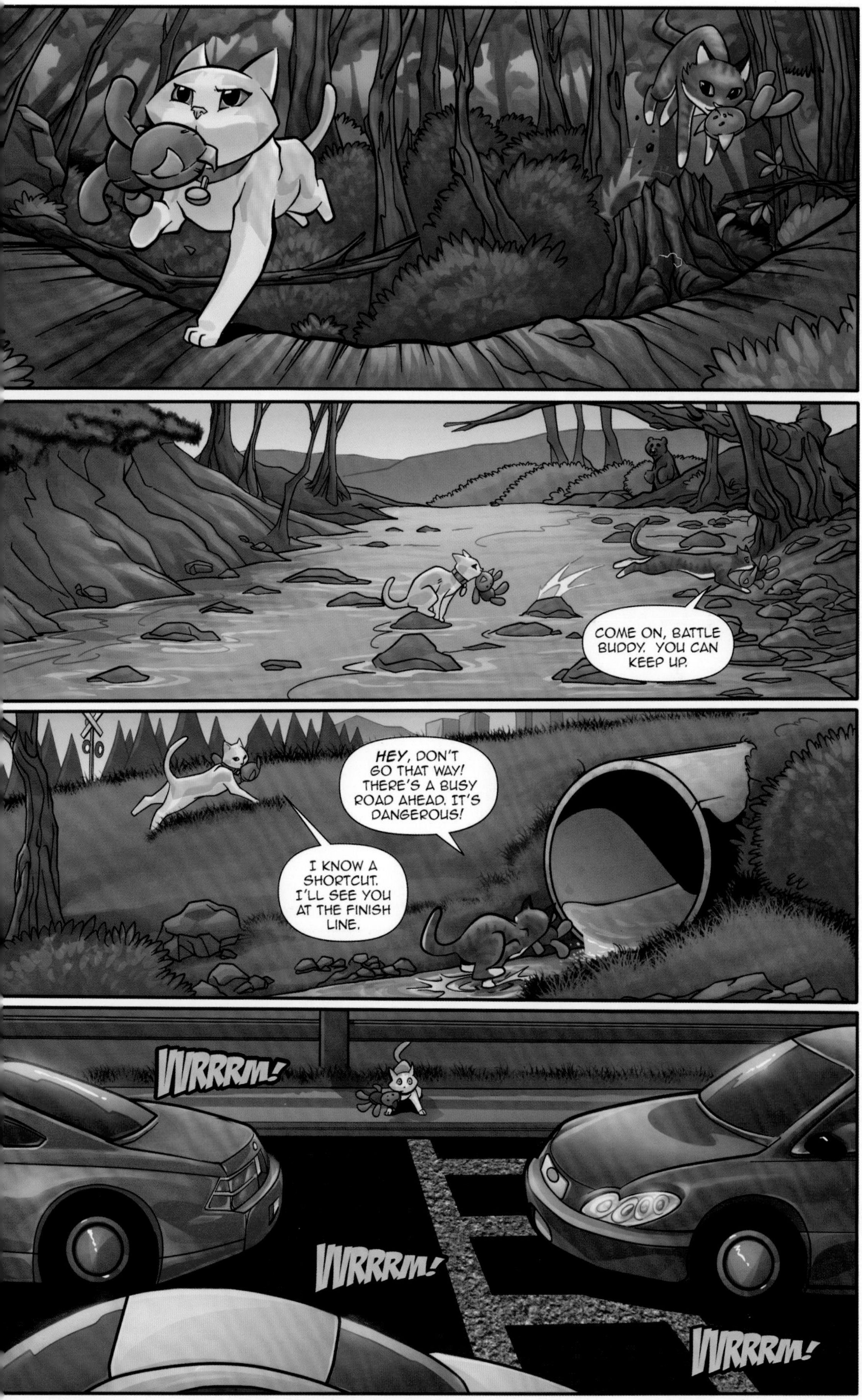
COME ON, BATTLE BUDDY. YOU CAN KEEP UP.
HEY, DON'T GO THAT WAY! THERE'S A BUSY ROAD AHEAD. IT'S DANGEROUS!
I KNOW A SHORTCUT. I'LL SEE YOU AT THE FINISH LINE.
VVRRRM!
VVRRRM!
VVRRRM!

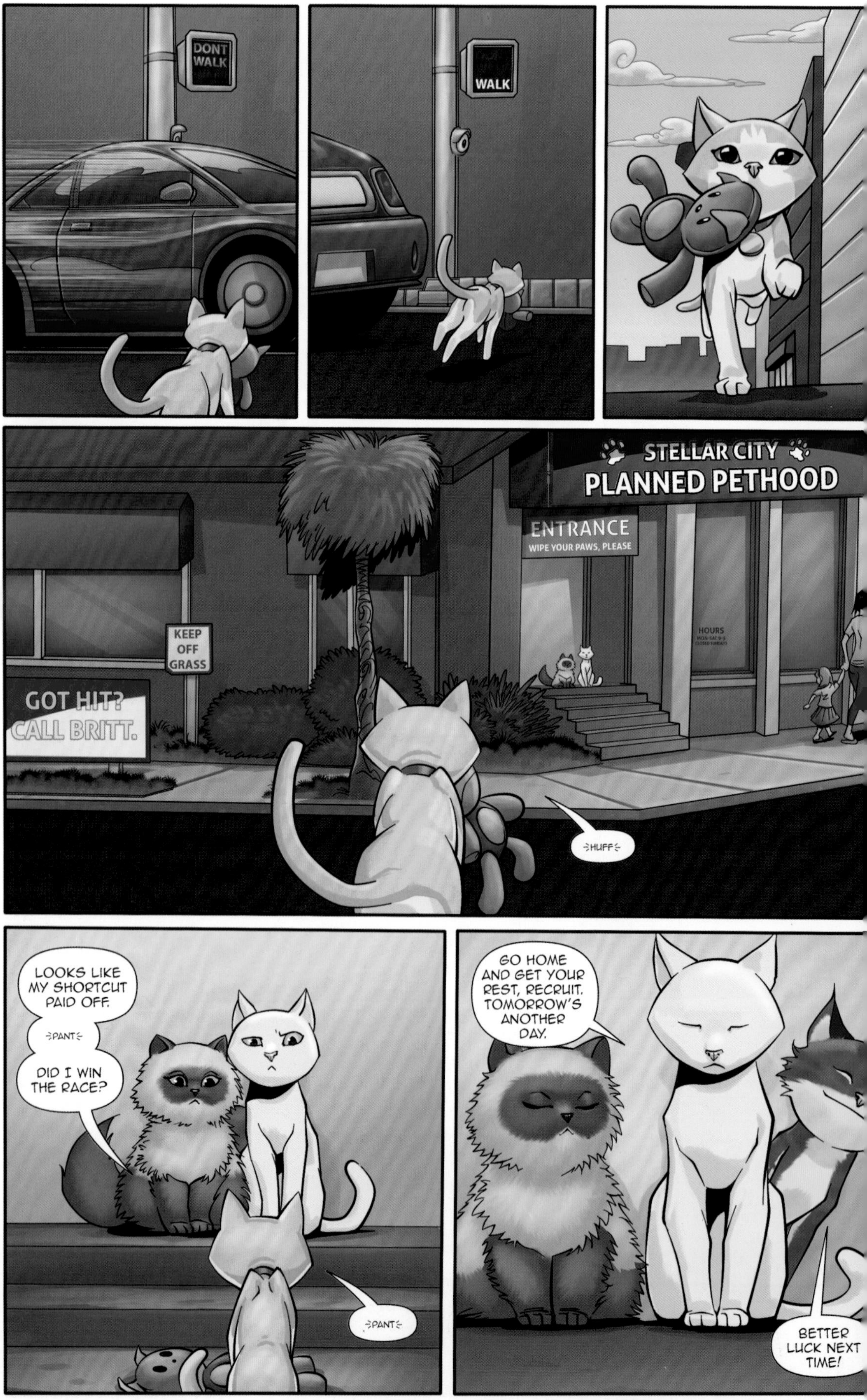
DONT WALK
WALK
STELLAR CITY
PLANNED PETHOOD
ENTRANCE
WIPE YOUR PAWS, PLEASE
KEEP OFF GRASS
GOT HIT? CALL BRITT.
HOURS
HUFF
LOOKS LIKE MY SHORTCUT PAID OFF.
PANT
DID I WIN THE RACE?
PANT
GO HOME AND GET YOUR REST, RECRUIT. TOMORROW'S ANOTHER DAY.
BETTER LUCK NEXT TIME!

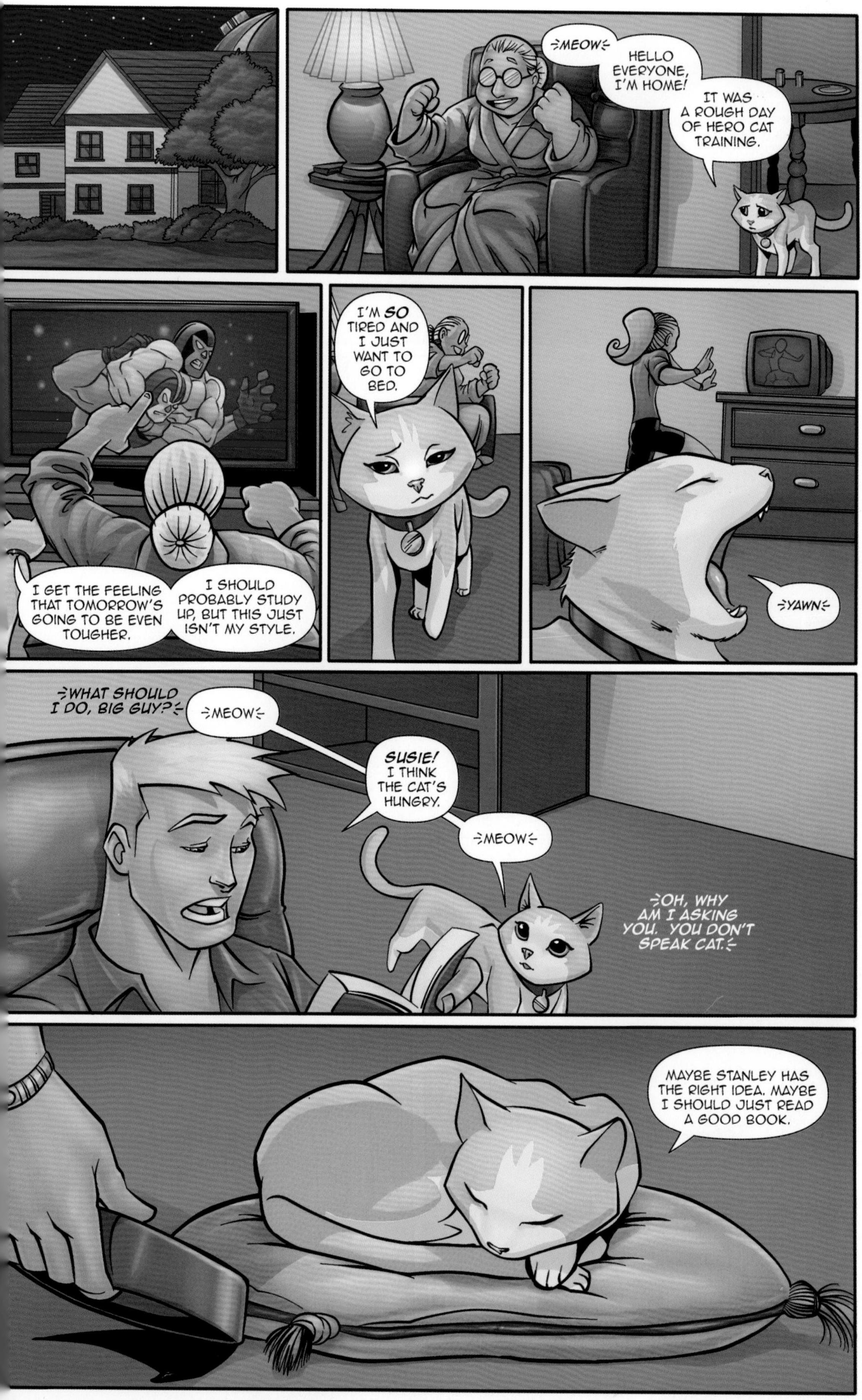

MEOW
HELLO EVERYONE, I'M HOME!
IT WAS A ROUGH DAY OF HERO CAT TRAINING.
I GET THE FEELING THAT TOMORROW'S GOING TO BE EVEN TOUGHER.
I SHOULD PROBABLY STUDY UP, BUT THIS JUST ISN'T MY STYLE.
I'M **SO** TIRED AND I JUST WANT TO GO TO BED.
YAWN
WHAT SHOULD I DO, BIG GUY?
MEOW
SUSIE! I THINK THE CAT'S HUNGRY.
MEOW
OH, WHY AM I ASKING YOU. YOU DON'T SPEAK CAT.
MAYBE STANLEY HAS THE RIGHT IDEA. MAYBE I SHOULD JUST READ A GOOD BOOK.

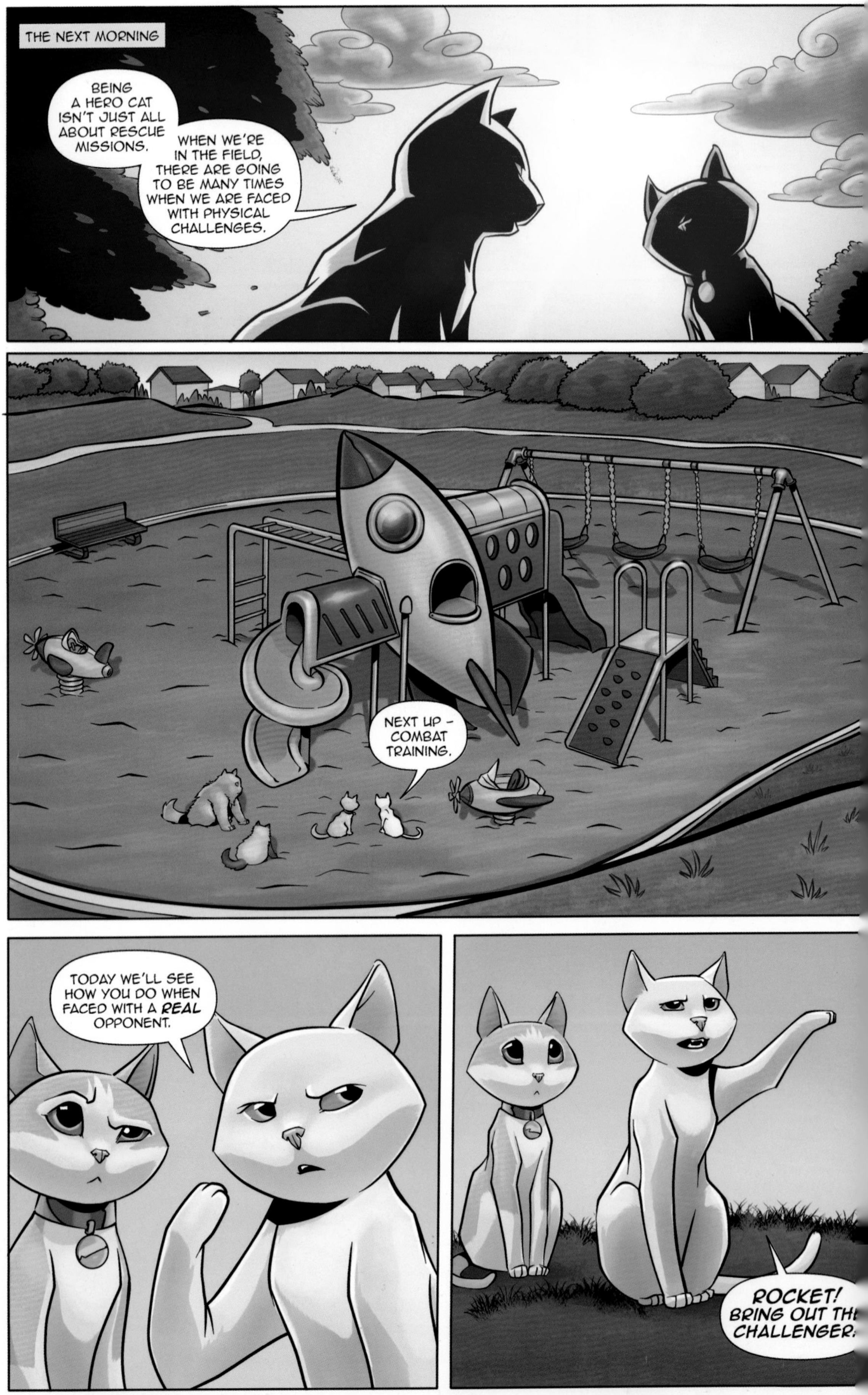
THE NEXT MORNING
BEING A HERO CAT ISN'T JUST ALL ABOUT RESCUE MISSIONS.
WHEN WE'RE IN THE FIELD, THERE ARE GOING TO BE MANY TIMES WHEN WE ARE FACED WITH PHYSICAL CHALLENGES.
NEXT UP - COMBAT TRAINING.
TODAY WE'LL SEE HOW YOU DO WHEN FACED WITH A REAL OPPONENT.
ROCKET! BRING OUT THE CHALLENGER!

ALMOST GOT IT.

KLANK!

TINK!

TINK!

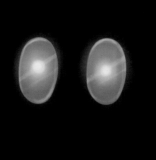

ANY *TIME* NOW!

GOT IT!

BZZZ—Z-Z

BRUZZT

WHEEE!

LET'S GET READY TO **RUMBLE!**

YOU HAVE A ROBOT?!

OF COURSE I HAVE A ROBOT... I'M FROM OUTER SPACE.

YOU'RE FROM OUTER SPACE?!

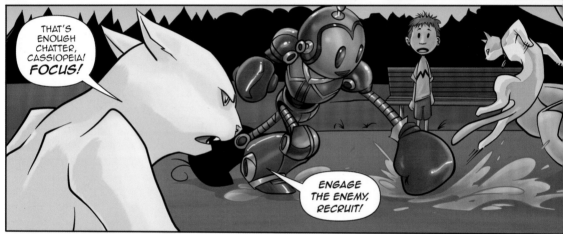

THAT'S ENOUGH CHATTER, CASSIOPEIA! FOCUS!

ENGAGE THE ENEMY, RECRUIT!

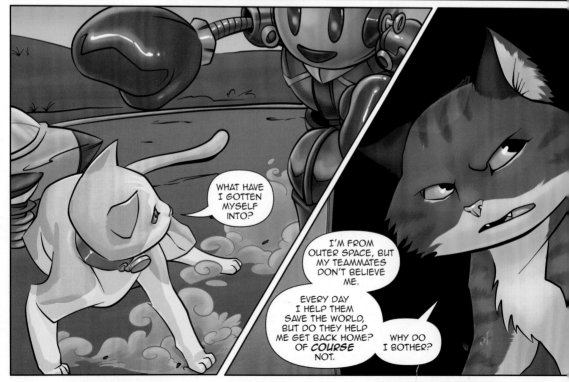

WHAT HAVE I GOTTEN MYSELF INTO?

I'M FROM OUTER SPACE, BUT MY TEAMMATES DON'T BELIEVE ME.

EVERY DAY I HELP THEM SAVE THE WORLD, BUT DO THEY HELP ME GET BACK HOME? OF COURSE NOT.

WHY DO I BOTHER?

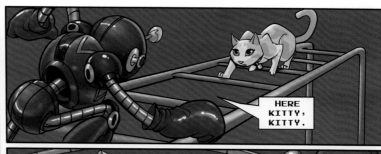

HERE, KITTY, KITTY.

SOMETIMES, I WONDER IF I'LL EVER UNDERSTAND *YOU*, ROCKET.

YOU CAN DO THIS!

EYE OF THE TIGER, CASSIE!

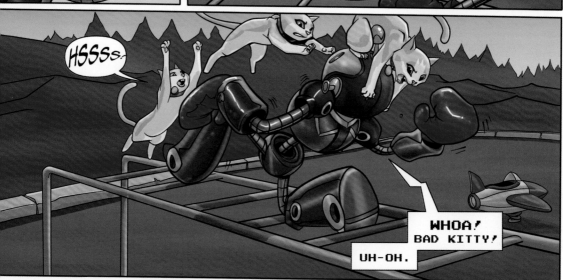

HSSSS.

WHOA! BAD KITTY!

UH-OH.

KRASH!

HOW DID I DO, DRILL SERGEANT? GOOD, RIGHT?

RECRUIT, THIS WAS ABOUT COMBAT TRAINING, *NOT* A GAME OF KEEP AWAY!

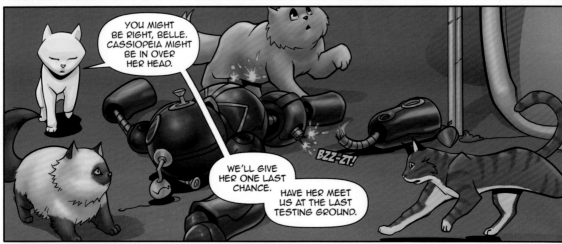

YOU MIGHT BE RIGHT, BELLE. CASSIOPEIA MIGHT BE IN OVER HER HEAD.

BZZ-ZT!

WE'LL GIVE HER ONE LAST CHANCE. HAVE HER MEET US AT THE LAST TESTING GROUND.

WELL YOUNG LADY, YOU BETTER GET YOUR REST TONIGHT.

WE'LL SEE YOU TOMORROW.

GREAT! TH-THAT'S *GREAT*. THIS WAS FUN GUYS.

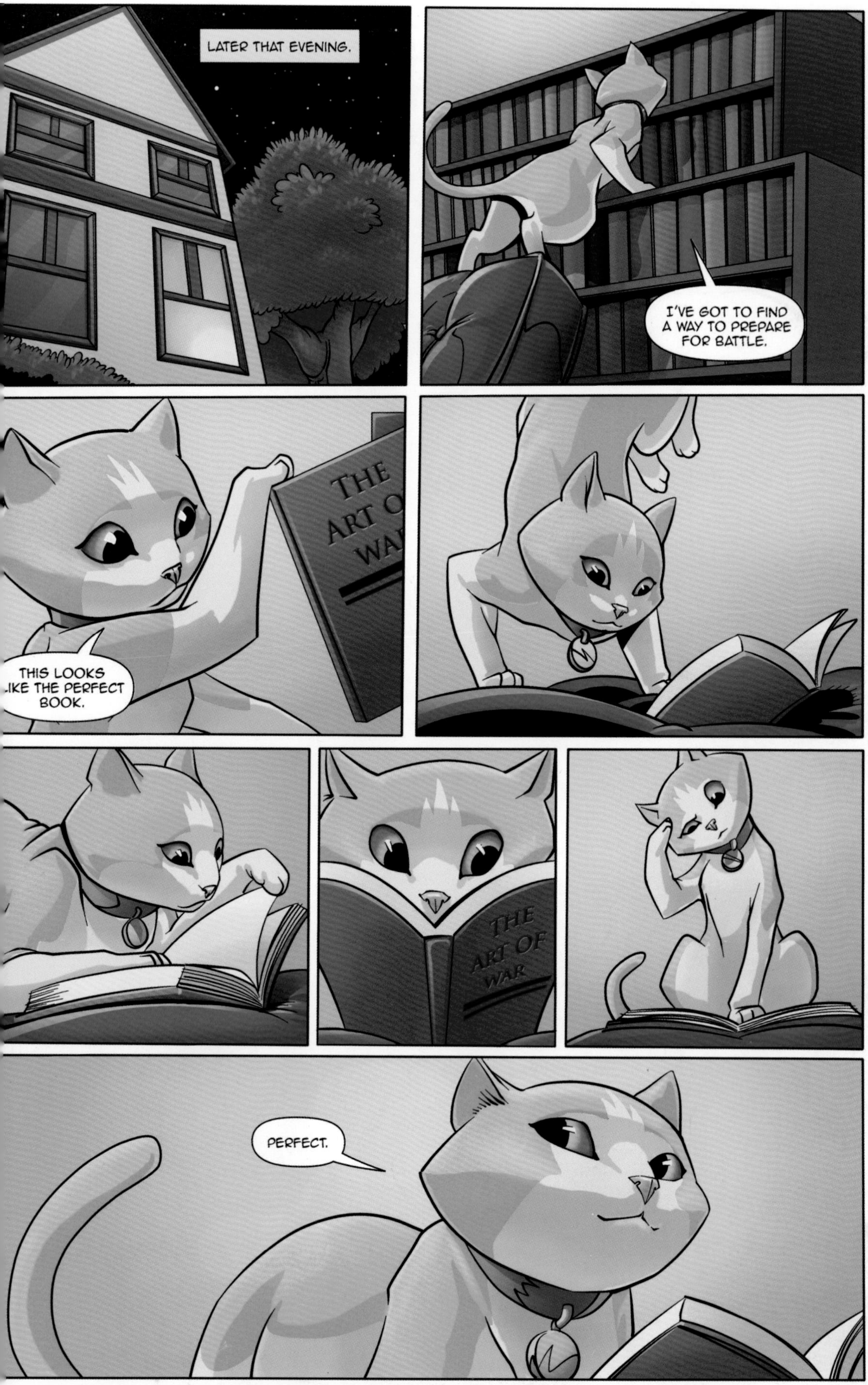
LATER THAT EVENING.
I'VE GOT TO FIND A WAY TO PREPARE FOR BATTLE.
THE ART OF WAR
THIS LOOKS LIKE THE PERFECT BOOK.
THE ART OF WAR
PERFECT.

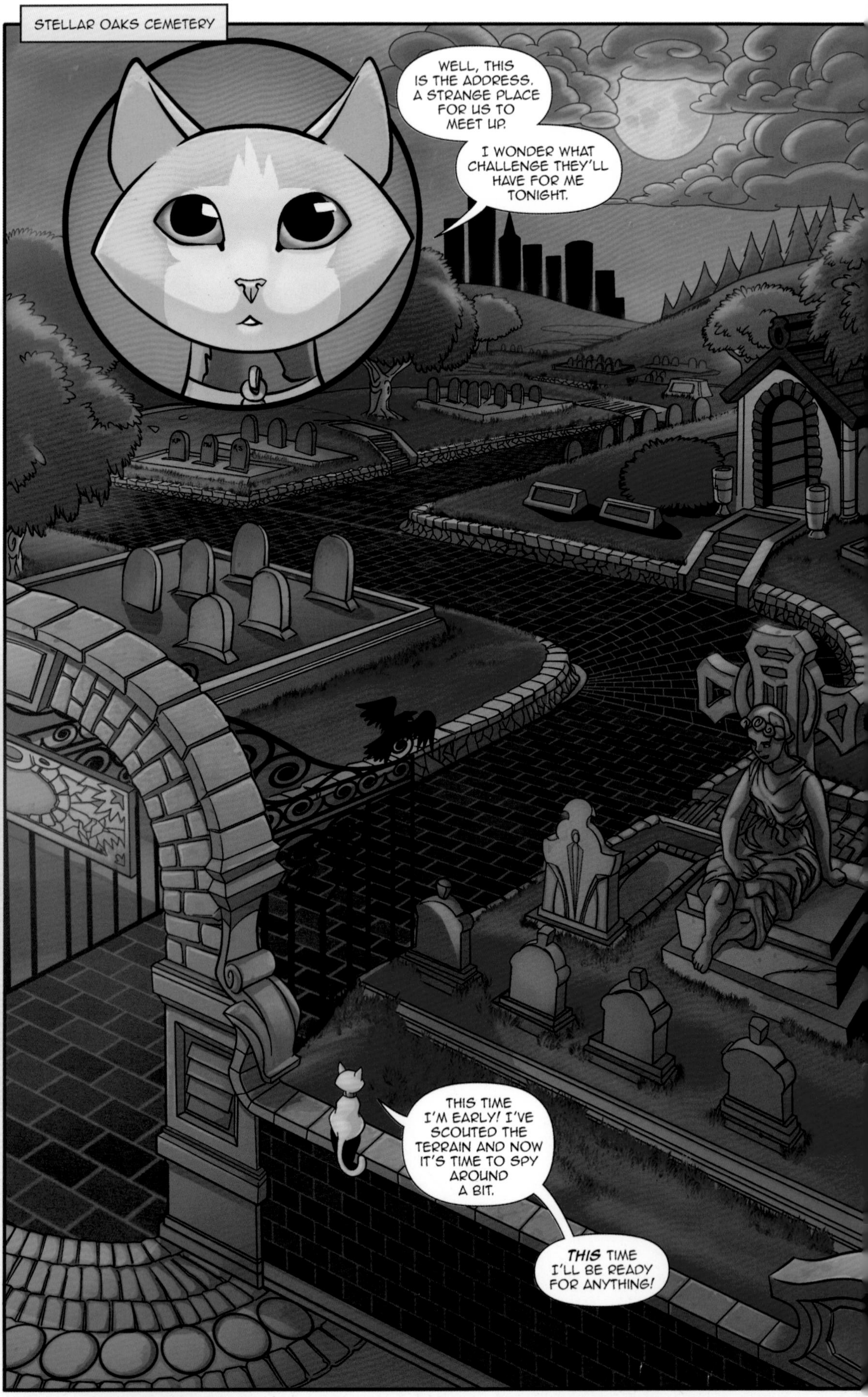
STELLAR OAKS CEMETERY
WELL, THIS IS THE ADDRESS. A STRANGE PLACE FOR US TO MEET UP.
I WONDER WHAT CHALLENGE THEY'LL HAVE FOR ME TONIGHT.
THIS TIME I'M EARLY! I'VE SCOUTED THE TERRAIN AND NOW IT'S TIME TO SPY AROUND A BIT.
THIS TIME I'LL BE READY FOR ANYTHING!

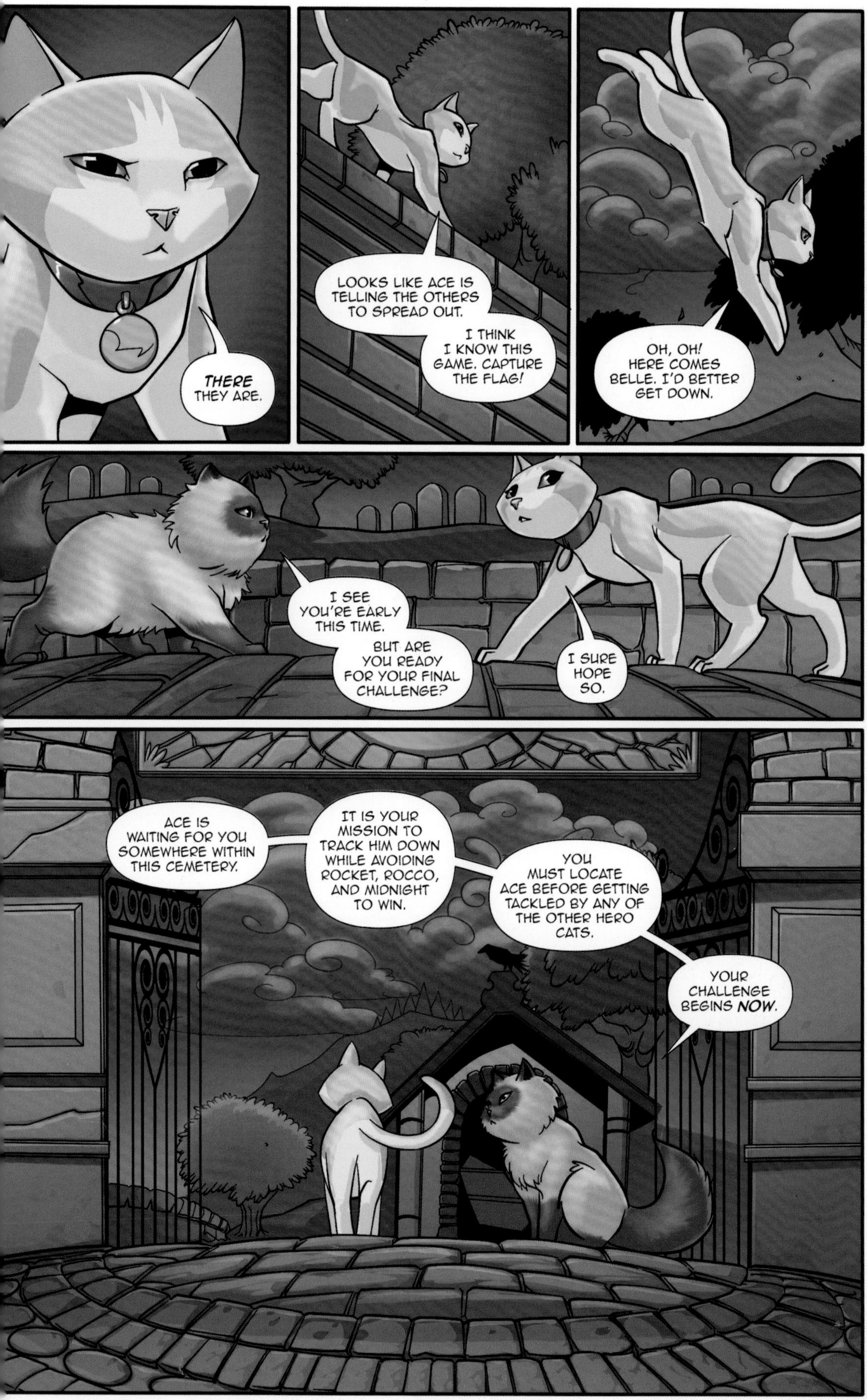

THERE THEY ARE.
LOOKS LIKE ACE IS TELLING THE OTHERS TO SPREAD OUT.
I THINK I KNOW THIS GAME. CAPTURE THE FLAG!
OH, OH! HERE COMES BELLE. I'D BETTER GET DOWN.
I SEE YOU'RE EARLY THIS TIME.
BUT ARE YOU READY FOR YOUR FINAL CHALLENGE?
I SURE HOPE SO.
ACE IS WAITING FOR YOU SOMEWHERE WITHIN THIS CEMETERY.
IT IS YOUR MISSION TO TRACK HIM DOWN WHILE AVOIDING ROCKET, ROCCO, AND MIDNIGHT TO WIN.
YOU MUST LOCATE ACE BEFORE GETTING TACKLED BY ANY OF THE OTHER HERO CATS.
YOUR CHALLENGE BEGINS **NOW**.

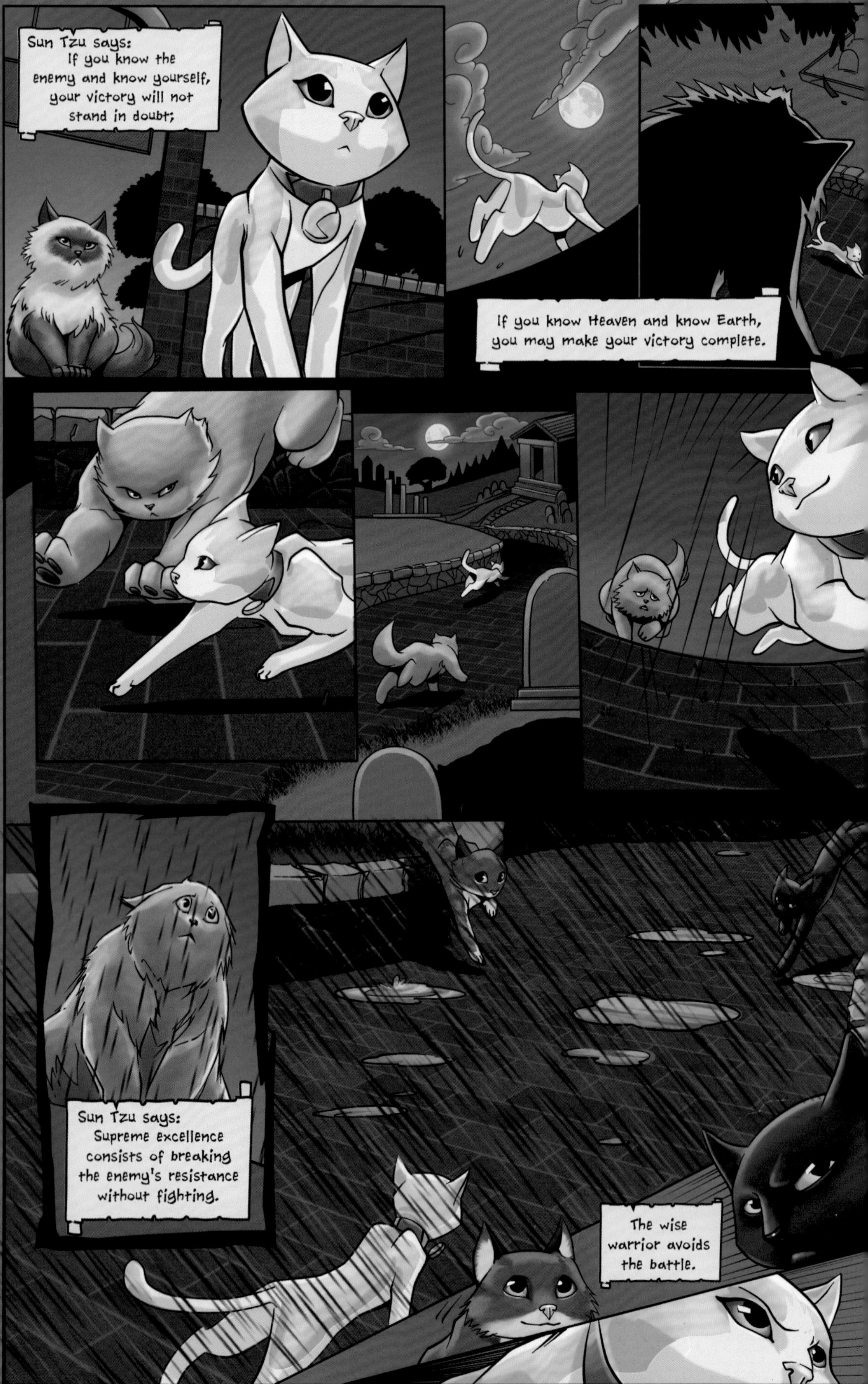
Sun Tzu says:
If you know the enemy and know yourself, your victory will not stand in doubt;
If you know Heaven and know Earth, you may make your victory complete.
Sun Tzu says:
Supreme excellence consists of breaking the enemy's resistance without fighting.
The wise warrior avoids the battle.

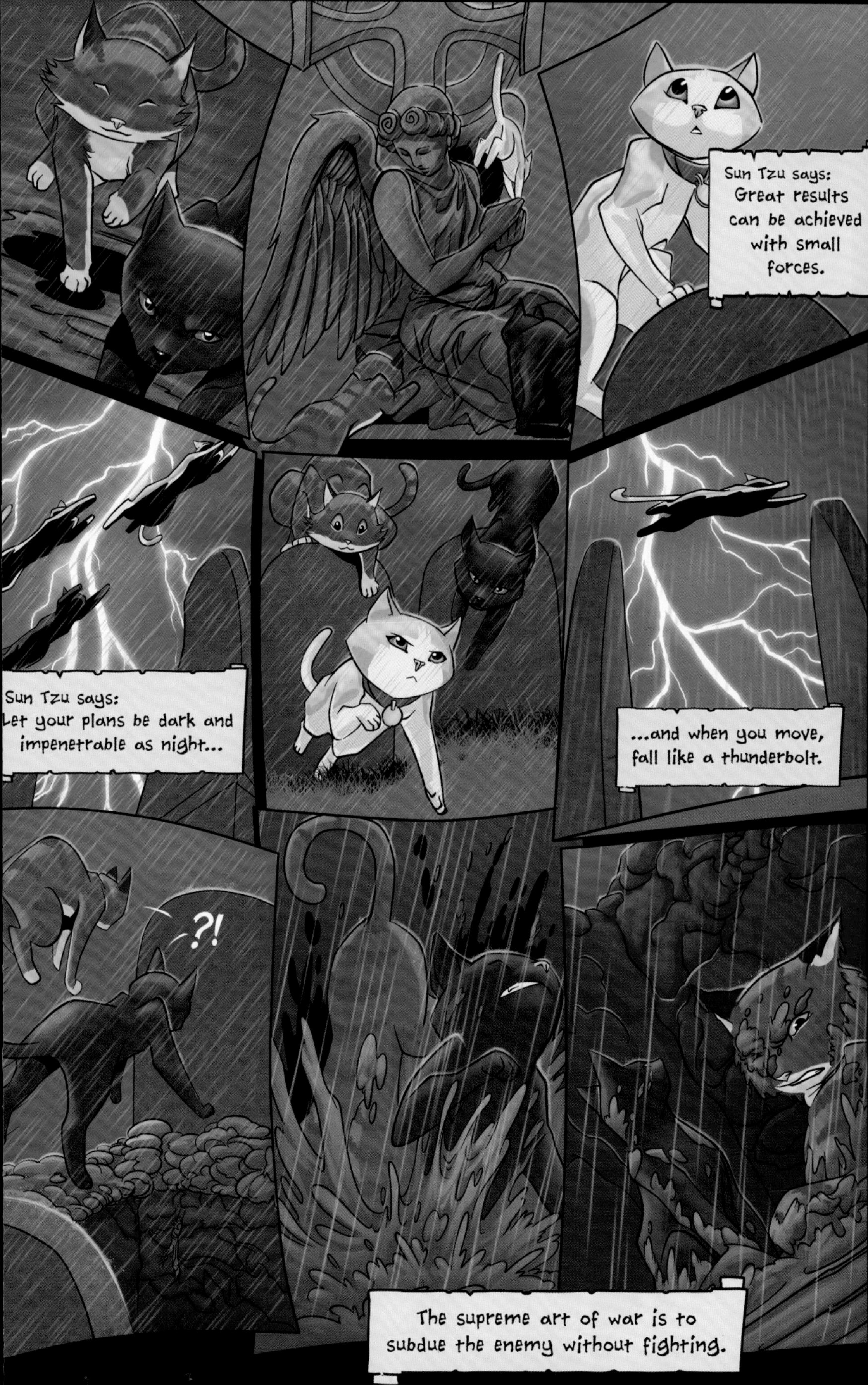
Sun Tzu says:
Great results can be achieved with small forces.
Sun Tzu says:
Let your plans be dark and impenetrable as night...
...and when you move, fall like a thunderbolt.
?!
The supreme art of war is to subdue the enemy without fighting.

"The opportunity of defeating the enemy is provided by the enemy himself."

— Sun Tzu, The Art of War

I DID IT!

I'VE WON!

I CAN JOIN YOUR TEAM NOW, RIGHT? I'VE PASSED ALL YOUR TESTS, RIGHT?

YES RECRUIT. YOU'VE EXHIBITED EXTRAORDINARY COURAGE, STRENGTH AND CUNNING. YOU'VE PROVEN THAT YOU HAVE WHAT IT TAKES.

BUT WHY?

EVERY MISSION CARRIES WITH IT A RISK? THIS ISN'T JUST SOME GAME WE PLAY THE DANGERS ARE VERY REAL CASSIOPEIA.

WHY DO YOU WANT TO BE PART OF THIS TEAM?

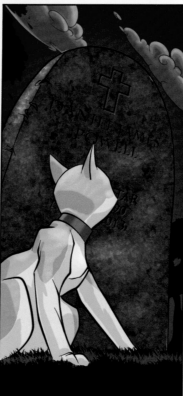

WHY LEAVE YOUR HOME WHEN YOU KNOW THERE ARE LOVED ONES WHO WORRY ABOUT YOU?

YOU HAVE A HUMAN FAMILY WHO LOVES AND TAKES CARE OF YOU. WHY WOULD YOU TAKE THE RISK OF LOSING THAT?

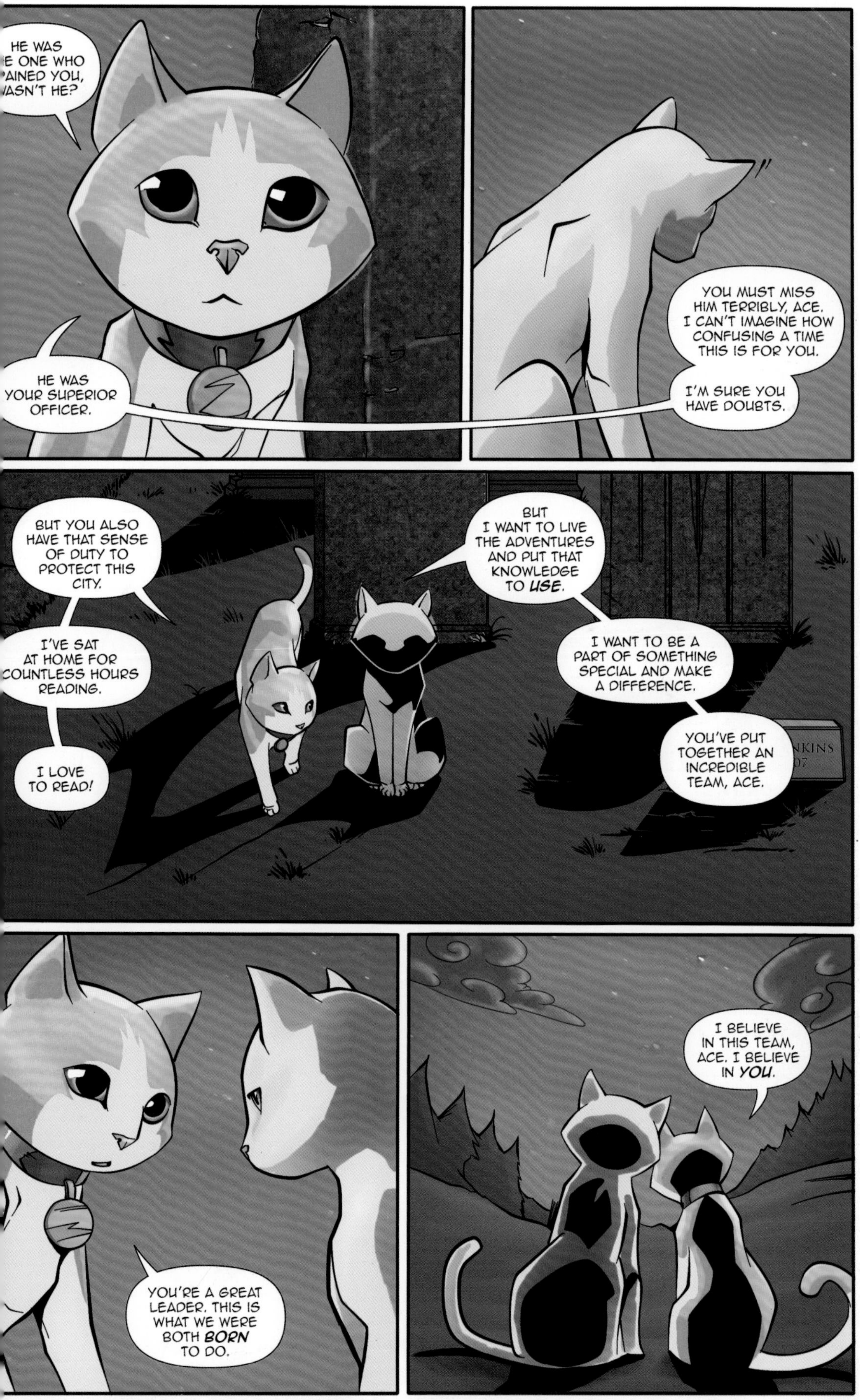
HE WAS
E ONE WHO
AINED YOU,
ASN'T HE?
HE WAS YOUR SUPERIOR OFFICER.
YOU MUST MISS HIM TERRIBLY, ACE. I CAN'T IMAGINE HOW CONFUSING A TIME THIS IS FOR YOU.
I'M SURE YOU HAVE DOUBTS.
BUT YOU ALSO HAVE THAT SENSE OF DUTY TO PROTECT THIS CITY.
I'VE SAT AT HOME FOR COUNTLESS HOURS READING.
I LOVE TO READ!
BUT I WANT TO LIVE THE ADVENTURES AND PUT THAT KNOWLEDGE TO USE.
I WANT TO BE A PART OF SOMETHING SPECIAL AND MAKE A DIFFERENCE.
YOU'VE PUT TOGETHER AN INCREDIBLE TEAM, ACE.
NKINS
07
YOU'RE A GREAT LEADER. THIS IS WHAT WE WERE BOTH BORN TO DO.
I BELIEVE IN THIS TEAM, ACE. I BELIEVE IN YOU.

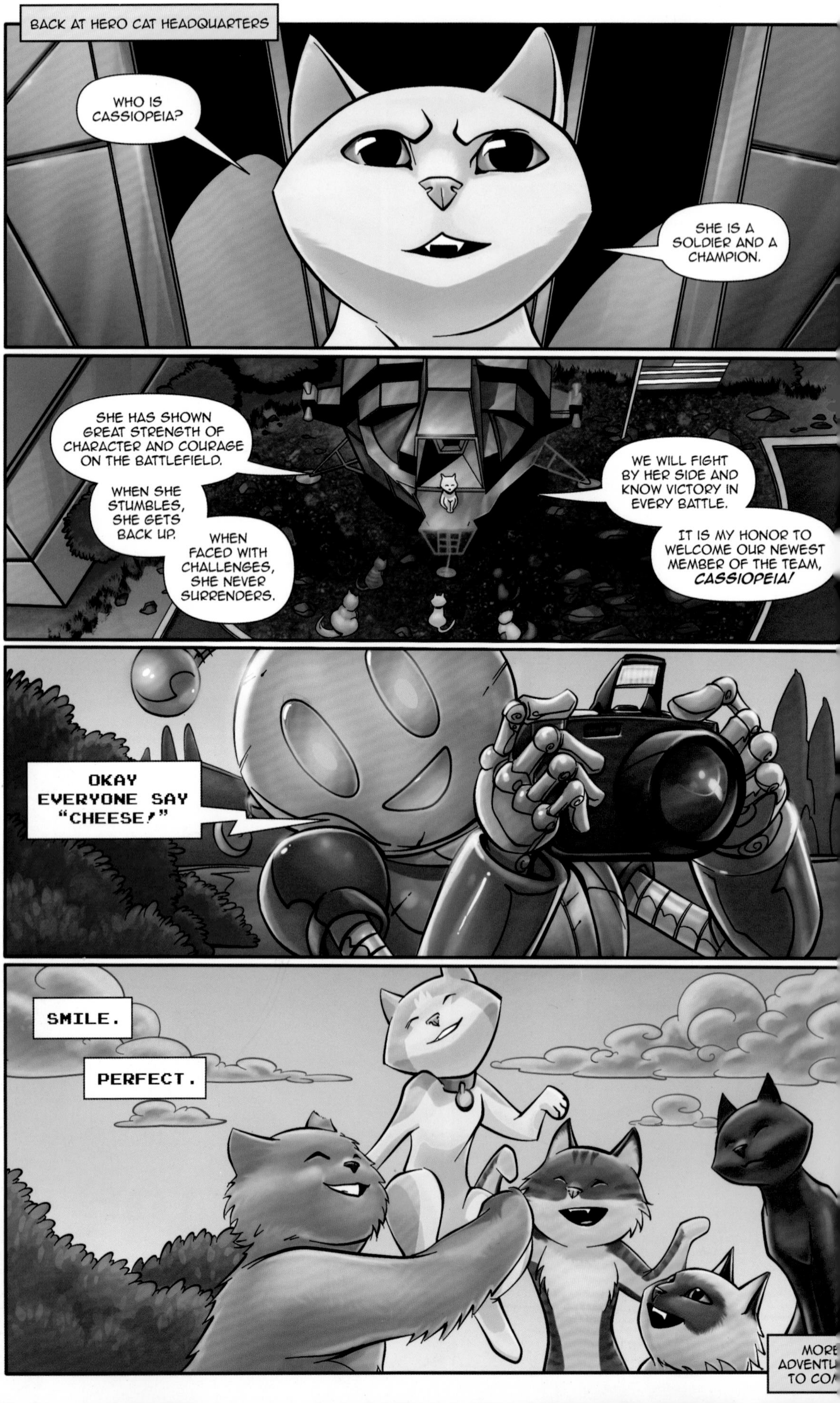
BACK AT HERO CAT HEADQUARTERS
WHO IS CASSIOPEIA?
SHE IS A SOLDIER AND A CHAMPION.
SHE HAS SHOWN GREAT STRENGTH OF CHARACTER AND COURAGE ON THE BATTLEFIELD.
WHEN SHE STUMBLES, SHE GETS BACK UP.
WHEN FACED WITH CHALLENGES, SHE NEVER SURRENDERS.
WE WILL FIGHT BY HER SIDE AND KNOW VICTORY IN EVERY BATTLE.
IT IS MY HONOR TO WELCOME OUR NEWEST MEMBER OF THE TEAM, CASSIOPEIA!
OKAY EVERYONE SAY "CHEESE!"
SMILE.
PERFECT.

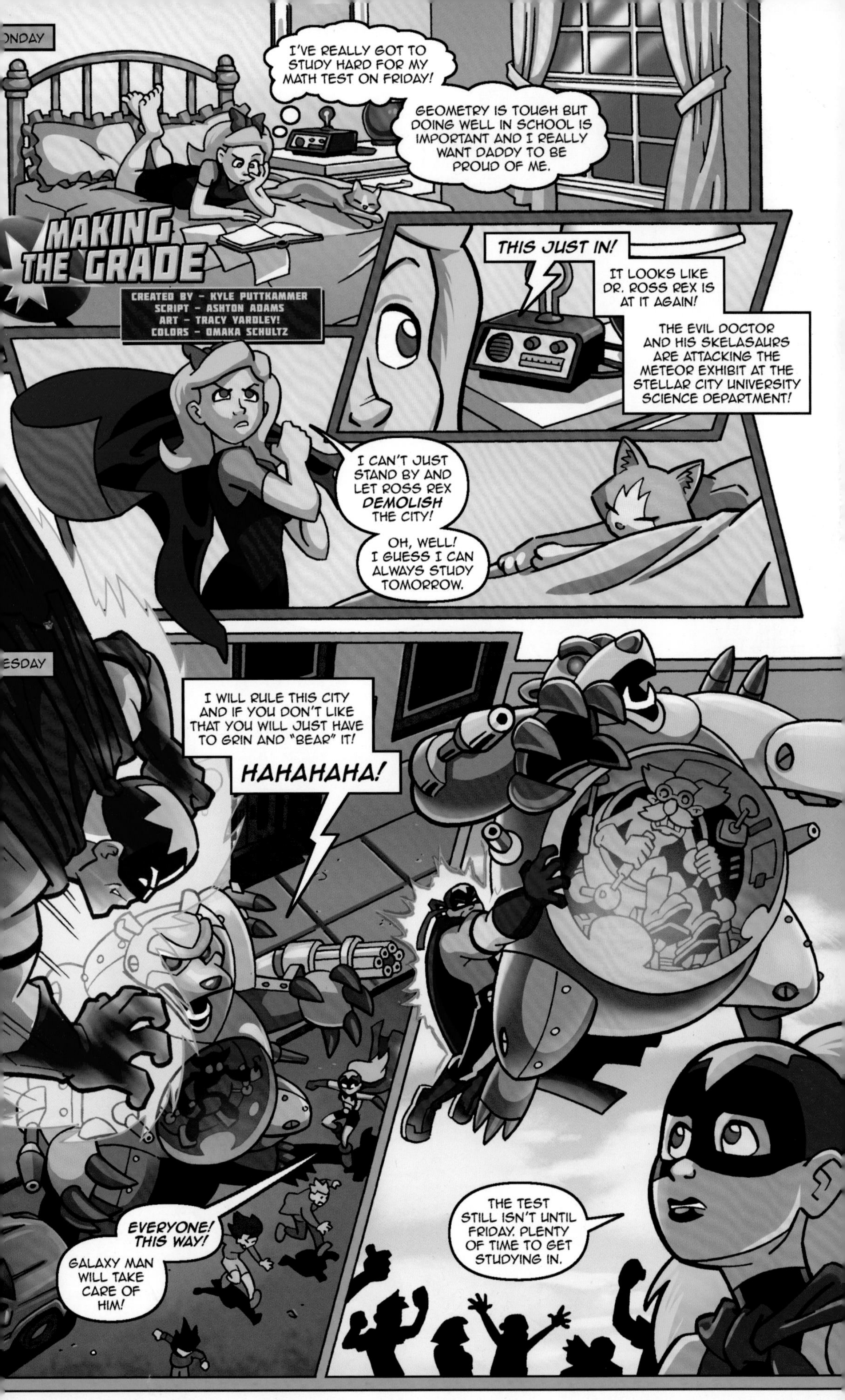

ONDAY
I'VE REALLY GOT TO STUDY HARD FOR MY MATH TEST ON FRIDAY!
GEOMETRY IS TOUGH BUT DOING WELL IN SCHOOL IS IMPORTANT AND I REALLY WANT DADDY TO BE PROUD OF ME.
MAKING THE GRADE
CREATED BY - KYLE PUTTKAMMER
SCRIPT - ASHTON ADAMS
ART - TRACY YARDLEY!
COLORS - OMAKA SCHULTZ
THIS JUST IN!
IT LOOKS LIKE DR. ROSS REX IS AT IT AGAIN!
THE EVIL DOCTOR AND HIS SKELASAURS ARE ATTACKING THE METEOR EXHIBIT AT THE STELLAR CITY UNIVERSITY SCIENCE DEPARTMENT!
I CAN'T JUST STAND BY AND LET ROSS REX DEMOLISH THE CITY!
OH, WELL! I GUESS I CAN ALWAYS STUDY TOMORROW.
ESDAY
I WILL RULE THIS CITY AND IF YOU DON'T LIKE THAT YOU WILL JUST HAVE TO GRIN AND "BEAR" IT!
HAHAHAHA!
EVERYONE! THIS WAY!
GALAXY MAN WILL TAKE CARE OF HIM!
THE TEST STILL ISN'T UNTIL FRIDAY. PLENTY OF TIME TO GET STUDYING IN.

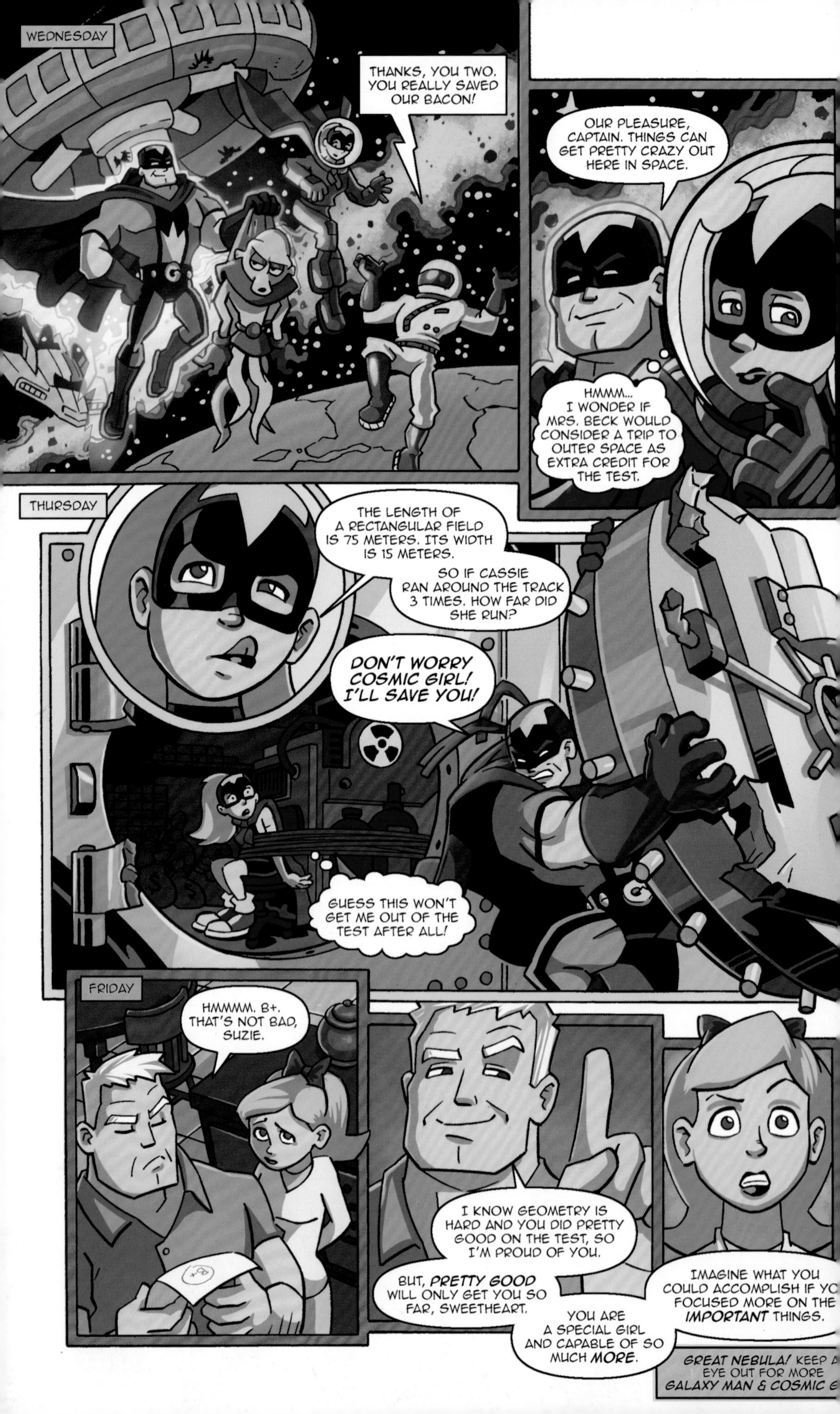
WEDNESDAY
THANKS, YOU TWO. YOU REALLY SAVED OUR BACON!
OUR PLEASURE, CAPTAIN. THINGS CAN GET PRETTY CRAZY OUT HERE IN SPACE.
HMMM... I WONDER IF MRS. BECK WOULD CONSIDER A TRIP TO OUTER SPACE AS EXTRA CREDIT FOR THE TEST.
THURSDAY
THE LENGTH OF A RECTANGULAR FIELD IS 75 METERS. ITS WIDTH IS 15 METERS.
SO IF CASSIE RAN AROUND THE TRACK 3 TIMES. HOW FAR DID SHE RUN?
DON'T WORRY COSMIC GIRL! I'LL SAVE YOU!
GUESS THIS WON'T GET ME OUT OF THE TEST AFTER ALL!
FRIDAY
HMMMM. B+. THAT'S NOT BAD, SUZIE.
B+
I KNOW GEOMETRY IS HARD AND YOU DID PRETTY GOOD ON THE TEST, SO I'M PROUD OF YOU.
BUT, PRETTY GOOD WILL ONLY GET YOU SO FAR, SWEETHEART.
YOU ARE A SPECIAL GIRL AND CAPABLE OF SO MUCH MORE.
IMAGINE WHAT YOU COULD ACCOMPLISH IF YO FOCUSED MORE ON THE IMPORTANT THINGS.
GREAT NEBULA! KEEP A EYE OUT FOR MORE GALAXY MAN & COSMIC G

CHAPTER 4:
THE WORLD BENEATH OUR FEET

WRITER: KYLE PUTTKAMMER

PENCILS: MARCUS WILLIAMS

INKS: RYAN SELLERS

COLORS: MATT HERMS

LETTERING: BRIANA HIGGINS

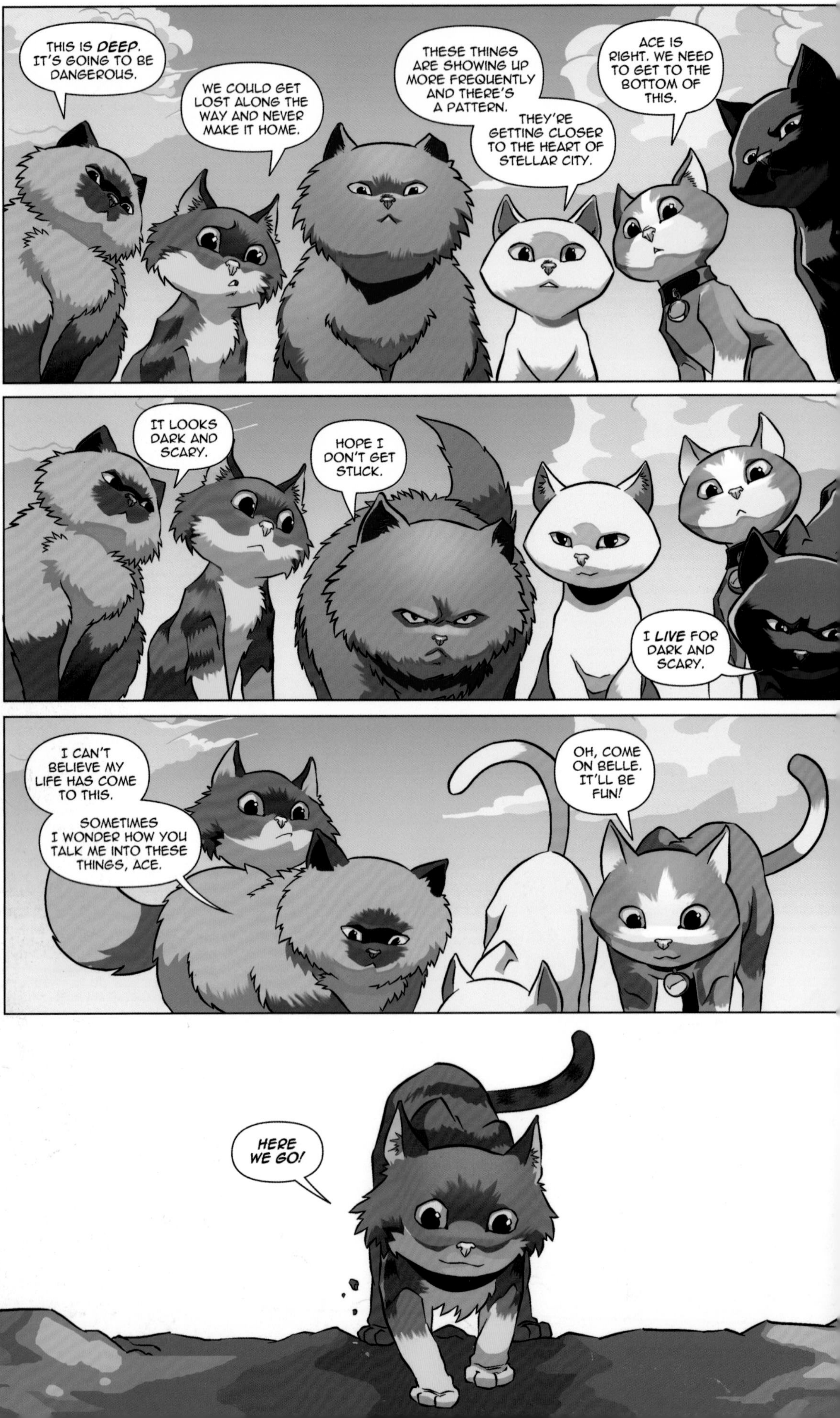
THIS IS *DEEP*. IT'S GOING TO BE DANGEROUS.
WE COULD GET LOST ALONG THE WAY AND NEVER MAKE IT HOME.
THESE THINGS ARE SHOWING UP MORE FREQUENTLY AND THERE'S A PATTERN.
THEY'RE GETTING CLOSER TO THE HEART OF STELLAR CITY.
ACE IS RIGHT. WE NEED TO GET TO THE BOTTOM OF THIS.
IT LOOKS DARK AND SCARY.
HOPE I DON'T GET STUCK.
I *LIVE* FOR DARK AND SCARY.
I CAN'T BELIEVE MY LIFE HAS COME TO THIS.
SOMETIMES I WONDER HOW YOU TALK ME INTO THESE THINGS, ACE.
OH, COME ON BELLE. IT'LL BE FUN!
HERE WE GO!

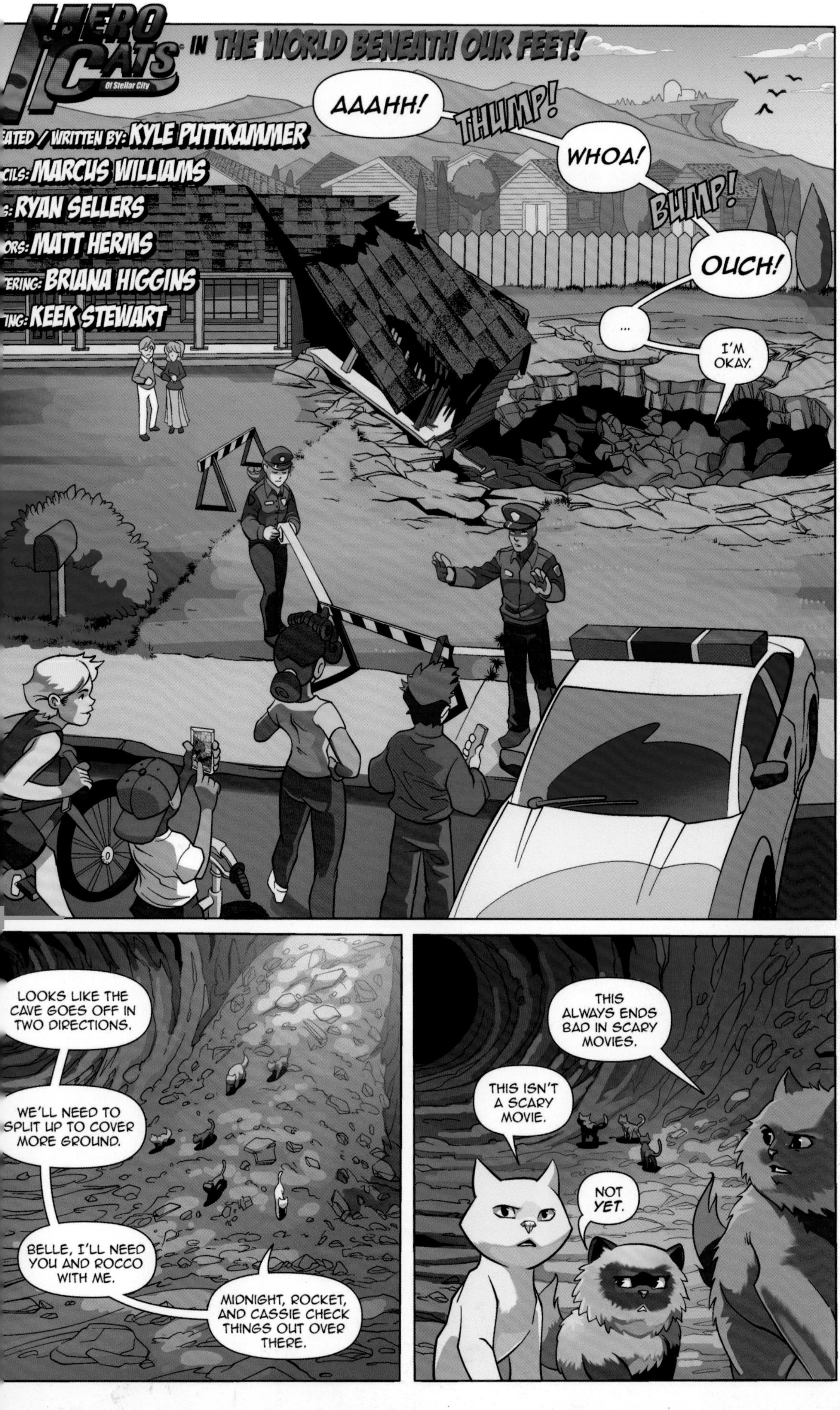
HERO CATS of Stellar City
IN THE WORLD BENEATH OUR FEET!
EATED / WRITTEN BY: KYLE PUTTKAMMER
CILS: MARCUS WILLIAMS
S: RYAN SELLERS
ORS: MATT HERMS
TERING: BRIANA HIGGINS
TING: KEEK STEWART
AAAHH!
THUMP!
WHOA!
BUMP!
OUCH!
...
I'M OKAY.
LOOKS LIKE THE CAVE GOES OFF IN TWO DIRECTIONS.
WE'LL NEED TO SPLIT UP TO COVER MORE GROUND.
BELLE, I'LL NEED YOU AND ROCCO WITH ME.
MIDNIGHT, ROCKET, AND CASSIE CHECK THINGS OUT OVER THERE.
THIS ALWAYS ENDS BAD IN SCARY MOVIES.
THIS ISN'T A SCARY MOVIE.
NOT YET.

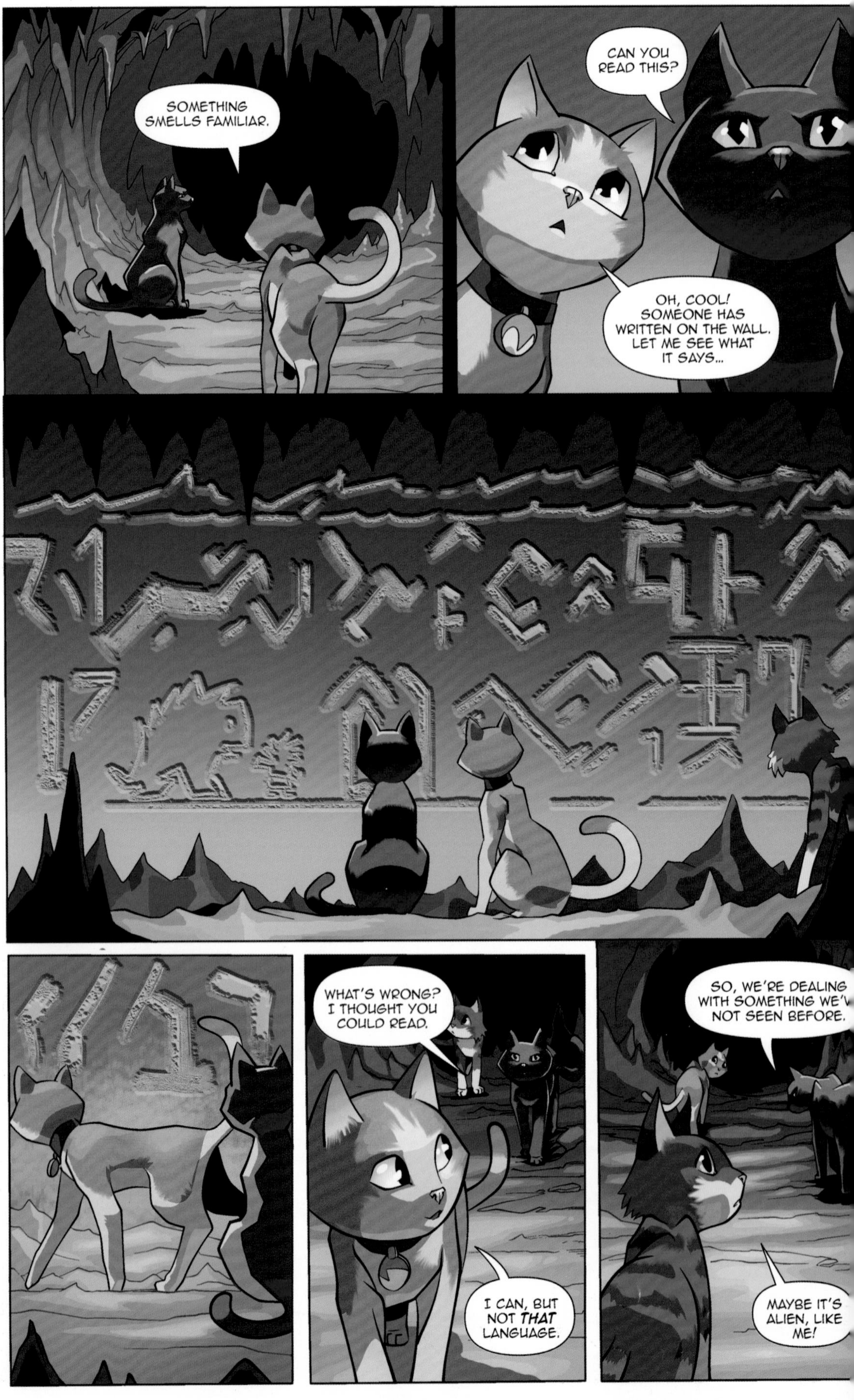
SOMETHING SMELLS FAMILIAR.
CAN YOU READ THIS?
OH, COOL! SOMEONE HAS WRITTEN ON THE WALL. LET ME SEE WHAT IT SAYS...
WHAT'S WRONG? I THOUGHT YOU COULD READ.
I CAN, BUT NOT *THAT* LANGUAGE.
SO, WE'RE DEALING WITH SOMETHING WE'V NOT SEEN BEFORE.
MAYBE IT'S ALIEN, LIKE ME!

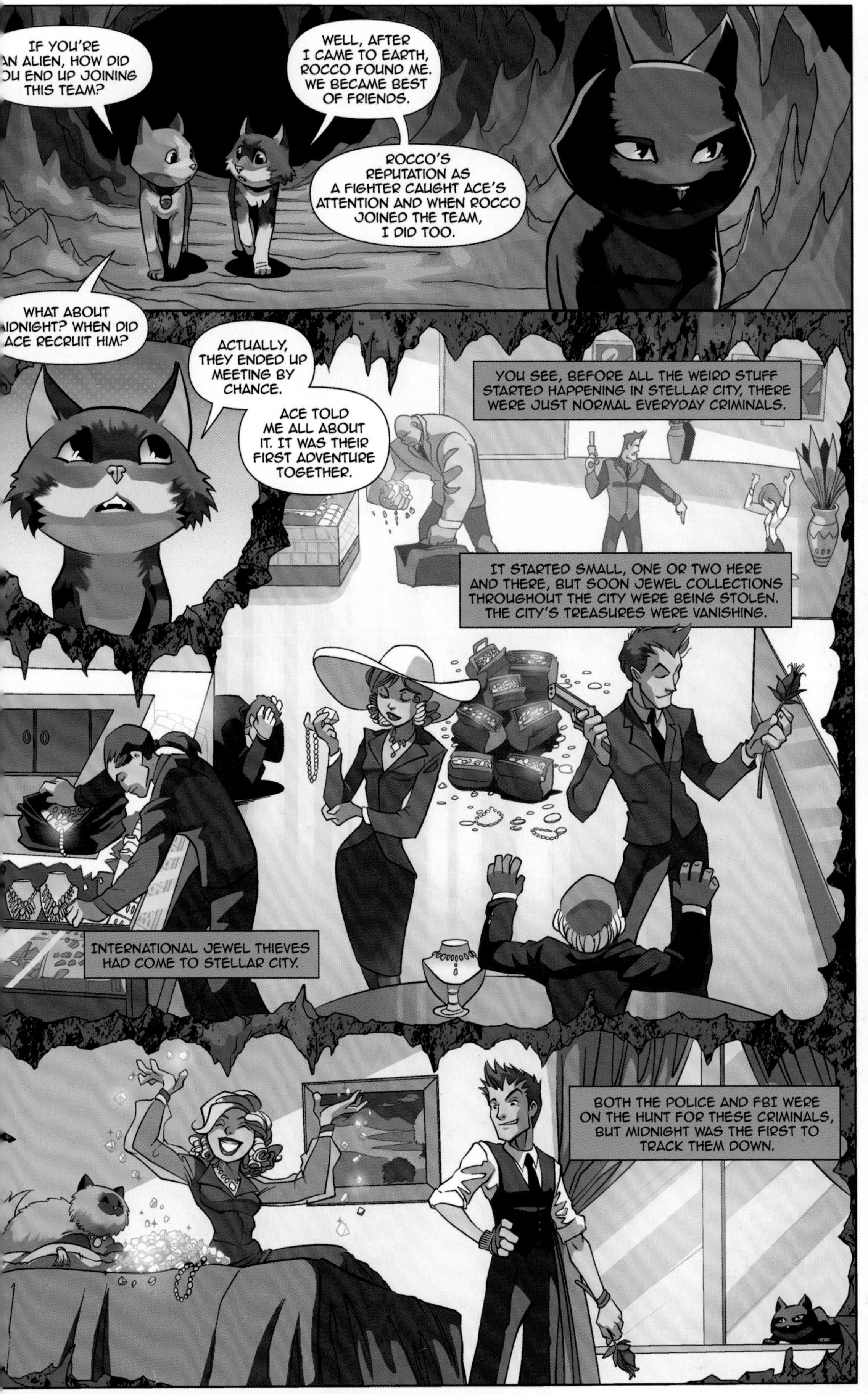
IF YOU'RE
AN ALIEN, HOW DID
OU END UP JOINING
THIS TEAM?
WELL, AFTER I CAME TO EARTH, ROCCO FOUND ME. WE BECAME BEST OF FRIENDS.
ROCCO'S REPUTATION AS A FIGHTER CAUGHT ACE'S ATTENTION AND WHEN ROCCO JOINED THE TEAM, I DID TOO.
WHAT ABOUT
IDNIGHT? WHEN DID
ACE RECRUIT HIM?
ACTUALLY, THEY ENDED UP MEETING BY CHANCE.
ACE TOLD ME ALL ABOUT IT. IT WAS THEIR FIRST ADVENTURE TOGETHER.
YOU SEE, BEFORE ALL THE WEIRD STUFF STARTED HAPPENING IN STELLAR CITY, THERE WERE JUST NORMAL EVERYDAY CRIMINALS.
IT STARTED SMALL, ONE OR TWO HERE AND THERE, BUT SOON JEWEL COLLECTIONS THROUGHOUT THE CITY WERE BEING STOLEN. THE CITY'S TREASURES WERE VANISHING.
INTERNATIONAL JEWEL THIEVES HAD COME TO STELLAR CITY.
BOTH THE POLICE AND FBI WERE ON THE HUNT FOR THESE CRIMINALS, BUT MIDNIGHT WAS THE FIRST TO TRACK THEM DOWN.

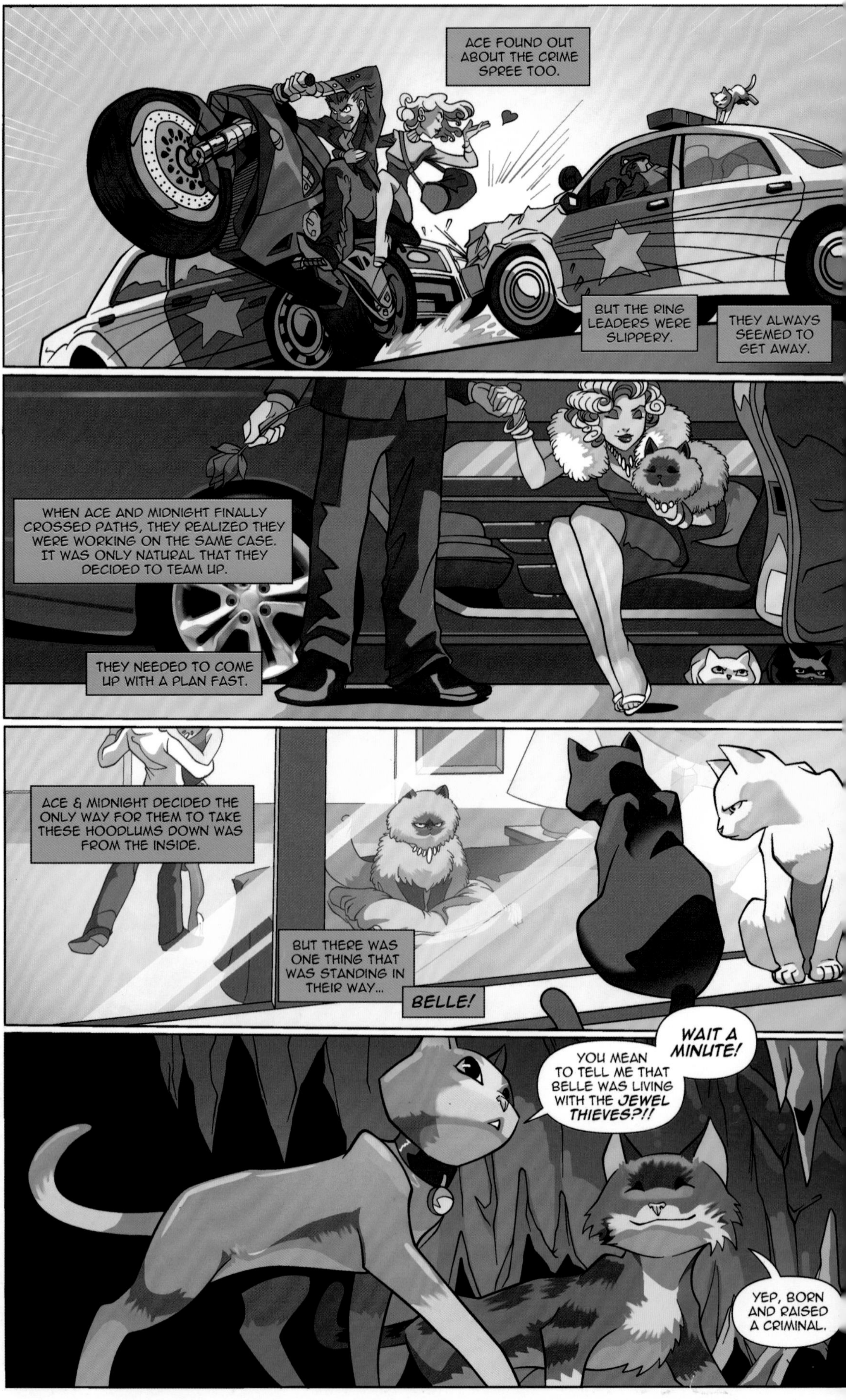
ACE FOUND OUT ABOUT THE CRIME SPREE TOO.
BUT THE RING LEADERS WERE SLIPPERY.
THEY ALWAYS SEEMED TO GET AWAY.
WHEN ACE AND MIDNIGHT FINALLY CROSSED PATHS, THEY REALIZED THEY WERE WORKING ON THE SAME CASE. IT WAS ONLY NATURAL THAT THEY DECIDED TO TEAM UP.
THEY NEEDED TO COME UP WITH A PLAN FAST.
ACE & MIDNIGHT DECIDED THE ONLY WAY FOR THEM TO TAKE THESE HOODLUMS DOWN WAS FROM THE INSIDE.
BUT THERE WAS ONE THING THAT WAS STANDING IN THEIR WAY...
BELLE!
WAIT A MINUTE!
YOU MEAN TO TELL ME THAT BELLE WAS LIVING WITH THE JEWEL THIEVES?!!
YEP, BORN AND RAISED A CRIMINAL.

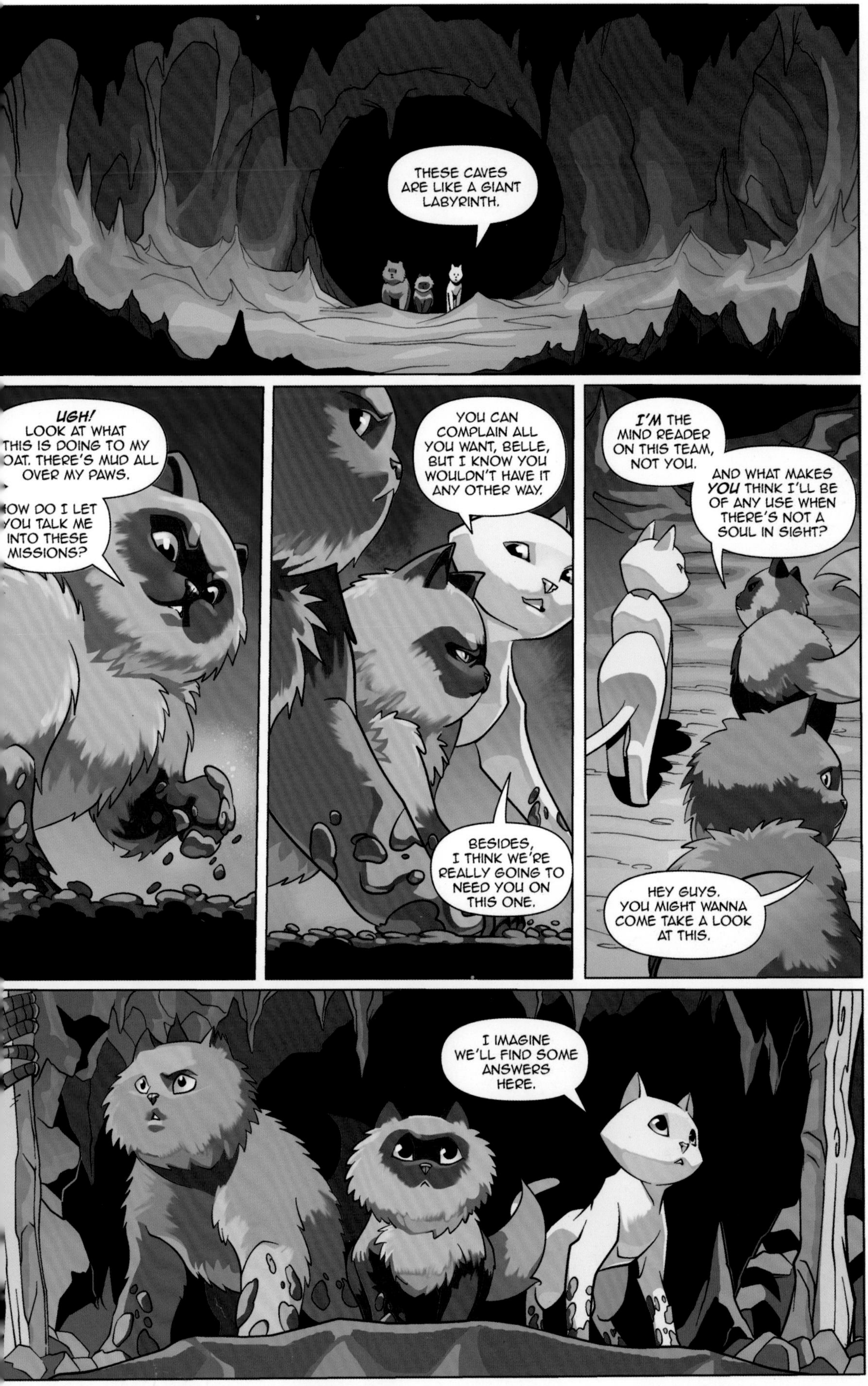

THESE CAVES ARE LIKE A GIANT LABYRINTH.
UGH! LOOK AT WHAT THIS IS DOING TO MY OAT. THERE'S MUD ALL OVER MY PAWS.
OW DO I LET YOU TALK ME INTO THESE MISSIONS?
YOU CAN COMPLAIN ALL YOU WANT, BELLE, BUT I KNOW YOU WOULDN'T HAVE IT ANY OTHER WAY.
BESIDES, I THINK WE'RE REALLY GOING TO NEED YOU ON THIS ONE.
I'M THE MIND READER ON THIS TEAM, NOT YOU.
AND WHAT MAKES YOU THINK I'LL BE OF ANY USE WHEN THERE'S NOT A SOUL IN SIGHT?
HEY GUYS. YOU MIGHT WANNA COME TAKE A LOOK AT THIS.
I IMAGINE WE'LL FIND SOME ANSWERS HERE.

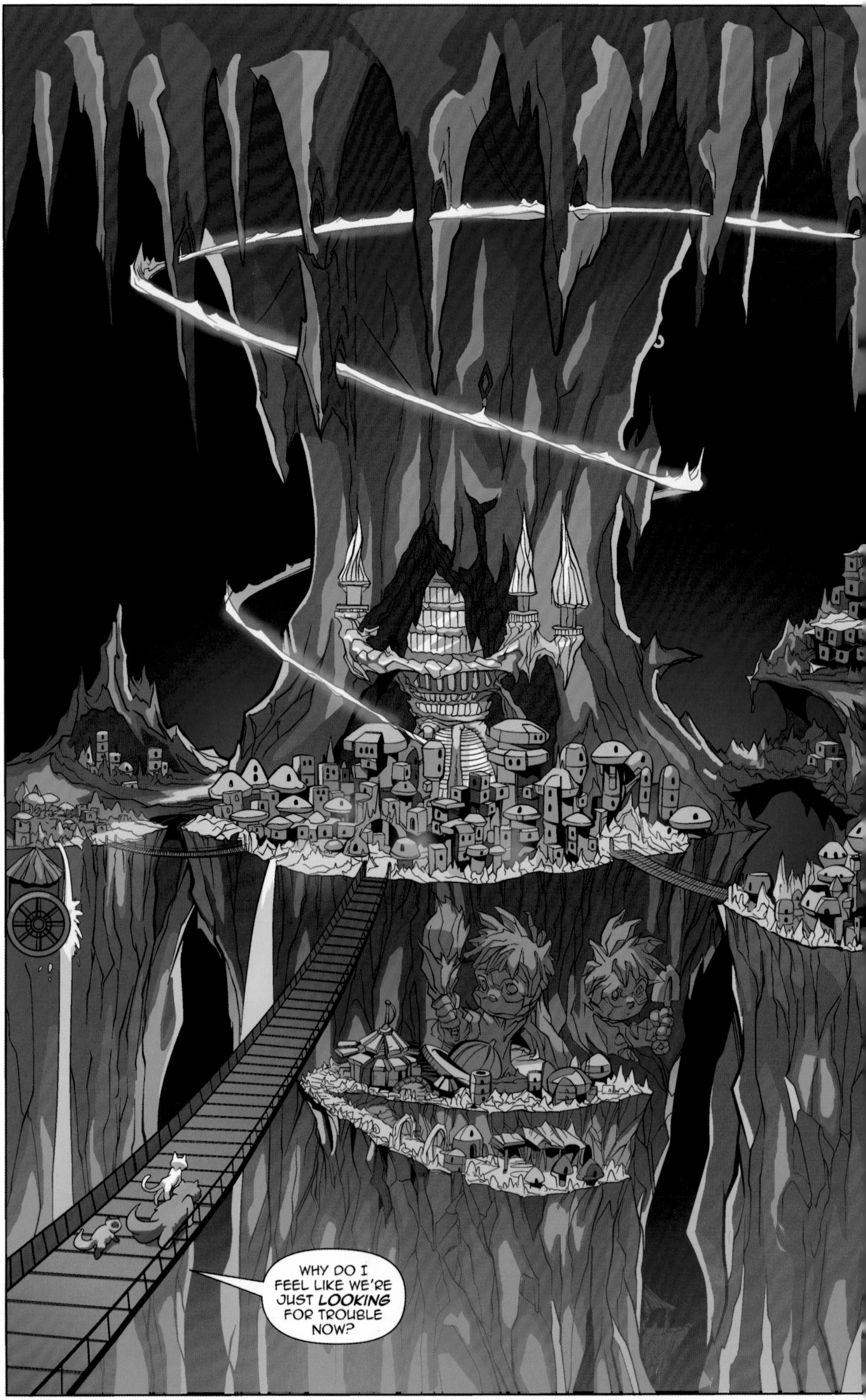
WHY DO I FEEL LIKE WE'RE JUST LOOKING FOR TROUBLE NOW?

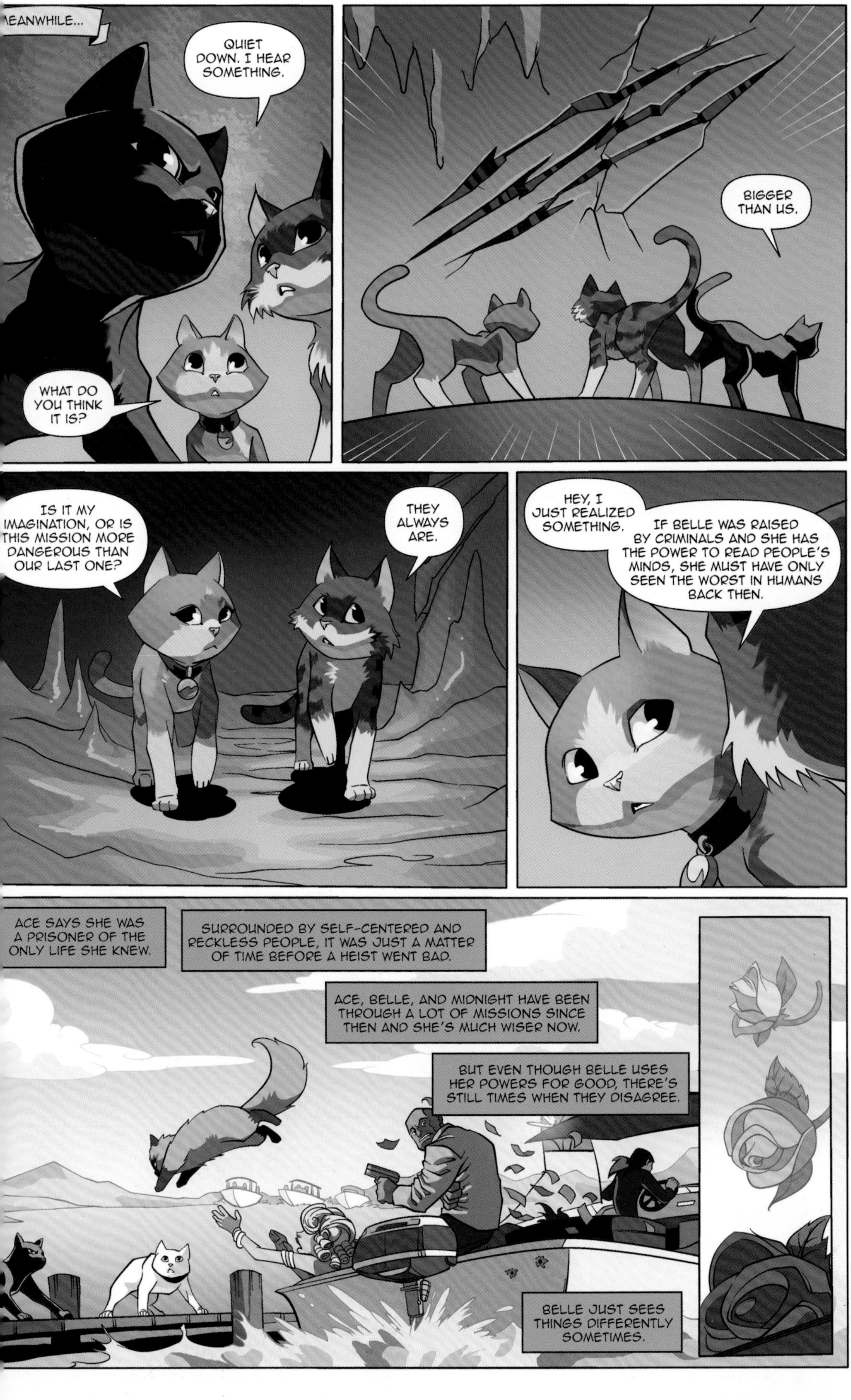
MEANWHILE...
QUIET DOWN. I HEAR SOMETHING.
WHAT DO YOU THINK IT IS?
BIGGER THAN US.
IS IT MY IMAGINATION, OR IS THIS MISSION MORE DANGEROUS THAN OUR LAST ONE?
THEY ALWAYS ARE.
HEY, I JUST REALIZED SOMETHING.
IF BELLE WAS RAISED BY CRIMINALS AND SHE HAS THE POWER TO READ PEOPLE'S MINDS, SHE MUST HAVE ONLY SEEN THE WORST IN HUMANS BACK THEN.
ACE SAYS SHE WAS A PRISONER OF THE ONLY LIFE SHE KNEW.
SURROUNDED BY SELF-CENTERED AND RECKLESS PEOPLE, IT WAS JUST A MATTER OF TIME BEFORE A HEIST WENT BAD.
ACE, BELLE, AND MIDNIGHT HAVE BEEN THROUGH A LOT OF MISSIONS SINCE THEN AND SHE'S MUCH WISER NOW.
BUT EVEN THOUGH BELLE USES HER POWERS FOR GOOD, THERE'S STILL TIMES WHEN THEY DISAGREE.
BELLE JUST SEES THINGS DIFFERENTLY SOMETIMES.

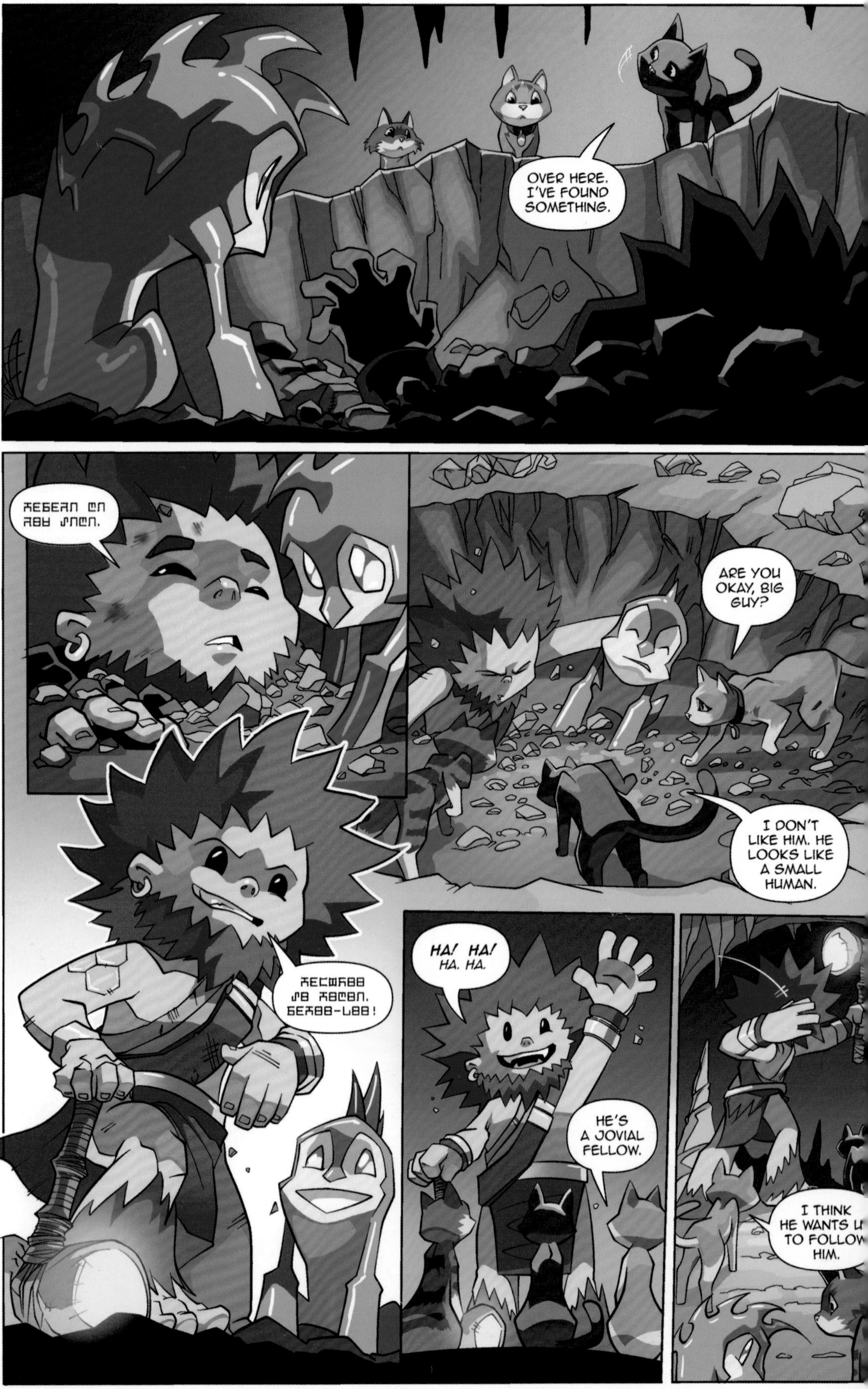
OVER HERE. I'VE FOUND SOMETHING.
ARE YOU OKAY, BIG GUY?
I DON'T LIKE HIM. HE LOOKS LIKE A SMALL HUMAN.
HA! HA! HA. HA.
HE'S A JOVIAL FELLOW.
I THINK HE WANTS U TO FOLLOW HIM.

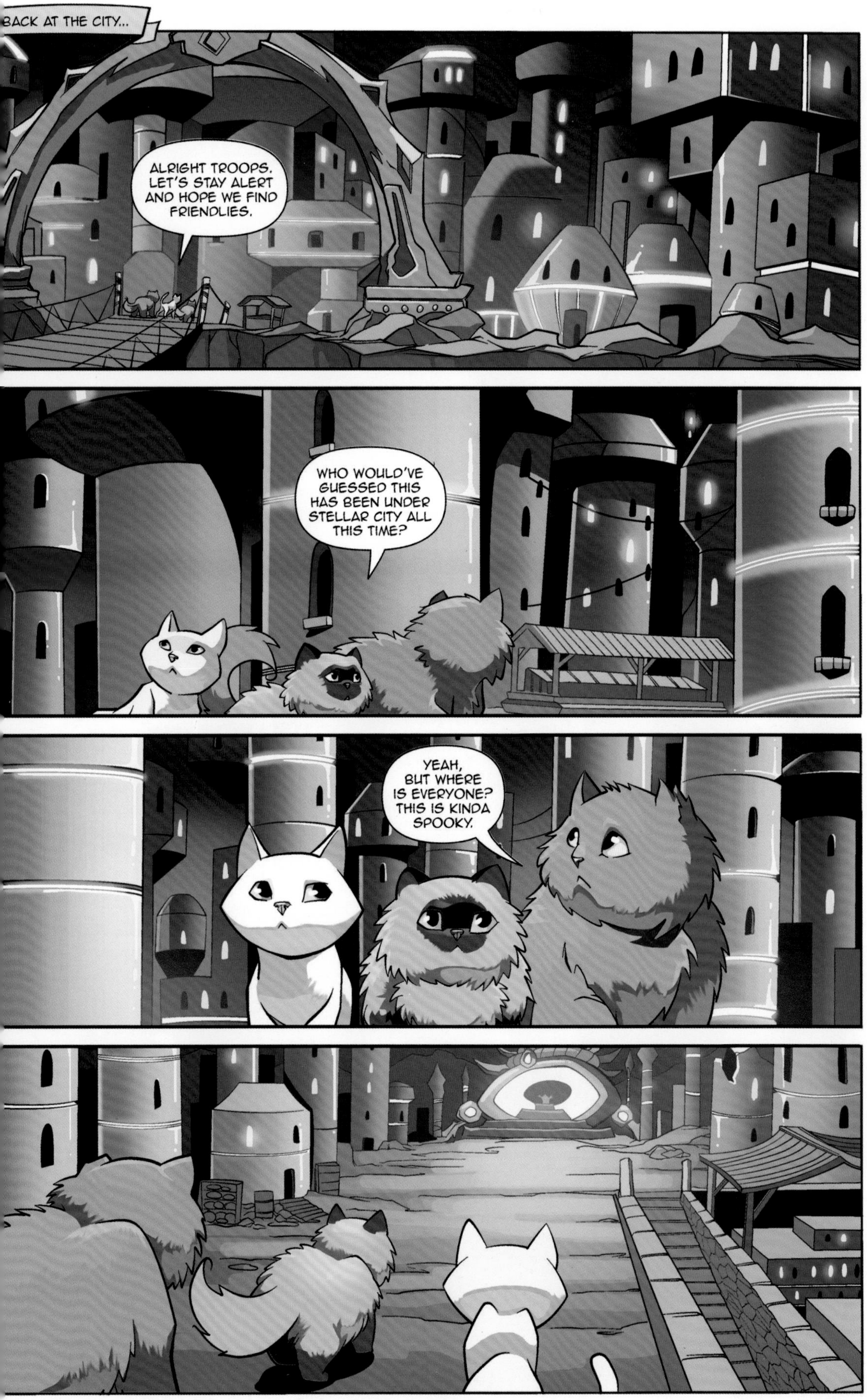

BACK AT THE CITY...
ALRIGHT TROOPS. LET'S STAY ALERT AND HOPE WE FIND FRIENDLIES.
WHO WOULD'VE GUESSED THIS HAS BEEN UNDER STELLAR CITY ALL THIS TIME?
YEAH, BUT WHERE IS EVERYONE? THIS IS KINDA SPOOKY.

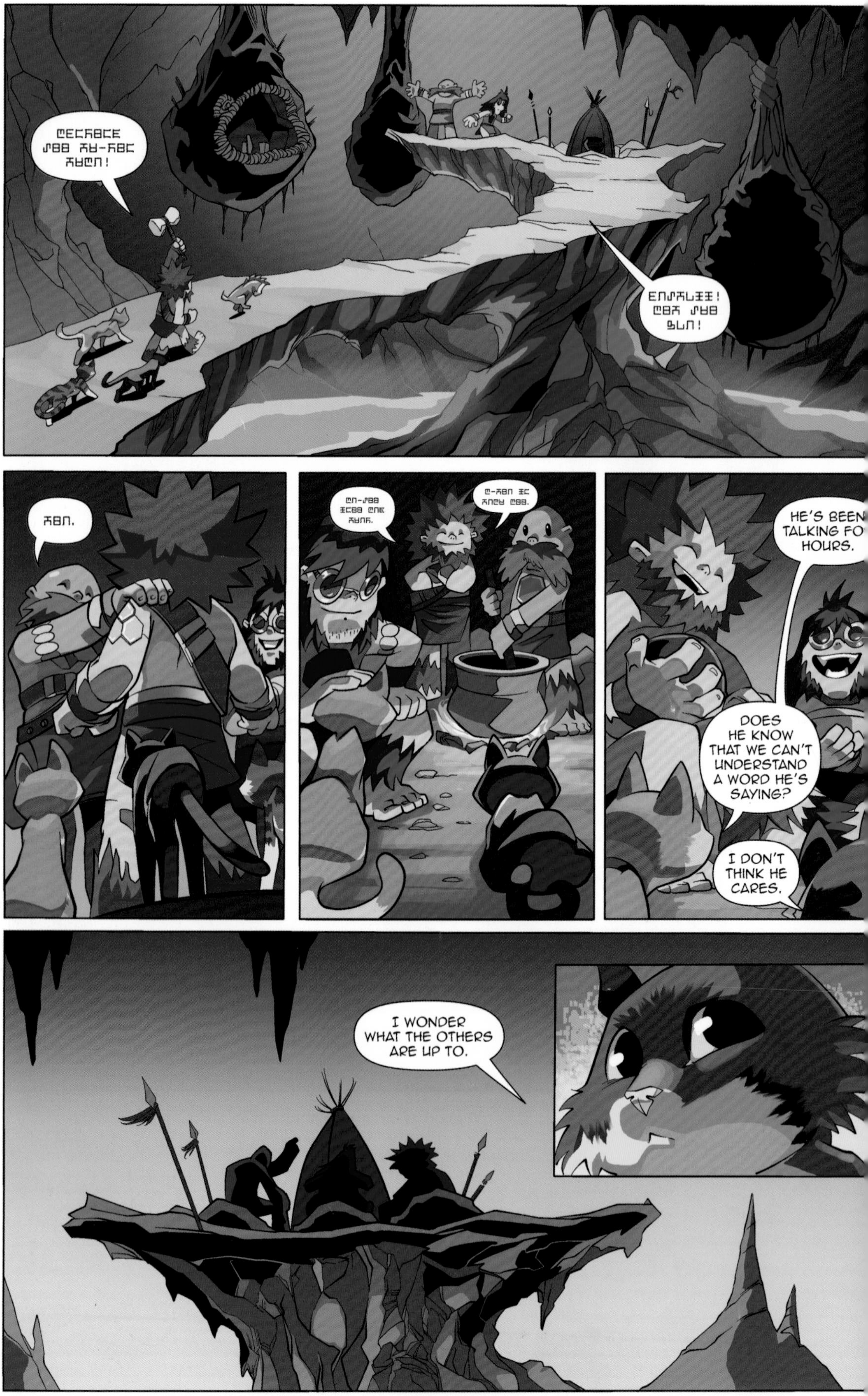
HE'S BEEN TALKING FO HOURS.
DOES HE KNOW THAT WE CAN'T UNDERSTAND A WORD HE'S SAYING?
I DON'T THINK HE CARES.
I WONDER WHAT THE OTHERS ARE UP TO.

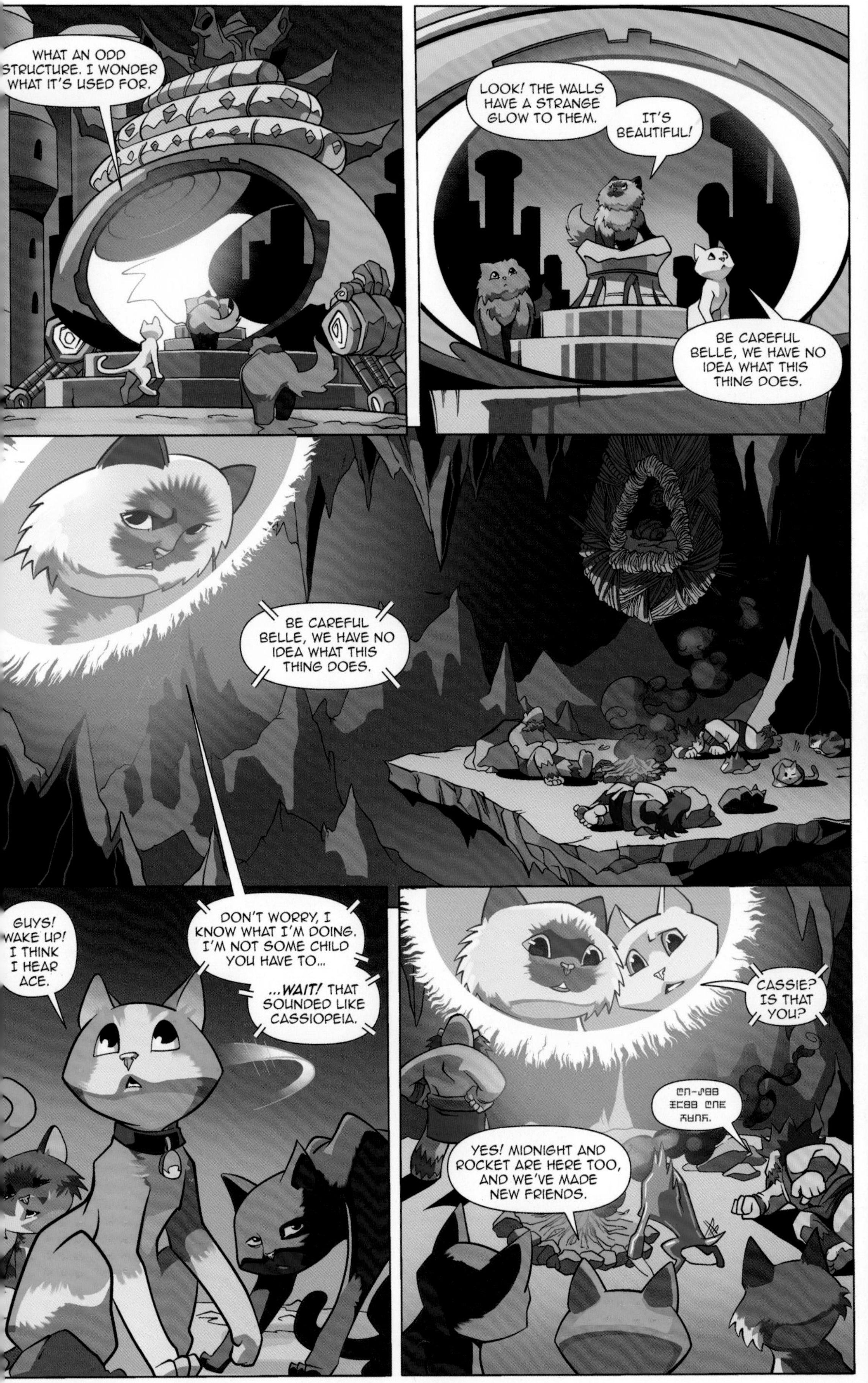
WHAT AN ODD STRUCTURE. I WONDER WHAT IT'S USED FOR.
LOOK! THE WALLS HAVE A STRANGE GLOW TO THEM.
IT'S BEAUTIFUL!
BE CAREFUL BELLE, WE HAVE NO IDEA WHAT THIS THING DOES.
BE CAREFUL BELLE, WE HAVE NO IDEA WHAT THIS THING DOES.
GUYS! WAKE UP! I THINK I HEAR ACE.
DON'T WORRY, I KNOW WHAT I'M DOING. I'M NOT SOME CHILD YOU HAVE TO...
...WAIT! THAT SOUNDED LIKE CASSIOPEIA.
CASSIE? IS THAT YOU?
YES! MIDNIGHT AND ROCKET ARE HERE TOO, AND WE'VE MADE NEW FRIENDS.

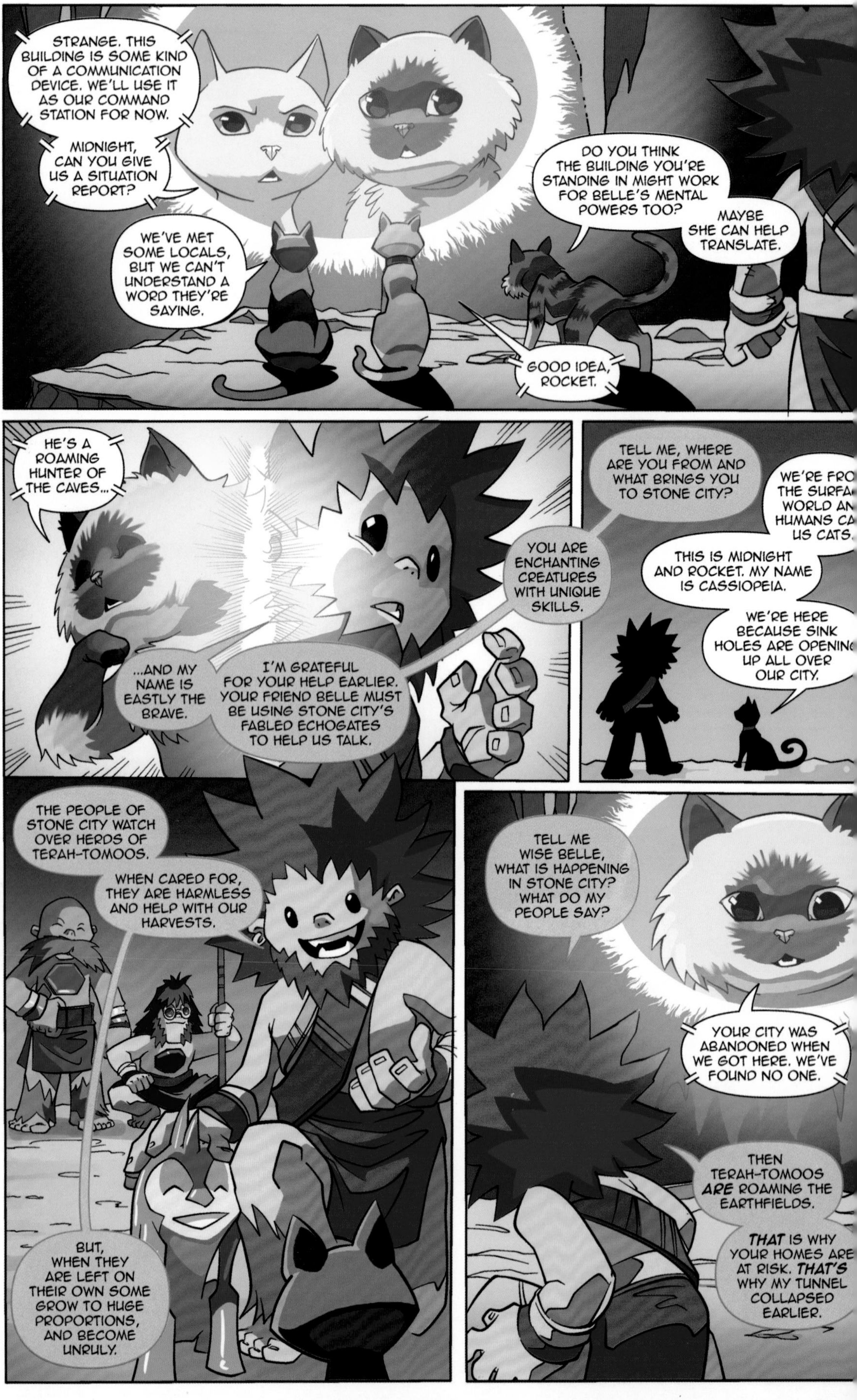

STRANGE. THIS BUILDING IS SOME KIND OF A COMMUNICATION DEVICE. WE'LL USE IT AS OUR COMMAND STATION FOR NOW.
MIDNIGHT, CAN YOU GIVE US A SITUATION REPORT?
WE'VE MET SOME LOCALS, BUT WE CAN'T UNDERSTAND A WORD THEY'RE SAYING.
DO YOU THINK THE BUILDING YOU'RE STANDING IN MIGHT WORK FOR BELLE'S MENTAL POWERS TOO?
MAYBE SHE CAN HELP TRANSLATE.
GOOD IDEA, ROCKET.
HE'S A ROAMING HUNTER OF THE CAVES...
...AND MY NAME IS EASTLY THE BRAVE.
I'M GRATEFUL FOR YOUR HELP EARLIER. YOUR FRIEND BELLE MUST BE USING STONE CITY'S FABLED ECHOGATES TO HELP US TALK.
YOU ARE ENCHANTING CREATURES WITH UNIQUE SKILLS.
TELL ME, WHERE ARE YOU FROM AND WHAT BRINGS YOU TO STONE CITY?
WE'RE FRO THE SURFA WORLD AN HUMANS CA US CATS.
THIS IS MIDNIGHT AND ROCKET. MY NAME IS CASSIOPEIA.
WE'RE HERE BECAUSE SINK HOLES ARE OPENING UP ALL OVER OUR CITY.
THE PEOPLE OF STONE CITY WATCH OVER HERDS OF TERAH-TOMOOS.
WHEN CARED FOR, THEY ARE HARMLESS AND HELP WITH OUR HARVESTS.
BUT, WHEN THEY ARE LEFT ON THEIR OWN SOME GROW TO HUGE PROPORTIONS, AND BECOME UNRULY.
TELL ME WISE BELLE, WHAT IS HAPPENING IN STONE CITY? WHAT DO MY PEOPLE SAY?
YOUR CITY WAS ABANDONED WHEN WE GOT HERE. WE'VE FOUND NO ONE.
THEN TERAH-TOMOOS *ARE* ROAMING THE EARTHFIELDS.
THAT IS WHY YOUR HOMES ARE AT RISK. *THAT'S* WHY MY TUNNEL COLLAPSED EARLIER.

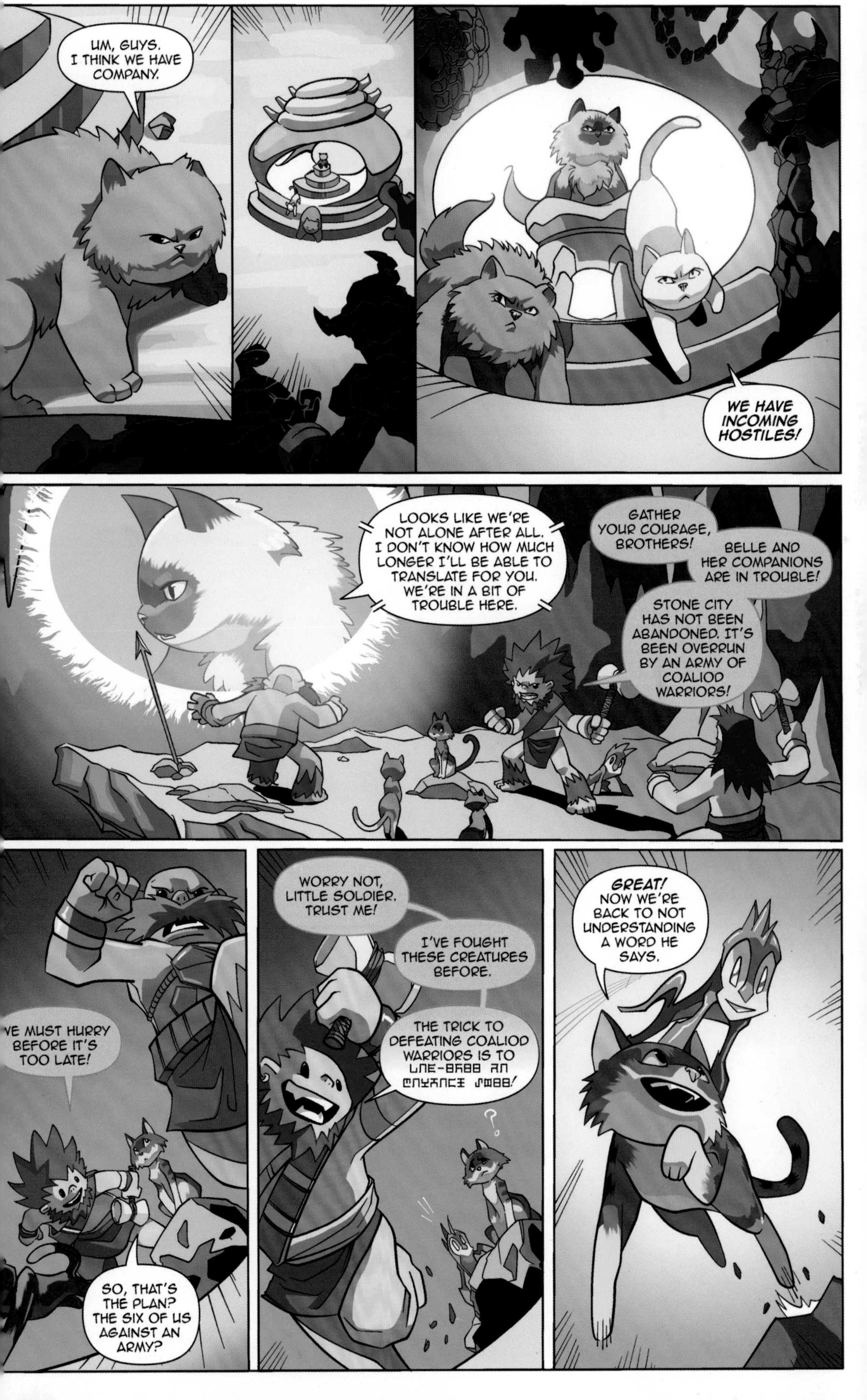
UM, GUYS. I THINK WE HAVE COMPANY.
WE HAVE INCOMING HOSTILES!
LOOKS LIKE WE'RE NOT ALONE AFTER ALL. I DON'T KNOW HOW MUCH LONGER I'LL BE ABLE TO TRANSLATE FOR YOU. WE'RE IN A BIT OF TROUBLE HERE.
GATHER YOUR COURAGE, BROTHERS!
BELLE AND HER COMPANIONS ARE IN TROUBLE!
STONE CITY HAS NOT BEEN ABANDONED. IT'S BEEN OVERRUN BY AN ARMY OF COALIOD WARRIORS!
WE MUST HURRY BEFORE IT'S TOO LATE!
SO, THAT'S THE PLAN? THE SIX OF US AGAINST AN ARMY?
WORRY NOT, LITTLE SOLDIER. TRUST ME!
I'VE FOUGHT THESE CREATURES BEFORE.
THE TRICK TO DEFEATING COALIOD WARRIORS IS TO
?
!!
GREAT! NOW WE'RE BACK TO NOT UNDERSTANDING A WORD HE SAYS.

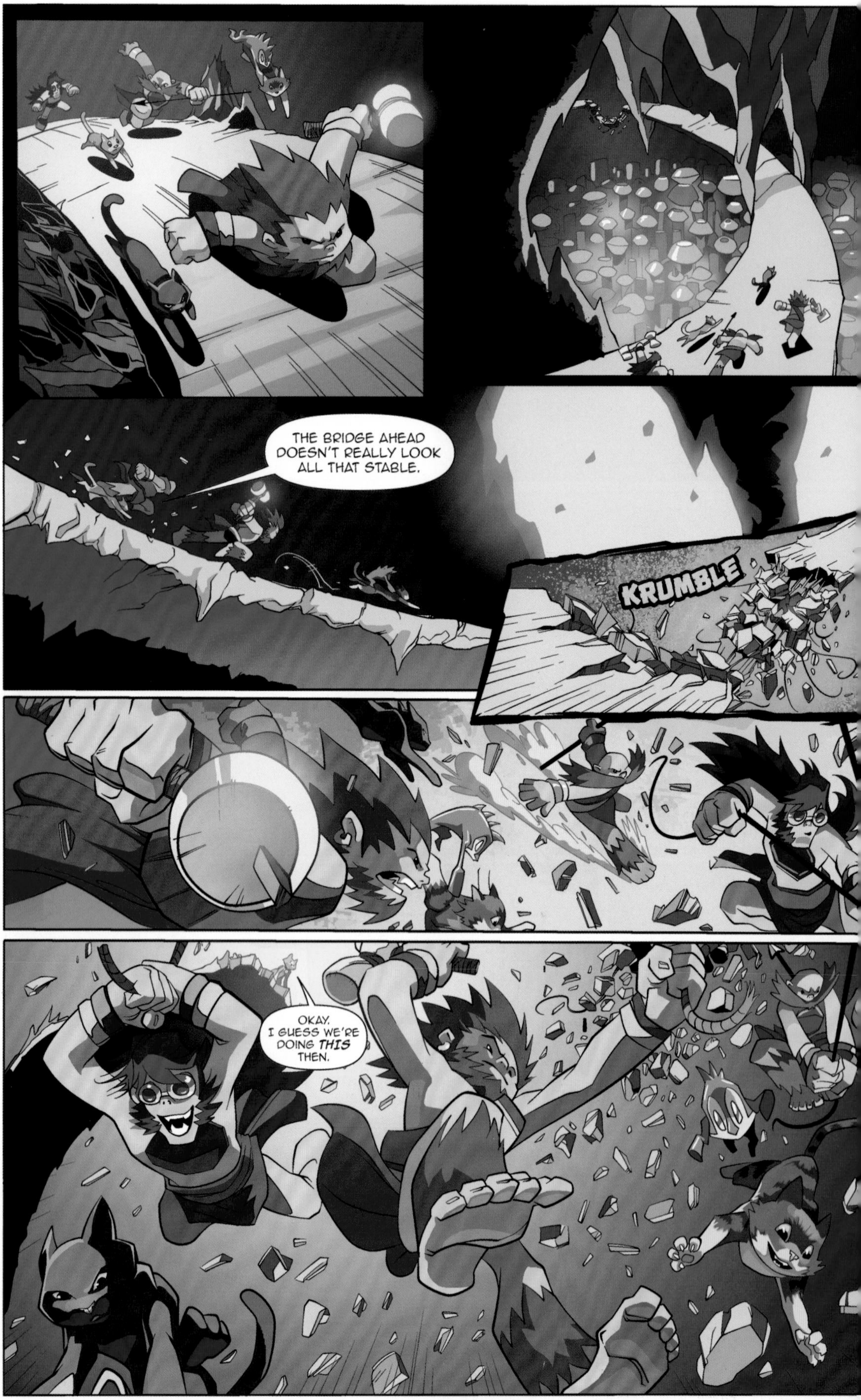
THE BRIDGE AHEAD DOESN'T REALLY LOOK ALL THAT STABLE.
KRUMBLE
OKAY. I GUESS WE'RE DOING *THIS* THEN.

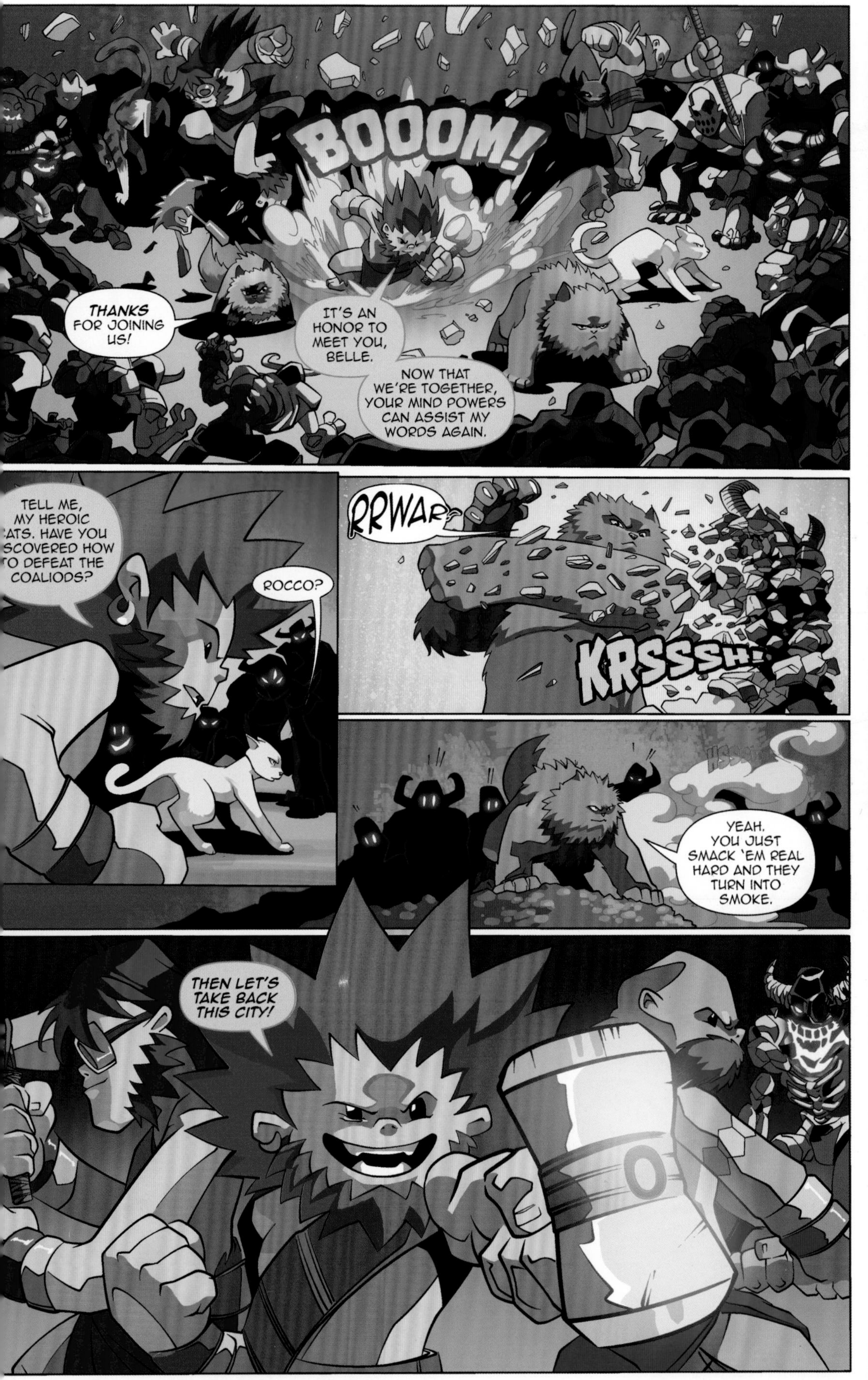
BOOOM!
THANKS FOR JOINING US!
IT'S AN HONOR TO MEET YOU, BELLE.
NOW THAT WE'RE TOGETHER, YOUR MIND POWERS CAN ASSIST MY WORDS AGAIN.
TELL ME, MY HEROIC CATS. HAVE YOU SCOVERED HOW TO DEFEAT THE COALIODS?
ROCCO?
RRWAR
KRSSSH!
YEAH. YOU JUST SMACK 'EM REAL HARD AND THEY TURN INTO SMOKE.
THEN LET'S TAKE BACK THIS CITY!

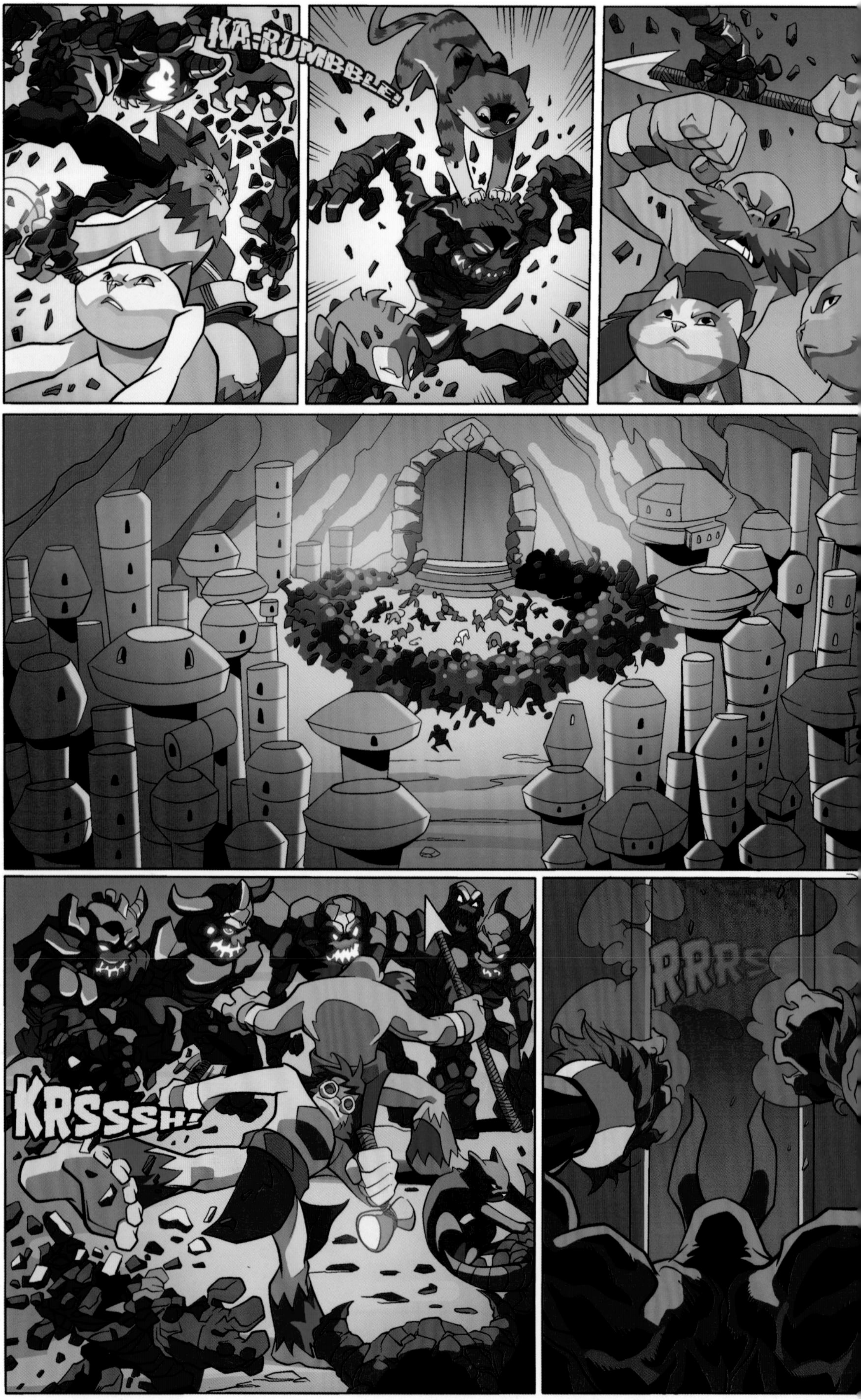

KA-RUMBBLE!
KRSSSH!
RRRS

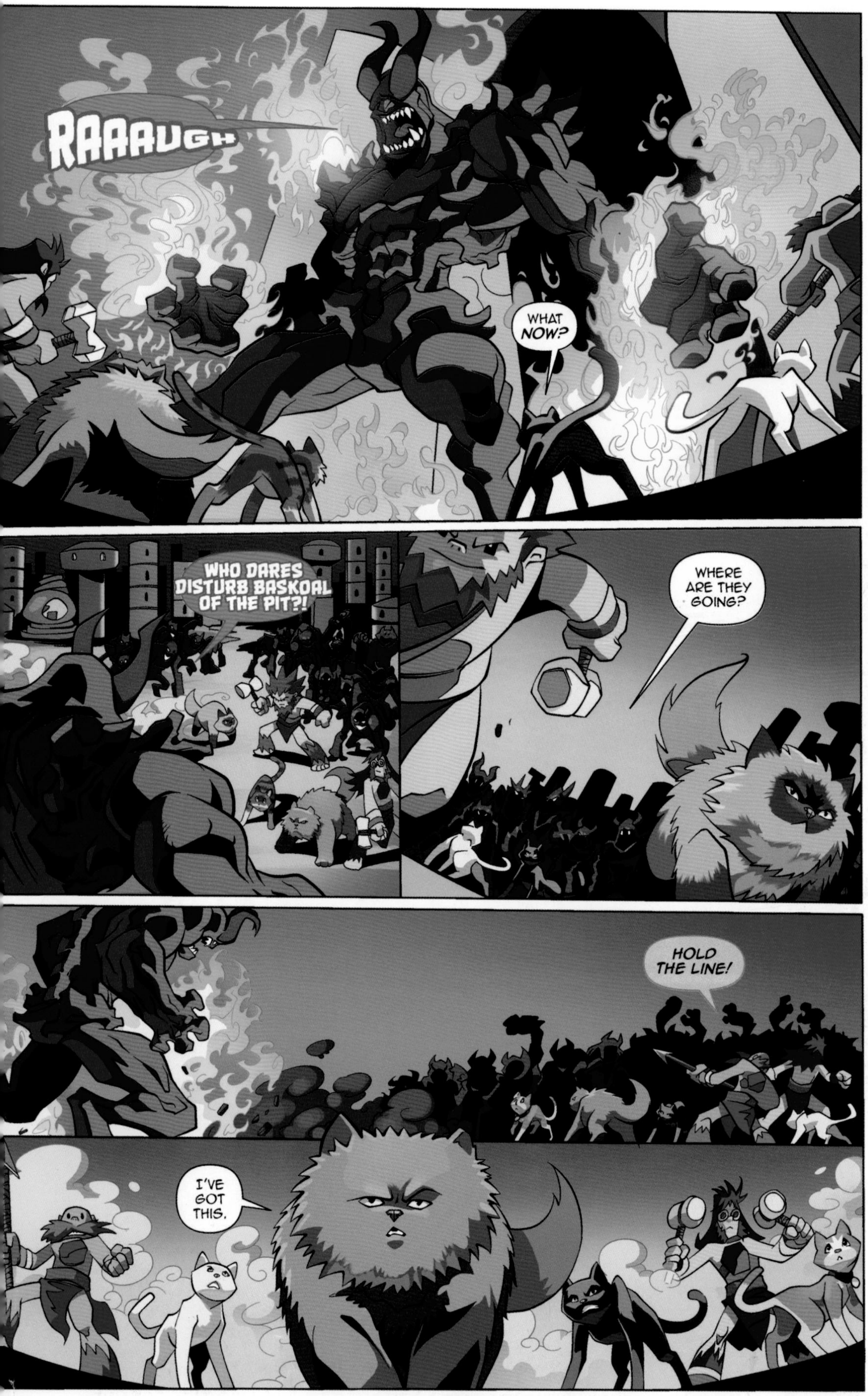
RAAAUGH
WHAT NOW?
WHO DARES DISTURB BASKOAL OF THE PIT?!
WHERE ARE THEY GOING?
HOLD THE LINE!
I'VE GOT THIS.

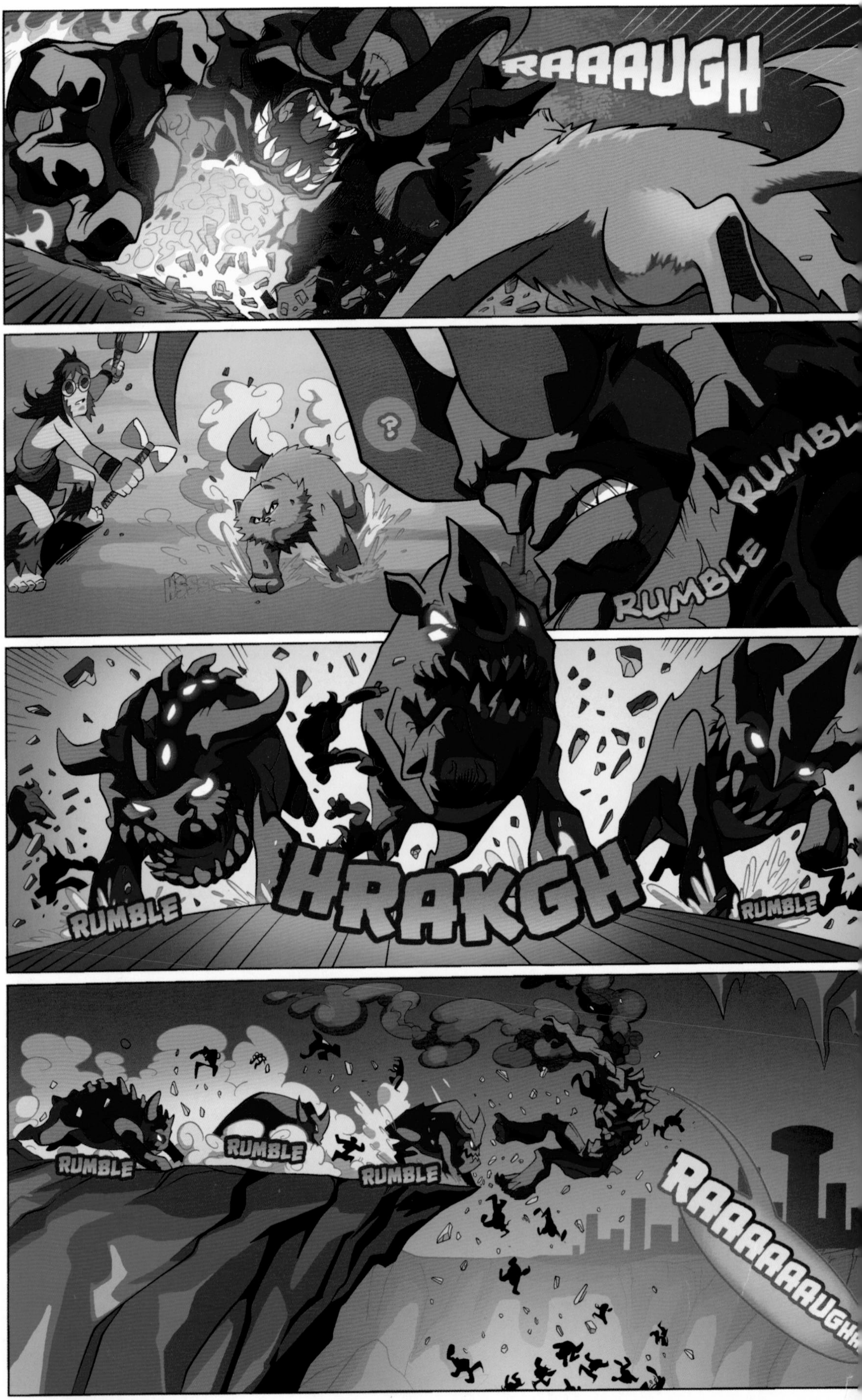

RAAAUGH
?
RUMBLE
RUMBLE
RUMBLE
RUMBLE
HRAKGH
RUMBLE
RUMBLE
RUMBLE
RUMBLE
RAAAAAAAUGH

WELL, WHAT DO YOU KNOW. WE ALL SURVIVED.

WHERE DID BELLE AND EASTLY GO?

LET'S FIND OUT.

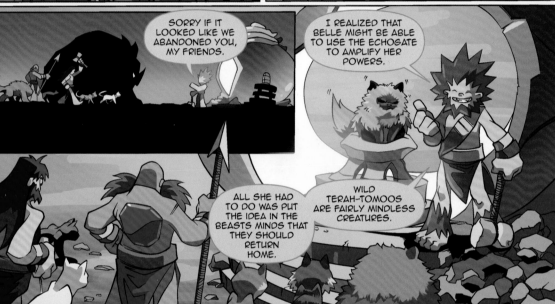

SORRY IF IT LOOKED LIKE WE ABANDONED YOU, MY FRIENDS.

I REALIZED THAT BELLE MIGHT BE ABLE TO USE THE ECHOGATE TO AMPLIFY HER POWERS.

ALL SHE HAD TO DO WAS PUT THE IDEA IN THE BEASTS MINDS THAT THEY SHOULD RETURN HOME.

WILD TERAH-TOMOOS ARE FAIRLY MINDLESS CREATURES.

COOL!

WELL DONE, SOLDIER.

THANKS FOR SAVING OUR SKINS, BELLE.

COULD YOU GUYS PLEASE BE QUIET?!

I'M TRYING TO KEEP THE TERAH-TOMOOS CALM.

WHILE YOU'RE IN THERE, PLEASE LET MY PEOPLE KNOW THE ENEMY HAS BEEN VANQUISHED.

IT IS SAFE FOR THEM TO RETURN TO STONE CITY. I WANT TO CELEBRATE!

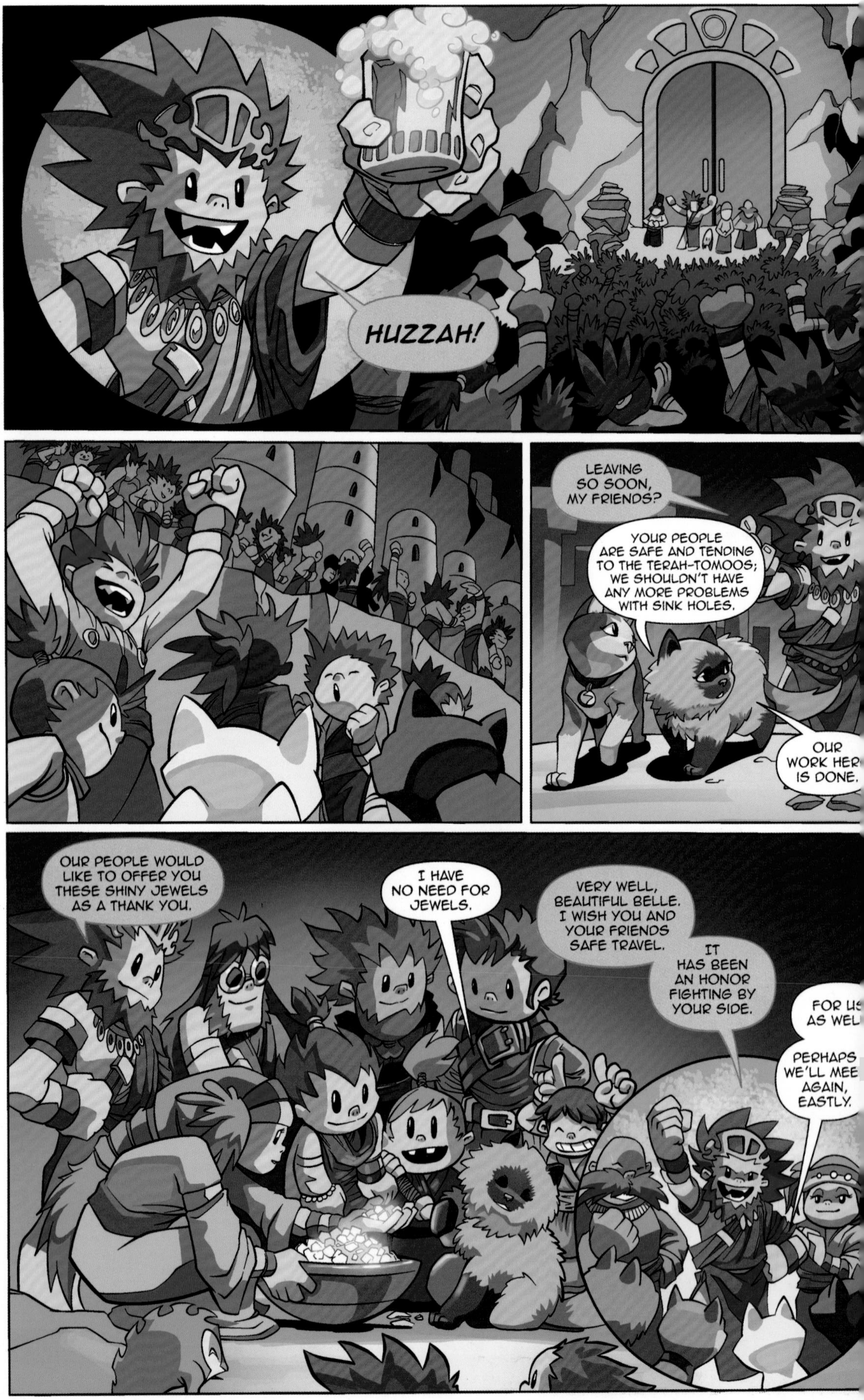
HUZZAH!
LEAVING SO SOON, MY FRIENDS?
YOUR PEOPLE ARE SAFE AND TENDING TO THE TERAH-TOMOOS; WE SHOULDN'T HAVE ANY MORE PROBLEMS WITH SINK HOLES.
OUR WORK HER IS DONE.
OUR PEOPLE WOULD LIKE TO OFFER YOU THESE SHINY JEWELS AS A THANK YOU.
I HAVE NO NEED FOR JEWELS.
VERY WELL, BEAUTIFUL BELLE. I WISH YOU AND YOUR FRIENDS SAFE TRAVEL.
IT HAS BEEN AN HONOR FIGHTING BY YOUR SIDE.
FOR US AS WEL
PERHAPS WE'LL MEE AGAIN, EASTLY.

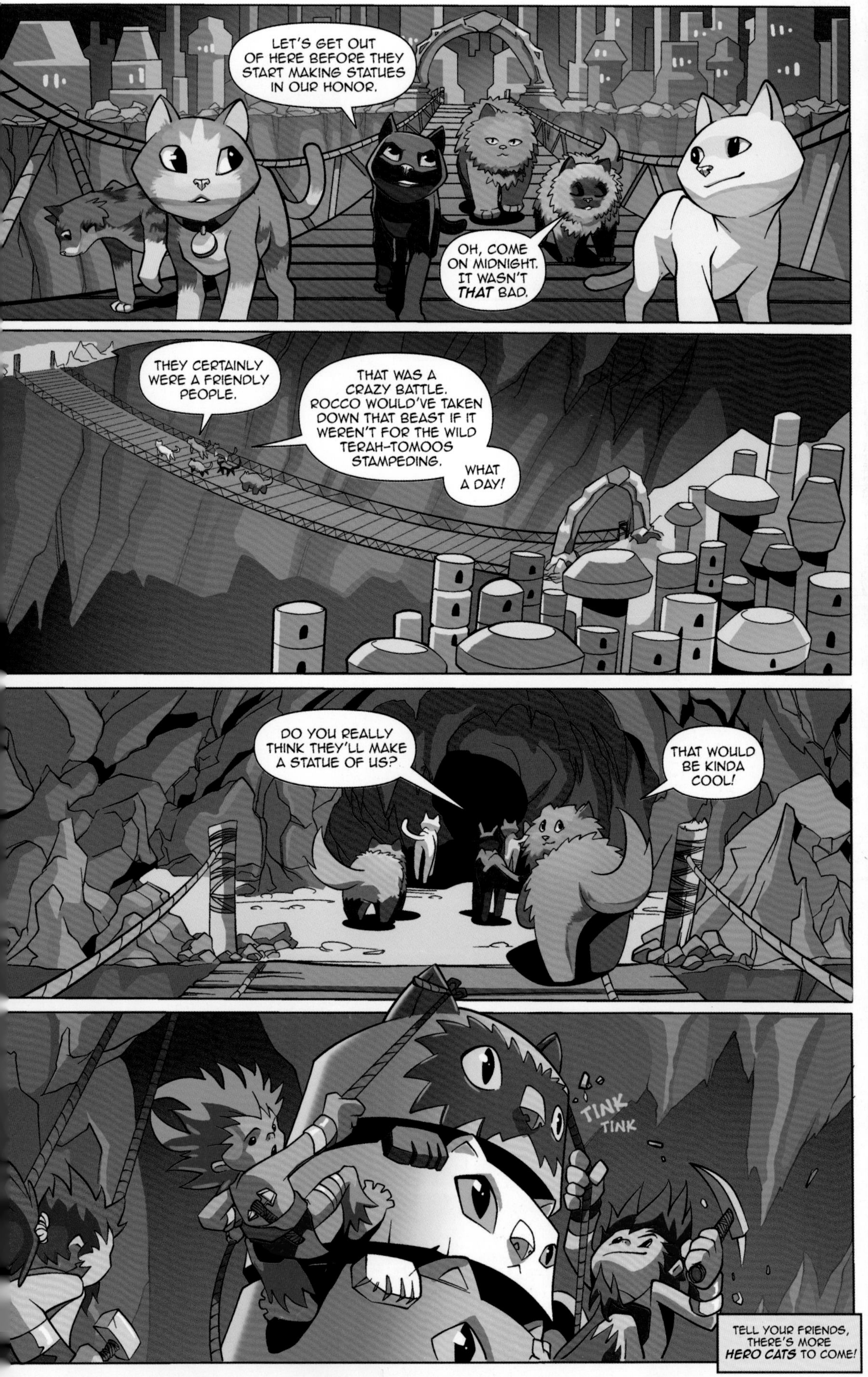
LET'S GET OUT OF HERE BEFORE THEY START MAKING STATUES IN OUR HONOR.
OH, COME ON MIDNIGHT. IT WASN'T *THAT* BAD.
THEY CERTAINLY WERE A FRIENDLY PEOPLE.
THAT WAS A CRAZY BATTLE. ROCCO WOULD'VE TAKEN DOWN THAT BEAST IF IT WEREN'T FOR THE WILD TERAH-TOMOOS STAMPEDING.
WHAT A DAY!
DO YOU REALLY THINK THEY'LL MAKE A STATUE OF US?
THAT WOULD BE KINDA COOL!
TINK
TINK
TELL YOUR FRIENDS, THERE'S MORE *HERO CATS* TO COME!

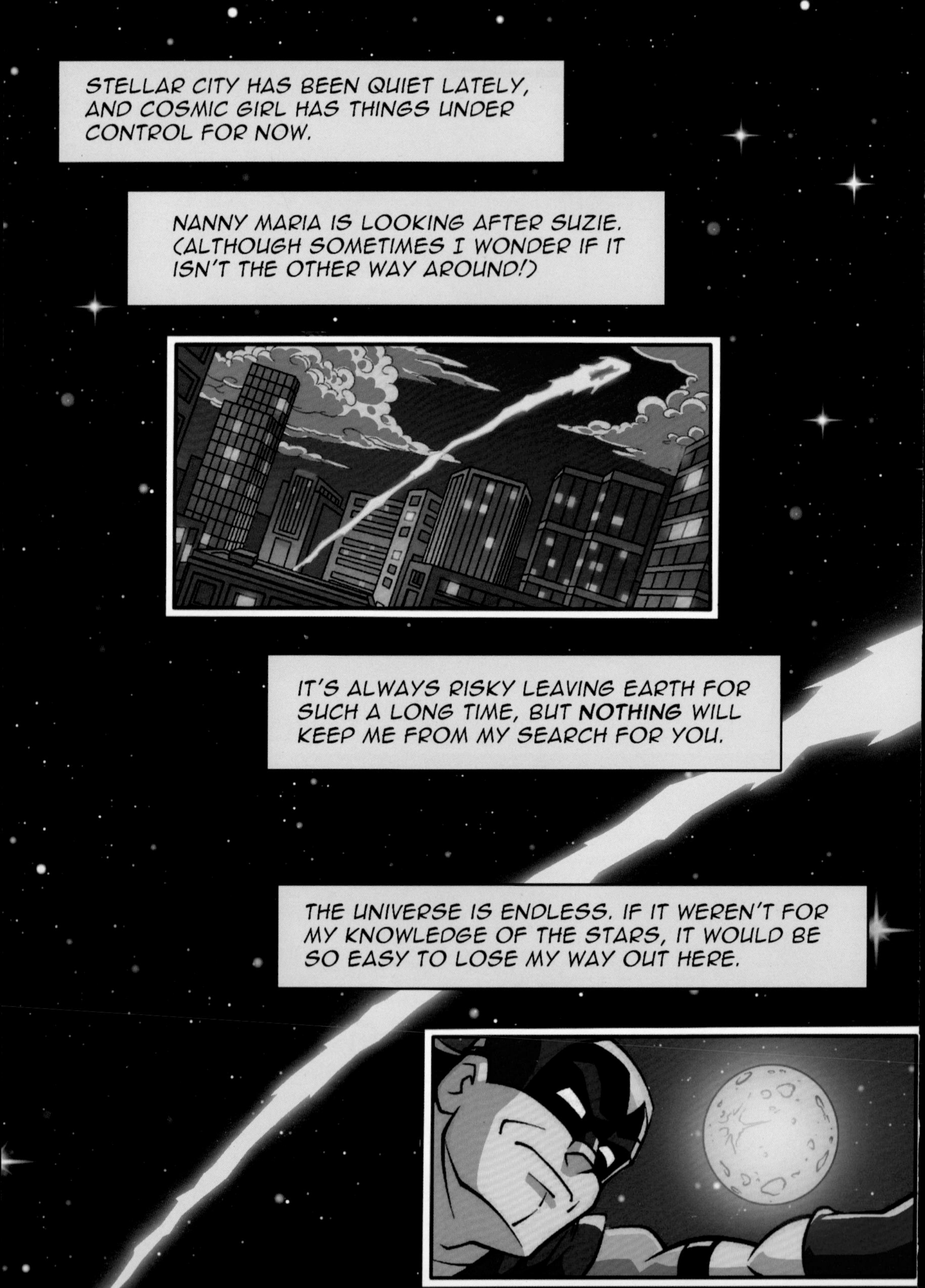
STELLAR CITY HAS BEEN QUIET LATELY, AND COSMIC GIRL HAS THINGS UNDER CONTROL FOR NOW.
NANNY MARIA IS LOOKING AFTER SUZIE. (ALTHOUGH SOMETIMES I WONDER IF IT ISN'T THE OTHER WAY AROUND!)
IT'S ALWAYS RISKY LEAVING EARTH FOR SUCH A LONG TIME, BUT **NOTHING** WILL KEEP ME FROM MY SEARCH FOR YOU.
THE UNIVERSE IS ENDLESS. IF IT WEREN'T FOR MY KNOWLEDGE OF THE STARS, IT WOULD BE SO EASY TO LOSE MY WAY OUT HERE.

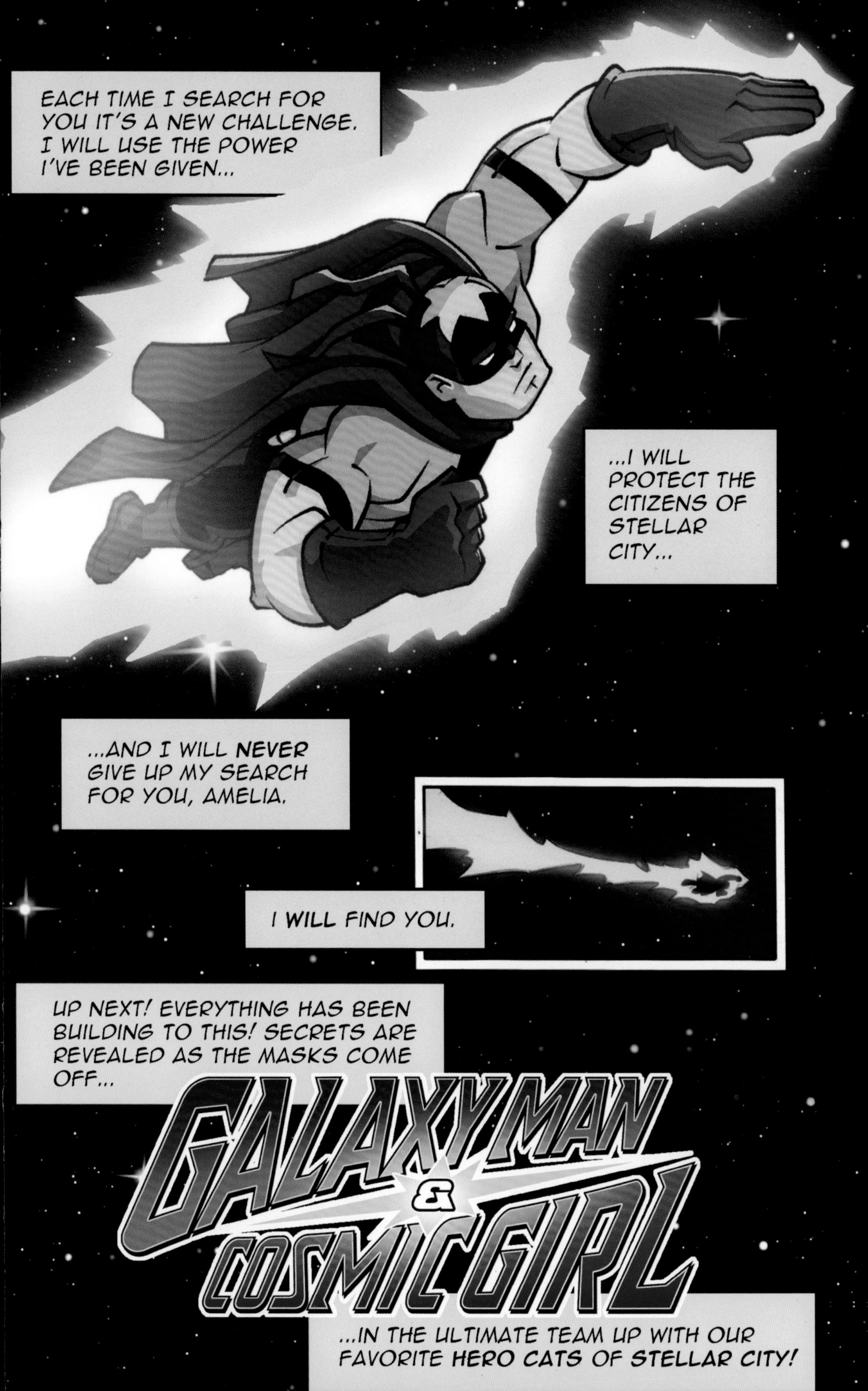
EACH TIME I SEARCH FOR YOU IT'S A NEW CHALLENGE. I WILL USE THE POWER I'VE BEEN GIVEN...
...I WILL PROTECT THE CITIZENS OF STELLAR CITY...
...AND I WILL NEVER GIVE UP MY SEARCH FOR YOU, AMELIA.
I WILL FIND YOU.
UP NEXT! EVERYTHING HAS BEEN BUILDING TO THIS! SECRETS ARE REVEALED AS THE MASKS COME OFF...
GALAXY MAN & COSMIC GIRL
...IN THE ULTIMATE TEAM UP WITH OUR FAVORITE HERO CATS OF STELLAR CITY!

CHAPTER 5:
SPACE BUGS

WRITER: KYLE PUTTKAMMER

PENCILS: MARCUS WILLIAMS

INKS: RYAN SELLERS

COLORS: OMAKA SCHULTZ

LETTERING: BRIANA HIGGINS

SPECIAL THANKS: NATE HILL

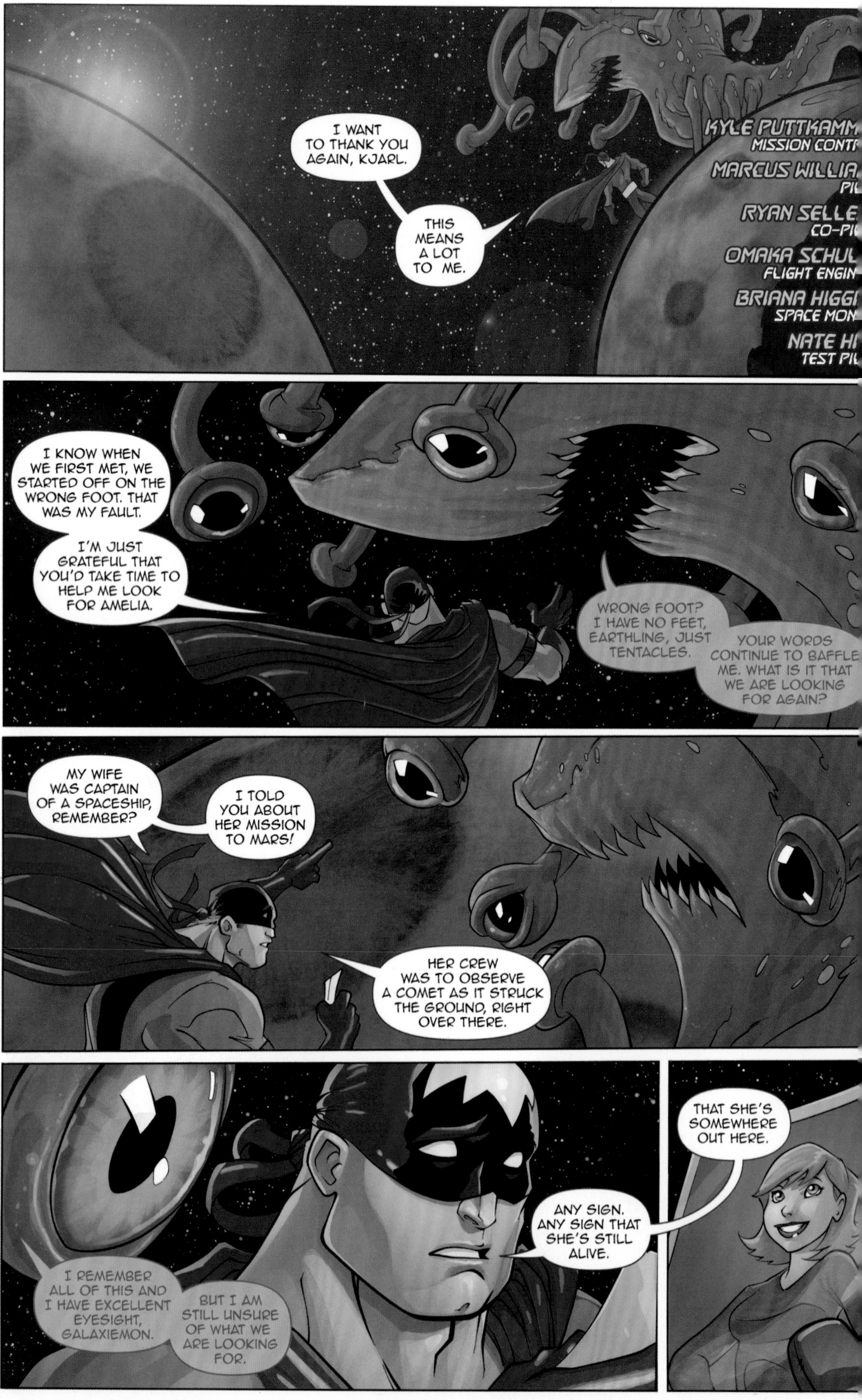
I WANT TO THANK YOU AGAIN, KJARL.
THIS MEANS A LOT TO ME.
KYLE PUTTKAMM
MISSION CONTR
MARCUS WILLIA
PI
RYAN SELLE
CO-PI
OMAKA SCHUL
FLIGHT ENGIN
BRIANA HIGGI
SPACE MON
NATE HI
TEST PI
I KNOW WHEN WE FIRST MET, WE STARTED OFF ON THE WRONG FOOT. THAT WAS MY FAULT.
I'M JUST GRATEFUL THAT YOU'D TAKE TIME TO HELP ME LOOK FOR AMELIA.
WRONG FOOT? I HAVE NO FEET, EARTHLING, JUST TENTACLES.
YOUR WORDS CONTINUE TO BAFFLE ME. WHAT IS IT THAT WE ARE LOOKING FOR AGAIN?
MY WIFE WAS CAPTAIN OF A SPACESHIP, REMEMBER?
I TOLD YOU ABOUT HER MISSION TO MARS!
HER CREW WAS TO OBSERVE A COMET AS IT STRUCK THE GROUND, RIGHT OVER THERE.
I REMEMBER ALL OF THIS AND I HAVE EXCELLENT EYESIGHT, GALAXIEMON.
BUT I AM STILL UNSURE OF WHAT WE ARE LOOKING FOR.
ANY SIGN. ANY SIGN THAT SHE'S STILL ALIVE.
THAT SHE'S SOMEWHERE OUT HERE.

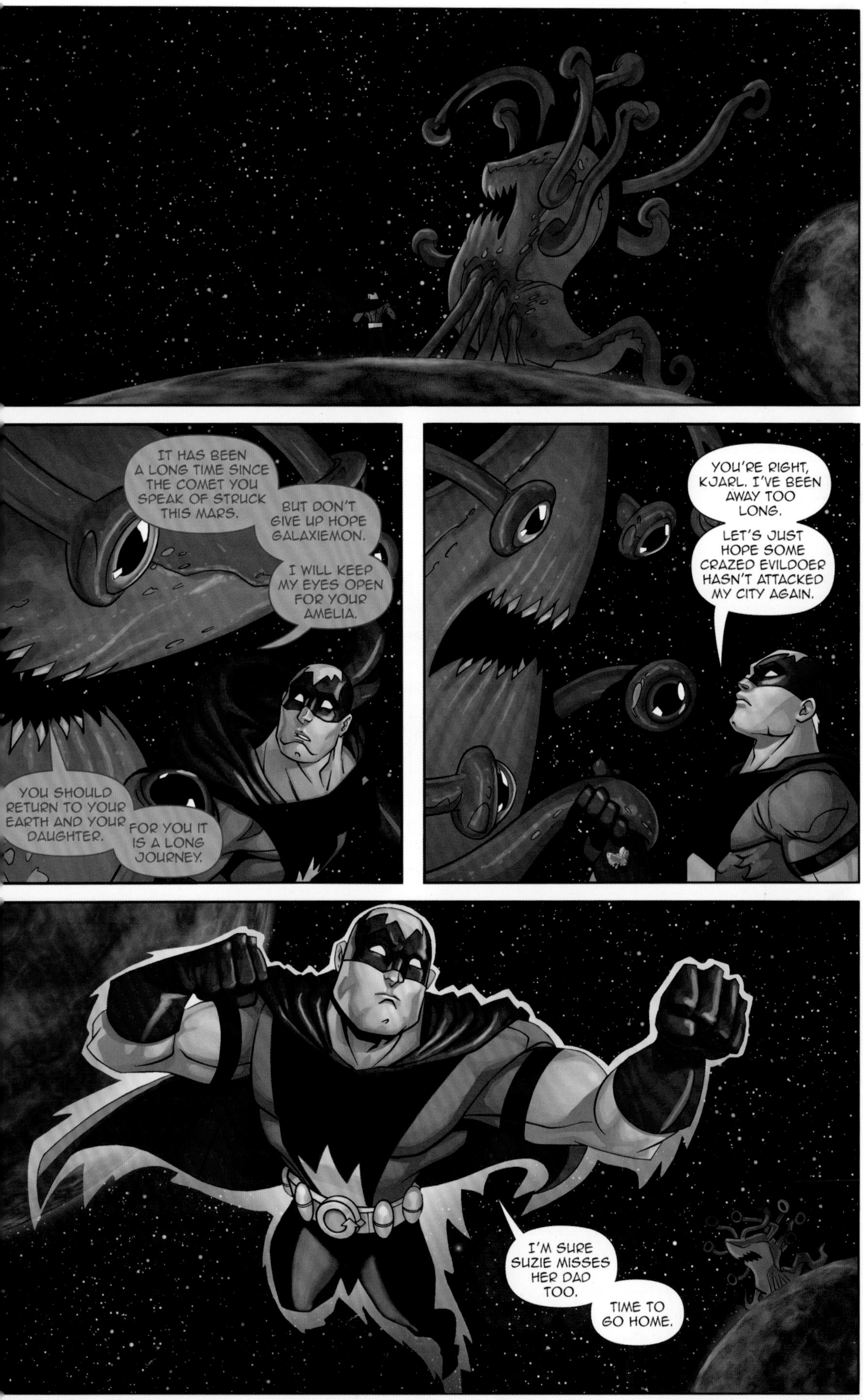
IT HAS BEEN A LONG TIME SINCE THE COMET YOU SPEAK OF STRUCK THIS MARS.
BUT DON'T GIVE UP HOPE GALAXIEMON.
I WILL KEEP MY EYES OPEN FOR YOUR AMELIA.
YOU SHOULD RETURN TO YOUR EARTH AND YOUR DAUGHTER.
FOR YOU IT IS A LONG JOURNEY.
YOU'RE RIGHT, KJARL. I'VE BEEN AWAY TOO LONG.
LET'S JUST HOPE SOME CRAZED EVILDOER HASN'T ATTACKED MY CITY AGAIN.
I'M SURE SUZIE MISSES HER DAD TOO.
TIME TO GO HOME.

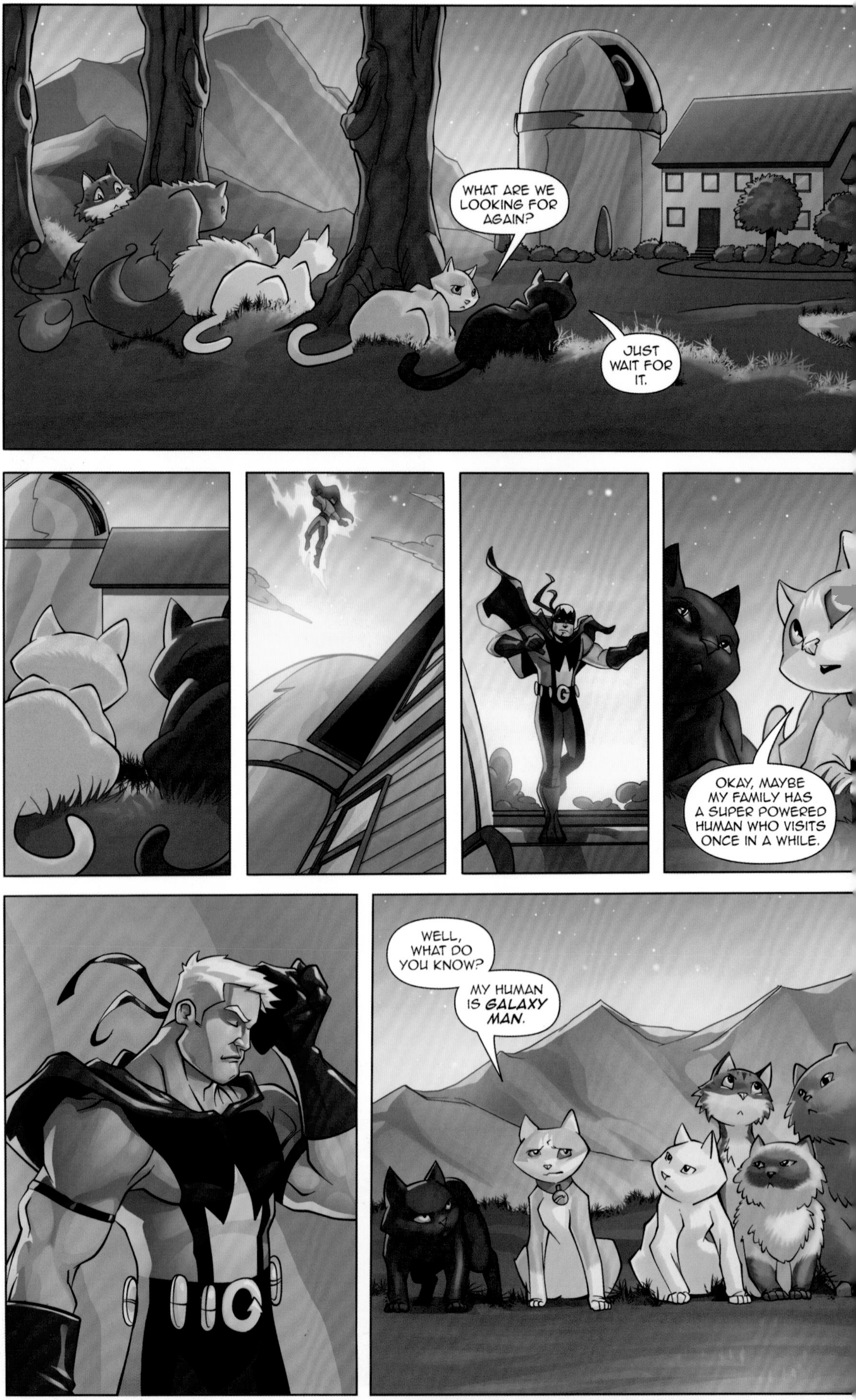
WHAT ARE WE LOOKING FOR AGAIN?
JUST WAIT FOR IT.
OKAY, MAYBE MY FAMILY HAS A SUPER POWERED HUMAN WHO VISITS ONCE IN A WHILE.
WELL, WHAT DO YOU KNOW?
MY HUMAN IS *GALAXY MAN*.

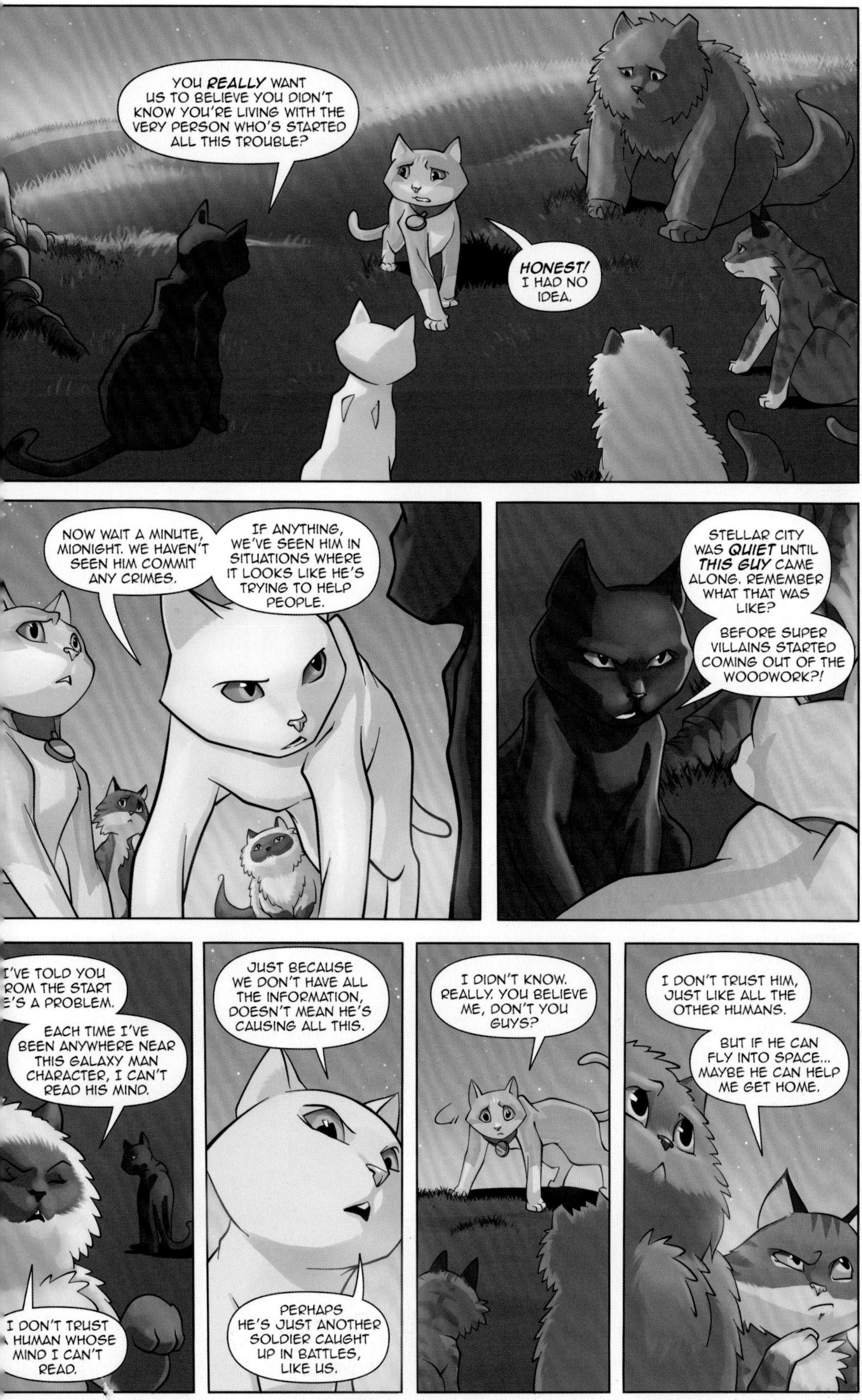
YOU REALLY WANT US TO BELIEVE YOU DIDN'T KNOW YOU'RE LIVING WITH THE VERY PERSON WHO'S STARTED ALL THIS TROUBLE?
HONEST! I HAD NO IDEA.
NOW WAIT A MINUTE, MIDNIGHT. WE HAVEN'T SEEN HIM COMMIT ANY CRIMES.
IF ANYTHING, WE'VE SEEN HIM IN SITUATIONS WHERE IT LOOKS LIKE HE'S TRYING TO HELP PEOPLE.
STELLAR CITY WAS QUIET UNTIL THIS GUY CAME ALONG. REMEMBER WHAT THAT WAS LIKE?
BEFORE SUPER VILLAINS STARTED COMING OUT OF THE WOODWORK?!
I'VE TOLD YOU ROM THE START E'S A PROBLEM.
EACH TIME I'VE BEEN ANYWHERE NEAR THIS GALAXY MAN CHARACTER, I CAN'T READ HIS MIND.
I DON'T TRUST HUMAN WHOSE MIND I CAN'T READ.
JUST BECAUSE WE DON'T HAVE ALL THE INFORMATION, DOESN'T MEAN HE'S CAUSING ALL THIS.
PERHAPS HE'S JUST ANOTHER SOLDIER CAUGHT UP IN BATTLES, LIKE US.
I DIDN'T KNOW. REALLY. YOU BELIEVE ME, DON'T YOU GUYS?
I DON'T TRUST HIM, JUST LIKE ALL THE OTHER HUMANS.
BUT IF HE CAN FLY INTO SPACE... MAYBE HE CAN HELP ME GET HOME.

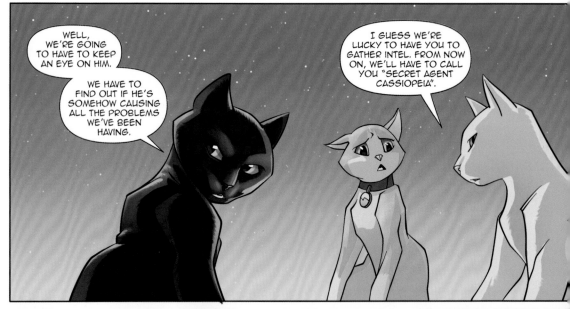

WELL, WE'RE GOING TO HAVE TO KEEP AN EYE ON HIM.

WE HAVE TO FIND OUT IF HE'S SOMEHOW CAUSING ALL THE PROBLEMS WE'VE BEEN HAVING.

I GUESS WE'RE LUCKY TO HAVE YOU TO GATHER INTEL. FROM NOW ON, WE'LL HAVE TO CALL YOU "SECRET AGENT CASSIOPEIA".

BUT... YOU... WHAT... UGH!

FINE. I'LL SEE WHAT I CAN FIND OUT.

THERE YOU ARE, SASSY CASSIE. HOW WAS YOUR DAY? WHAT HAVE YOU BEEN UP TO LATELY?

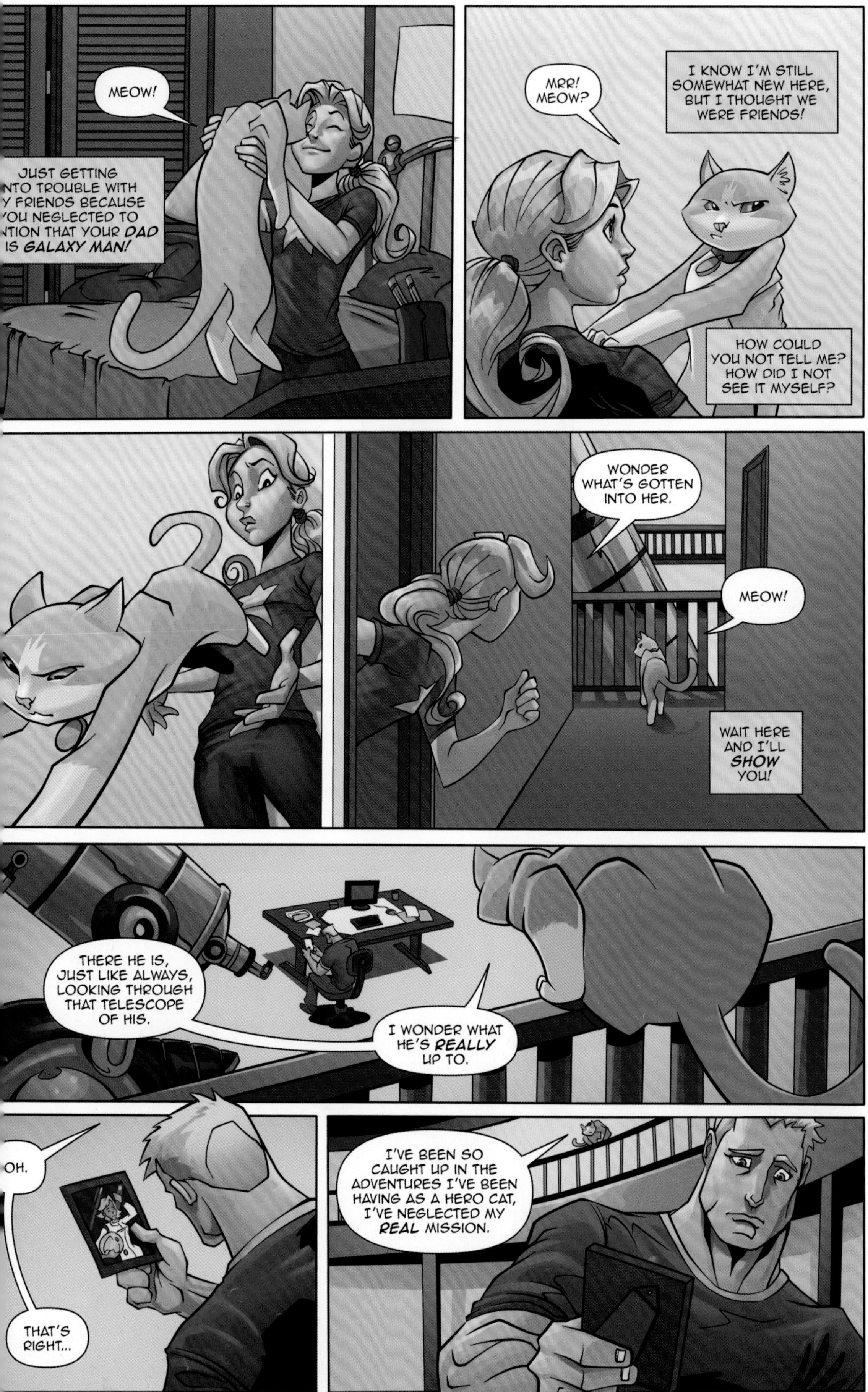

MEOW!
JUST GETTING INTO TROUBLE WITH Y FRIENDS BECAUSE YOU NEGLECTED TO NTION THAT YOUR DAD IS GALAXY MAN!
MRR! MEOW?
I KNOW I'M STILL SOMEWHAT NEW HERE, BUT I THOUGHT WE WERE FRIENDS!
HOW COULD YOU NOT TELL ME? HOW DID I NOT SEE IT MYSELF?
WONDER WHAT'S GOTTEN INTO HER.
MEOW!
WAIT HERE AND I'LL SHOW YOU!
THERE HE IS, JUST LIKE ALWAYS, LOOKING THROUGH THAT TELESCOPE OF HIS.
I WONDER WHAT HE'S REALLY UP TO.
OH.
THAT'S RIGHT...
I'VE BEEN SO CAUGHT UP IN THE ADVENTURES I'VE BEEN HAVING AS A HERO CAT, I'VE NEGLECTED MY REAL MISSION.

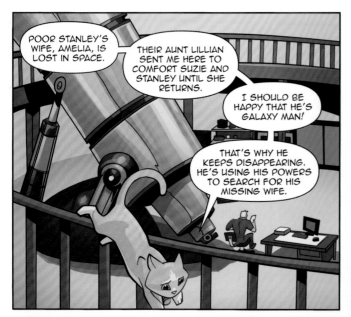

POOR STANLEY'S WIFE, AMELIA, IS LOST IN SPACE.

THEIR AUNT LILLIAN SENT ME HERE TO COMFORT SUZIE AND STANLEY UNTIL SHE RETURNS.

I SHOULD BE HAPPY THAT HE'S GALAXY MAN!

THAT'S WHY HE KEEPS DISAPPEARING. HE'S USING HIS POWERS TO SEARCH FOR HIS MISSING WIFE.

MAYBE I WAS TOO HARSH ON HER. MAYBE SUZIE DOESN'T KNOW THAT HER DAD IS GALAXY MAN.

I'M SO CONFUSED, BUT I SHOULD STILL LET HER KNOW.

I'VE GOT JUST THE WAY TO DO IT.

HE'S GOT TO KEEP IT IN HERE SOMEWHERE.

FUMP!

HERE IT IS! NOW ALL I HAVE TO DO IS BRING THE MASK BACK TO SUZIE AND I CAN GET SOME ANSWERS AS TO –

BZZT!

–OUCH!

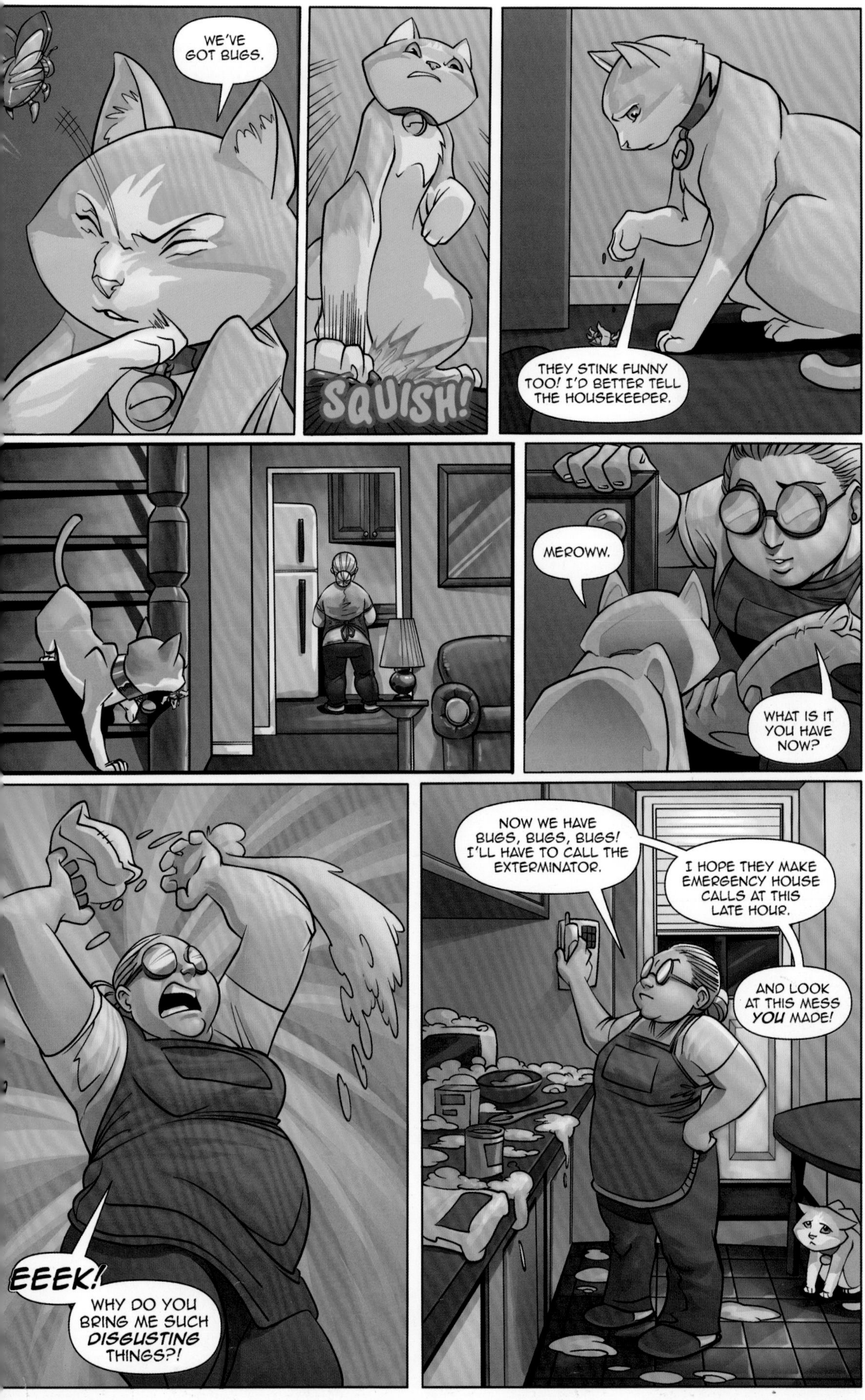

WE'VE GOT BUGS.
SQUISH!
THEY STINK FUNNY TOO! I'D BETTER TELL THE HOUSEKEEPER.
MEROWW.
WHAT IS IT YOU HAVE NOW?
EEEK!
WHY DO YOU BRING ME SUCH DISGUSTING THINGS?!
NOW WE HAVE BUGS, BUGS, BUGS! I'LL HAVE TO CALL THE EXTERMINATOR.
I HOPE THEY MAKE EMERGENCY HOUSE CALLS AT THIS LATE HOUR.
AND LOOK AT THIS MESS YOU MADE!

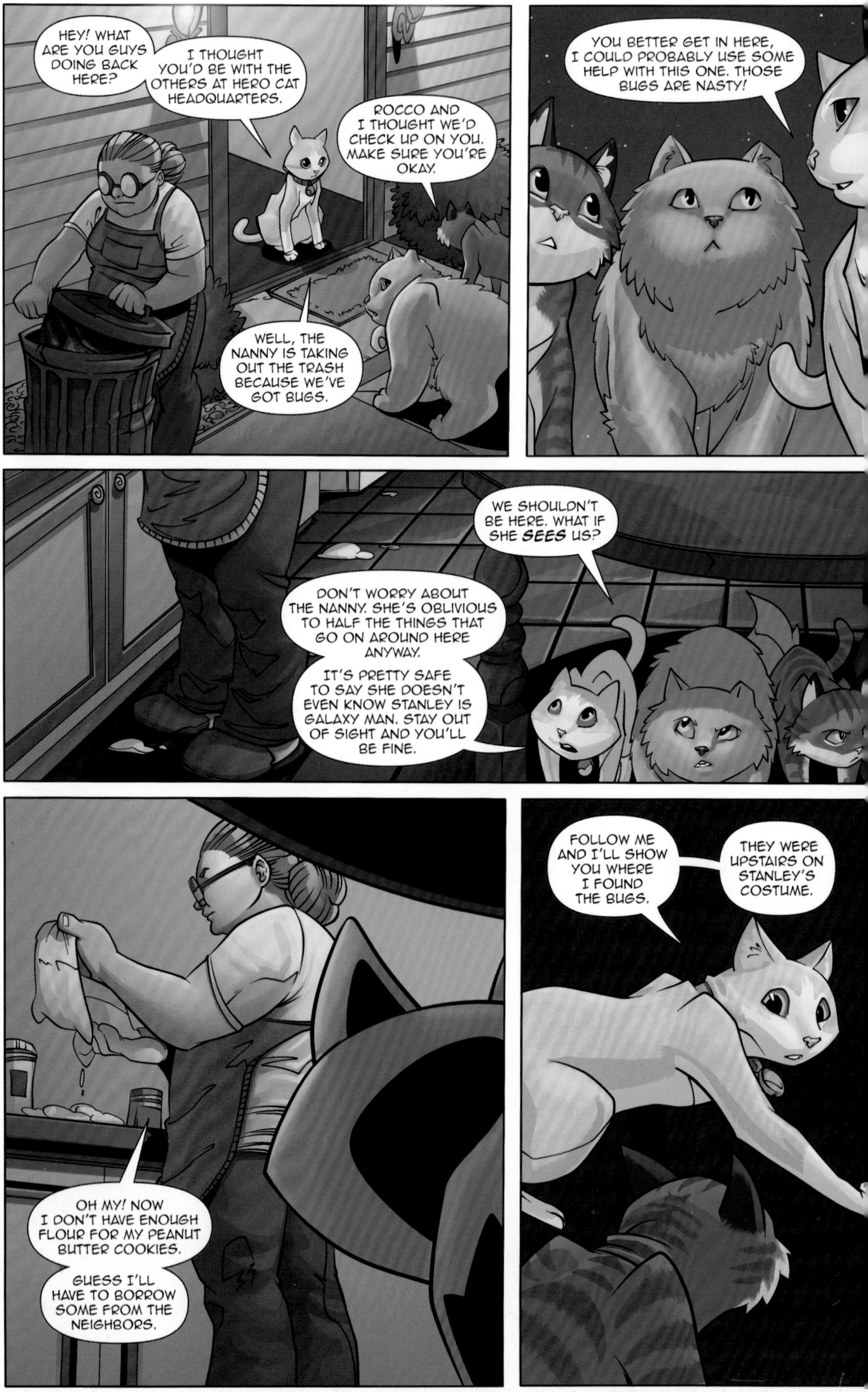
HEY! WHAT ARE YOU GUYS DOING BACK HERE?
I THOUGHT YOU'D BE WITH THE OTHERS AT HERO CAT HEADQUARTERS.
ROCCO AND I THOUGHT WE'D CHECK UP ON YOU. MAKE SURE YOU'RE OKAY.
WELL, THE NANNY IS TAKING OUT THE TRASH BECAUSE WE'VE GOT BUGS.
YOU BETTER GET IN HERE, I COULD PROBABLY USE SOME HELP WITH THIS ONE. THOSE BUGS ARE NASTY!
WE SHOULDN'T BE HERE. WHAT IF SHE *SEES* US?
DON'T WORRY ABOUT THE NANNY. SHE'S OBLIVIOUS TO HALF THE THINGS THAT GO ON AROUND HERE ANYWAY.
IT'S PRETTY SAFE TO SAY SHE DOESN'T EVEN KNOW STANLEY IS GALAXY MAN. STAY OUT OF SIGHT AND YOU'LL BE FINE.
OH MY! NOW I DON'T HAVE ENOUGH FLOUR FOR MY PEANUT BUTTER COOKIES.
GUESS I'LL HAVE TO BORROW SOME FROM THE NEIGHBORS.
FOLLOW ME AND I'LL SHOW YOU WHERE I FOUND THE BUGS.
THEY WERE UPSTAIRS ON STANLEY'S COSTUME.

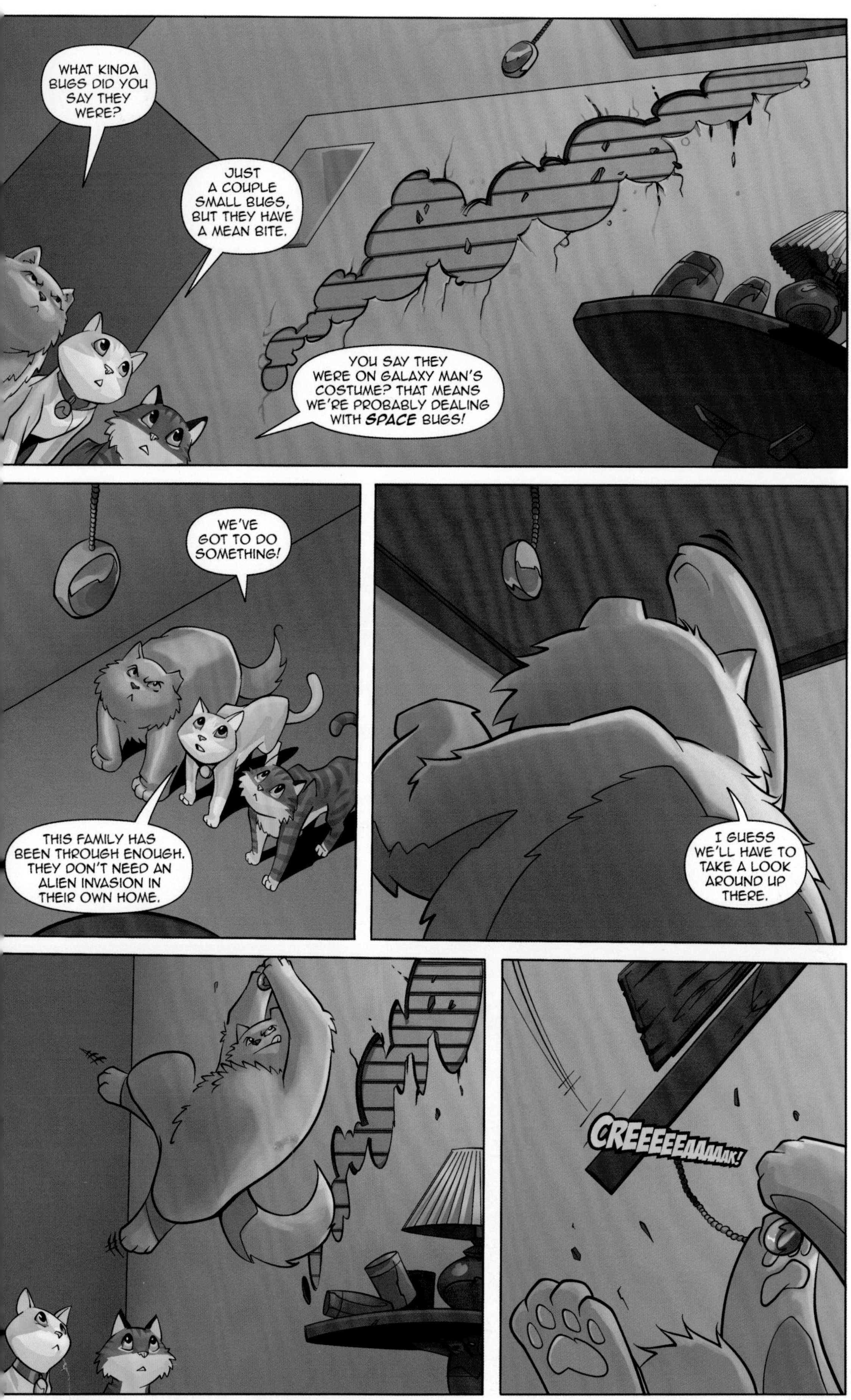
WHAT KINDA BUGS DID YOU SAY THEY WERE?
JUST A COUPLE SMALL BUGS, BUT THEY HAVE A MEAN BITE.
YOU SAY THEY WERE ON GALAXY MAN'S COSTUME? THAT MEANS WE'RE PROBABLY DEALING WITH SPACE BUGS!
WE'VE GOT TO DO SOMETHING!
THIS FAMILY HAS BEEN THROUGH ENOUGH. THEY DON'T NEED AN ALIEN INVASION IN THEIR OWN HOME.
I GUESS WE'LL HAVE TO TAKE A LOOK AROUND UP THERE.
CREEEEEAAAAAK!

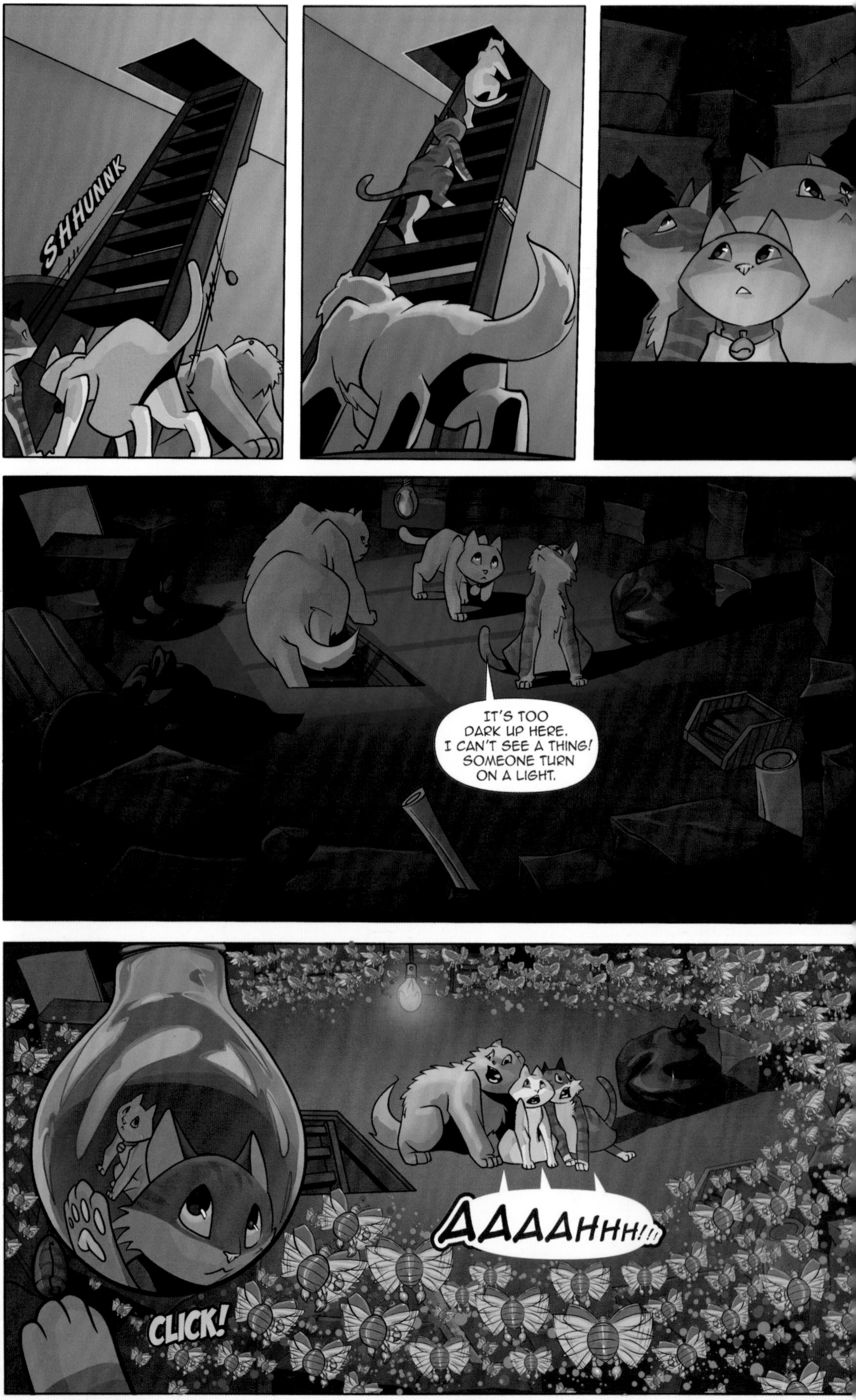
SHHUNNK
IT'S TOO DARK UP HERE. I CAN'T SEE A THING! SOMEONE TURN ON A LIGHT.
CLICK!
AAAAHHH!!!

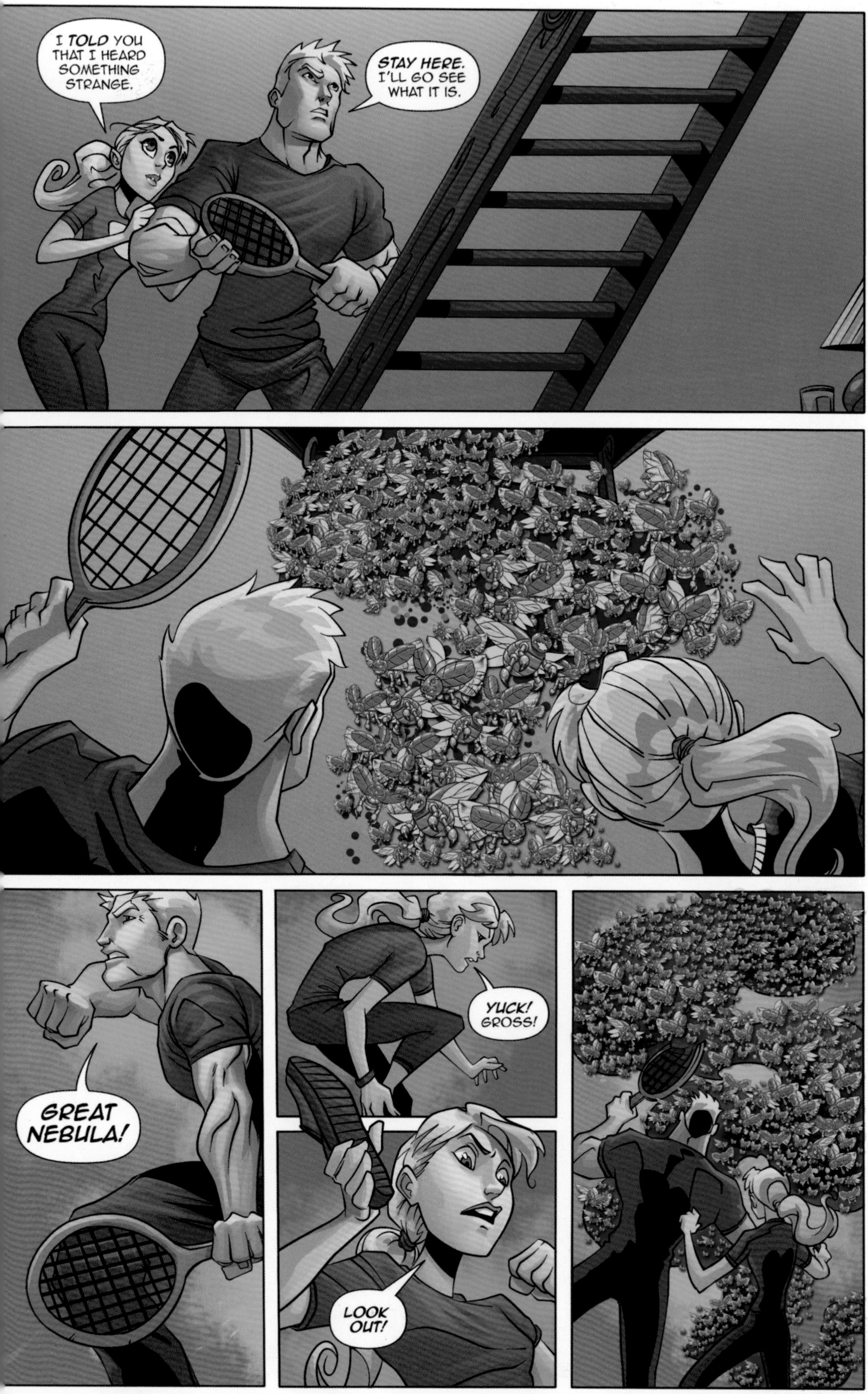

I TOLD YOU THAT I HEARD SOMETHING STRANGE.
STAY HERE. I'LL GO SEE WHAT IT IS.
GREAT NEBULA!
YUCK! GROSS!
LOOK OUT!

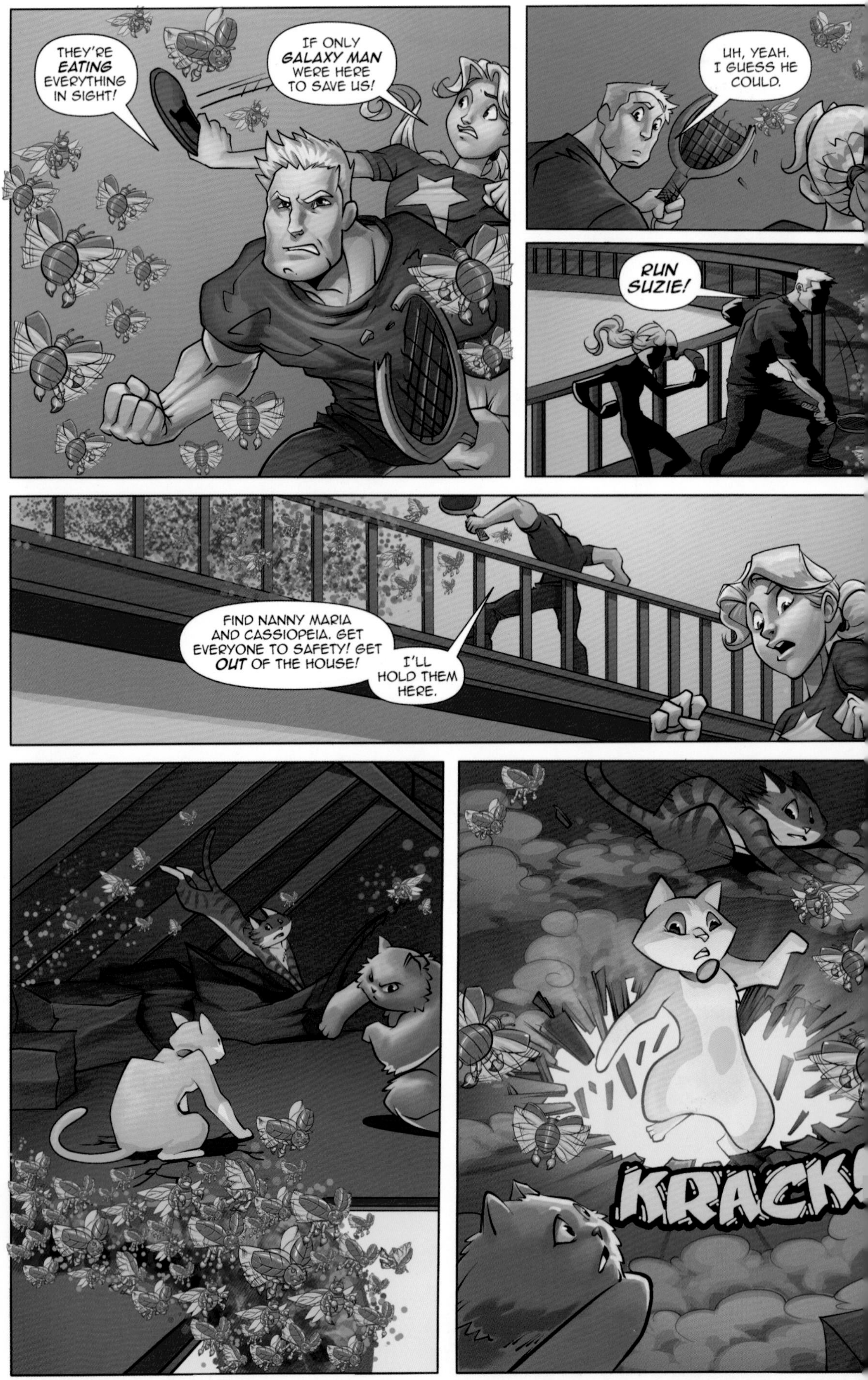

THEY'RE EATING EVERYTHING IN SIGHT!
IF ONLY GALAXY MAN WERE HERE TO SAVE US!
UH, YEAH. I GUESS HE COULD.
RUN SUZIE!
FIND NANNY MARIA AND CASSIOPEIA. GET EVERYONE TO SAFETY! GET OUT OF THE HOUSE!
I'LL HOLD THEM HERE.
KRACK

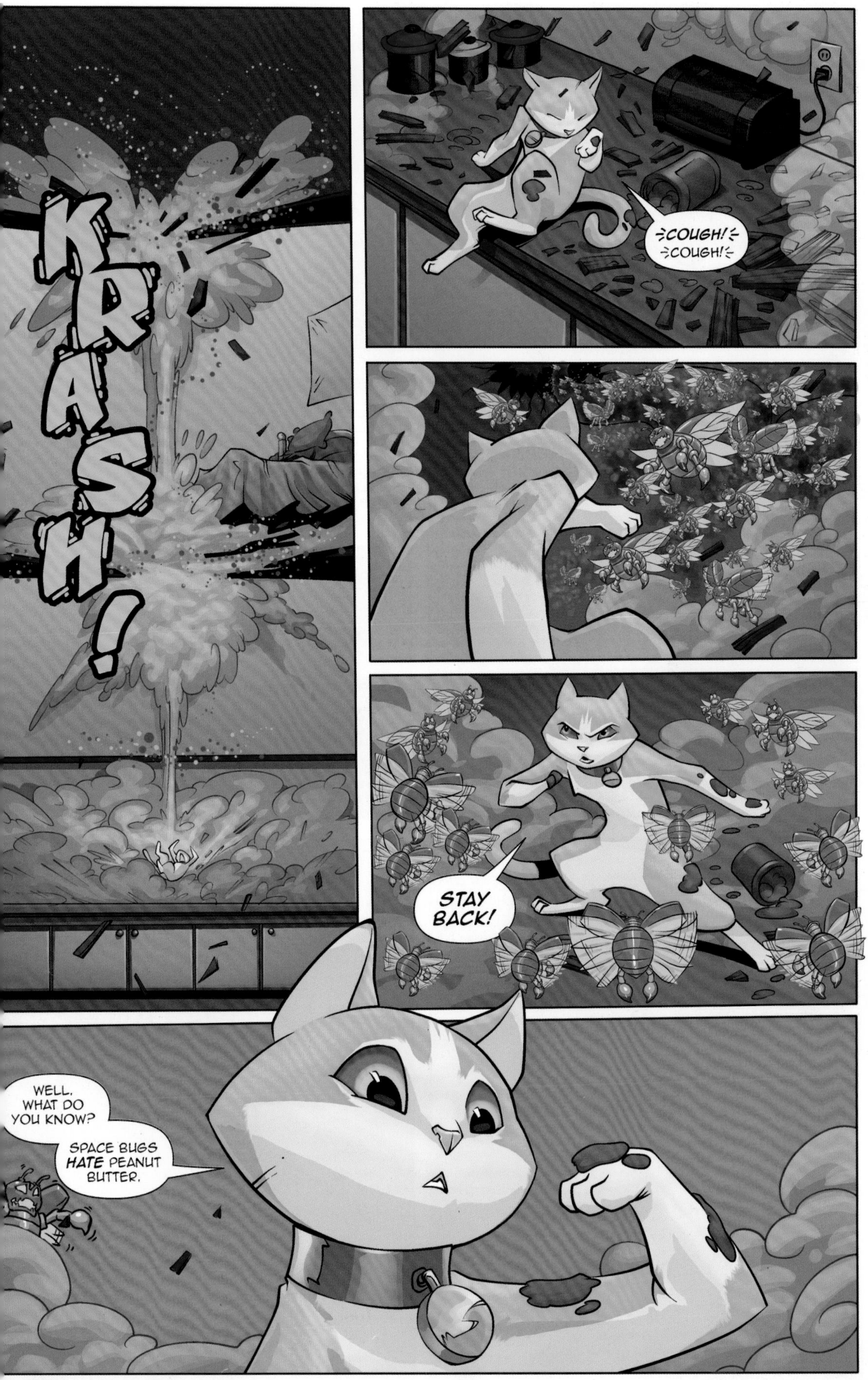
KRASH!
COUGH! COUGH!
STAY BACK!
WELL, WHAT DO YOU KNOW?
SPACE BUGS HATE PEANUT BUTTER.

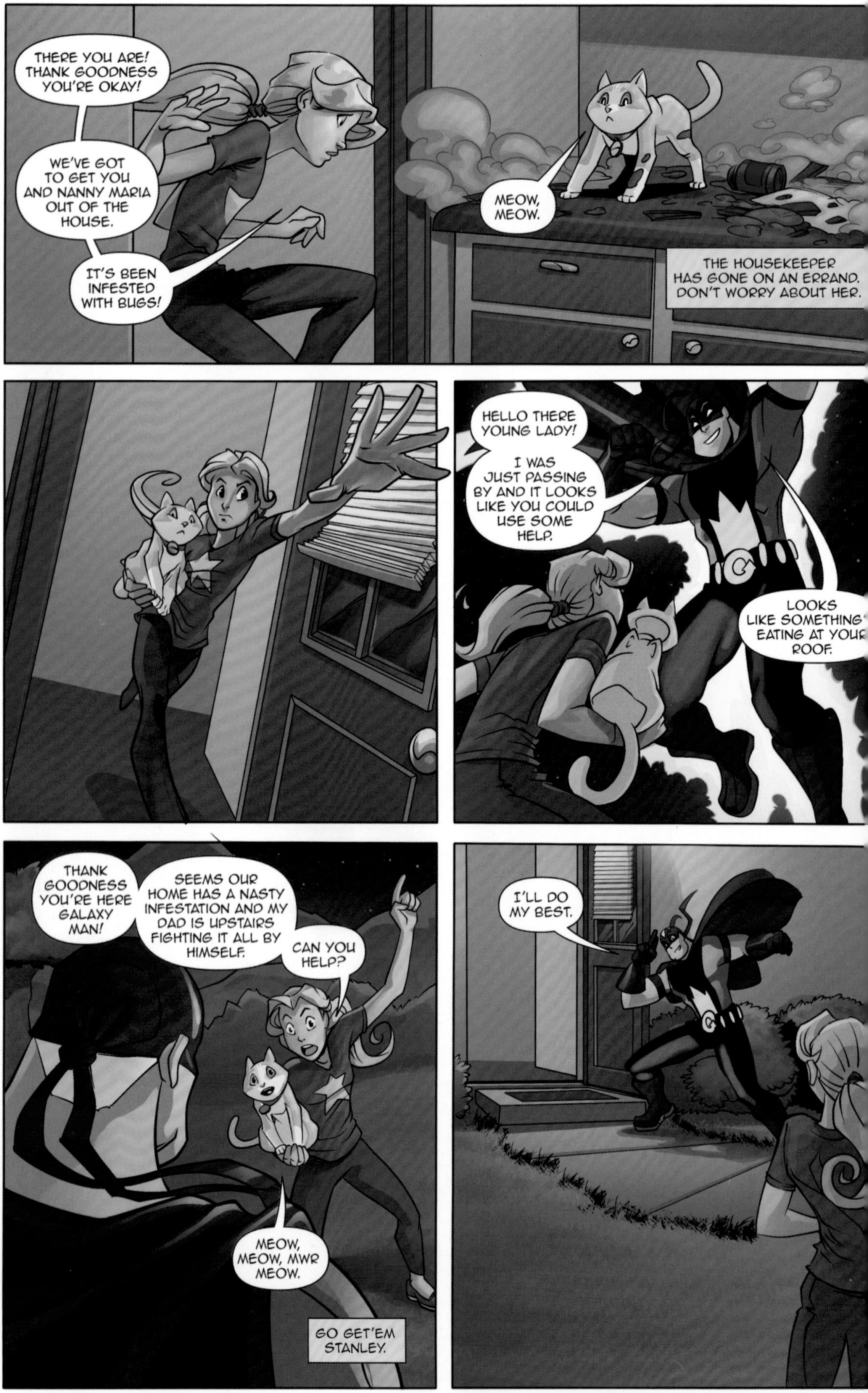
THERE YOU ARE! THANK GOODNESS YOU'RE OKAY!
WE'VE GOT TO GET YOU AND NANNY MARIA OUT OF THE HOUSE.
IT'S BEEN INFESTED WITH BUGS!
MEOW, MEOW.
THE HOUSEKEEPER HAS GONE ON AN ERRAND. DON'T WORRY ABOUT HER.
HELLO THERE YOUNG LADY!
I WAS JUST PASSING BY AND IT LOOKS LIKE YOU COULD USE SOME HELP.
LOOKS LIKE SOMETHING EATING AT YOUR ROOF.
THANK GOODNESS YOU'RE HERE GALAXY MAN!
SEEMS OUR HOME HAS A NASTY INFESTATION AND MY DAD IS UPSTAIRS FIGHTING IT ALL BY HIMSELF.
CAN YOU HELP?
MEOW, MEOW, MWR MEOW.
GO GET'EM STANLEY.
I'LL DO MY BEST.

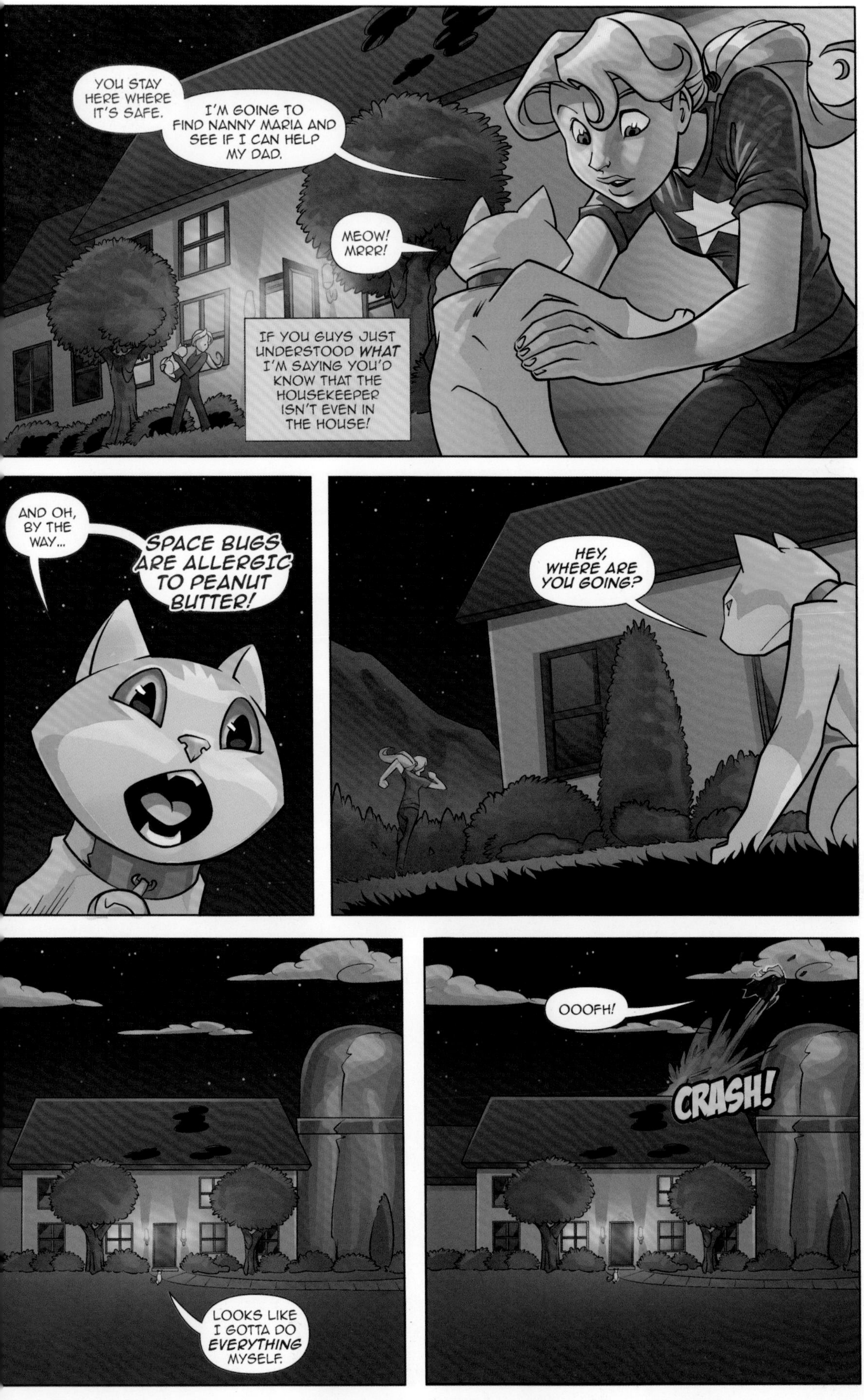
YOU STAY HERE WHERE IT'S SAFE.
I'M GOING TO FIND NANNY MARIA AND SEE IF I CAN HELP MY DAD.
MEOW! MRRR!
IF YOU GUYS JUST UNDERSTOOD WHAT I'M SAYING YOU'D KNOW THAT THE HOUSEKEEPER ISN'T EVEN IN THE HOUSE!
AND OH, BY THE WAY...
SPACE BUGS ARE ALLERGIC TO PEANUT BUTTER!
HEY, WHERE ARE YOU GOING?
LOOKS LIKE I GOTTA DO EVERYTHING MYSELF.
OOOFH!
CRASH!

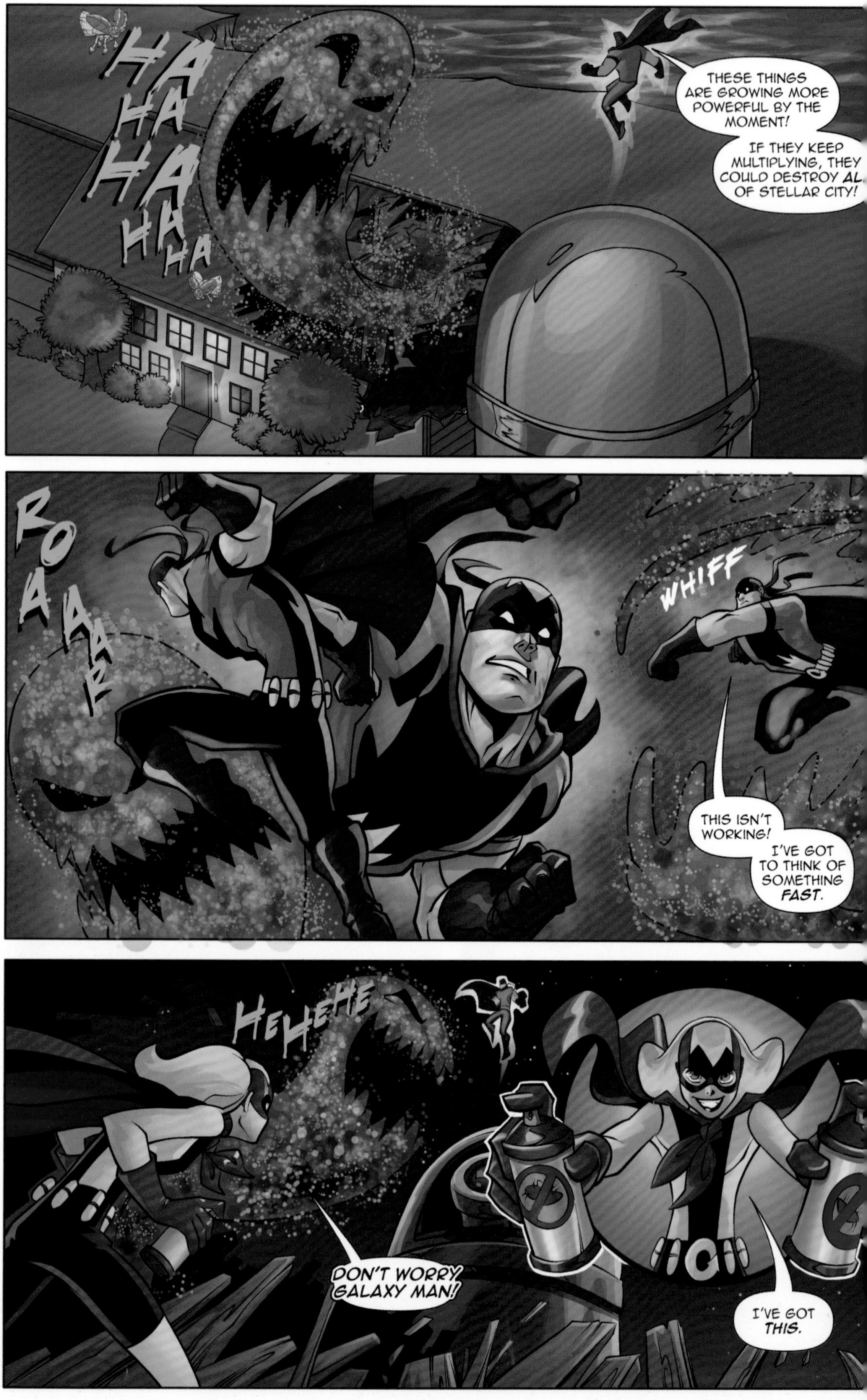
HA HA HA HA HA HA HA HA
THESE THINGS ARE GROWING MORE POWERFUL BY THE MOMENT!
IF THEY KEEP MULTIPLYING, THEY COULD DESTROY AL OF STELLAR CITY!
ROAAAAR
WHIFF
THIS ISN'T WORKING!
I'VE GOT TO THINK OF SOMETHING FAST.
HEHEHE
DON'T WORRY GALAXY MAN!
I'VE GOT THIS.

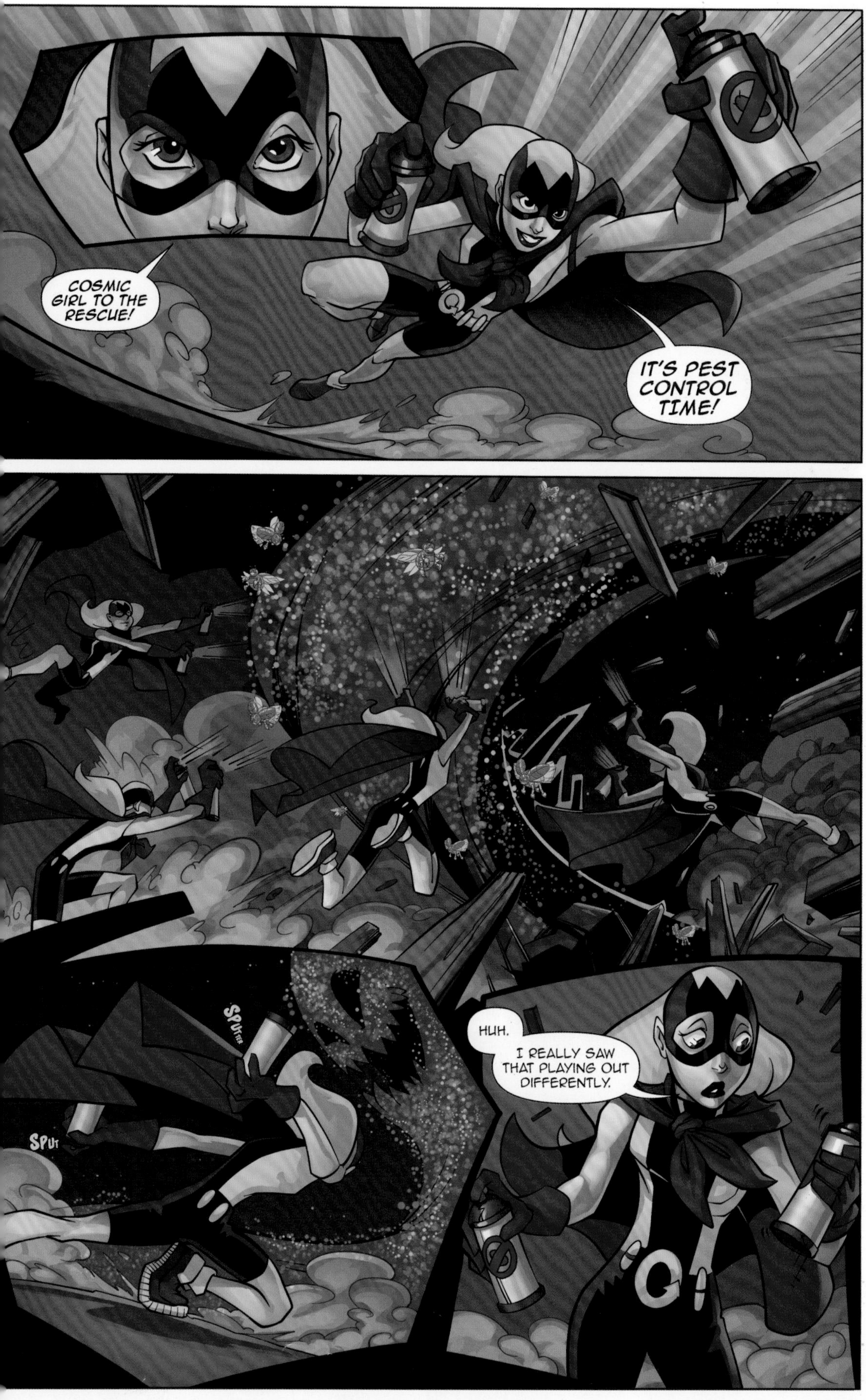
COSMIC GIRL TO THE RESCUE!
IT'S PEST CONTROL TIME!
SPUTTER
SPUT
HUH.
I REALLY SAW THAT PLAYING OUT DIFFERENTLY.

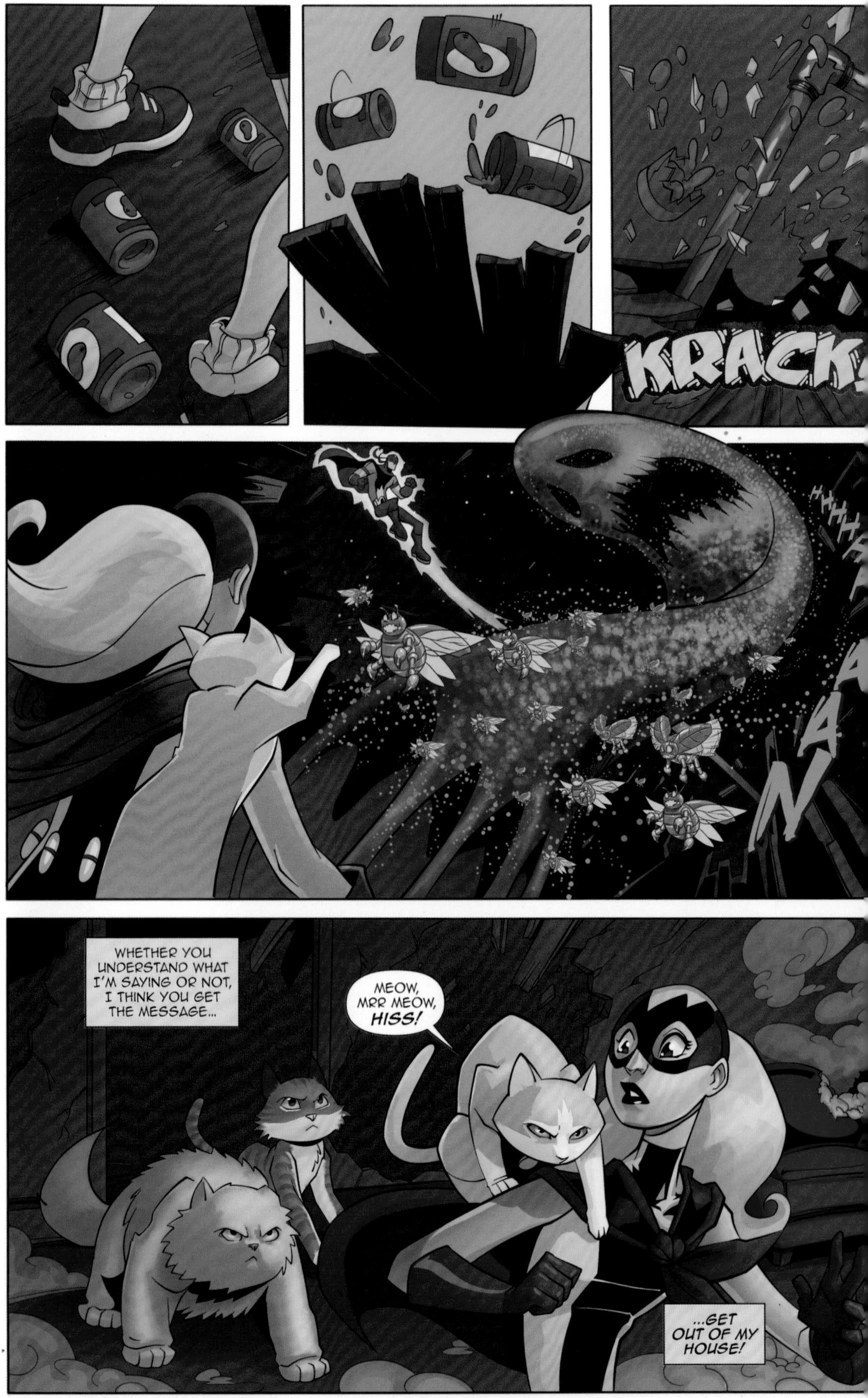
KRACK
WHETHER YOU UNDERSTAND WHAT I'M SAYING OR NOT, I THINK YOU GET THE MESSAGE...
MEOW, MRR MEOW, HISS!
...GET OUT OF MY HOUSE!

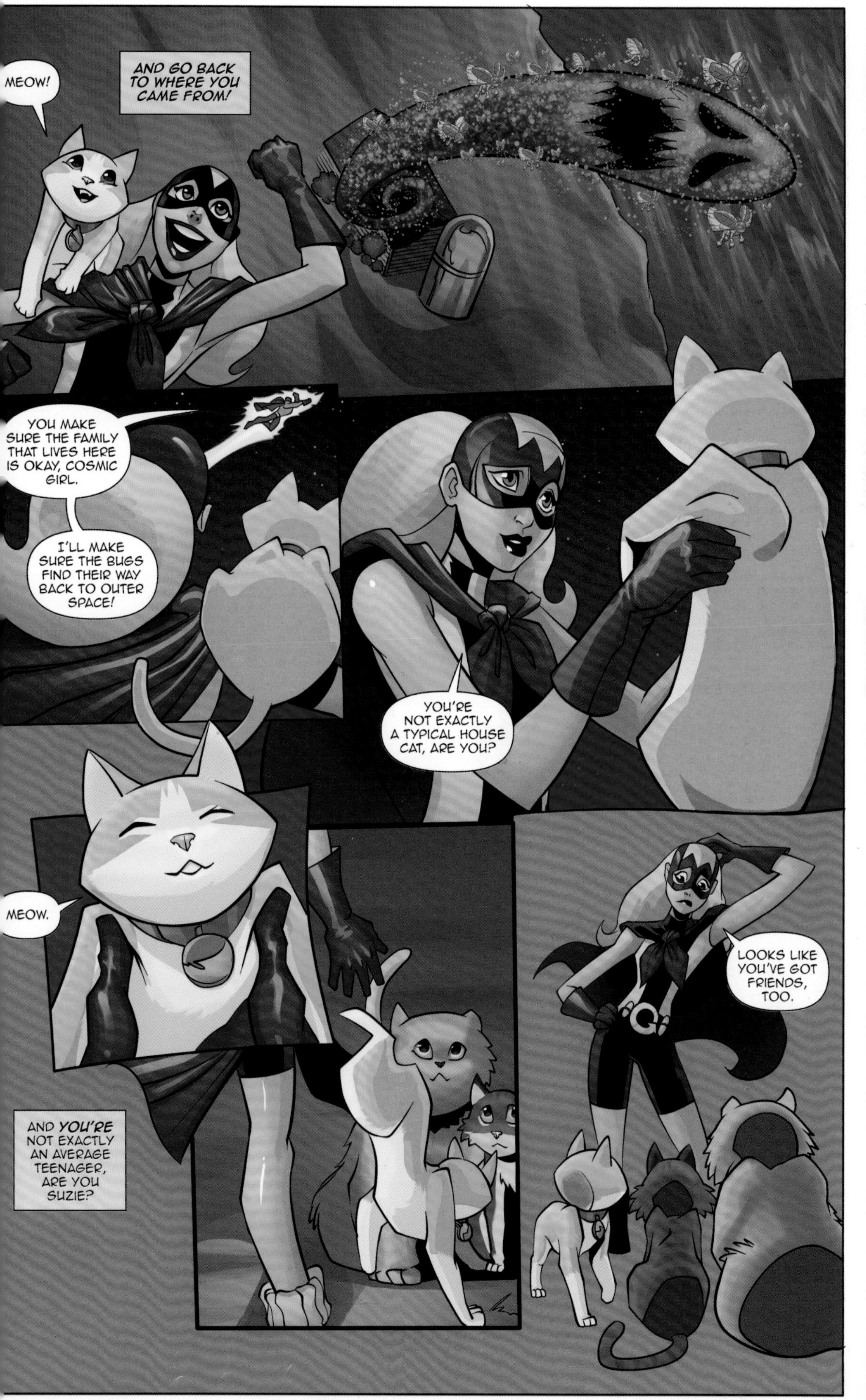
MEOW!
AND GO BACK TO WHERE YOU CAME FROM!
YOU MAKE SURE THE FAMILY THAT LIVES HERE IS OKAY, COSMIC GIRL.
I'LL MAKE SURE THE BUGS FIND THEIR WAY BACK TO OUTER SPACE!
YOU'RE NOT EXACTLY A TYPICAL HOUSE CAT, ARE YOU?
MEOW.
AND YOU'RE NOT EXACTLY AN AVERAGE TEENAGER, ARE YOU SUZIE?
LOOKS LIKE YOU'VE GOT FRIENDS, TOO.

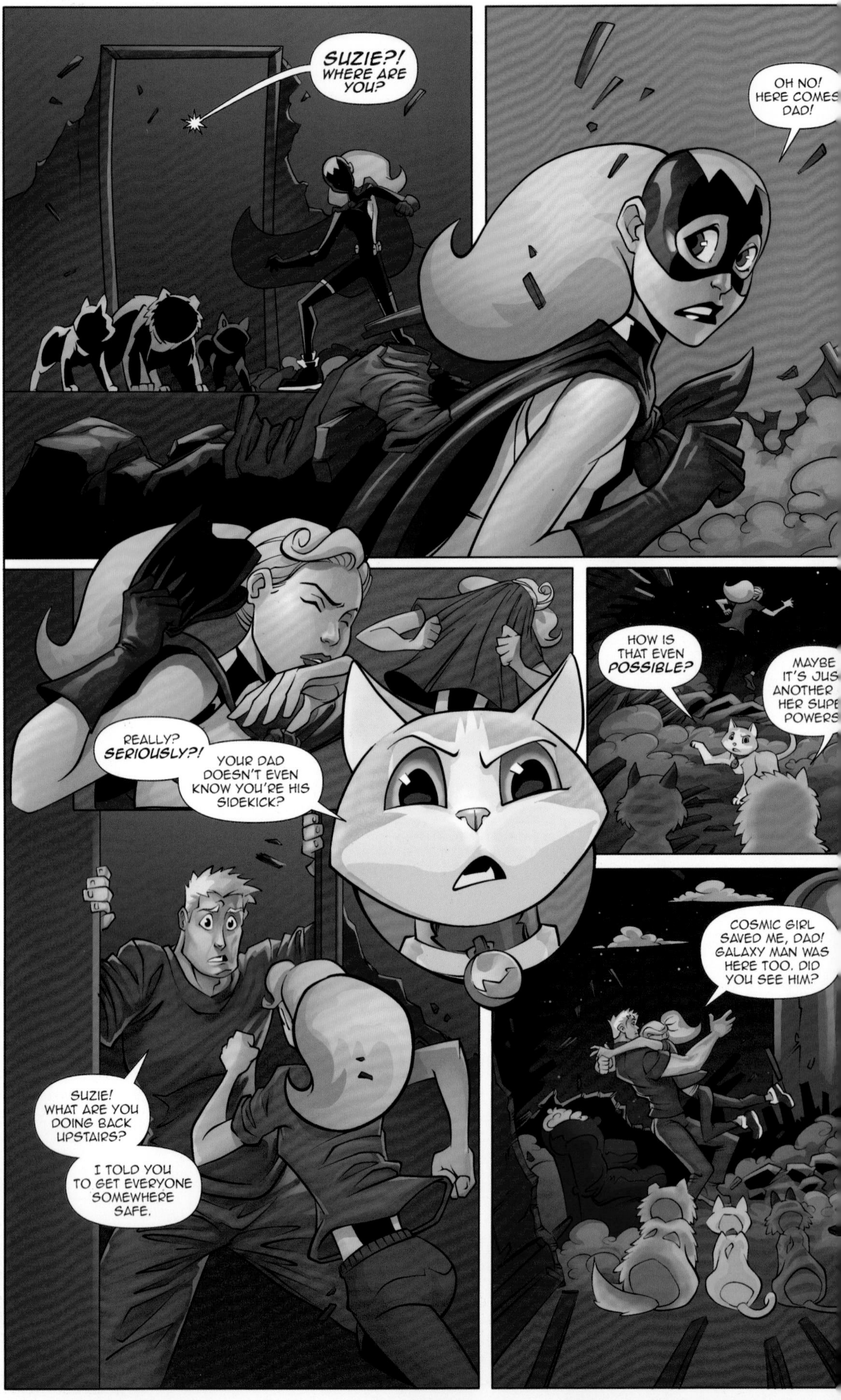
SUZIE?! WHERE ARE YOU?
OH NO! HERE COMES DAD!
REALLY? SERIOUSLY?!
YOUR DAD DOESN'T EVEN KNOW YOU'RE HIS SIDEKICK?
SUZIE! WHAT ARE YOU DOING BACK UPSTAIRS?
I TOLD YOU TO GET EVERYONE SOMEWHERE SAFE.
HOW IS THAT EVEN POSSIBLE?
MAYBE IT'S JUS ANOTHER HER SUPE POWERS
COSMIC GIRL SAVED ME, DAD! GALAXY MAN WAS HERE TOO. DID YOU SEE HIM?

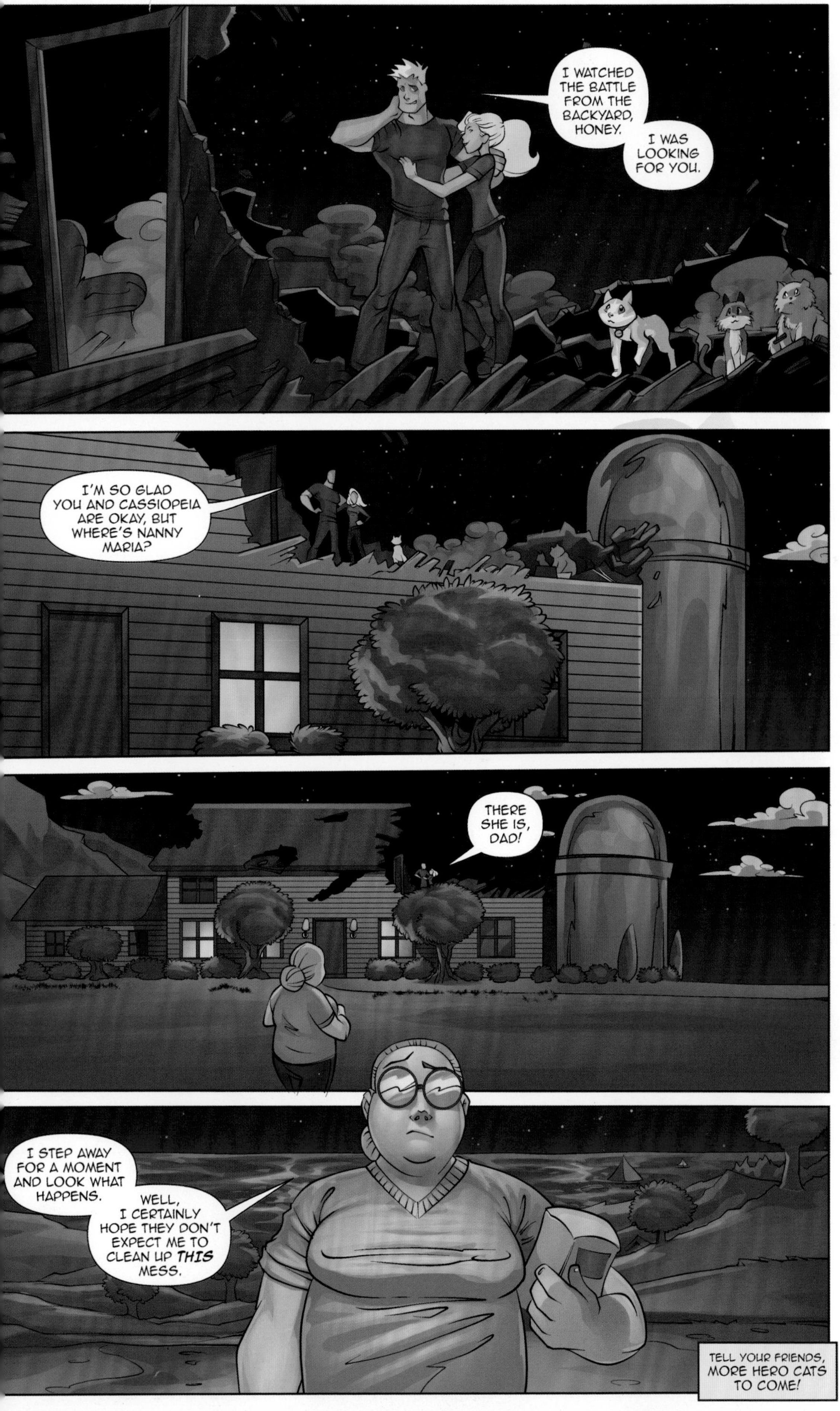
I WATCHED THE BATTLE FROM THE BACKYARD, HONEY.
I WAS LOOKING FOR YOU.
I'M SO GLAD YOU AND CASSIOPEIA ARE OKAY, BUT WHERE'S NANNY MARIA?
THERE SHE IS, DAD!
I STEP AWAY FOR A MOMENT AND LOOK WHAT HAPPENS.
WELL, I CERTAINLY HOPE THEY DON'T EXPECT ME TO CLEAN UP *THIS* MESS.
TELL YOUR FRIENDS, MORE HERO CATS TO COME!

CHAPTER 6:
MYSTERY ON CAMPUS

WRITER: KYLE PUTTKAMMER

PENCILS: MARCUS WILLIAMS

INKS: RYAN SELLERS

COLORS: OMAKA SCHULTZ

LETTERING: BRIANA HIGGINS

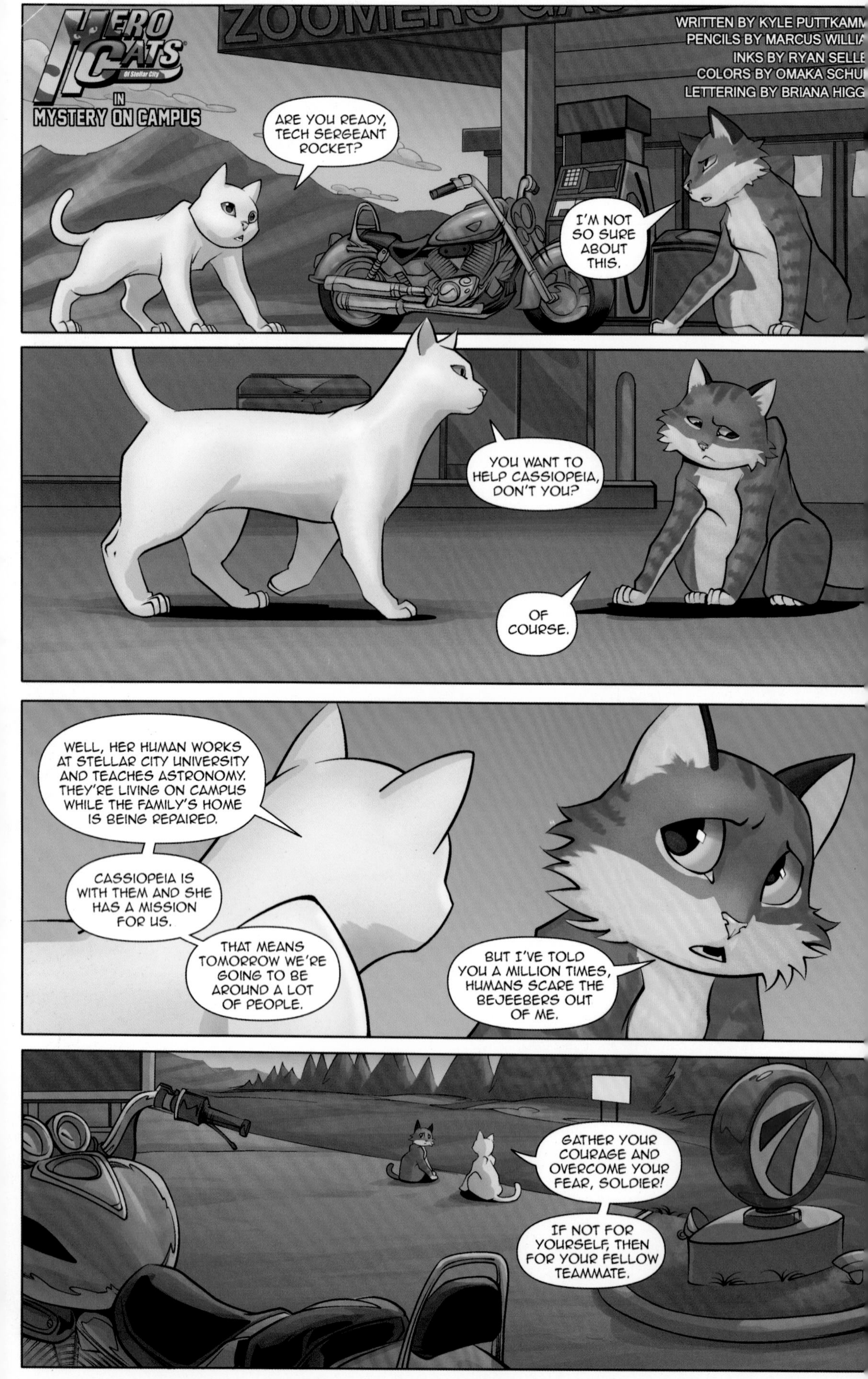
HERO CATS of Stellar City
IN
MYSTERY ON CAMPUS
WRITTEN BY KYLE PUTTKAMM
PENCILS BY MARCUS WILLIA
INKS BY RYAN SELLE
COLORS BY OMAKA SCHU
LETTERING BY BRIANA HIGG
ZOOMERS GAS
ARE YOU READY, TECH SERGEANT ROCKET?
I'M NOT SO SURE ABOUT THIS.
YOU WANT TO HELP CASSIOPEIA, DON'T YOU?
OF COURSE.
WELL, HER HUMAN WORKS AT STELLAR CITY UNIVERSITY AND TEACHES ASTRONOMY. THEY'RE LIVING ON CAMPUS WHILE THE FAMILY'S HOME IS BEING REPAIRED.
CASSIOPEIA IS WITH THEM AND SHE HAS A MISSION FOR US.
THAT MEANS TOMORROW WE'RE GOING TO BE AROUND A LOT OF PEOPLE.
BUT I'VE TOLD YOU A MILLION TIMES, HUMANS SCARE THE BEJEEBERS OUT OF ME.
GATHER YOUR COURAGE AND OVERCOME YOUR FEAR, SOLDIER!
IF NOT FOR YOURSELF, THEN FOR YOUR FELLOW TEAMMATE.

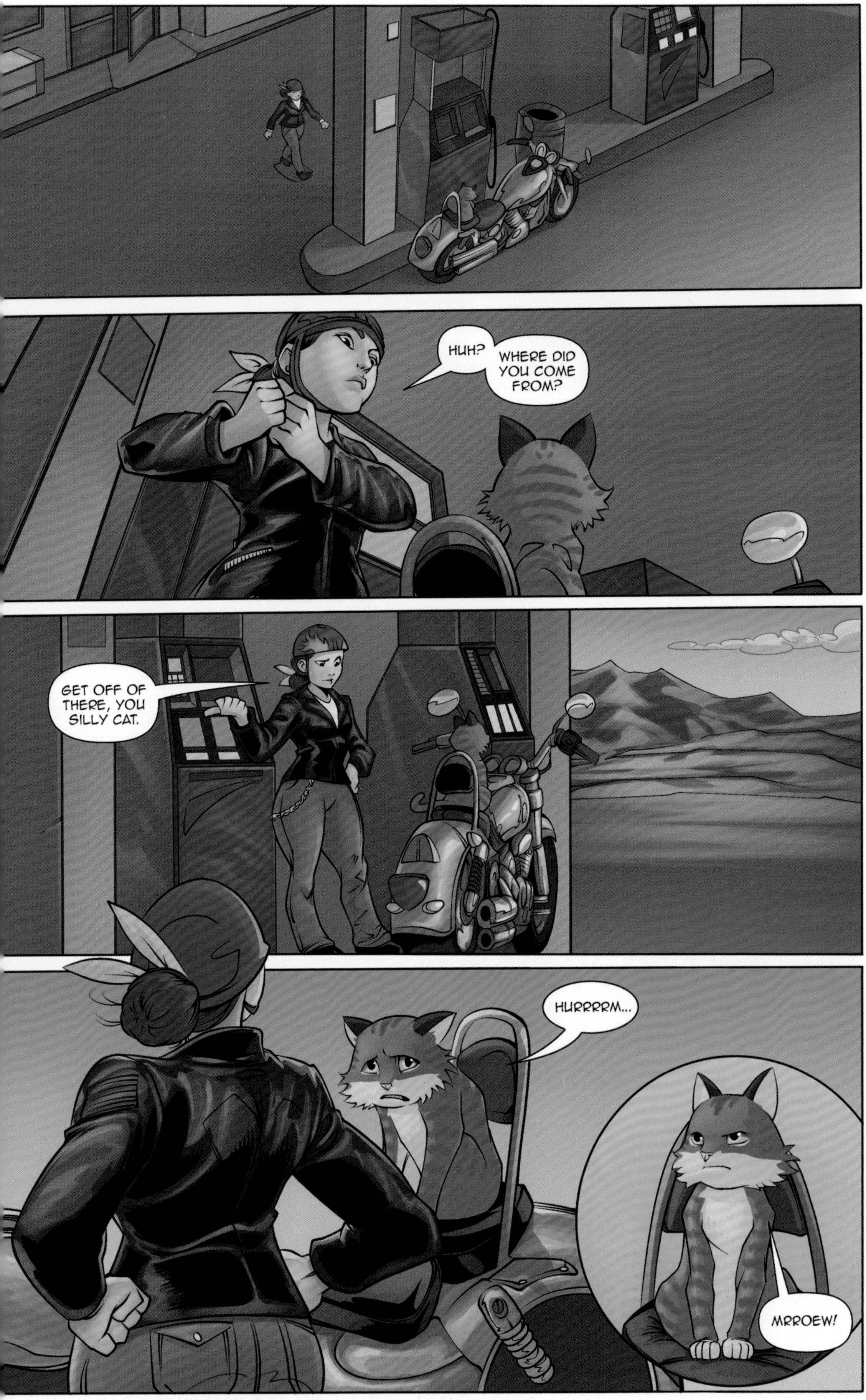
HUH?
WHERE DID YOU COME FROM?
GET OFF OF THERE, YOU SILLY CAT.
HURRRRM...
MRROEW!

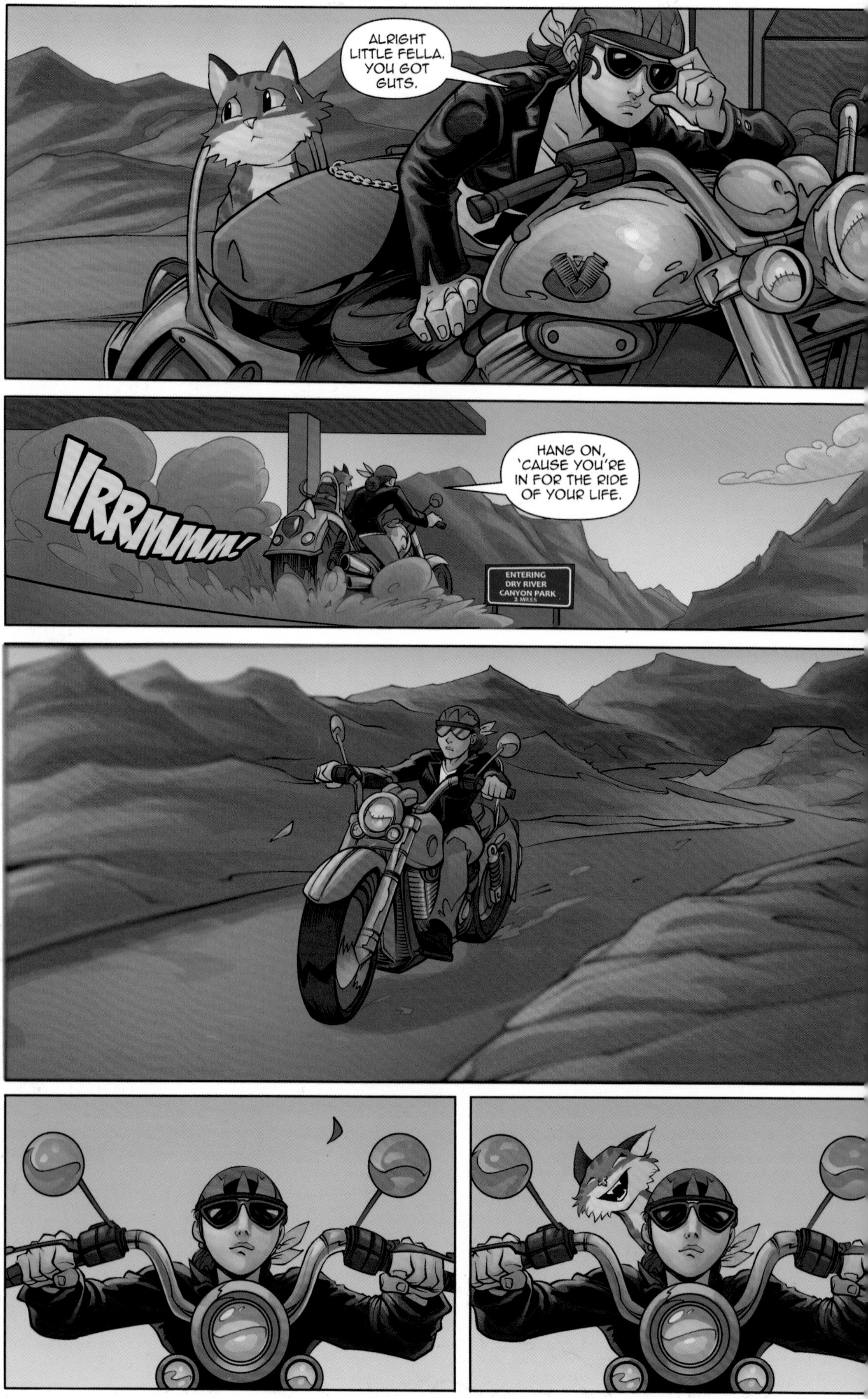
ALRIGHT LITTLE FELLA. YOU GOT GUTS.
VRRMMMM!
HANG ON, 'CAUSE YOU'RE IN FOR THE RIDE OF YOUR LIFE.
ENTERING DRY RIVER CANYON PARK 2 MILES

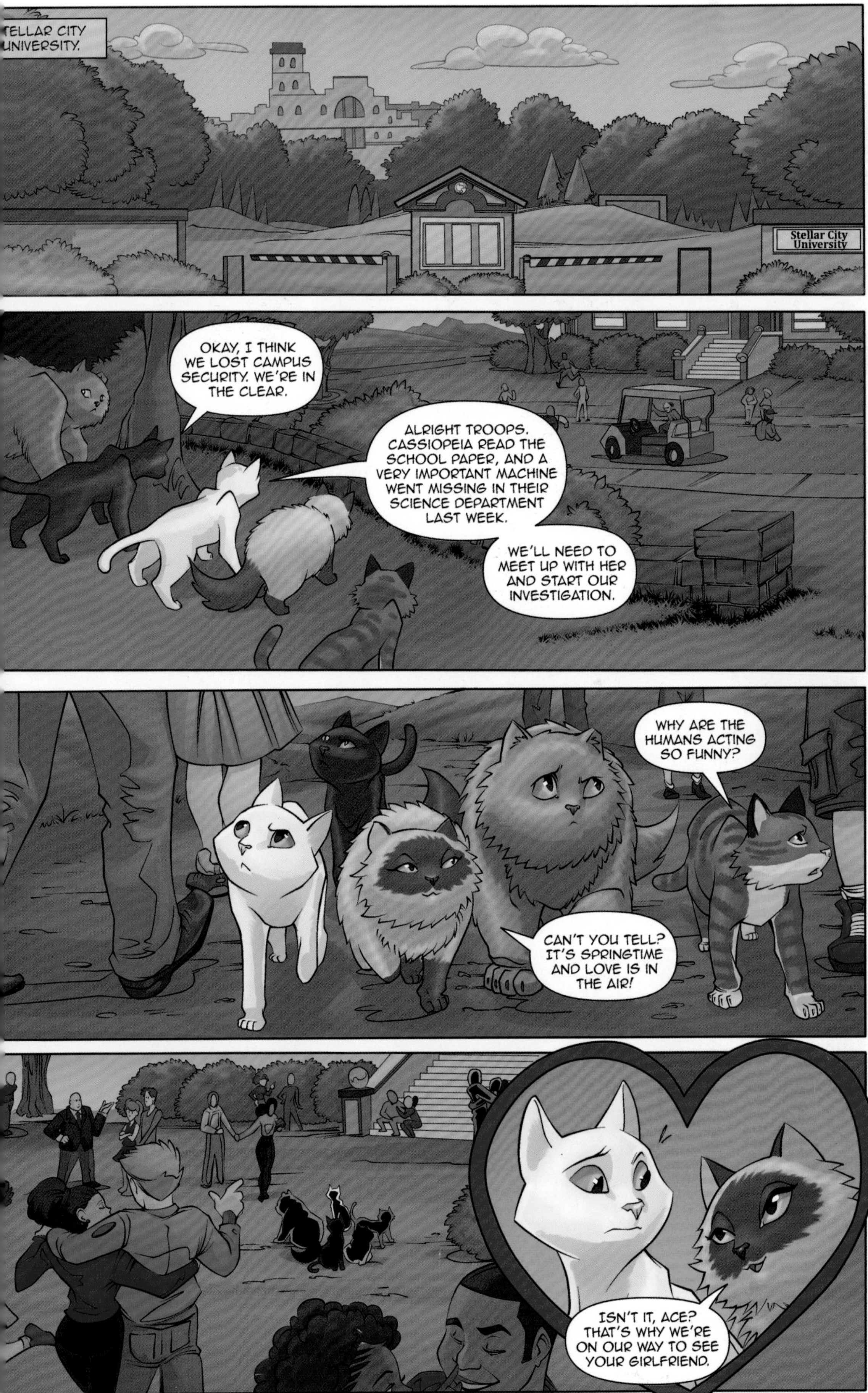
TELLAR CITY UNIVERSITY.
Stellar City University
OKAY, I THINK WE LOST CAMPUS SECURITY. WE'RE IN THE CLEAR.
ALRIGHT TROOPS. CASSIOPEIA READ THE SCHOOL PAPER, AND A VERY IMPORTANT MACHINE WENT MISSING IN THEIR SCIENCE DEPARTMENT LAST WEEK.
WE'LL NEED TO MEET UP WITH HER AND START OUR INVESTIGATION.
WHY ARE THE HUMANS ACTING SO FUNNY?
CAN'T YOU TELL? IT'S SPRINGTIME AND LOVE IS IN THE AIR!
ISN'T IT, ACE? THAT'S WHY WE'RE ON OUR WAY TO SEE YOUR GIRLFRIEND.

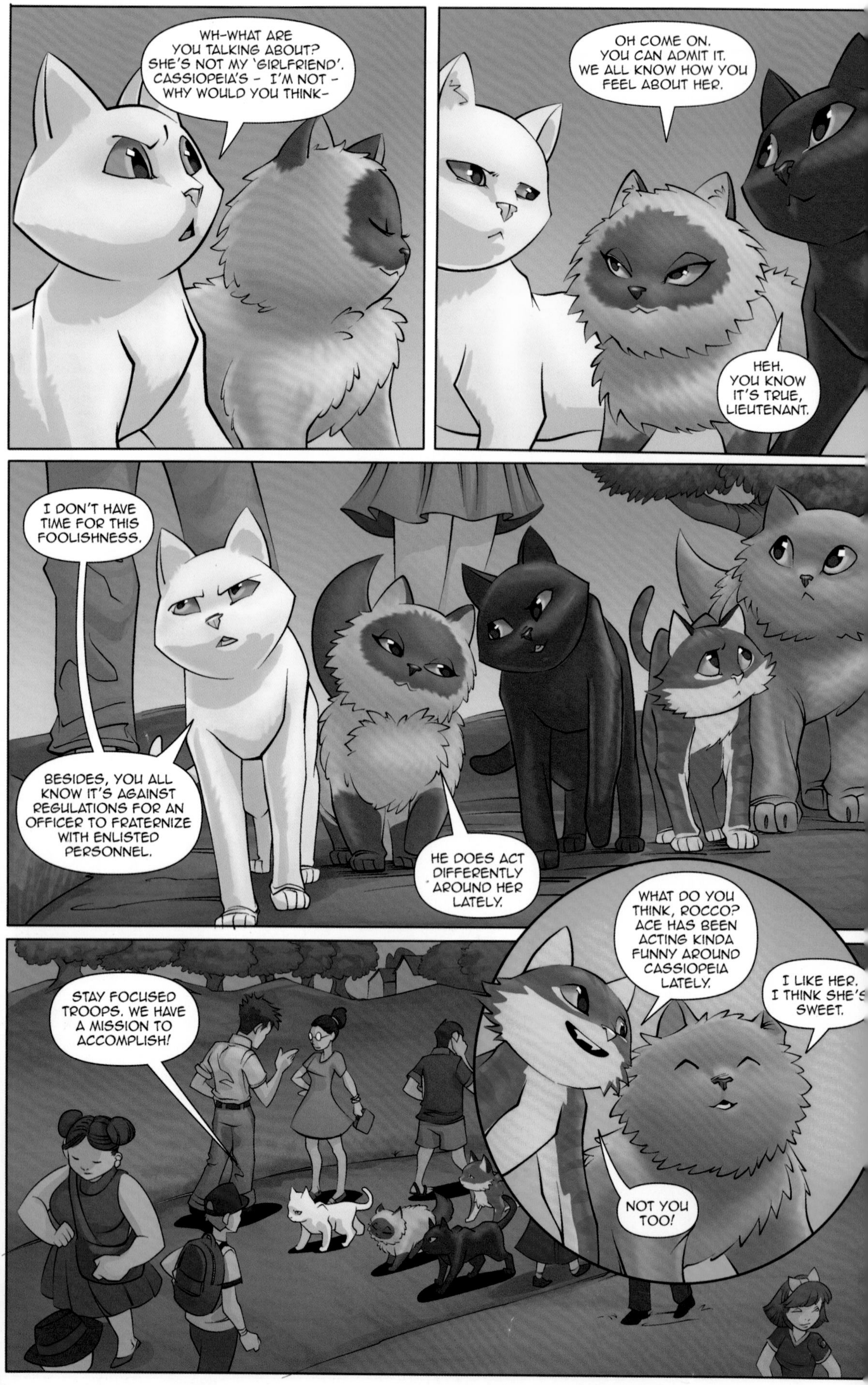
WH-WHAT ARE YOU TALKING ABOUT? SHE'S NOT MY 'GIRLFRIEND'. CASSIOPEIA'S - I'M NOT - WHY WOULD YOU THINK-
OH COME ON. YOU CAN ADMIT IT. WE ALL KNOW HOW YOU FEEL ABOUT HER.
HEH. YOU KNOW IT'S TRUE, LIEUTENANT.
I DON'T HAVE TIME FOR THIS FOOLISHNESS.
BESIDES, YOU ALL KNOW IT'S AGAINST REGULATIONS FOR AN OFFICER TO FRATERNIZE WITH ENLISTED PERSONNEL.
HE DOES ACT DIFFERENTLY AROUND HER LATELY.
STAY FOCUSED TROOPS. WE HAVE A MISSION TO ACCOMPLISH!
WHAT DO YOU THINK, ROCCO? ACE HAS BEEN ACTING KINDA FUNNY AROUND CASSIOPEIA LATELY.
I LIKE HER. I THINK SHE'S SWEET.
NOT YOU TOO!

THE QUEST FAMILY [CA]MPUS RESIDENCE.

THANKS FOR YOUR HELP WITH THIS, GUYS.

WHAT'S THE LATEST REPORT, SOLDIER?

SUZIE AND STANLEY ARE HERE WHILE THE HOME AND OBSERVATORY ARE BEING REPAIRED.

NANNY MARIA'S BEEN SENT ON A VACATION.

LATELY, STANLEY IS CONCERNED ABOUT ONE OF HIS COWORKERS, PROFESSOR TABART.

HE WAS WORKING ON AN IMPORTANT INVENTION THAT'S GONE MISSING.

WHAT DOES THE MACHINE DO?

THE PROFESSOR [IS] STUDYING HOW TO [SU]PERSIZE PLANTS TO [P]ROVIDE MORE FOOD [I]N NEEDY PARTS OF THE WORLD.

HIS EXPERIMENTS INVOLVE A MACHINE CALLED A MACRO-NUTRIATOR.

LAST WEEK IT WENT MISSING.

ANY CLUES AS TO WHO THE CULPRIT MAY BE?

FROM WHAT I'VE HEARD, THE POLICE ARE STUMPED.

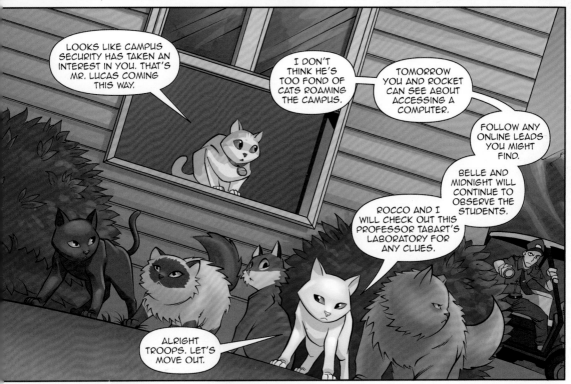

LOOKS LIKE CAMPUS SECURITY HAS TAKEN AN INTEREST IN YOU. THAT'S MR. LUCAS COMING THIS WAY.

I DON'T THINK HE'S TOO FOND OF CATS ROAMING THE CAMPUS.

TOMORROW YOU AND ROCKET CAN SEE ABOUT ACCESSING A COMPUTER.

FOLLOW ANY ONLINE LEADS YOU MIGHT FIND.

BELLE AND MIDNIGHT WILL CONTINUE TO OBSERVE THE STUDENTS.

ROCCO AND I WILL CHECK OUT THIS PROFESSOR TABART'S LABORATORY FOR ANY CLUES.

ALRIGHT TROOPS. LET'S MOVE OUT.

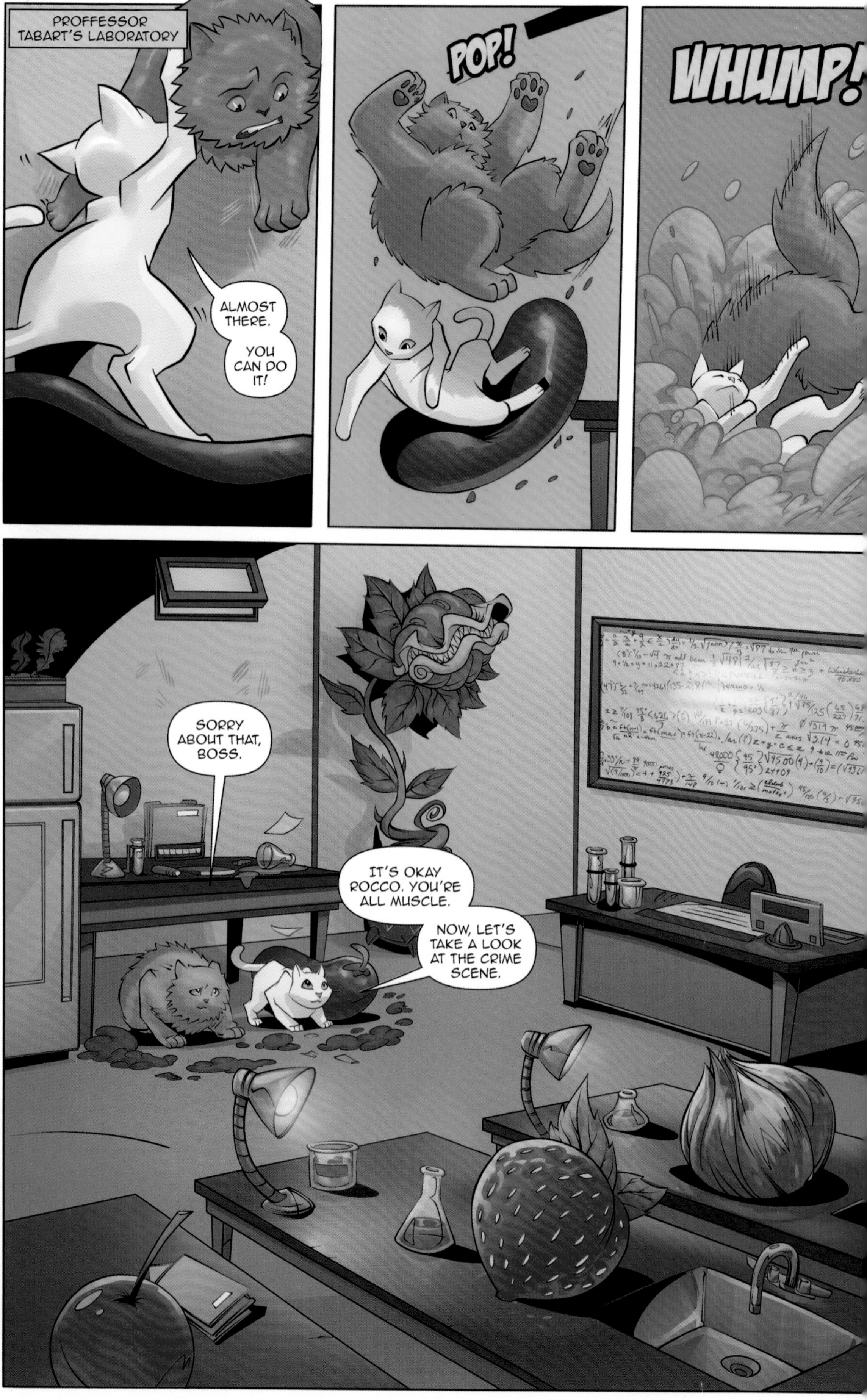
PROFFESSOR TABART'S LABORATORY
ALMOST THERE.
YOU CAN DO IT!
POP!
WHUMP!
SORRY ABOUT THAT, BOSS.
IT'S OKAY ROCCO. YOU'RE ALL MUSCLE.
NOW, LET'S TAKE A LOOK AT THE CRIME SCENE.

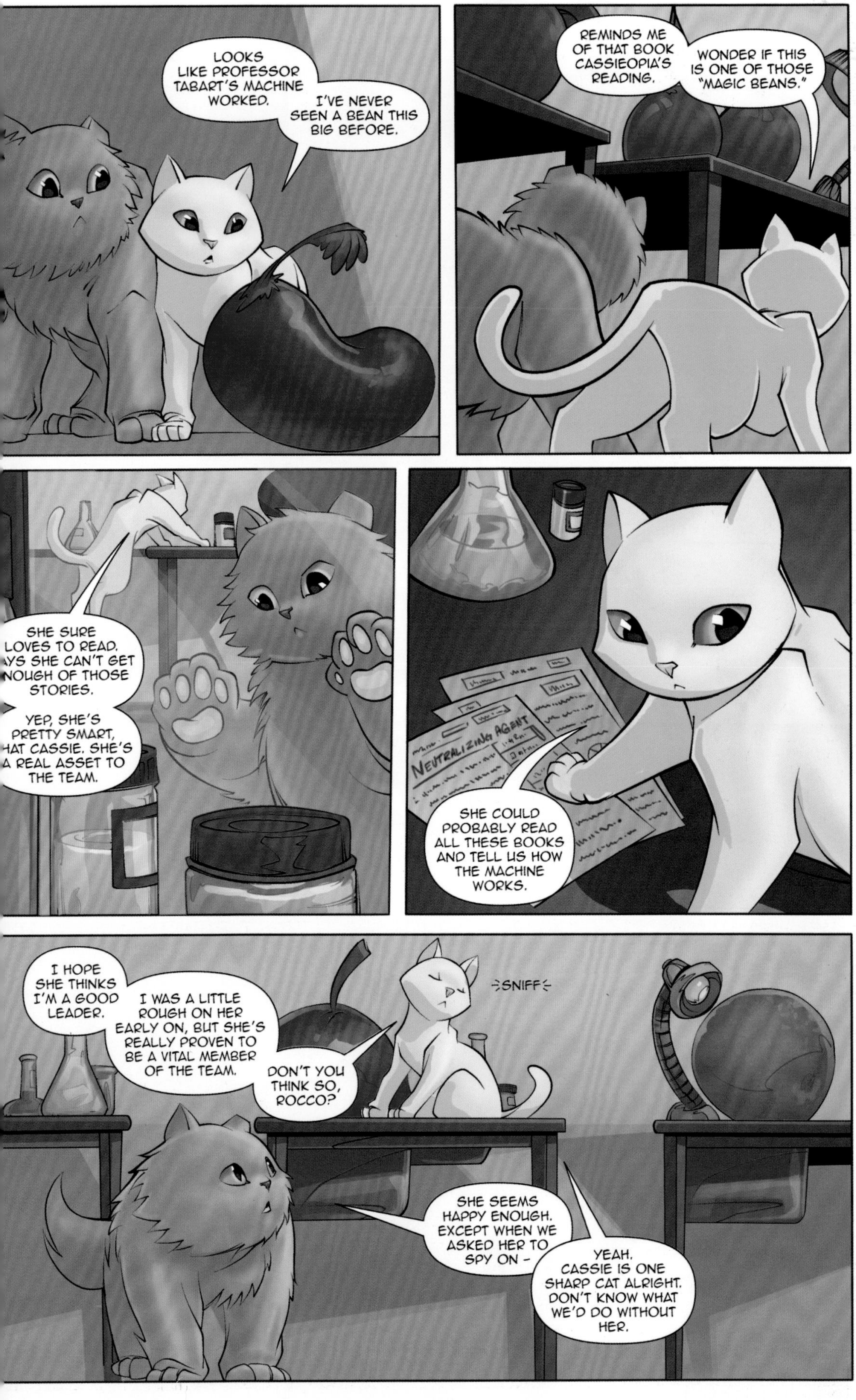

LOOKS LIKE PROFESSOR TABART'S MACHINE WORKED.
I'VE NEVER SEEN A BEAN THIS BIG BEFORE.
REMINDS ME OF THAT BOOK CASSIEOPIA'S READING.
WONDER IF THIS IS ONE OF THOSE "MAGIC BEANS."
SHE SURE LOVES TO READ. AYS SHE CAN'T GET NOUGH OF THOSE STORIES.
YEP, SHE'S PRETTY SMART, HAT CASSIE. SHE'S A REAL ASSET TO THE TEAM.
NEUTRALIZING AGENT
SHE COULD PROBABLY READ ALL THESE BOOKS AND TELL US HOW THE MACHINE WORKS.
I HOPE SHE THINKS I'M A GOOD LEADER.
I WAS A LITTLE ROUGH ON HER EARLY ON, BUT SHE'S REALLY PROVEN TO BE A VITAL MEMBER OF THE TEAM.
DON'T YOU THINK SO, ROCCO?
SNIFF
SHE SEEMS HAPPY ENOUGH. EXCEPT WHEN WE ASKED HER TO SPY ON –
YEAH. CASSIE IS ONE SHARP CAT ALRIGHT. DON'T KNOW WHAT WE'D DO WITHOUT HER.

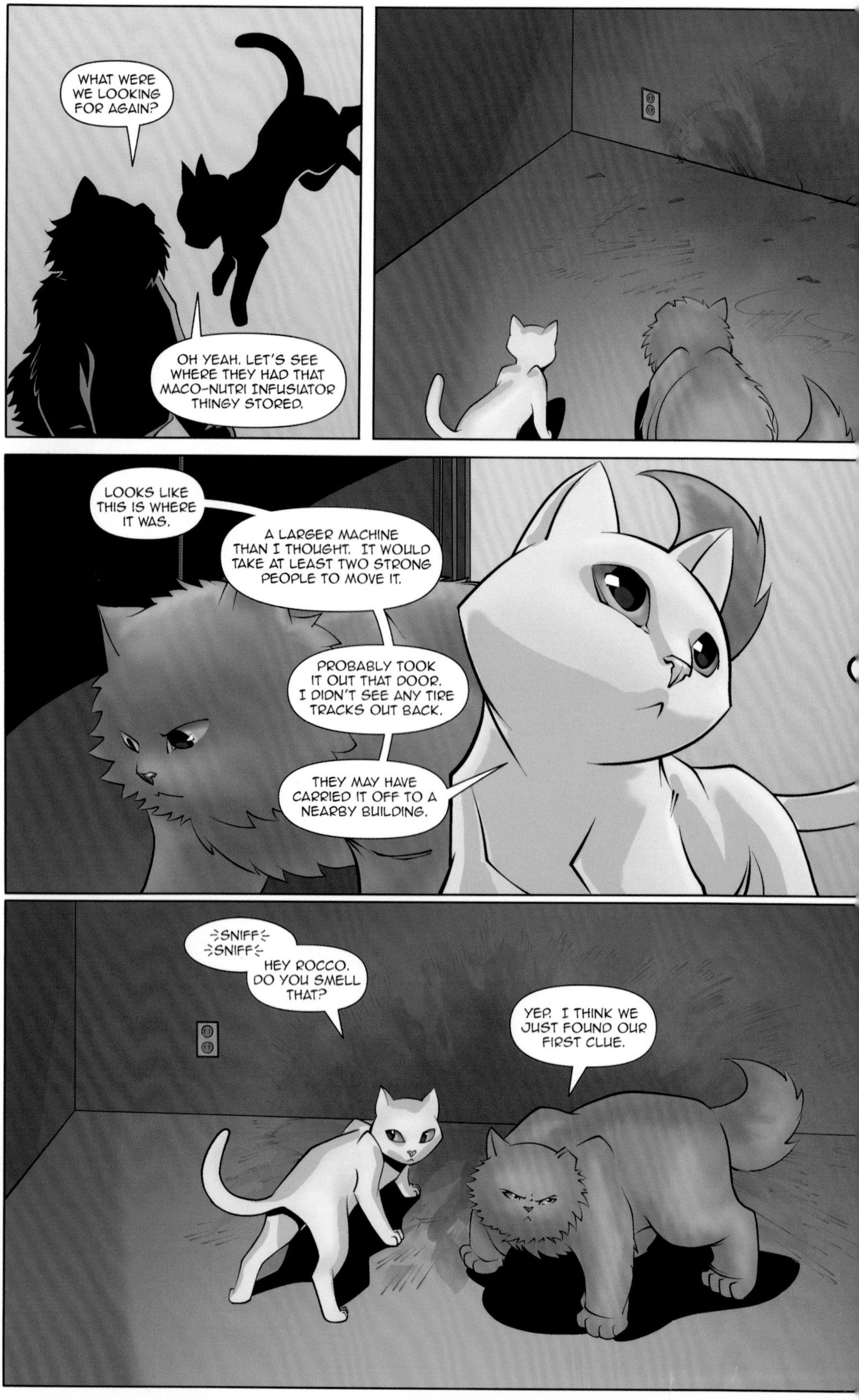
WHAT WERE WE LOOKING FOR AGAIN?
OH YEAH. LET'S SEE WHERE THEY HAD THAT MACO-NUTRI INFUSIATOR THINGY STORED.
LOOKS LIKE THIS IS WHERE IT WAS.
A LARGER MACHINE THAN I THOUGHT. IT WOULD TAKE AT LEAST TWO STRONG PEOPLE TO MOVE IT.
PROBABLY TOOK IT OUT THAT DOOR. I DIDN'T SEE ANY TIRE TRACKS OUT BACK.
THEY MAY HAVE CARRIED IT OFF TO A NEARBY BUILDING.
SNIFF SNIFF HEY ROCCO. DO YOU SMELL THAT?
YEP. I THINK WE JUST FOUND OUR FIRST CLUE.

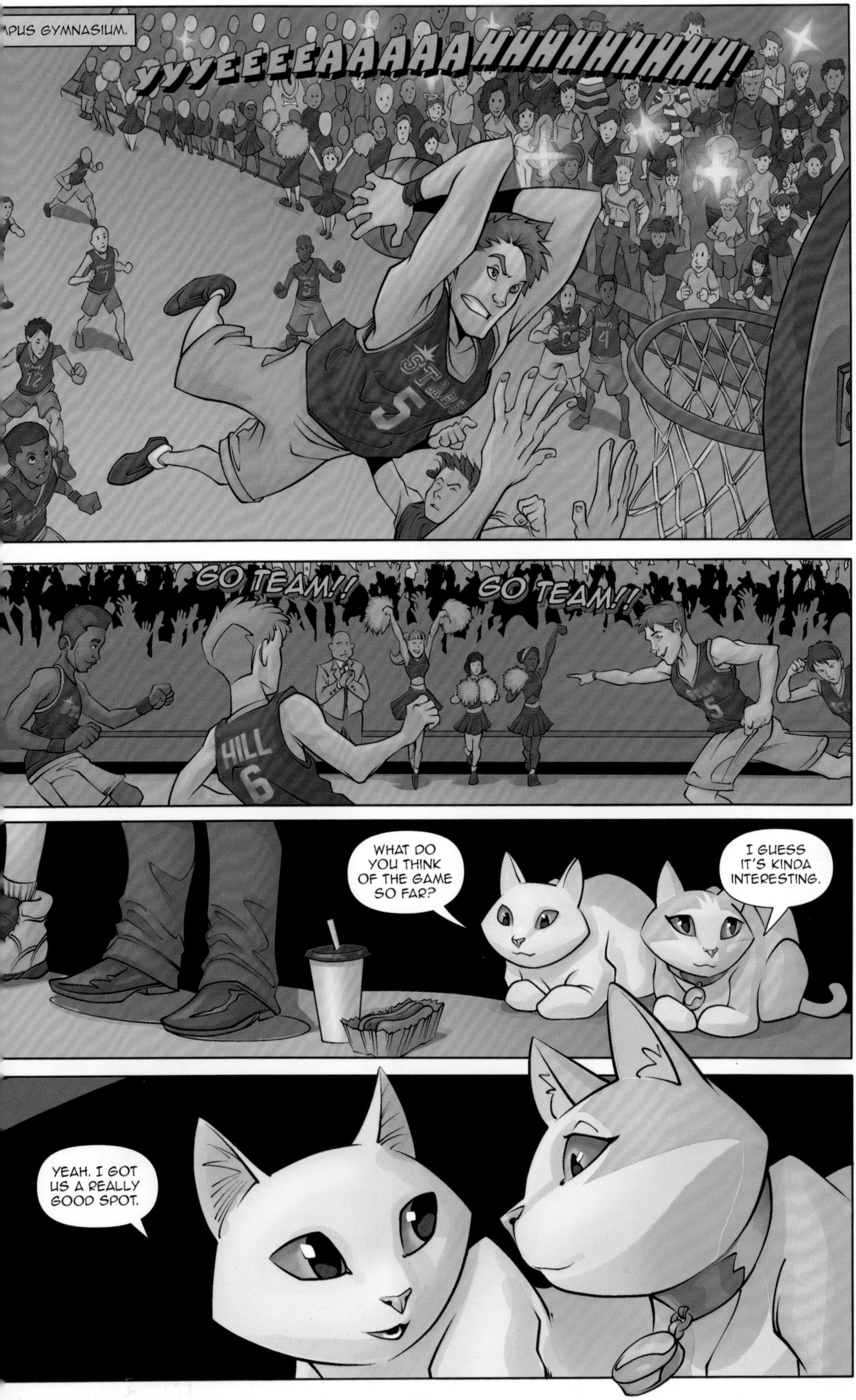
MPUS GYMNASIUM.
YYYEEEEAAAAAHHHHHHHHHH!
GO TEAM!!
GO TEAM!!
WHAT DO YOU THINK OF THE GAME SO FAR?
I GUESS IT'S KINDA INTERESTING.
YEAH. I GOT US A REALLY GOOD SPOT.

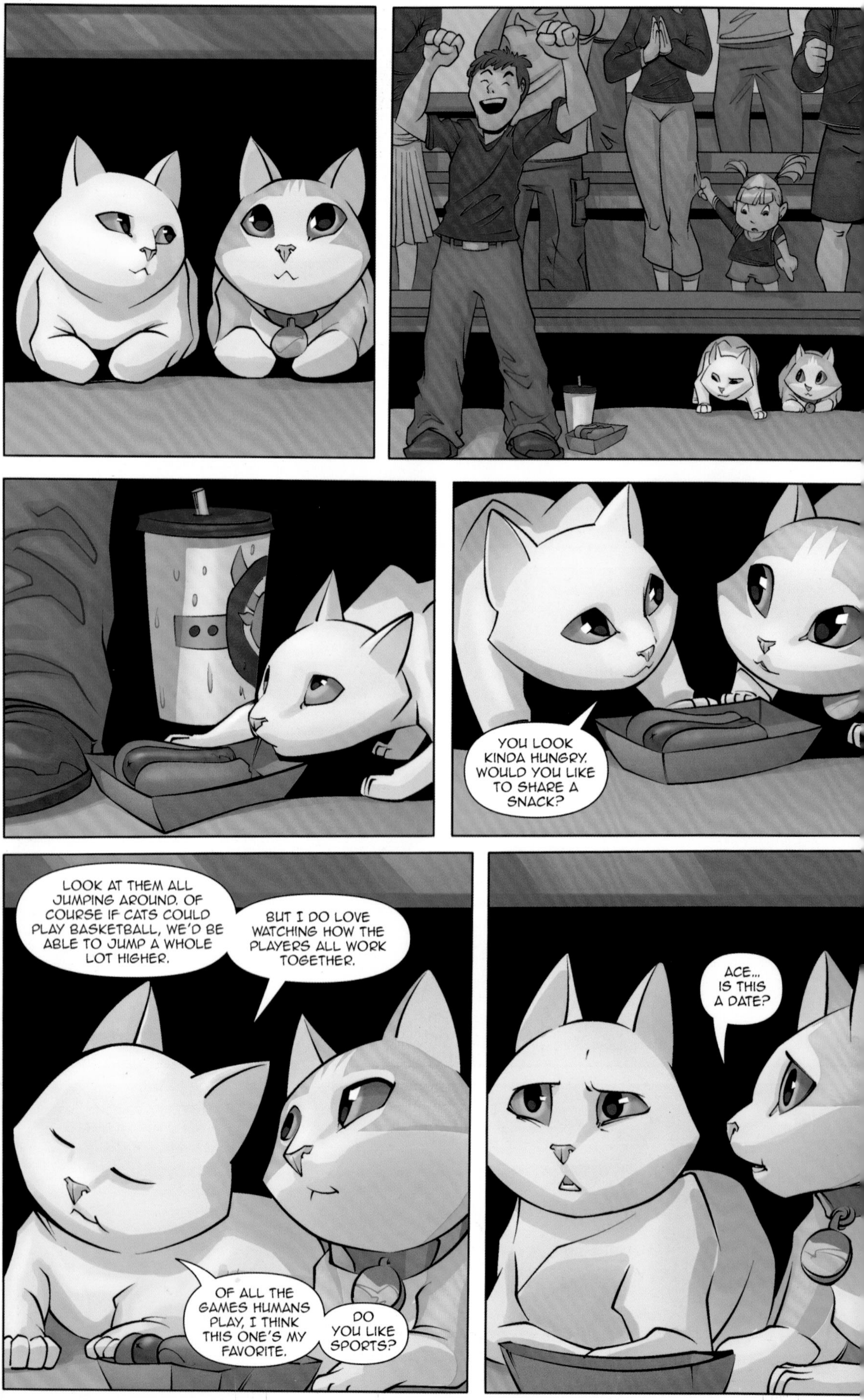
YOU LOOK KINDA HUNGRY. WOULD YOU LIKE TO SHARE A SNACK?
LOOK AT THEM ALL JUMPING AROUND. OF COURSE IF CATS COULD PLAY BASKETBALL, WE'D BE ABLE TO JUMP A WHOLE LOT HIGHER.
BUT I DO LOVE WATCHING HOW THE PLAYERS ALL WORK TOGETHER.
OF ALL THE GAMES HUMANS PLAY, I THINK THIS ONE'S MY FAVORITE.
DO YOU LIKE SPORTS?
ACE... IS THIS A DATE?

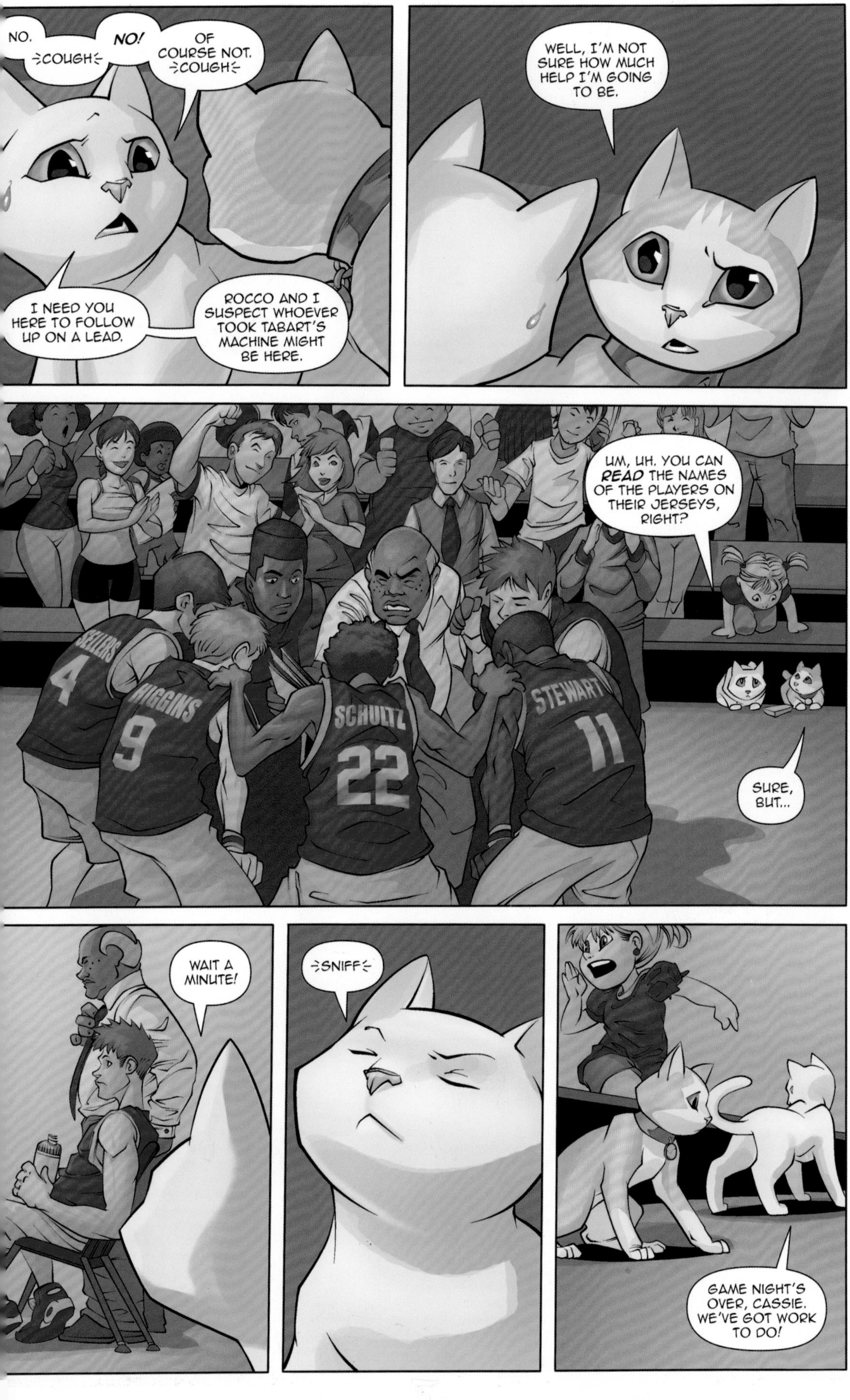
NO.
⇉COUGH⇇
NO!
OF COURSE NOT. ⇉COUGH⇇
I NEED YOU HERE TO FOLLOW UP ON A LEAD.
ROCCO AND I SUSPECT WHOEVER TOOK TABART'S MACHINE MIGHT BE HERE.
WELL, I'M NOT SURE HOW MUCH HELP I'M GOING TO BE.
UM, UH. YOU CAN READ THE NAMES OF THE PLAYERS ON THEIR JERSEYS, RIGHT?
SELLERS 4
HIGGINS 9
SCHULTZ 22
STEWART 11
SURE, BUT...
WAIT A MINUTE!
⇉SNIFF⇇
GAME NIGHT'S OVER, CASSIE. WE'VE GOT WORK TO DO!

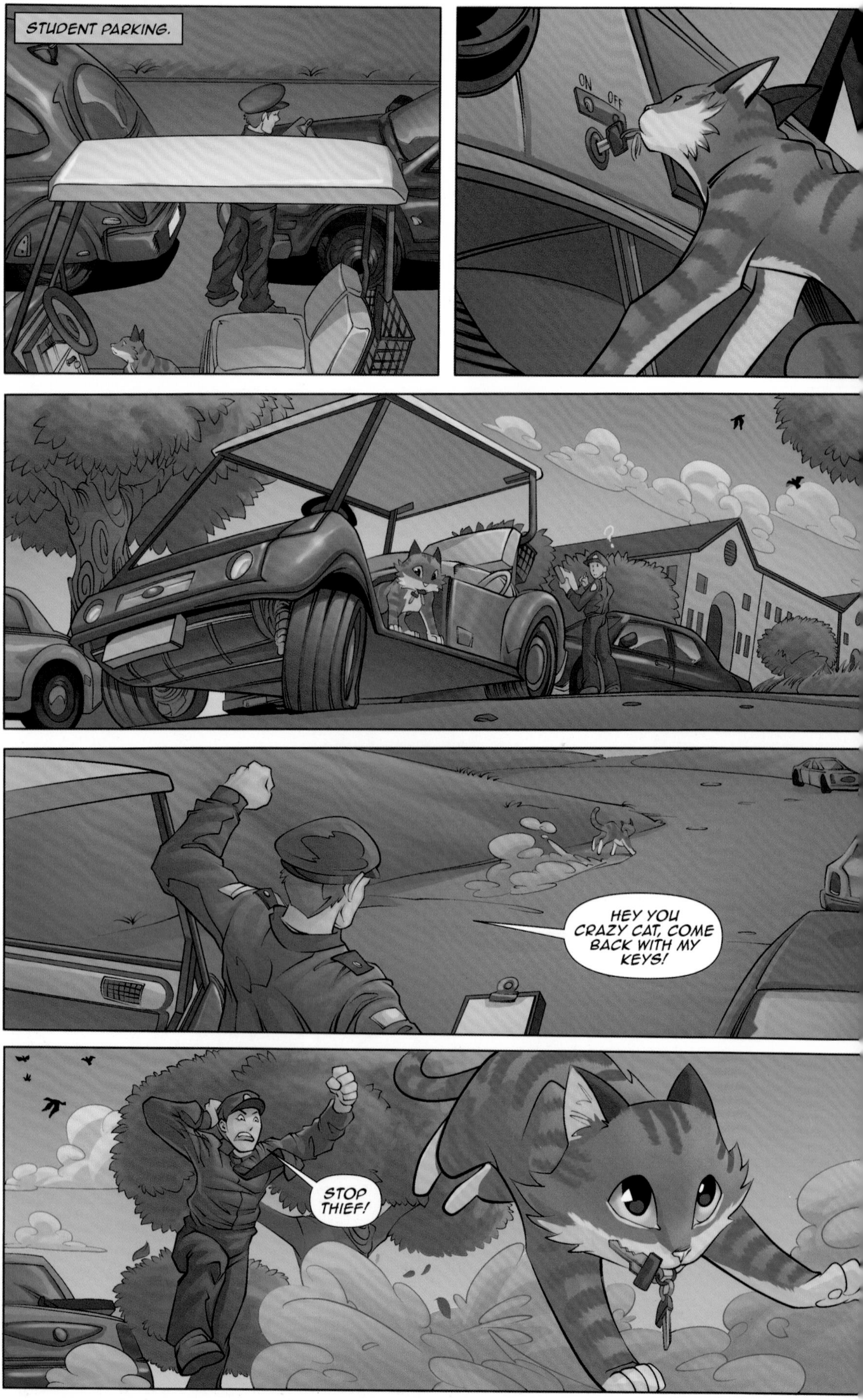
STUDENT PARKING.
ON
OFF
HEY YOU CRAZY CAT, COME BACK WITH MY KEYS!
STOP THIEF!

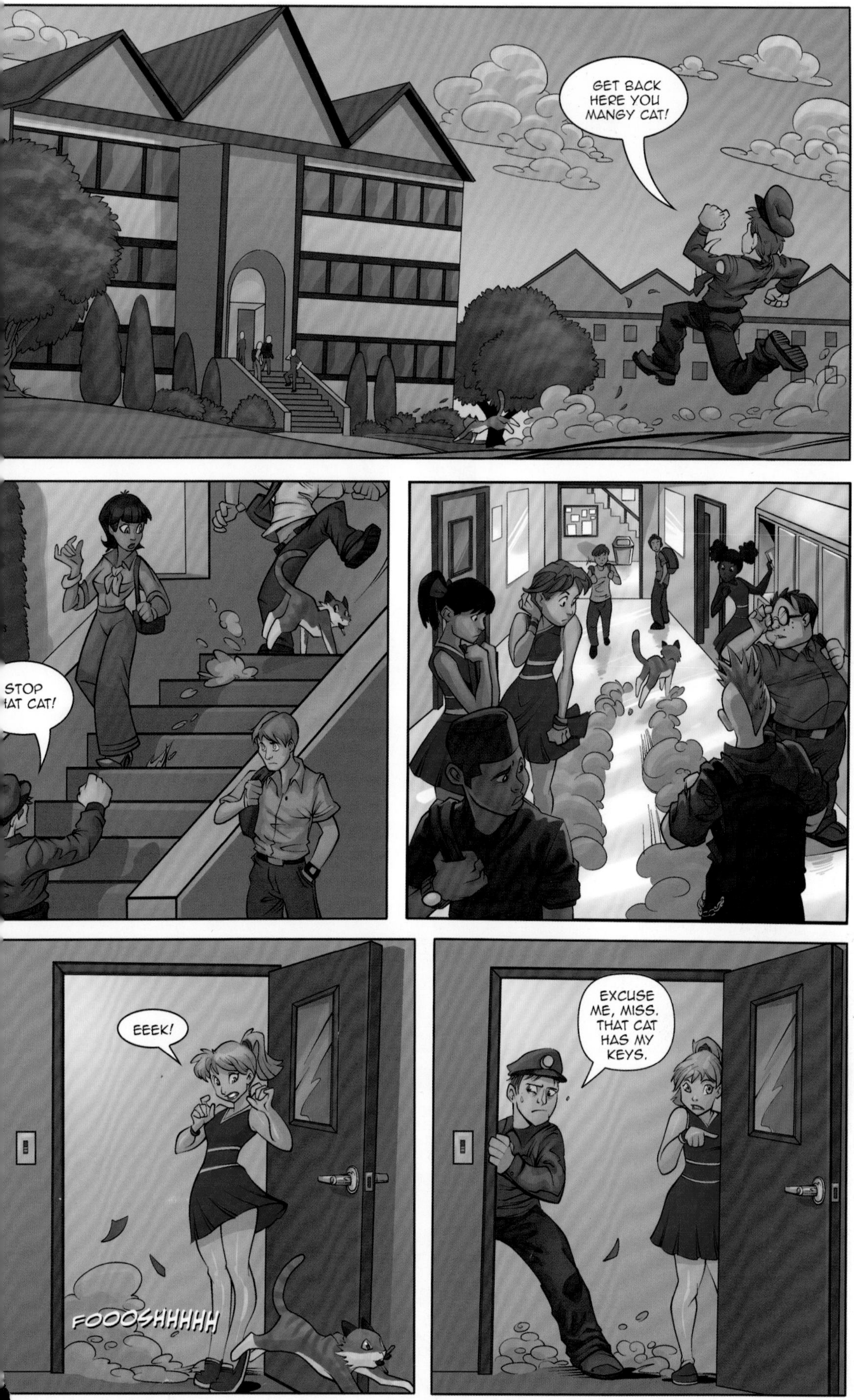
GET BACK HERE YOU MANGY CAT!
STOP THAT CAT!
EEEK!
FOOOSHHHHH
EXCUSE ME, MISS. THAT CAT HAS MY KEYS.

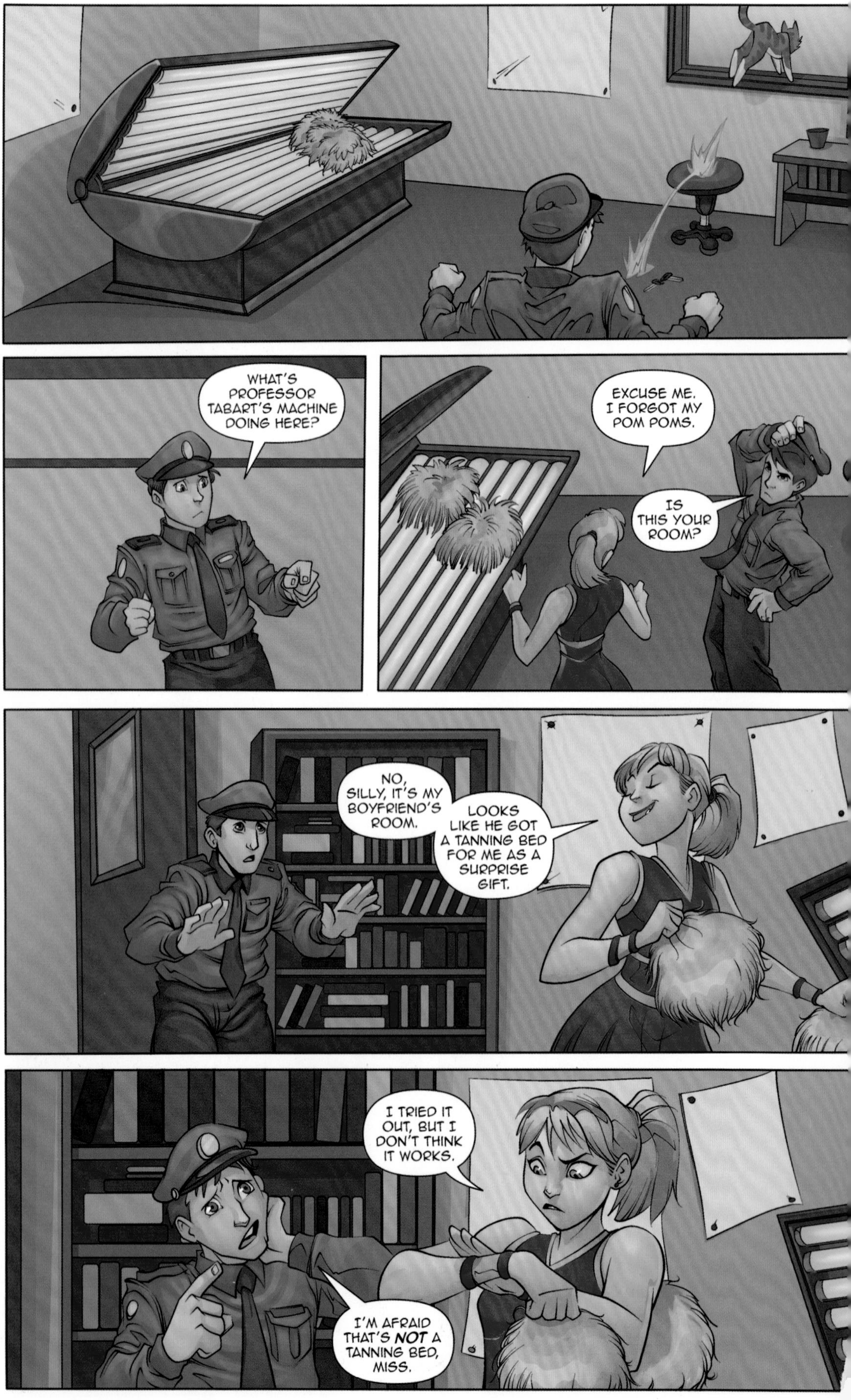
WHAT'S PROFESSOR TABART'S MACHINE DOING HERE?
EXCUSE ME. I FORGOT MY POM POMS.
IS THIS YOUR ROOM?
NO, SILLY, IT'S MY BOYFRIEND'S ROOM.
LOOKS LIKE HE GOT A TANNING BED FOR ME AS A SURPRISE GIFT.
I TRIED IT OUT, BUT I DON'T THINK IT WORKS.
I'M AFRAID THAT'S ***NOT*** A TANNING BED, MISS.

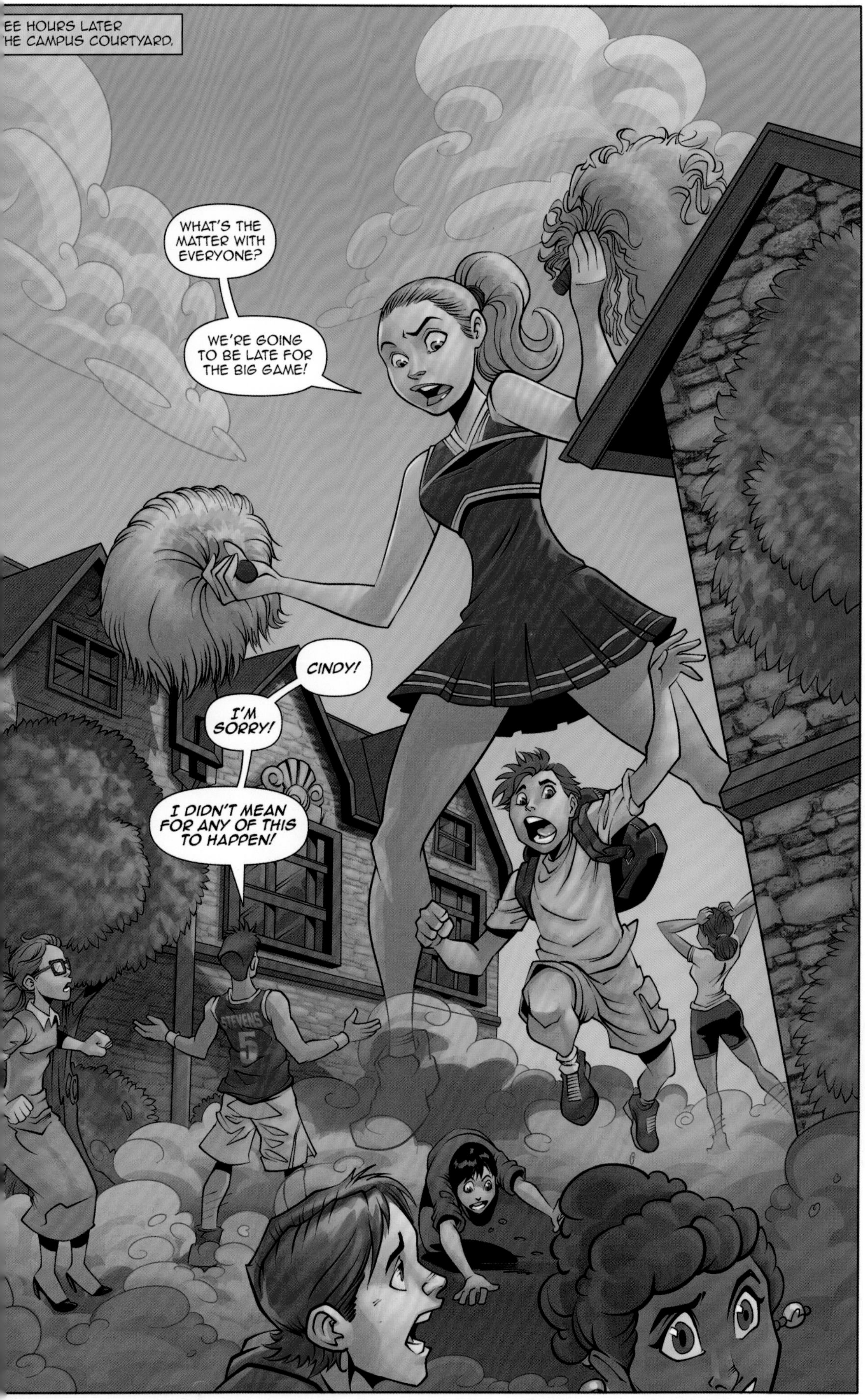
EE HOURS LATER
HE CAMPUS COURTYARD.
WHAT'S THE MATTER WITH EVERYONE?
WE'RE GOING TO BE LATE FOR THE BIG GAME!
CINDY!
I'M SORRY!
I DIDN'T MEAN FOR ANY OF THIS TO HAPPEN!
STEVENS
5

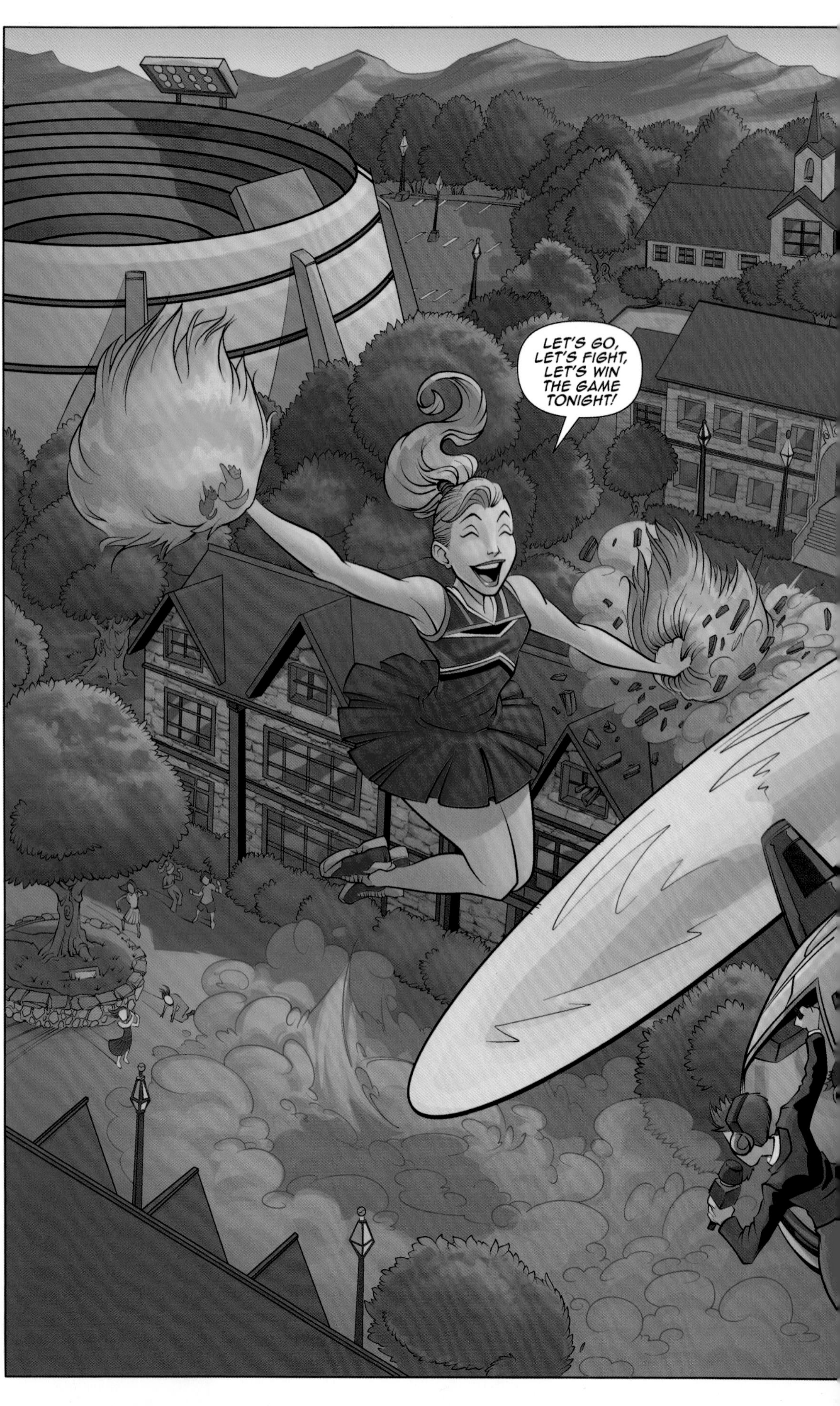
LET'S GO, LET'S FIGHT, LET'S WIN THE GAME TONIGHT!

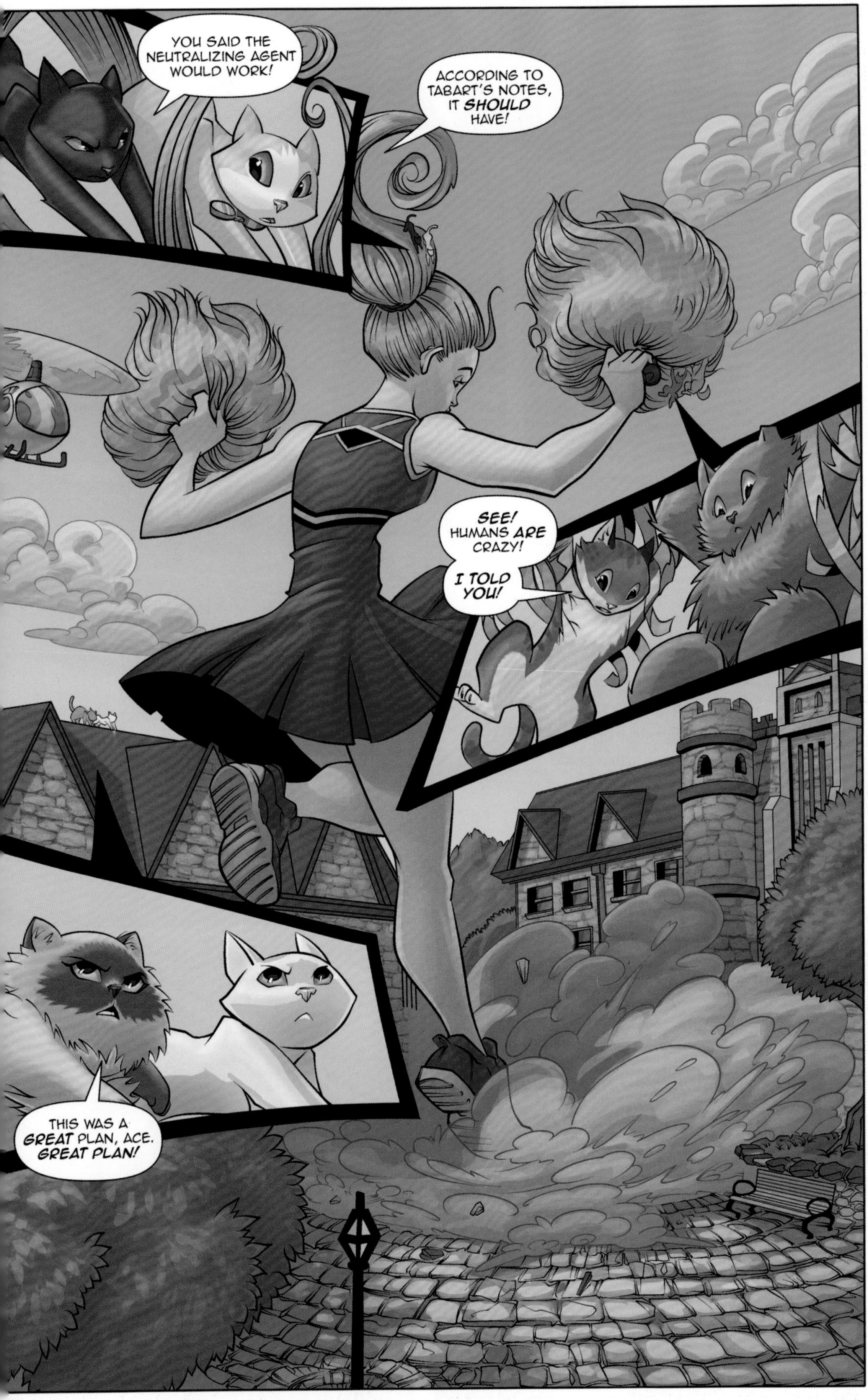
YOU SAID THE NEUTRALIZING AGENT WOULD WORK!
ACCORDING TO TABART'S NOTES, IT SHOULD HAVE!
SEE! HUMANS ARE CRAZY!
I TOLD YOU!
THIS WAS A GREAT PLAN, ACE. GREAT PLAN!

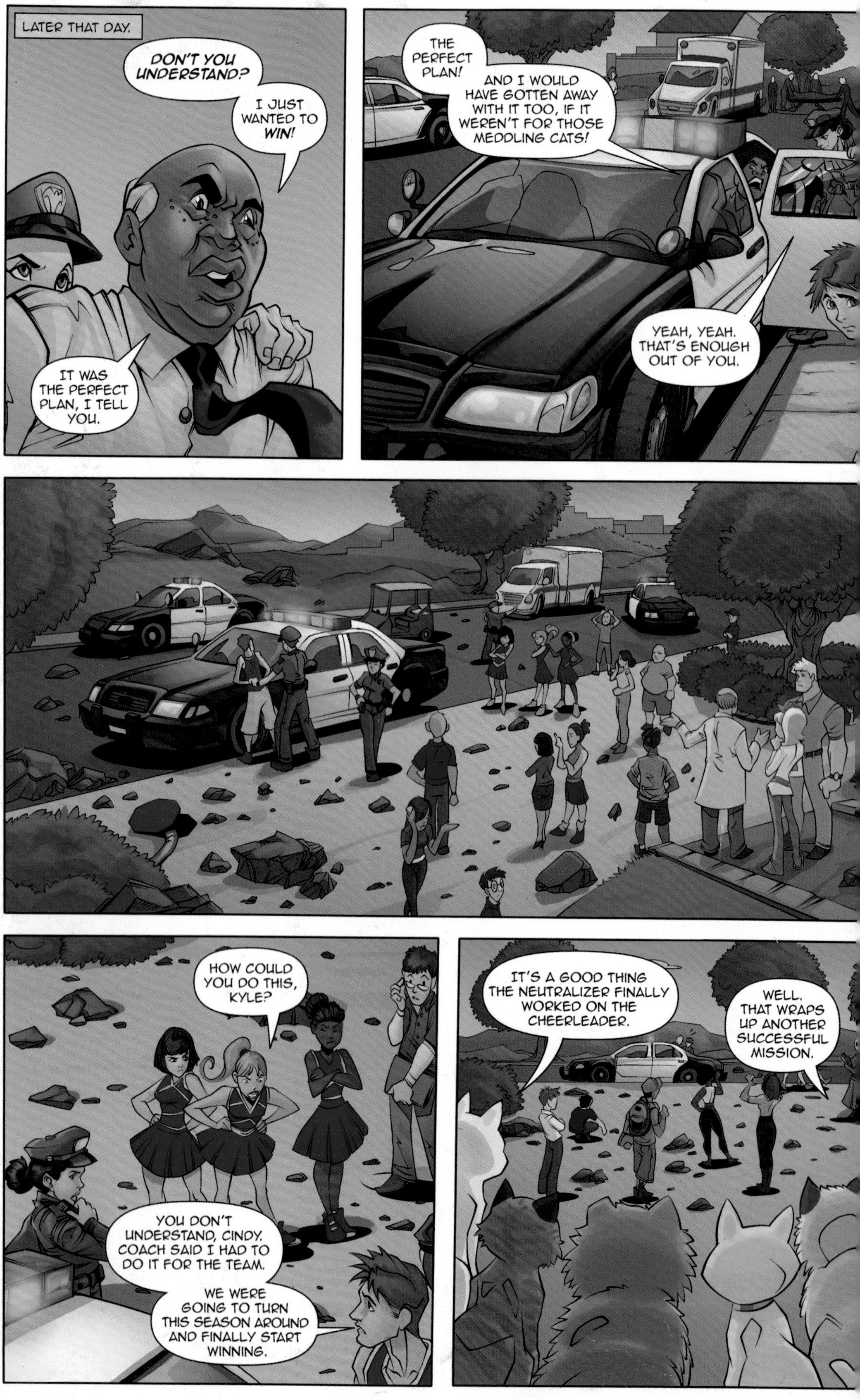
LATER THAT DAY.
DON'T YOU UNDERSTAND?
I JUST WANTED TO WIN!
IT WAS THE PERFECT PLAN, I TELL YOU.
THE PERFECT PLAN!
AND I WOULD HAVE GOTTEN AWAY WITH IT TOO, IF IT WEREN'T FOR THOSE MEDDLING CATS!
YEAH, YEAH. THAT'S ENOUGH OUT OF YOU.
HOW COULD YOU DO THIS, KYLE?
YOU DON'T UNDERSTAND, CINDY. COACH SAID I HAD TO DO IT FOR THE TEAM.
WE WERE GOING TO TURN THIS SEASON AROUND AND FINALLY START WINNING.
IT'S A GOOD THING THE NEUTRALIZER FINALLY WORKED ON THE CHEERLEADER.
WELL. THAT WRAPS UP ANOTHER SUCCESSFUL MISSION.

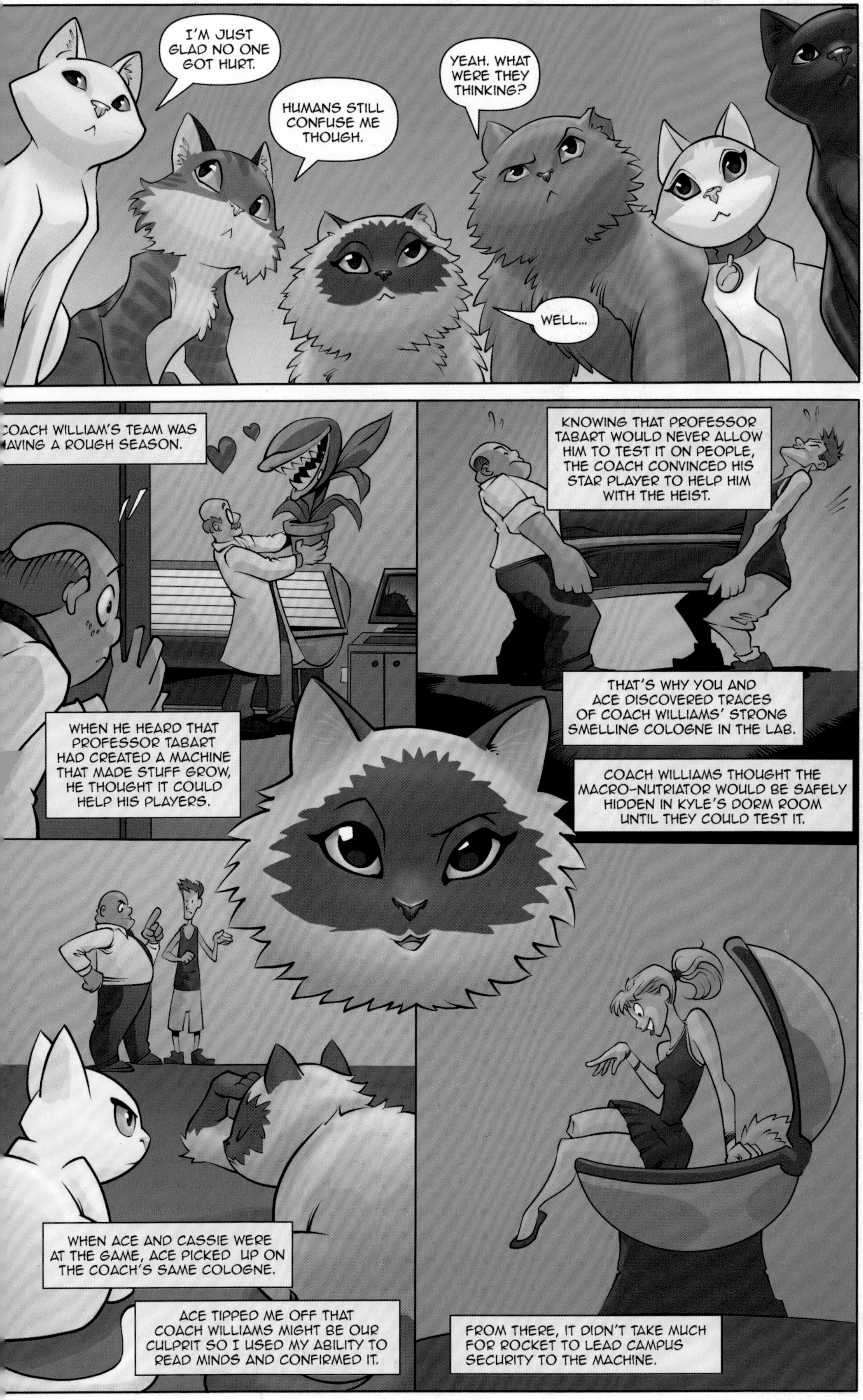

I'M JUST GLAD NO ONE GOT HURT.
HUMANS STILL CONFUSE ME THOUGH.
YEAH. WHAT WERE THEY THINKING?
WELL...
COACH WILLIAM'S TEAM WAS HAVING A ROUGH SEASON.
WHEN HE HEARD THAT PROFESSOR TABART HAD CREATED A MACHINE THAT MADE STUFF GROW, HE THOUGHT IT COULD HELP HIS PLAYERS.
KNOWING THAT PROFESSOR TABART WOULD NEVER ALLOW HIM TO TEST IT ON PEOPLE, THE COACH CONVINCED HIS STAR PLAYER TO HELP HIM WITH THE HEIST.
THAT'S WHY YOU AND ACE DISCOVERED TRACES OF COACH WILLIAMS' STRONG SMELLING COLOGNE IN THE LAB.
COACH WILLIAMS THOUGHT THE MACRO-NUTRIATOR WOULD BE SAFELY HIDDEN IN KYLE'S DORM ROOM UNTIL THEY COULD TEST IT.
WHEN ACE AND CASSIE WERE AT THE GAME, ACE PICKED UP ON THE COACH'S SAME COLOGNE.
ACE TIPPED ME OFF THAT COACH WILLIAMS MIGHT BE OUR CULPRIT SO I USED MY ABILITY TO READ MINDS AND CONFIRMED IT.
FROM THERE, IT DIDN'T TAKE MUCH FOR ROCKET TO LEAD CAMPUS SECURITY TO THE MACHINE.

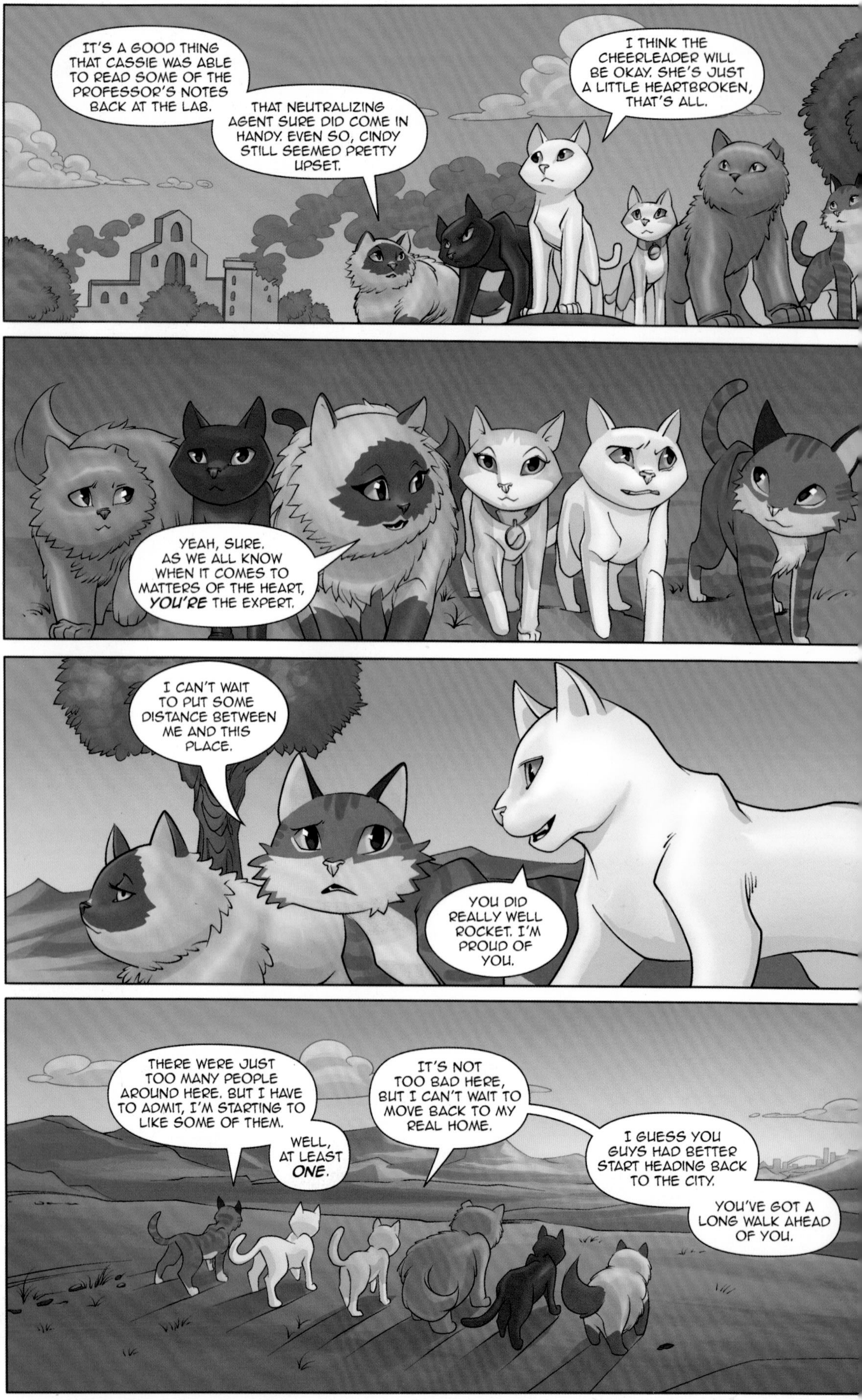
IT'S A GOOD THING THAT CASSIE WAS ABLE TO READ SOME OF THE PROFESSOR'S NOTES BACK AT THE LAB.
THAT NEUTRALIZING AGENT SURE DID COME IN HANDY. EVEN SO, CINDY STILL SEEMED PRETTY UPSET.
I THINK THE CHEERLEADER WILL BE OKAY. SHE'S JUST A LITTLE HEARTBROKEN, THAT'S ALL.
YEAH, SURE. AS WE ALL KNOW WHEN IT COMES TO MATTERS OF THE HEART, ***YOU'RE*** THE EXPERT.
I CAN'T WAIT TO PUT SOME DISTANCE BETWEEN ME AND THIS PLACE.
YOU DID REALLY WELL ROCKET. I'M PROUD OF YOU.
THERE WERE JUST TOO MANY PEOPLE AROUND HERE. BUT I HAVE TO ADMIT, I'M STARTING TO LIKE SOME OF THEM.
WELL, AT LEAST ***ONE***.
IT'S NOT TOO BAD HERE, BUT I CAN'T WAIT TO MOVE BACK TO MY REAL HOME.
I GUESS YOU GUYS HAD BETTER START HEADING BACK TO THE CITY.
YOU'VE GOT A LONG WALK AHEAD OF YOU.

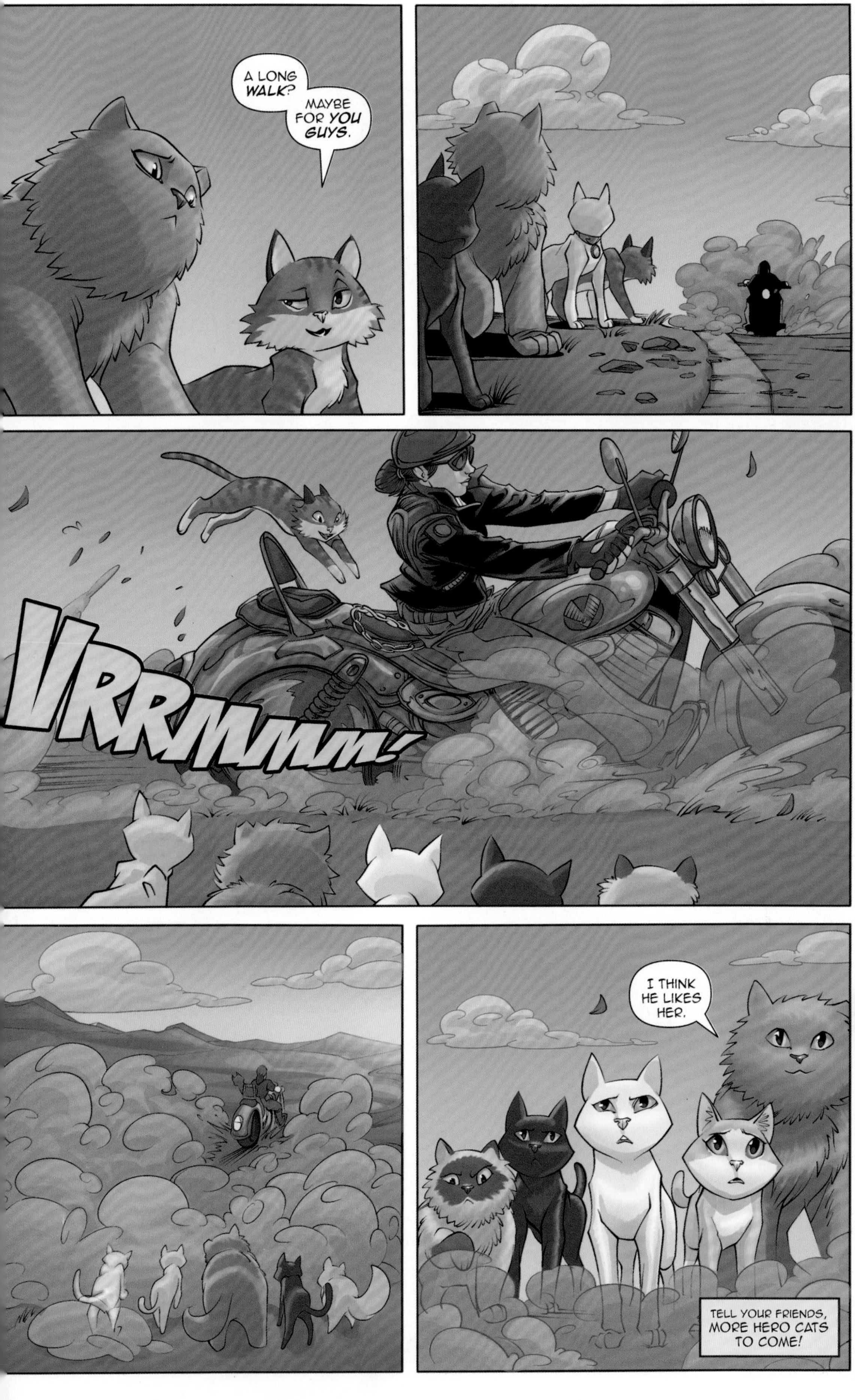
A LONG WALK?
MAYBE FOR YOU GUYS.
VRRMMMM!
I THINK HE LIKES HER.
TELL YOUR FRIENDS, MORE HERO CATS TO COME!

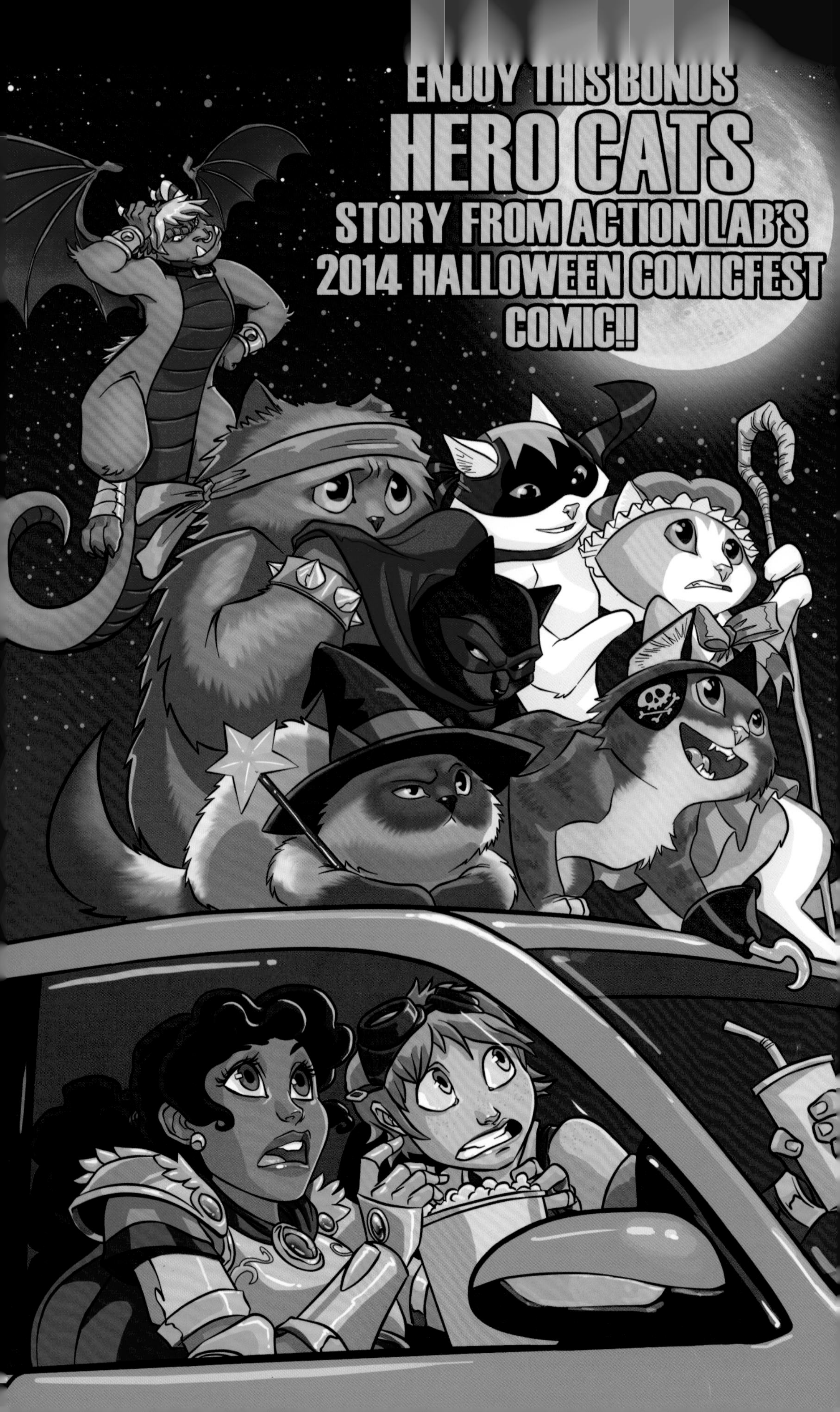
ENJOY THIS BONUS
HERO CATS
STORY FROM ACTION LAB'S
2014 HALLOWEEN COMICFEST
COMIC!!

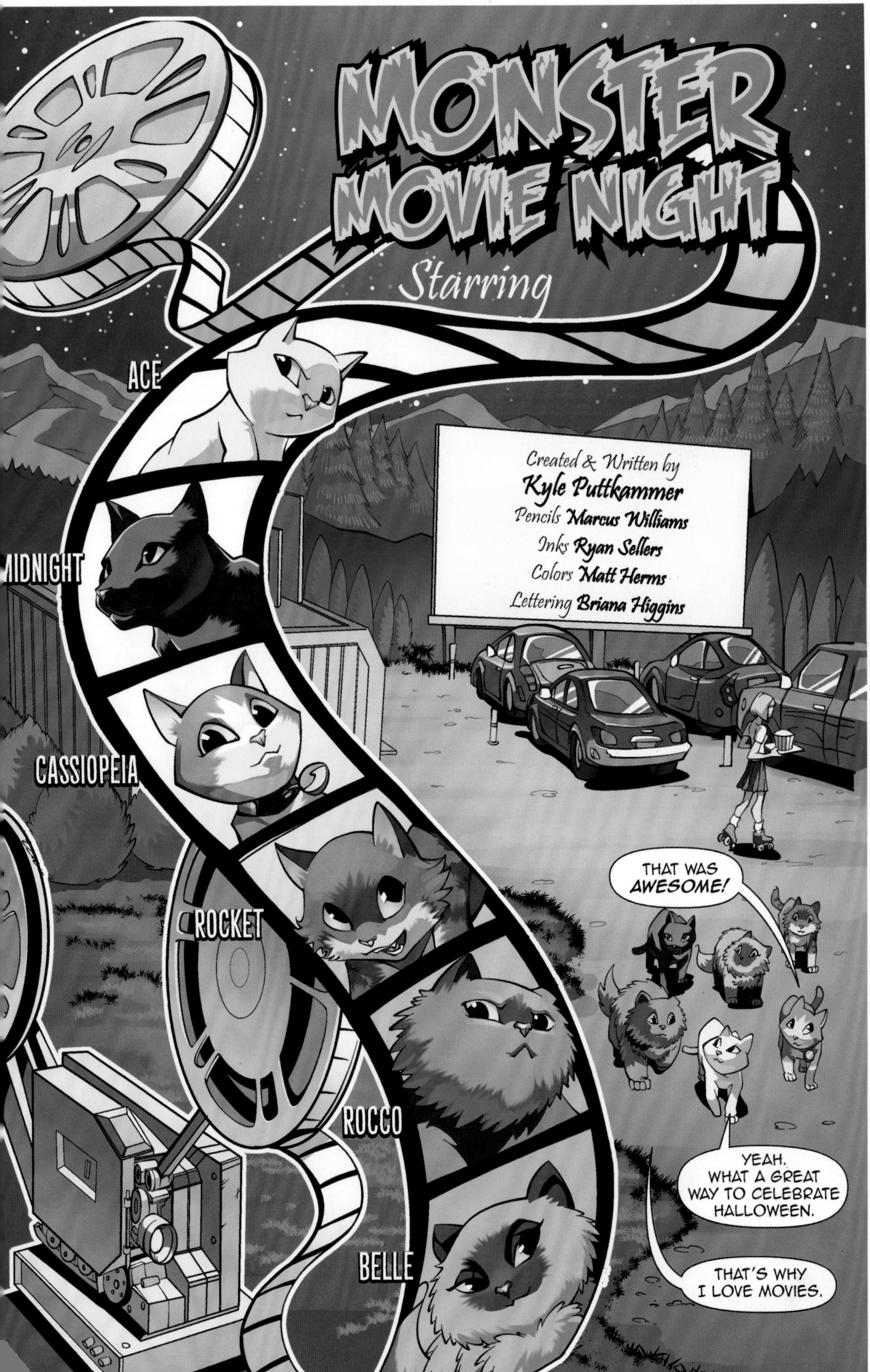

MONSTER MOVIE NIGHT
Starring
ACE
MIDNIGHT
CASSIOPEIA
ROCKET
ROCCO
BELLE
Created & Written by
Kyle Puttkammer
Pencils Marcus Williams
Inks Ryan Sellers
Colors Matt Herms
Lettering Briana Higgins
THAT WAS AWESOME!
YEAH. WHAT A GREAT WAY TO CELEBRATE HALLOWEEN.
THAT'S WHY I LOVE MOVIES.

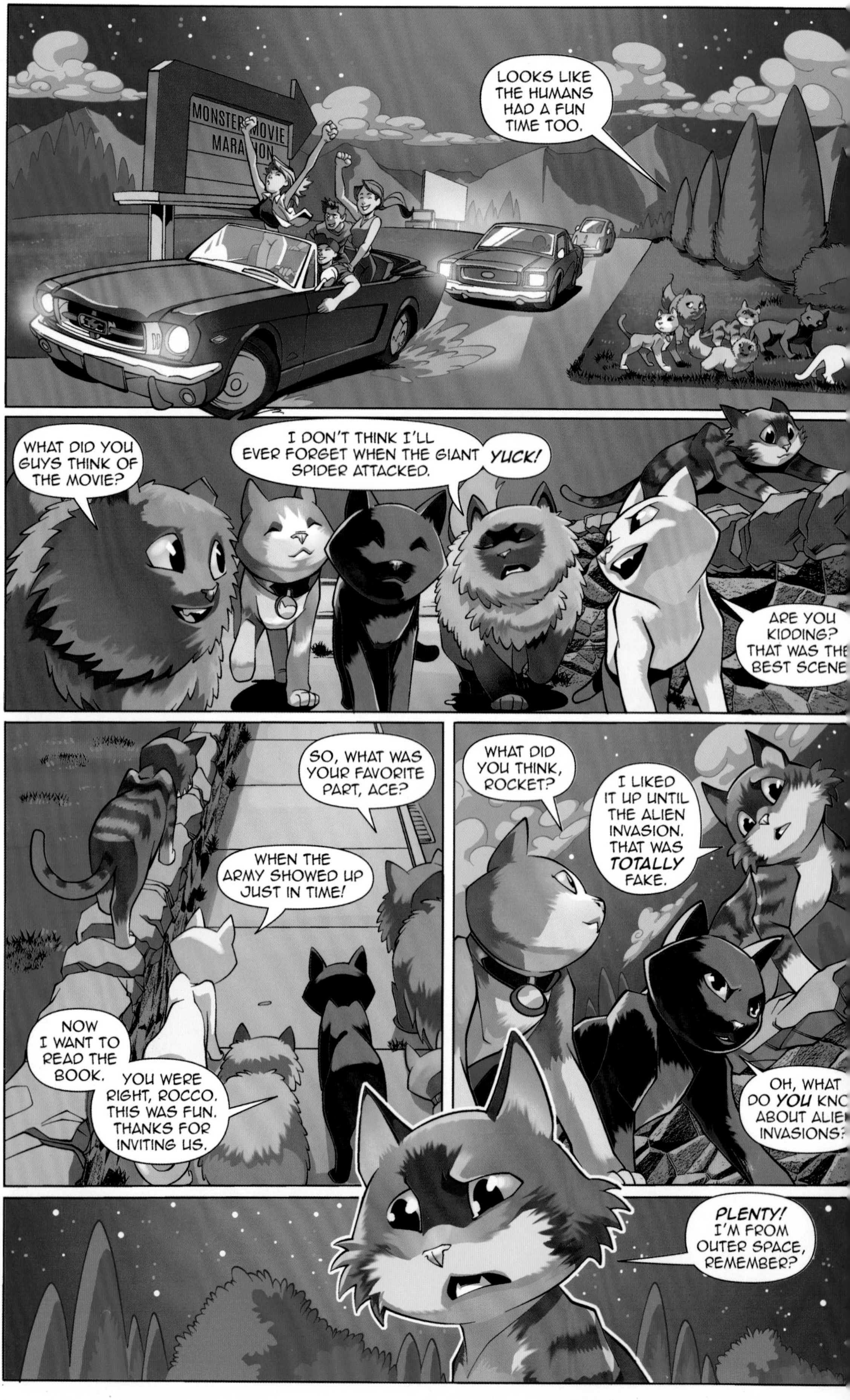
MONSTER MOVIE MARATHON
LOOKS LIKE THE HUMANS HAD A FUN TIME TOO.
WHAT DID YOU GUYS THINK OF THE MOVIE?
I DON'T THINK I'LL EVER FORGET WHEN THE GIANT SPIDER ATTACKED.
YUCK!
ARE YOU KIDDING? THAT WAS THE BEST SCENE
SO, WHAT WAS YOUR FAVORITE PART, ACE?
WHEN THE ARMY SHOWED UP JUST IN TIME!
NOW I WANT TO READ THE BOOK.
YOU WERE RIGHT, ROCCO. THIS WAS FUN. THANKS FOR INVITING US.
WHAT DID YOU THINK, ROCKET?
I LIKED IT UP UNTIL THE ALIEN INVASION. THAT WAS TOTALLY FAKE.
OH, WHAT DO YOU KNO ABOUT ALIE INVASIONS?
PLENTY! I'M FROM OUTER SPACE, REMEMBER?

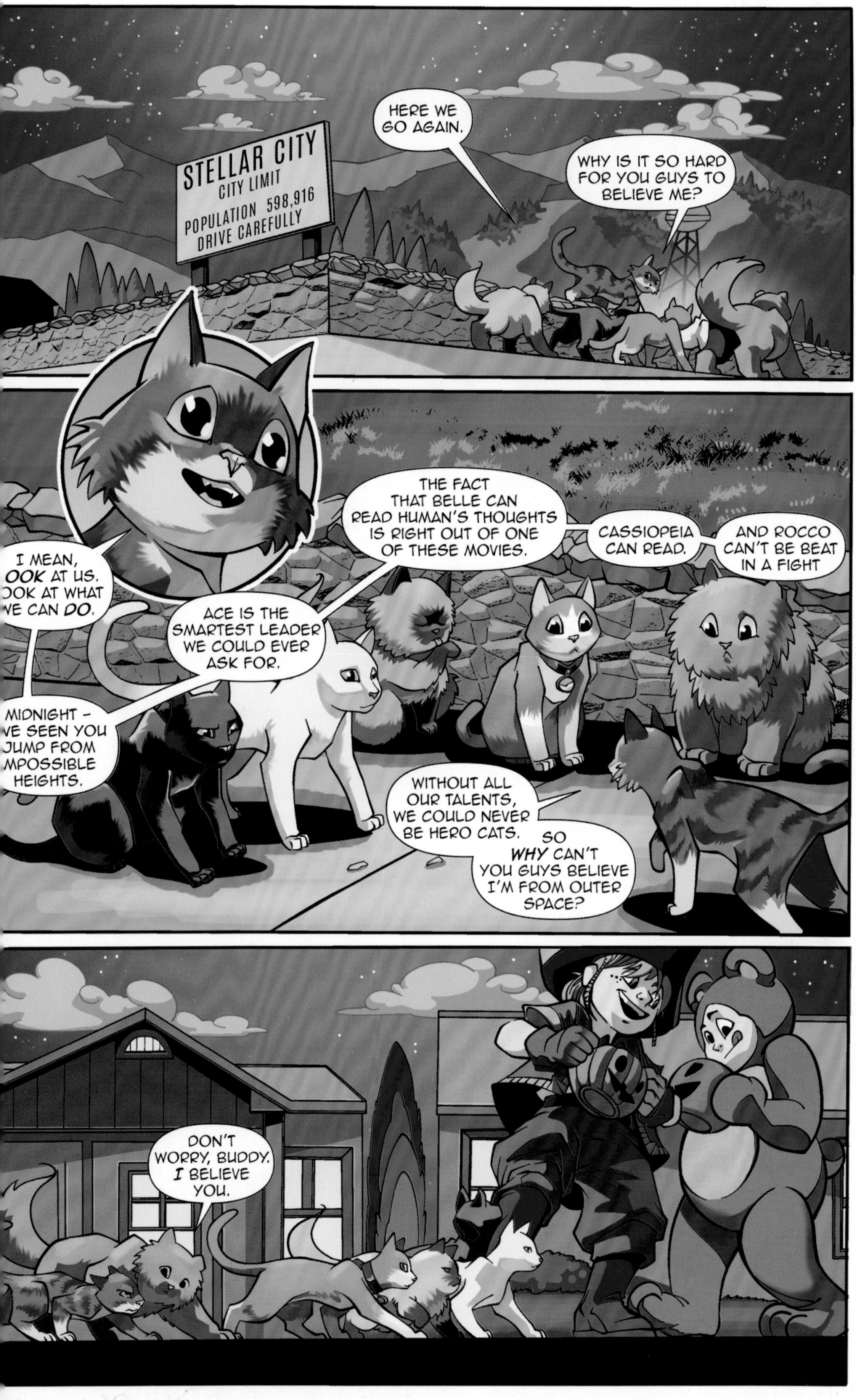
STELLAR CITY
CITY LIMIT
POPULATION 598,916
DRIVE CAREFULLY
HERE WE GO AGAIN.
WHY IS IT SO HARD FOR YOU GUYS TO BELIEVE ME?
I MEAN, OOK AT US. OOK AT WHAT VE CAN *DO*.
ACE IS THE SMARTEST LEADER WE COULD EVER ASK FOR.
MIDNIGHT – VE SEEN YOU JUMP FROM MPOSSIBLE HEIGHTS.
THE FACT THAT BELLE CAN READ HUMAN'S THOUGHTS IS RIGHT OUT OF ONE OF THESE MOVIES.
CASSIOPEIA CAN READ.
AND ROCCO CAN'T BE BEAT IN A FIGHT
WITHOUT ALL OUR TALENTS, WE COULD NEVER BE HERO CATS.
SO *WHY* CAN'T YOU GUYS BELIEVE I'M FROM OUTER SPACE?
DON'T WORRY, BUDDY. *I* BELIEVE YOU.

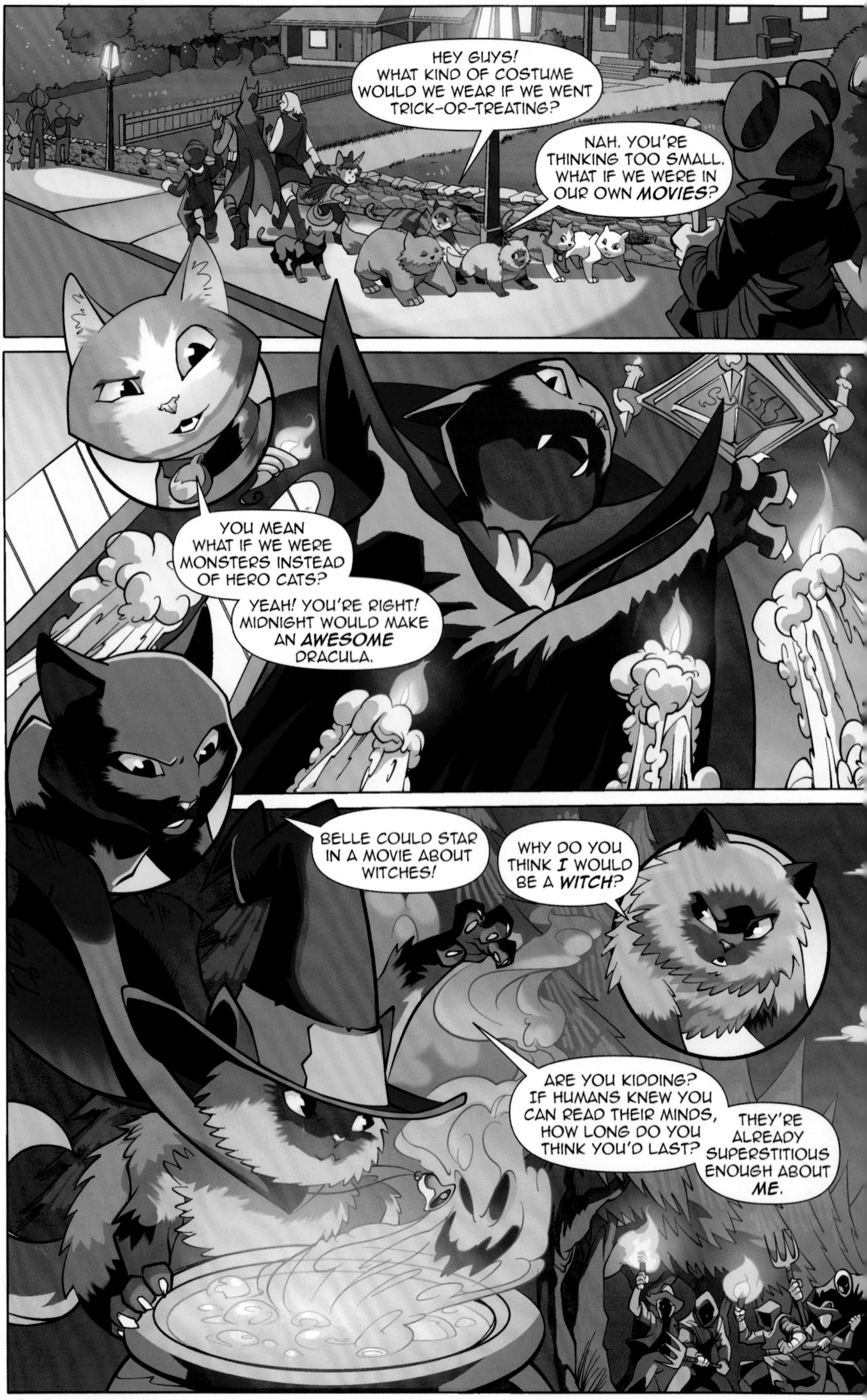
HEY GUYS! WHAT KIND OF COSTUME WOULD WE WEAR IF WE WENT TRICK-OR-TREATING?
NAH. YOU'RE THINKING TOO SMALL. WHAT IF WE WERE IN OUR OWN MOVIES?
YOU MEAN WHAT IF WE WERE MONSTERS INSTEAD OF HERO CATS?
YEAH! YOU'RE RIGHT! MIDNIGHT WOULD MAKE AN AWESOME DRACULA.
BELLE COULD STAR IN A MOVIE ABOUT WITCHES!
WHY DO YOU THINK I WOULD BE A WITCH?
ARE YOU KIDDING? IF HUMANS KNEW YOU CAN READ THEIR MINDS, HOW LONG DO YOU THINK YOU'D LAST?
THEY'RE ALREADY SUPERSTITIOUS ENOUGH ABOUT ME.

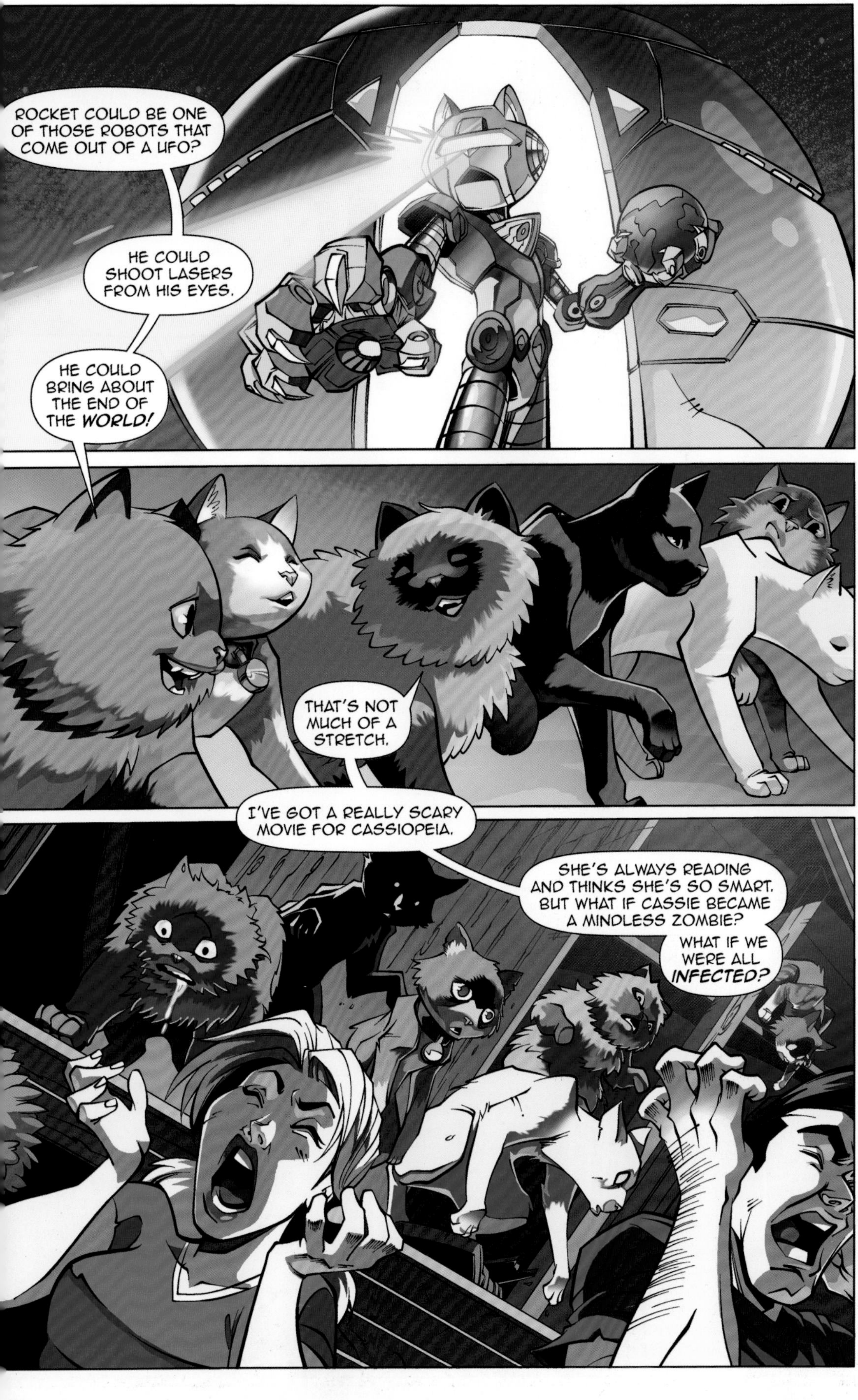
ROCKET COULD BE ONE OF THOSE ROBOTS THAT COME OUT OF A UFO?
HE COULD SHOOT LASERS FROM HIS EYES.
HE COULD BRING ABOUT THE END OF THE *WORLD!*
THAT'S NOT MUCH OF A STRETCH.
I'VE GOT A REALLY SCARY MOVIE FOR CASSIOPEIA.
SHE'S ALWAYS READING AND THINKS SHE'S SO SMART. BUT WHAT IF CASSIE BECAME A MINDLESS ZOMBIE?
WHAT IF WE WERE ALL *INFECTED?*

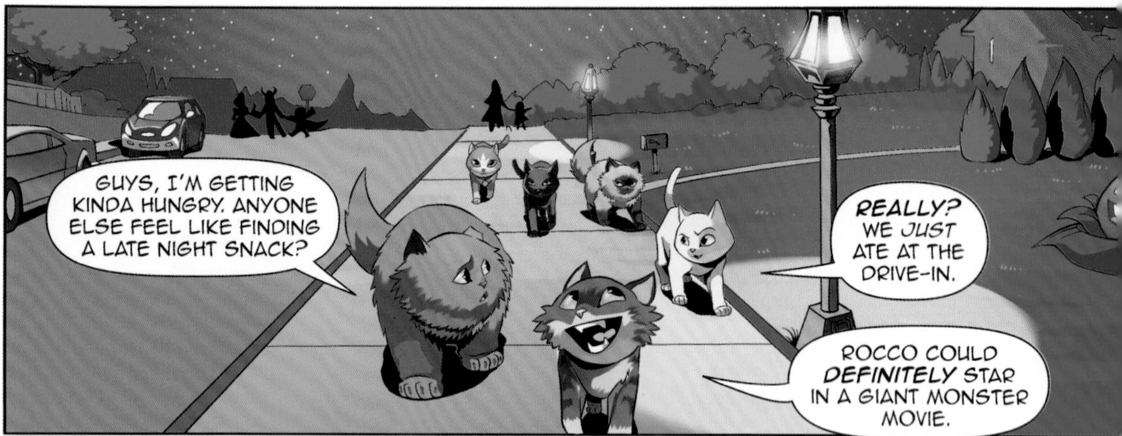
GUYS, I'M GETTING KINDA HUNGRY. ANYONE ELSE FEEL LIKE FINDING A LATE NIGHT SNACK?
REALLY? WE JUST ATE AT THE DRIVE-IN.
ROCCO COULD DEFINITELY STAR IN A GIANT MONSTER MOVIE.

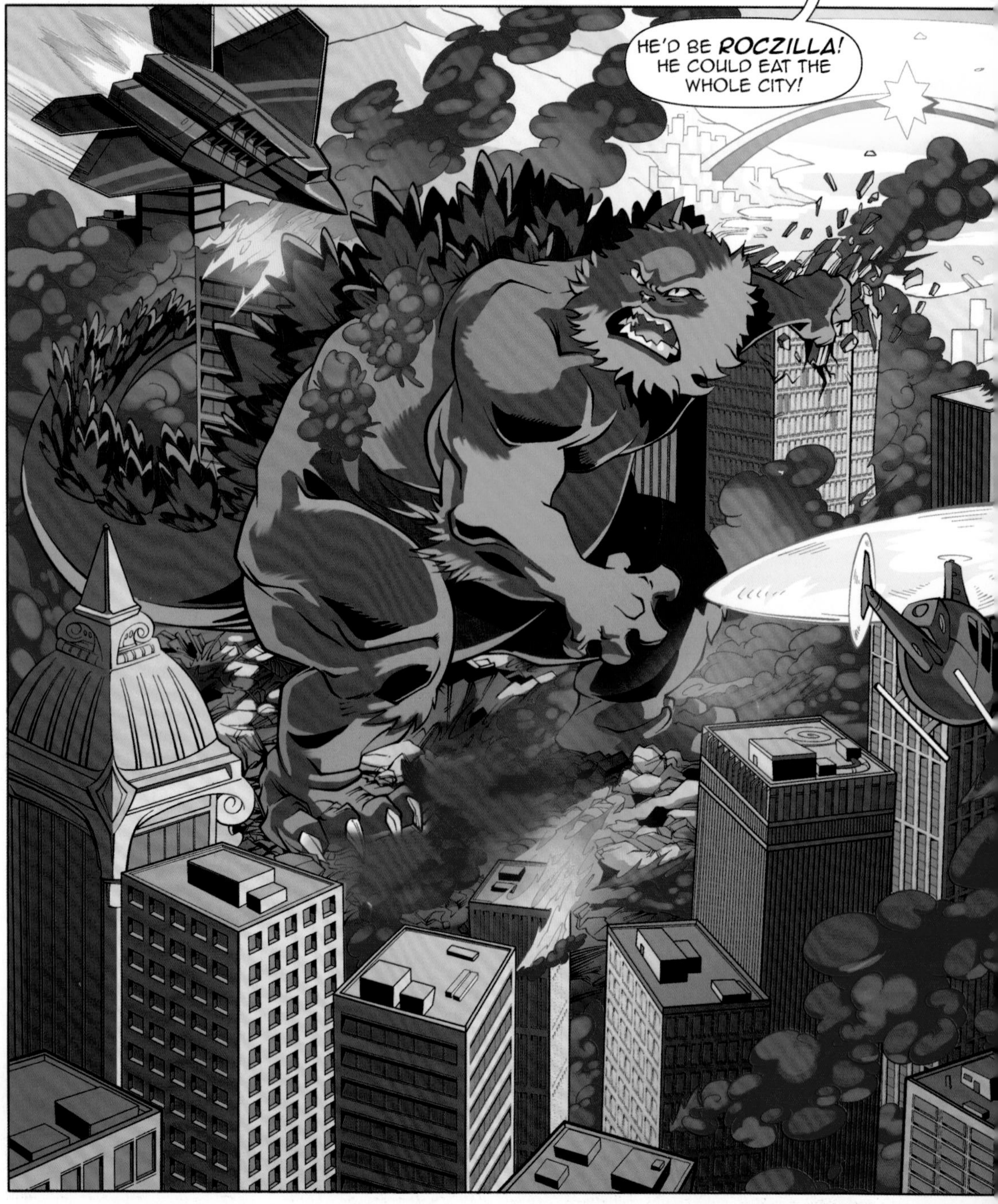
HE'D BE ROCZILLA! HE COULD EAT THE WHOLE CITY!

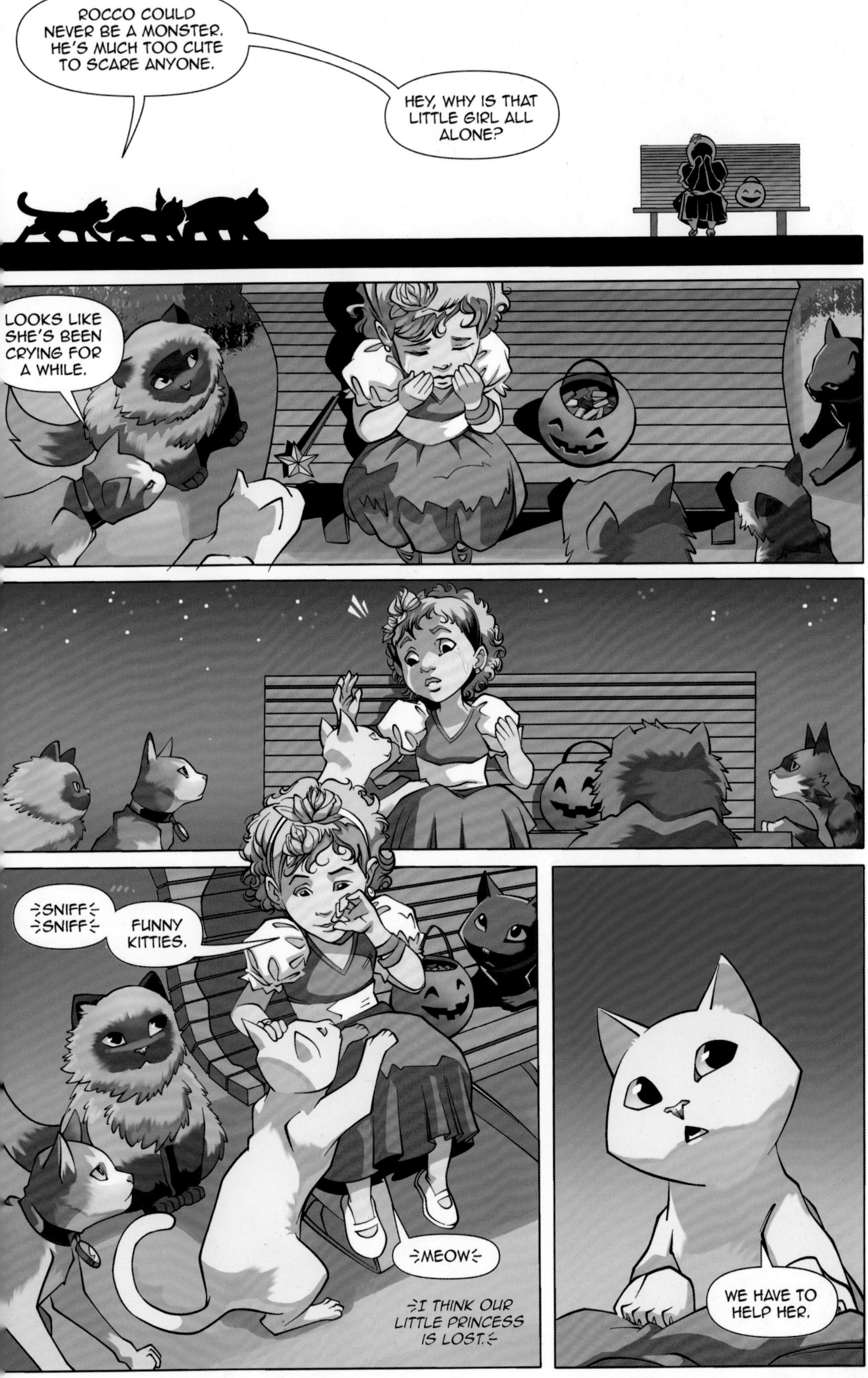
ROCCO COULD NEVER BE A MONSTER. HE'S MUCH TOO CUTE TO SCARE ANYONE.
HEY, WHY IS THAT LITTLE GIRL ALL ALONE?
LOOKS LIKE SHE'S BEEN CRYING FOR A WHILE.
SNIFF SNIFF
FUNNY KITTIES.
MEOW
I THINK OUR LITTLE PRINCESS IS LOST.
WE HAVE TO HELP HER.

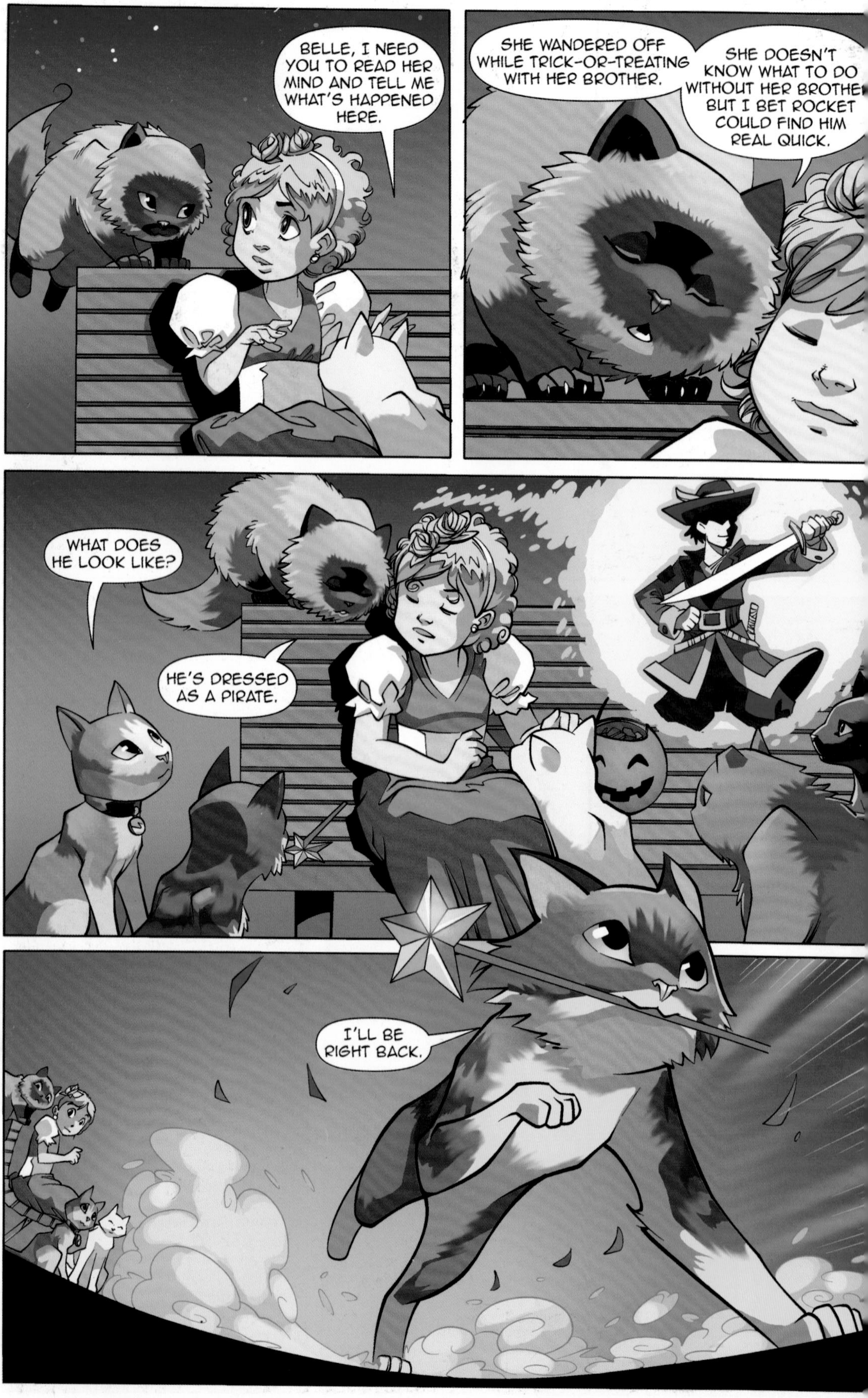
BELLE, I NEED YOU TO READ HER MIND AND TELL ME WHAT'S HAPPENED HERE.
SHE WANDERED OFF WHILE TRICK-OR-TREATING WITH HER BROTHER.
SHE DOESN'T KNOW WHAT TO DO WITHOUT HER BROTHE
BUT I BET ROCKET COULD FIND HIM REAL QUICK.
WHAT DOES HE LOOK LIKE?
HE'S DRESSED AS A PIRATE.
I'LL BE RIGHT BACK.

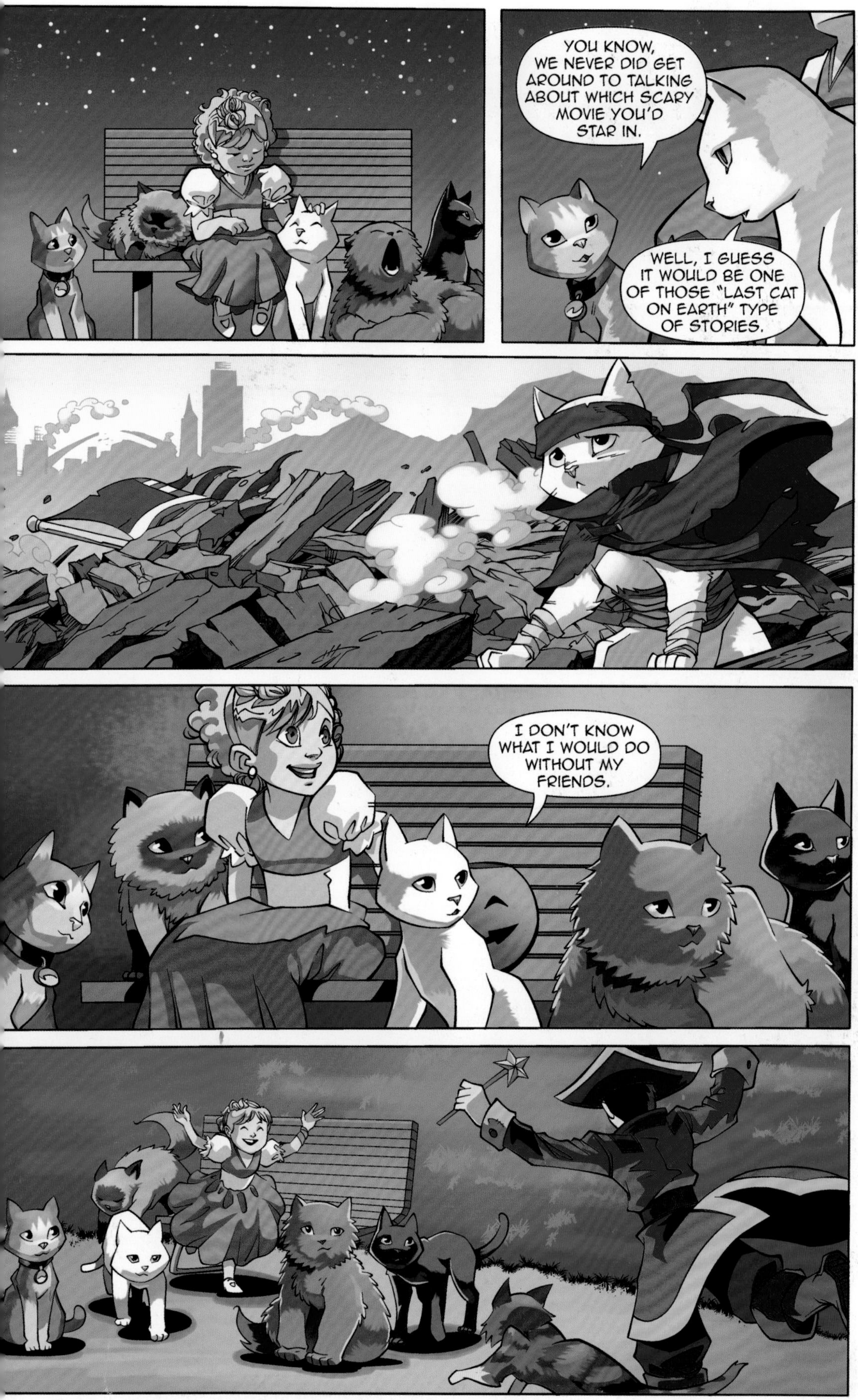
YOU KNOW, WE NEVER DID GET AROUND TO TALKING ABOUT WHICH SCARY MOVIE YOU'D STAR IN.
WELL, I GUESS IT WOULD BE ONE OF THOSE "LAST CAT ON EARTH" TYPE OF STORIES.
I DON'T KNOW WHAT I WOULD DO WITHOUT MY FRIENDS.

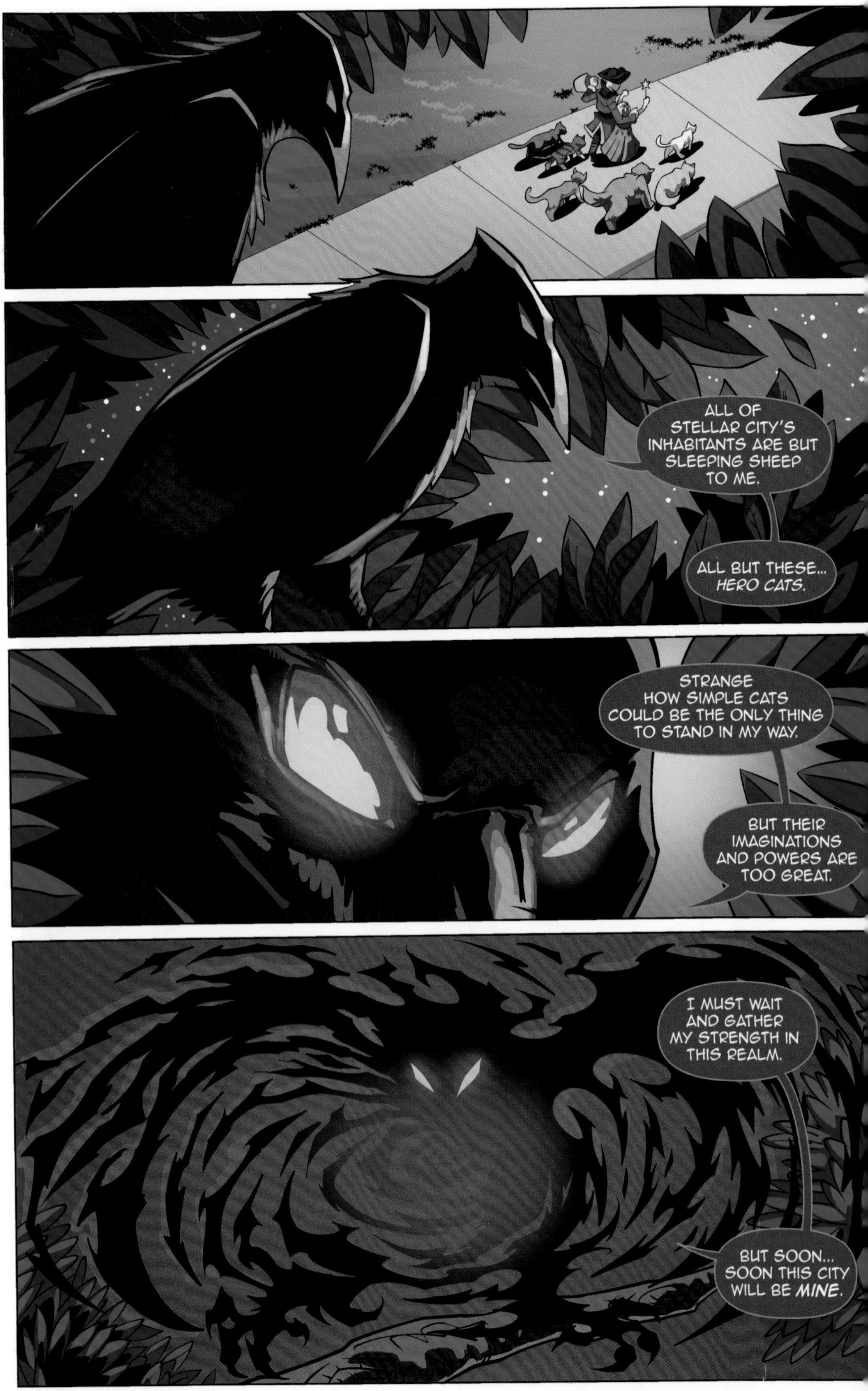
ALL OF STELLAR CITY'S INHABITANTS ARE BUT SLEEPING SHEEP TO ME.
ALL BUT THESE... *HERO CATS.*
STRANGE HOW SIMPLE CATS COULD BE THE ONLY THING TO STAND IN MY WAY.
BUT THEIR IMAGINATIONS AND POWERS ARE TOO GREAT.
I MUST WAIT AND GATHER MY STRENGTH IN THIS REALM.
BUT SOON... SOON THIS CITY WILL BE ***MINE***.

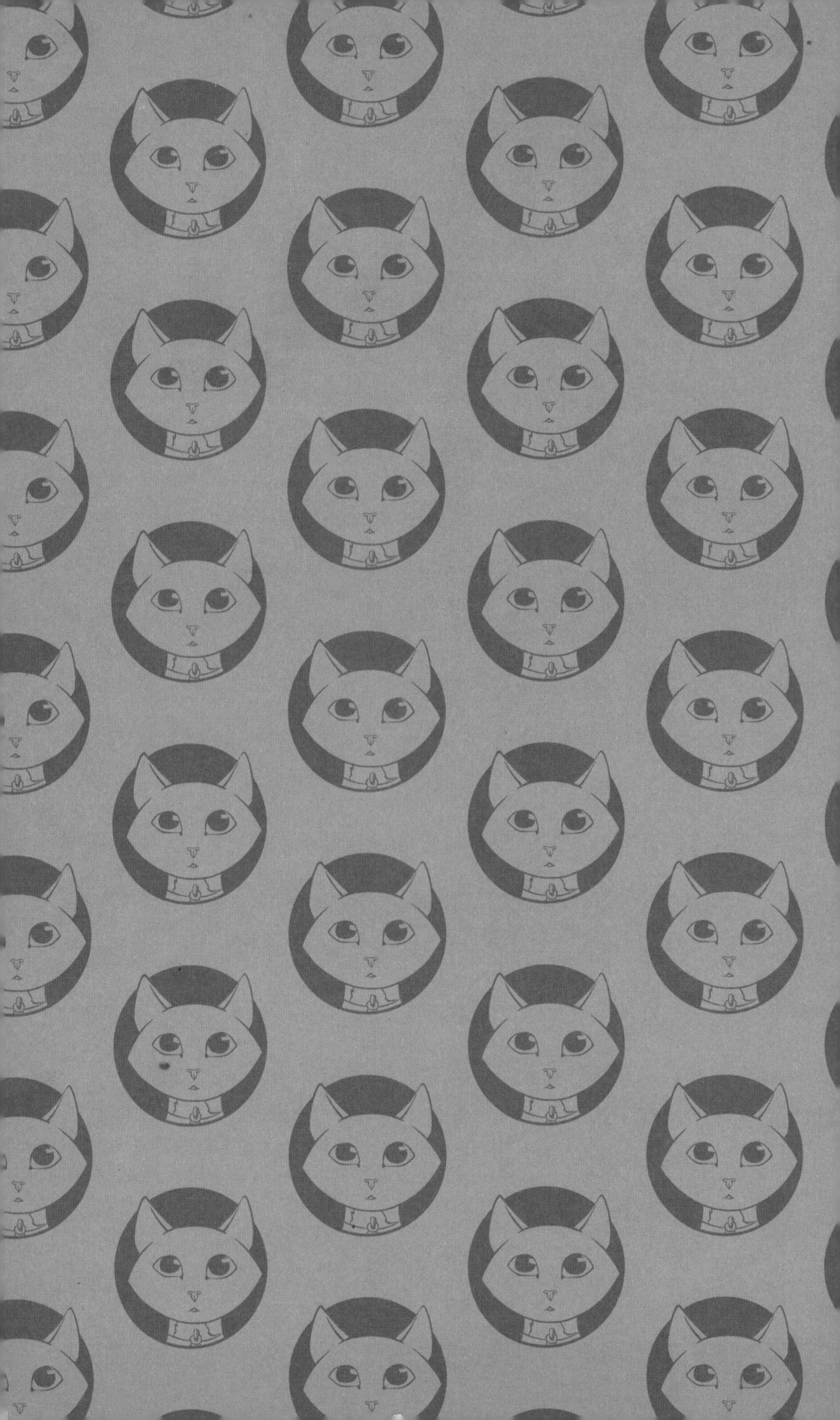